Stonehill Downs

STONEHILL DOWNS

A NOVEL

SARAH REMY

HARPER

VOYAGER
IMPULSE

An Imprint of HarperCollinsPublishers

STONEHILL DOWNS. Copyright © 2014 by Sarah Remy. All rights reserved under International and Pan-American Copyright Conventions. By payment of the required fees, you have been granted the nonexclusive, nontransferable right to access and read the text of this e-book on screen. No part of this text may be reproduced, transmitted, decompiled, reverse-engineered, or stored in or introduced into any information storage and retrieval system, in any form or by any means, whether electronic or mechanical, now known or hereafter invented, without the express written permission of HarperCollins e-books.

EPub Edition DECEMBER 2014 ISBN: 9780062383426
Print Edition ISBN: 9780062383433

10 9 8 7 6 5 4 3 2 1

For Willem's Hobblings.

Dusk

ANDREW STRUGGLED.

Mal held him down. The old man's skin burned, and sweat turned his mottled flesh slick, but still he shuddered as if chilled. Where Mal's long fingers encircled his wrists, bruises blossomed.

Perspiration dampened Mal's own brow, running in rivulets along his nose and into the corners of his eyes, stinging. He didn't move to wipe them away. All of his strength was focused on the man convulsing beneath his hands.

"Let him go, Mal."

"No." He refused to spare Siobahn a glance. He refused to acknowledge the disapproval he felt vibrating across the room.

"Malachi. You mustn't keep him back. It's too painful."

"For him? Or for you?" He knew the words were unkind. He didn't care.

The air moved as Siobahn shifted. The candles in the close room flickered, shedding plumes of smoke. Her breath stirred the hair on the back of his head.

Still, he wouldn't look around.

The dying man twisted on silken bedclothes. His mouth gaped open, showing yellow teeth, and his eyes rolled in his skull.

Mal knew the old man was all but senseless, but he couldn't help himself; he bent forward and peered into the wizened face.

"Andrew," he whispered, willing the other man to hear.

"Mal." Siobahn forced the issue, stepping away from the shadows and into his line of sight.

Her gown rustled. He could hear the soft pad of her slippers along the stone floor. She slid through the haze of incense, and set her palms flat on the edge of the bed, leaning across the mattress until he was forced to meet her gaze.

"Let him go," she said again. This time she put just a touch of ice into the words.

Mal no longer took orders, not even from the young woman who had once been his wife. But she could still pierce him through with her deep blue eyes, and she knew it.

No matter how often he wished it otherwise, Siobahn never failed to move him. She knew that, also.

So he looked away from Andrew's gaping mouth, and let her rake him with her gaze. She was angry, he saw, and disappointed. Maybe she was frightened, but she kept her smile sweet.

"You're holding him back," she warned. "Don't make him struggle."

"He might still be saved," Mal argued, even though his heart knew better. Already the bitter tang of grief roughened the back of his throat.

Andrew was the last, and Mal didn't want to be alone.

Siobahn lifted one hand from the mattress, and set it on Mal's arm. His tendons quivered at her touch. Beneath his own fingers Andrew's muscles convulsed in response. The ravaged body arched up off the bed, then snapped back onto the bedclothes.

Blooded scented the air; a trickle of the dark liquid stained Andrew's chin. The old man had bitten through his tongue.

The violence of the struggle touched Mal at last. He flinched away from the bed, releasing frail bones. The moment his fingers left Andrew's flesh, the old man convulsed again, as though plucked off the mattress by the hands of the gods. Mal heard bones in the tortured spine snap.

"He's on his way," Siobahn whispered, relieved.

Mal shuddered. The gods were never gentle with the ones they favored.

He bent over the bed, and took Andrew's right hand in his own. There was no response. The old man was well and truly gone.

Mal stroked Andrew's cooling palm with his thumb. Tears still scratched at the back of his throat. He forced them down, waited until he knew his eyes were dry, and then he reached over and wiped the blood from Andrew's mouth with the edge of his sleeve.

The blood disappeared into the grain of the dark

leather he wore. Mal studied the cuff, searching for a stain that didn't show. Then he straightened his shoulders and set Andrew's hand back onto the silks.

He turned from the canopied bed and stepped off the sleeping dais. The suite was gloomy, the air too thick. The smoke from the massive candles Andrew had so loved twined with the fumes of eastern incense.

Mal stumbled over the flagstones, intending to wrench open the windows. He wanted to breath in the night air, to clear away the headache lurking behind his eyes.

"Malachi," Siobahn warned, just as his hand settled on the window latch. "Tradition. Renault would not be pleased . . ."

She broke off, sensing his silent fury.

She was correct. He almost lifted the latch anyway. If only he could get a taste of fresh air. He needed the breeze across his face to cool his growing rage. And Renault would never know.

He pulled his hand back from the latch and curled his fingers carefully behind his back. Standing alone in the hazy darkness, he could almost feel the chill of the night through the windowpane.

Glass was dearly bought. Only the king's most beloved were lucky enough to have paned windows. Mal had glass in his own rooms, but not so much.

Andrew had been Renualt's most beloved.

"And now he's dead." Mal forced himself to say it aloud. Briefly, he set his brow against one cool pane.

"You need to tell him," Siobahn said from somewhere over his left shoulder. "You've already waited too long. Renault should have been here earlier. To order the windows covered and—"

This time he stopped her words with a snarl. He heard her teeth click as she bit back the rest of her lecture. He sighed. Again, she was correct. She almost always was.

"I'll go to him now," he allowed, turning away from his reflection in the glass.

Siobahn lingered over the bed, poised as though in mid grasp, her fingers still hovering over Andrew's face. Mal followed the drift of her unnatural blue gaze to the glitter of yellow on the dead man's thumb.

Now it was his turn to use the power of their connection, to twist her guilt into a weapon. He strode back across the room until he could pin her with his frown. She flinched beneath his stare. Her cheeks pinked soft rose in embarrassment or fear.

"I thought you had forgotten," she said.

He loomed at her side, towering four full handspans above the crown of her head, and regarded the yellow stone in Andrew's ring with distaste.

"And you hoped to remove it for me?" His laugh was bitter, his mouth hard.

"You know better."

She stood in the soft gown she had worn on their wedding day and faced his fury with dignity.

He set his hands on her small shoulders and shook her once, gently, but with passion. Siobahn allowed his touch for a heartbeat. Then she slipped from under his grasp. Mal almost went after her, but something in her half smile stopped him.

He watched as she moved to stand before one of Andrew's giant candelabras. The flames bowed, drawn by her very breath.

For an instant Mal heard as she did; the king's heavy footsteps echoed between his ears, pounding with the headache behind his nose.

He swallowed hard, blinked the pain away, and lifted Andrew's fingers.

The ring slid easily over a bony knuckle. The true gold was warm in Mal's hand. The yellow jewel burst to life, sending a scattering of starbursts across dead man, bedclothes, and wall.

"The king!" she whispered, starbursts glittering in her hair. She let him hear again. Renault's footfall almost punched holes in Mal's tender skull.

He shoved Andrew's ring into the small pouch he kept on his belt. Then he moved away from the canopy, standing where he could be seen from the massive wooden door Andrew never barred.

He could hear the march of booted feet in truth, now. It sounded as though Renault had gathered his entire guard.

"He knows," Siobahn murmured from her place among the candles and smoke.

"How?"

"He slept," she replied. "He dreamed, as Andrew died. I sent him a vision."

Mal heard regret in her admission. No doubt she feared he would be angry.

He was too exhausted to fume any longer, weighed by grief. He looked over his shoulder, thinking to reassure, but at that moment the footsteps rolled to a stop in the corridor outside Andrew's suite. The heavy door slammed open, rattling the antechamber.

A gust of cool air made the candles gutter and go out. Smoke wreathed the room. Mal's eyes watered in response.

He blinked. When his vision cleared, Siobahn was gone, snuffed out along with Andrew's pretty tapers.

Mal rubbed his throbbing brow. Then he set his shoulders, touched the pouch at his belt, and went to greet his king.

Chapter One

AVANI FOUND THE corpse two days after first snowfall.

Enough slush remained on the ground to stain the Downs gray in the early morning light. The cold made her bones ache even though she'd wrapped herself from head to toe in an old cape she had traded from the Widow. Fashioned from mismatched animal pelts, the cape fell nearly to her knees.

Avani disliked the smell of death that lingered still on the cape, but she disliked the cold even more, and she could be grateful for the wolf, and weasel, and squirrel that had fallen to the Widow's traps. The patches of mottled fur still clinging to the cape kept most of the bitter air from her skin.

Avani's feet were another matter. Her sheepskin boots were worn and thin. She'd meant to fashion a new pair over the summer, but time had slipped away.

Only a few moments out on the Downs, and she could barely feel her heels. Her toes were pinpricks of icy pain.

Jacob fared somewhat better, but even the raven disliked the slush that clung to his claws and the frost that gilded his tail feathers. The ice made it difficult and uncomfortable to fly, so the bird rode on Avani's shoulder, growling complaints low in the back of his throat.

As it was, they made slow progress over the Downs. The morning sun had nearly peaked when Jacob launched himself into the sky. He flapped hard, buffeted by the wind, and then began to circle in large, endless loops. Soon after, Avani spotted a huddled lump on the frozen grass.

At first she thought it was one of her sheep and made a sound of distress, unwilling to give up another of the valuable creatures as lost. But then Jacob began to call, and she knew something different had died on her borrowed land.

Avani's pace slowed to a near crawl. She almost went back to Stonehill for help. She had seen enough death already in her lifetime. She wasn't eager to witness another. She stopped once, glancing back across the rolling hills in the direction of the village, but Jacob swooped and called until she heaved a sigh and forced herself to continue on.

The dead man lay in a hollow, sheltered from the wind. His arms were stretched out along the grass at odd angles. It looked as though his limbs had been twisted until his bones had shattered.

Frozen blood caked his tunic, staining the hard ground beneath his torso. He had neither face nor throat. Something had torn open his belly and left his entrails spread on the Downs.

Avani crouched in the brown grass. She propped her

elbows on her knees and cupped her chin in her hands. Frost crackled beneath the bottoms of her boots, and the cold seeped through sheepskin soles. She considered the dead man's ruined face, and frowned.

Jacob squawked, plummeting. He settled on the dead man's chest. The raven walked up and down along the length of the corpse, head tilted, beak working. When at last he returned to Avani's shoulder, he had blood on his feathers and the gleam of wisdom in his black eyes.

"A Kingsman," she agreed, noting the remains of the royal insignia on the man's ripped tunic. "Torn apart on our Downs. And left to rot beneath the winter sky."

She scanned the grass, but couldn't pick out any tracks around the body. The Downs were frozen, the soil too hard.

Jacob muttered and hissed. He ruffled his dark wings, and ducked from side to side, and then pressed his sleek head against the curve of Avani's jaw.

She lifted her hand to his head in resignation, and when she did, her Goddess spoke, and Avani saw.

The man had died brutally, and in terror. That was not a surprise. But the darkness surrounding his death made Avani's heart clench. It was more than a shadow of sorrow, of a life cut short too soon.

Here was something different; a pitch-black venom tasting of rotted blood, and of the deep earth.

"Murder," she said. "Nothing so simple as a mad wolf or a wild weasel."

She looked deeper, trying to understand. There was another, lighter scent beneath the rotted perfume. One that was somehow familiar.

But Jacob moved from beneath her hand, and the vision shredded away to nothing. Avani rubbed the back of her fist across her mouth. Her stomach rolled. She shut her eyes, waiting for her innards to still.

She crouched on the frozen ground, unmoving, until a light snow began to drift from the sky and coat the grass. Avani watched tiny crystals settle across the Kingsman's bloodied skull. Then she sighed, her breath a puff of smoke in the winter air.

"*Ai*, Jacob!" She rocked to her feet, calling the raven from where he poked idly at the corpse's scalp. "Storm is coming. We need to get the sheep in."

She rubbed her hand across her mouth again, then caught the accusatory gleam in Jacob's beady eye.

"The sheep come first," she repeated firmly, because it was true. The wooly creatures were her livelihood. She couldn't allow the storm to damage their worth.

Avani made herself turn from the Kingsman, made herself leave the corpse alone on the frozen ground.

She walked carefully away down the slippery hill, setting one foot in front of the other. After a moment Jacob joined her, arrowing through the snow until he found her right shoulder. He clicked his beak irritably as she walked. Usually Avani found his small tantrums amusing. Now her heart lay heavy in her chest.

She thought of the shadow over the murdered man all the way across the Downs. She couldn't let the vision go even as she found her sheep, and began the long process of herding the animals back up rolling hills to the shelter of the village.

Shepherding was not simple work, and by the time Avani had managed to coax every last sheep into the village pen, she was exhausted and wet to the bone. She couldn't feel her fingers. She thought the tip of her nose had frozen.

Even so, as soon as the final lamb was safely penned, Avani trudged up through the village to Stonehill's one tavern. There she knew she would find the village lord, and possibly justice for the dead man on the Downs.

AVANI LIVED ON the very edge of town in a clapboard-and-graystone house not far from the sheep pen. It was a small house, but it had a solid roof and a deep well, and a pretty stretch of grass that sloped behind it onto the Downs.

In the summer she spread her fabrics on the grass to dry. In the winter she had to break the rime on the well water with stones, but the water was always fresh. And in the evenings, no matter what the season, if she stood on tiptoe in her backyard, she could see away across the Downs to the River Mors.

Avani's house was not tightly crafted. She learned quickly her first year how to hang her rugs and blankets and tapestries from the rafters. When tacked up correctly, the heavy fabrics blocked drafts, and kept Avani from succumbing to the cold.

She scattered more of the brightly colored rugs and blankets on the floor, and managed to turn the little house into a warm shelter even in the middle of winter.

The small cellar under the back room belonged to the Goddess. Avani kept a fat beeswax candle burning on Her shrine day and night. She'd loomed a small kneeling rug for the hard floor. She kept the rest of the room bare.

Avani never felt cold in the little cellar. She could spend hours on her knees on the rug, unconcerned and unaware, while the outside world froze.

In the fall the house shuddered beneath wind and rain, and in the winter the weight of ice made the roof whisper and groan. But in the summer Avani's home was always cool, and in the springtime the slope along the Downs sprouted tiny colored flowers.

Avani hadn't yet learned to love Stonehill; three years was too short a time to forget her past. But she had managed to nurture a thriving business, and to turn an abandoned graystone house into a home.

Almost, she had learned to belong.

THREE NIGHTS AFTER Avani and Jacob found the dead Kingsman out on the Downs, Stonehill's lord came calling.

He rapped on Avani's clapboard door. She welcomed him with genuine pleasure, letting him into the warmth of her home.

He knocked snow from heavy boots before he stepped onto the rugs, and smiled.

"Good eve, mistress."

"Good eve, my lord," she replied, hiding her own smile as the big man was forced to duck beneath the drape of her fabrics.

Stonehill's lord was a giant of a man. Already into his fifth decade, he still stood straight and strong. An aesthetic soul, he kept his peppered beard neatly trimmed, and his boots carefully polished.

The village loved him. Young and old respected his judgments.

He had a soft spot for Avani, and through the turn of seasons he had become her champion. He was a bachelor, gentle in his own gruff way. Avani found him sweet. She fed him stews and curries, and looked to his comfort the way she had her own father.

"A bitter night," he said, out of habit more than complaint. He ducked through fabric until he found the pile of embroidered cushions Avani kept for guests.

He dropped onto the pillows, stretching booted feet across Avani's rugs with a sigh. Jacob, lurking in the rafters, clattered his beak and turned his back. The raven didn't approve of his lordship.

"Ah, child. Can you believe it? A Kingsman dead on our own Downs."

The village lord's given name was Thom. Avani was one of the few in the village who knew it. She also knew his secret love of spiced cider, and so as the big man began to relax, she crossed to her old stove, and ladled hot liquid into her largest mug.

"Murdered," she corrected.

His lordship arched his brows as he accepted the drink, frowning as he took a sip.

"Murdered, aye. But by what man?"

Avani settled cross-legged in the cushions at his side.

"Perhaps no man," she said.

He took another sip. Steam from the mug wreathed his face and clung to his beard. Up in the rafters Jacob rustled his wings and danced from foot to foot.

"Is that what you think?" his lordship asked.

Avani shrugged. "There was nothing human in the feel of his death. It was horrible. Beastly. And what man would flay another so violently?"

"An animal, then. A crazed wolf, or a water-mad stag."

"Mayhap." Avani linked her fingers around her knee. "I don't think so."

His lordship set his mug carefully on the patterned rug. He shifted forward until he could meet her gaze. "Tell me."

She rolled one shoulder, and glanced up at Jacob's nervous dance.

"It was dark," she said, slowly. "It tasted . . . wrong. He suffered. And he was still alive when they left him."

"They?" he pounced on the word.

Avani tried to recall the vision, but it flittered in and out of reach on the edges of her conscious.

"They," she agreed at last. "Shadows, vague forms. Hungry. More than one."

"More than one what, that's the question."

Avani only shrugged again. She got up to replenish his drink.

"I've called a gathering," the village lord said. He watched as she dippered up the cider.

She spilled a little of the drink, scalding her thumb. Absently, she licked her fingers clean. "When?"

"Tomorrow, after supper. He was a Kingsman, far from home. And murdered in my village. We'll send a message, at least to the keep."

Avani agreed, but she shook her head.

"Tempers will flare."

"Nobody in Stonehill will want to involve king or keep," he allowed. "But this time . . ."

" . . . it's necessary," she finished.

It didn't matter that she was a foreigner, or that his king was not her own. Removed as she was, still she understood his loyalty.

"Will you come?"

Avani tilted her chin, watching as he fingered a swatch of recently dyed fabric. He was one of her best customers, and she saw immediately that the dark blue wool had snagged his interest.

"I thought I'd make a winter tunic with that," she said, hiding a grin. "Maybe a pair of hose."

"A tunic," his lordship murmured as he pinched the wool. He studied the fabric a heartbeat longer, then shot her a glance. "They respect you, child."

Amused, Avani brushed a tangle of hair from her brow. "They fear me."

"They'll want you there," he insisted. "*I* want you there. You'll come."

"If the sheep are comfortable." She was reluctant to agree, but she saw the worry on his face, and didn't want to disappoint.

"*Ai*, the sheep," he teased, mimicking her own accented tones. "Does this world exist only for your sheep?"

"It does," Avani replied, solemn. And then she laughed.

His lordship finished the last of the cider in one swig. He rose to his feet.

"Tomorrow after supper," he said. "And the blue wool there, set that aside for me. I'm in need of a new winter tunic."

She laughed again, following him to the door. Outside the snow came down in swirls. The wind whispered of more cold to come.

"Good night, Avani," the village lord said as he stepped out into the storm.

"Good night, Thom."

She stood on the doorstep and watched his broad back until he disappeared into the night.

BEFORE DAWN SHE left her warm nest of blankets and staggered out into the cold to check on her sheep. She slogged through weather that had turned overnight to sleet, kicking up mud as she stumbled. Jacob rode on her shoulder, muttering his disgust all the way to the pen.

The driving wet splattered Avani's face and hair. She slipped once, and almost went down in the mud.

The sheep waited, huddled in a damp group at the low end of the fenced circle, as far from the bite of the wind as possible. Avani clambered over the old rails. She staggered and slid across the pen to her herd. She could smell the steam off their wool even before she reached the animals.

The sheep knew her. They paid Avani little attention as

she walked among them, shouldering aside wet noses and springy withers, checking for injury or blight.

They were hardy animals, mountain raised. The weather rarely seemed to bother their placid minds. Only Jacob sparked their interest. The sheep raised their heads as he took to the air, flapping about in their midst.

"Watch your beak," Avani warned as she tugged a ewe's muddy ear. Jacob tolerated the sheep about as well as he did Thom.

She couldn't blame him. She winced to wonder what her Goddess thought of a daughter tending flatland creatures. She sometimes worried that the raven would slip her control and terrorize the herd. Unhappy sheep produced thin, hard-to-spin wool.

Once Avani was assured that her livelihood had survived the night, and that they had plenty of dried grass still to eat, she hopped the fence and made her way slowly up into town.

Stonehill was the oldest settlement on the Downs, and the smallest. It was far enough away from true civilization that the king's whim rarely interfered with daily life. The people were proud of their land, and tended the village with something close to religious fervor.

The main street, cobbled long ago and cracking, was swept clean daily, rain or shine, summer or winter. The clapboard buildings were kept whitewashed. Once a year, on Saint Katherine's Day, Stonehillers gathered together to bleach every piece of graystone in the village, scrubbing and polishing until the rock gleamed.

They took as much pride in their Saints' days and festivals as they did in their holdings. No celebration passed without recognition and decoration. Already, as Avani hurried down slick cobblestones, she noted ongoing preparations for Winter Ceilidh.

Candles burned in sheltering tins on most doorsteps. Ropes of holly looped several chimneys. The sleet made the pretty red berries shine, even in the gloom of early morning.

At the very center of the village crouched Crooked Creek Inn. The tavern was named after the cascade of water that frothed along the Downs to the River Mors. The bedrooms on the second floor had long ago been closed to the public. The sign swinging above the entrance was painted red as the setting sun.

Avani had mixed the latest coat of paint for the Widow, stirring in dye after dye until the old woman was satisfied with the color.

As Avani knocked her boots on rough-hewn steps, Jacob leaped from her shoulder and rose into the morning sky. Avani watched the raven spiral out of sight, then she stepped into the warmth of the tavern.

The Widow kept the massive hearth in the common room stocked and burning all year long. Flames cracked and spat, and over the years smoke had saturated walls and ceiling.

Avani loved the scent of the smoke. She loved the soot stains on the thick beams overhead, and she loved the equally sooty massive dining tables, each large enough to seat at least ten men.

Early in the day as it was, the commons was full. Avani

knew every face in the room. No one looked up as she entered, but she knew her arrival had been noted.

She slid into an empty seat close to the fire and stretched out her limbs, hoping to dry hose and cape and tunic. The murmur of conversation rose and fell, a soft counterpoint to the snap of the hearth.

Eventually Avani's cape stopped dripping, and one of the Widow's two servers found his way to her spot. He carried a broken bowl and a wedge of black bread. Avani accepted the fare with a smile, dipping the bread eagerly into the stew.

She picked vegetables and chunks of lamb from the bowl with her fingers, gingerly trying to avoid globs of salted fat, the Widow's specialty.

By the time Avani had finished most of the stew and all of the bread, her cape had dried out, and her hose were no longer sopping. She could feel her toes again. She heaved a sigh of relief as she licked grease from her fingers.

"As fastidious as a cat."

The Widow's bulk blocked the firelight. The scent of pine smoke clinging to her ancient clothes made Avani's nose itch.

"Good morn," Avani said. She eyed the Widow carefully, trying to guess her mood.

"A nasty morn," the Widow argued. "Fall is waning."

"It is."

Avani picked a boiled turnip from the stew. She finished it in two bites.

"They've taken your dead soldier down to the keep," the Widow said. She brushed a hand over her coarse, curly hair.

"*My* dead soldier?" Avani titled her chin.

"You found him, eh?"

"Jacob found him," Avani corrected, stretching the truth just a little.

The Widow huffed. "That bird is drawn to trouble."

Avani knew it was meant as an insult, but she didn't bother to disagree. She dug through her stew until she found a last chunk of meat, and devoured the treat with regret. Her stomach growled.

"I need a new rug for my bedchamber," the Widow said. She gathered up Avani's empty bowl.

Avani swallowed back a protest. Their deal was long-standing; Avani got two meals a day and whatever seconds the Widow decided to toss her way. In exchange she was expected to keep the Widow and her tavern in rugs, and blankets, and woolens.

"Something blue or green," the Widow continued. "Large enough to stretch from window to bed. You remember the room."

Avani did indeed. The Widow's bedroom had once been the inn's best chamber, reserved for royalty when royalty came calling. As far as Avani knew, the Widow had been but a child during the last Progress. Royalty had long ago turned its back on Stonehill.

Rubbing her palms on her thighs, Avani considered her inventory.

"I've got nothing finished in blue. A large rug in grass green, and a patterned in black and red?"

The Widow shook her head. "Grass green is too light for the room."

Avani fisted her hands on her knees. "If I start a new rug now, I'll have it finished by Winter Ceilidh. Any color you like."

"Only if you work night and day. Bring me the black and red. It will have to do for the nonce."

Avani had planned the black and red for her own floor, but she nodded. "Tomorrow?"

"This eve," the Widow said. "At the gathering."

Avani sighed. She nodded, shoving away from the table.

The Widow bent her considerable weight to look Avani in the eye. "You be careful, hey? It's nasty out there, not for the faint of heart."

Avani kept her mouth shut. She gave the Widow a tight smile, and made her way around the great tables to the door.

Jacob was waiting for her in the wind.

JUST AFTER SUNSET Avani rolled the black and red rug into a thick bundle. She wrapped the bundle in old burlap for protection. The finished roll was heavy. When Avani hefted the rug over her shoulders her spine twinged, but she came from a tradition of hard work, and ignored the pain.

Outside the weather had cleared, but dusk was ice cold. Frost broke beneath Avani's boots. The air burned her lungs. Taking shallow breaths, she tracked over the brown grass. By the time she reached the sheep pen her nose and eyes were watering from cold.

The sun had dropped behind the Downs, and the sky had turned purple. Avani could smell the smoke from the Widow's ever-burning fire.

The thought of dinner lightened her load. She increased her pace.

But the roll of carpet was awkward across her neck. It forced her head at an angle and her eyes to the ground, and so she saw the splash of blood before the spreading puddle stained her sheepskin boots.

She stopped, rocking back on her heels, and almost dropped the Widow's carpet.

"*Ai*. Jacob!"

The raven didn't answer her call. Alarmed, she lifted her gaze from the ground, and searched the sky.

When she finally located the bird, she did drop her burden.

"Jacob!" she scolded, desperate.

Jacob didn't listen. He flew low over the grass, up the slope and back around toward the sheep pen, following a bloody trail across frozen ground.

Avani ran after. Even in her fear she took care not to step in the blood. The trail hadn't iced over, she realized, as she overtook the bird. The blood was still fresh.

She called for Jacob again. The raven screamed and took to her shoulder, claws piercing her cape. His nails pricked her bare skin, and the world turned sideways.

Pain burst in her skull. Six shadows loomed on the dim horizon, spreading like smoke. Avani cried out, fighting free of their grasp, but the wisdom of her Goddess held her fast.

She could smell venom; decay, brutality. She didn't know whether it was the stink of the shadows or the perfume of the dead.

Avani struggled to her feet. She tried to run, but the vision made the air around her thick as the bile she tasted in the back of her throat. She heard screaming and thought the sound was Jacob's rage. Then she tripped, and ran up against something hard.

The shock sent her tumbling, freeing the shadows from her head.

She lay sprawled on the cold ground. Jacob sat on her chest. The raven was still screaming, challenging the gloom. Avani wanted to calm him, but she was afraid to touch him again.

He jumped from her chest, mincing off across the grass. Avani managed to roll to her hands and knees. She lifted her head.

Her hands were dark with blood. She wondered if it was her own.

She lurched to her feet, and found that in her terror she had crashed up against the village pen. She could see her sheep at the farthest curve, and in the center of their huddle, something else.

She looked again at the blood on her hands. Then she focused on the fence, on the splash of black dripping across graystone and rail. Her gorge rose, but Jacob was already nearing the sheep, so she forced herself over the rails and across the field.

It seemed to take forever. Her eyes teared. Her stomach churned. Twice she had to stop to catch her breath, and steady her whirling head. The vision lurked still in her skull, threatening, and the winter air seemed thick as grease.

Jacob stopped before the mess in the middle of the herd. Avani could see the raven's eyes gleam in the dusk. He lifted his wings and called. Avani thought she could hear an echo of the Goddess in his cries.

She pressed on across the grass.

By the time she reached the horror, Jacob had stopped his screams and hunched silently on the ground. He turned his head and looked at her once, beak parted as though tasting the wind. Then he spread his wings and left her alone.

Avani folded her hands at her breast, schooled her courage, and looked down at the bodies tangled in the middle of her pen.

There were three. Two of the men wore the king's insignia. Their bodies had been torn apart. Blood was just beginning to freeze on their limbs.

The third man had collapsed several paces away from the dead Kingsmen. He was missing his left arm and most of his right thigh. His chest had been broken open, just like the first dead man Avani had found, below on the Downs.

The lower half of his face was still intact, and Avani recognized the kind mouth and the neatly trimmed beard. She recognized the tunic she had made for him more than a year earlier. She recognized the newly dyed cloak, even beneath the soak of blood. The one she had made for him a season past. Pinned to the cloak was a silver brooch, the badge of honor the king awarded each of his flatland lords.

Avani pressed a trembling hand against her mouth. She tried to speak his name, but it wouldn't come. Instead the world wavered, and the vision came rushing in again from every side.

Chapter Two

MAL REACHED MORS Keep on his sixth day in the saddle. The horse he rode, an old favorite, had lost flesh on the journey. Mal had pushed the animal too hard, and although the pace of travel had been necessary, he regretted the gelding's discomfort.

So he dropped the reins as they circled into the river valley, and let the horse slow to an easy walk. Stretching back in the saddle to relieve his own aching muscles, he lifted his gaze to the horizon, and considered the hills that rolled upward and away from the river.

Even from a distance the Downs looked harsh and unforgiving, nothing but an endless flow of stone broken here and there by sparse, dry grass. If he squinted, he could make out a smattering of white along the uppermost hills.

Winter weather arrived early on the Downs.

Along the river, fall chilled the air, but the wind was mild. Small groves of sheltering trees bent along the riverbank. Yellow leaves fluttered from gnarled branches. As Mal passed through a grove, a handful of the leaves burst free of the trees and took to the air in a small whirlwind, swirling above his head.

Acting on a whim, Mal jolted upright in his stirrups. He managed to snag one of the leaves midair.

Bringing the leaf back to earth for examination, he twirled it between his fingers, admiring the delicate veins and the gentle reddish stain along the broken stem.

The wind whistled, flinging more of the leaves into the air, but Mal settled back into his saddle, content with a lone treasure.

He let his eyes droop shut, enjoying the faint warmth of the rising sun on his face. He allowed his mind to drift, and by the time the Keep appeared around an island of rustling trees, he was nearly relaxed again, nearly ready to deal with the grisly task ahead.

Even so, as he dismounted in the shadow of the portcullis, his heart sank like a stone in his chest.

The only king's post for days in either direction, Mors Keep was very old, and as stark as the surrounding hills. A single tower rose halfheartedly into the sky. A thick wall of graystone and mortar encircled the spire. The portcullis was steel, and probably an antique.

Renault's pennant flew from the very top of the tower, as tattered as the crumbling leaf Mal still held.

A branch of the river rushed by only yards from the graystone wall. The remains of a rotting water wheel slumped against the far bank. The spray from the river wet Mal's face, and made his horse twitch and stomp.

Leading the animal carefully across stony ground, Mal approached the portcullis. He rapped the gate with the toe of his boot. The resulting sound was muffled at best. Showers of rust and grime fell from the metal. The portcullis looked as though it hadn't been opened in seasons.

Resigned, Mal stripped the glove from his right hand, put fingers to lips, and split the morning with a shrill whistle.

Response was a long time in coming. Mal hobbled his cooling horse to a clump of thick weeds, and stole an icy drink from the river. He had started to wonder if he would have to go over the daunting graystone wall when at last he heard an answering hail.

Mal gloved his cold hands again. He waited patiently before the gate.

"Lord Vocent!" The man regarding Mal through the rusting portcullis looked decidedly relieved.

"My lord," Mal replied, noting the badge on the man's breast. He cocked a brow at the man's expression. "You were expecting me, I think?"

"Aye!" The man's voice echoed off graystone. He stepped momentarily out of sight.

Mal could hear the squeaks of a winch turning. The portcullis inched its way upward with surprising speed. As soon as the way was clear, he led his horse under the gate and into the keep.

His lordship was a broad man, and young for his title. Sweat glistened on his upper lip as he brought the portcullis back to ground. His cheeks were very pale and his eyes were frightened.

"Trouble, my lord?" Mal asked gently, wondering at the man's unease.

"No, Lord Vocent," The man puffed out his breath. He released the winch. "That is, I wasn't expecting you until this eve. I was with the . . ." He swallowed. "I was in the temple when I heard your call."

Mal understood at once. "You shouldn't trouble yourself with the dead, my lord. It's my job." He tried a smile, but the man only flinched.

"I knew Thom," his lordship explained, rubbing a hand across his jaw. "Stonehill's lord. He was a good fellow. I couldn't believe it, when I heard." He squared his shoulders. "Well. I'll take you there now, shall I?"

"No. First I'll see to my horse. It's been a long journey for the both of us. Do you have mash?"

His lordship nodded. "We have a small stables. We have but one horse in the keep, but there are two extra stalls. I cleaned one when I understood you were on your way."

"Thank you," Mal replied. He followed the younger man across the bailey.

The stables were nearly as run-down as the keep. A lone pony munched happily in a small stall. It showed no interest in the new arrivals.

Mal led his horse to an empty stall and began to untack. His lordship went after the mash. By the time he returned with a steaming bucket, Mal had rubbed his mount clean, and found the horse fresh water.

"A lovely animal, Lord Vocent," his lordship said, briefly distracted from his sorrows. He watched the gelding eat. "I've never seen quite that shade of red before. Does he have a name?"

"Bran," Mal replied, hiding his amusement.

His lordship slapped Bran gently on the shoulder. Then he turned to Mal. "Galen FitzGerald, Lord Blackwater. You're welcome here, very welcome."

"Thank you." Mal gathered up his saddlebags. He bowed to the other man. "The temple?"

Blackwater nodded. Any color he'd regained left his cheeks. They set off together across the inner courtyard.

Mors Keep's temple was little more than a barn decorated with the proper saints and runes. His lordship made his obeisance at the door. Mal automatically followed suit.

They stepped over the threshold and onto a floor of packed earth. No fire warmed the building. The only real light fell in a weak glaze from high windows. A group of candles burned at the altar's base, but the votives were old, and they shed more smoke than light.

"Over here, Lord Vocent."

The bodies were laid out on a graystone bier at the very back of the temple. Someone had tossed dried winter flowers across the floor and altar, but the buds did little to hide the stench of decomposition in the air. Mal knew the stink well; his stomach stayed steady.

"Thank you, my lord." He set his saddlebags in the rushes at the foot of the bier. "I need some time alone with the dead."

The younger man twitched just a little. "I'll be outside. If you're wanting anything."

Mal nodded, already dismissing Blackwater from his world.

He approached the bier, bent over the bodies, and inhaled the perfume of the dead.

"I count four," Siobahn said from where she stood at the foot of the altar. "You only mentioned three."

"The first man died somewhat earlier," Mal answered, without pausing his examination. "His death might have been a forgotten murmur in Renault's ear if not for the last three. Come and look."

She stepped to his side, small hands folded neatly at her waist. She sniffed at the foul air, then lowered her head over the bier.

A strand of her long hair fell over her brow and clung to the tip of her nose, sparking red even in the dim light.

"Well?" Mal prompted, when she didn't speak.

Siobahn wrinkled her brow. "There isn't much left of them. An animal, perhaps. A wolf."

"Are you certain?"

She shook her head. More of her hair fell around her shoulders and over her face, framing her cheeks in a silken curtain.

"Three Kingsmen and Stonehill's village lord," Mal murmured, running a critical eye over the ruined bodies. "Torn to pieces on the Downs. And what were Kingsmen—*three* Kingsmen—doing in this bitter place, a sennight's ride from home?"

"Renault?"

"Woke me in the night and sent me here in haste. He didn't bother with explanations. His Majesty hasn't yet forgiven me Andrew."

Mal glanced down the side of his nose at his wife. "What do you see? They're not long dead, there must be something. Did they travel here with a purpose? Together?"

Siobahn pressed her mouth into a line.

"Nothing?" Mal challenged. "You've nothing?"

Siobahn nibbled at her bottom lip, frowning. Mal scowled back.

He paced twice around the bier, thinking. At last he stopped beside the largest of the dead men, Stonehill's lord. Mal picked up one of the man's stiff hands, studying the tips of his fingers. Flesh came away at his touch.

Mal grimaced. Carefully, he pinched each of the corpse's fingers between his own.

"Not broken. The nails are undamaged."

"No struggle," said Siobahn. "It happened quickly. Or they knew their assailant."

Mal looked up. "They speak to you?"

"No." She shrugged a little in her wedding dress. "But I know how you think."

"Do you?" he returned. "I think I don't like their silence."

Siobahn brushed her hair from her face. "It's happened before."

"Not often, and not without obvious explanation." Mal left the village lord, and moved to study the Kingsmen.

The first two yielded nothing of interest. The third . . .

He drew a breath.

"What is it?"

"I know this man. His name is Piers. He was one of Renault's private guardsmen. He was quite young."

"Young and far from home." Siobahn frowned at the torn face. "How do you know him?"

"His crest." Mal poked at the signet on the dead man's thumb. "His father was a friend to my mother. Piers had just made page when I was called to court."

"Far from home," Siobahn repeated. Mal wasn't sure whether she spoke of the dead youth, or of himself. "And lost for it."

Mal touched the body, stroked the matted beard. The yellow stone on his own finger glittered, mirroring the shifting light in the high windows.

"I don't like this."

Siobahn saw his anger. She responded in kind. "Their silence is not my failing."

"No." Mal took a deep breath. He started to apologize, but the light in the temple moved again as Blackwater hurried through the door.

"Lord Vocent?" Blackwater's voice trembled and cracked on a high note. "The day is growing dark; an afternoon storm blows our way. Will you shelter in the keep? This temple is old and not always safe in winter winds. The tower is warmer, and sturdy."

Mal arched his brows.

"The tower will withstand your storm?" he asked, dry.

Blackwater's expression was somber. "Aye. As I said, the tower is sturdily built. And as the king has charged me with your safety . . ."

"Of course." Mal slung his saddlebags over one arm. He let Blackwater usher him from the temple. "I've learned all I can. I'm afraid these men tell me nothing. I have no answers for His Majesty."

His lordship paused in the temple door. The surprise on his face had Mal's eyes narrowing.

"What is it?"

Blackwater looked away. The younger man blinked at the packed dirt floor. Mal balanced his saddlebags and touched his lordship's arm.

"What is it?" he repeated, more gently.

"There is a woman, Lord Vocent," Blackwater muttered. "Up on the Downs. They say she saw things."

"A Stonehiller?"

Blackwater nodded. "A foreigner. But she's lived up on the Downs for nigh on four winters. They say she found the three men, penned in with her sheep. They say, after, she was struck mute for an entire day. They say whatever she saw drove her mad."

"More likely it was fear, and the shock of finding corpses among her sheep."

"Aye, Lord Vocent," answered Blackwater, doubtfully.

Mal sighed. He looked up past the high graystone walls to the heights of the snowy Downs. The sky above the hills was black with temper, and Mal could indeed smell the coming storm.

"His Majesty will want to hear her story, no doubt."

"No doubt." Blackwater seemed to cheer a little.

"She has a name? This Stonehiller?"

"Avani, Lord Vocent."

"Avani," Mal tried the unfamiliar syllables. He studied racing black clouds. "Will the storm clear overnight?"

"Most likely, Lord Vocent."

"Good." Mal stepped around the other man, starting for the tower. "I'll make for the Downs at dawn, hear the woman's tale, and be back on low ground by tomorrow eve."

"Aye," Blackwater agreed. "I hope so."

THE STORM RAN its course overnight as promised, leaving behind only a light drizzle in the pale sunrise. Even the small rain was cold. Mal wrapped his cloak around his shoulders, and pulled the low hood over his face.

Great yellow and red clouds of leaves hung in circling whirlwinds over the ground. Made heavier by the rain, shredded by overnight winds, the leaves clung in bits and pieces to Mal's boots and trousers.

Blackwater had been happy enough to see Mal go, but unwilling to let the bodies of the dead linger overlong in his temple. Only Mal's quiet reassurances had kept his lordship from hysteria.

Siobahn paced alongside Mal's horse as they climbed the Downs, her hand set just behind the Bran's girth. The gelding tolerated her touch, although the rustle of the wind through her skirts made the animal snort.

Mal sat quietly in the saddle, watching as wind sculpted the mist. His bride didn't speak until the path became more stone than grass.

"Why," she asked, brushing rain from her cheeks, "would any person live in a place such as this?"

Mal studied her out of the corner of his eye. He kept a smile from his mouth.

"It *is* unpleasant. Stonehill itself sits in a dip on the Downs. The village is somewhat sheltered from the passions of the seasons."

"Passions," she snorted, leaning into the warmth of the horse. "You've traveled this way before?"

"Once. Many years ago. With Gerald."

Siobahn looked up into his face, gauging his expression, but didn't press. Instead, she scraped wet hair from her neck, shaking droplets from her curls.

"Why up here? Why not down along the river? The land on the water is lovely, the air mild."

This time he did smile, a wry twist of the lips in response to her veiled complaint.

"The keep is there. Stonehillers have no use for king or creed."

"Ah. Trouble," she decided. "Hidden away in the hills."

Bran stumbled. Mal took a firmer grip on the reins.

"Not trouble. Merely discontent. There are many similar pockets scattered throughout the kingdom. These people"—he nodded at the hills—"want nothing more than to be left alone."

Siobahn considered. "Perhaps so much so that they murdered three Kingsmen? And their lord when he tried to put a stop to the violence?"

"Thom was a Stonehiller born and bred. Well beloved, according to Blackwater."

"Even so." Lost in thought, she tapped Bran's wet shoulder. "He was the king's soldier, and wore His Majesty's favor."

"He was a village man," Mal corrected. "No matter the fancy badge on his breast."

Siobahn huffed. Irritation turned her eyes into slits of boiling blue. To Mal's surprise, she didn't argue further.

He reached down to grip her hand. After a moment she awarded him a quick smile.

Clouds cut the sky and the rain eased. Mal slouched in the saddle, trying to outwit a cutting wind. The hills above grew less distant. He could see snow falling across stony shoulders.

Siobahn moved, lifting her palm from Bran's coat, and gripping Mal's calf. He could feel the heat of her through the leather of his boot.

As they climbed, drizzle grew heavy again, and turned to drifting snow. Thin flakes caught in Bran's dark mane, and immediately began to melt. But where snow touched ground it stuck, coating rock with a fine layer of sparkle.

When Mal sucked in a breath of white-frozen air, his lung hitched at the shock of cold.

"Beautiful," he remarked through a dry throat. He pulled Bran up, pausing for a moment to admire the scenery. Harsh as the land was, it touched something deep in his gut, and made him want to run free and feral as he had in his boyhood.

Siobahn blinked up at his face. She laughed.

"Wait until we freeze to the ground." She rested her chin on his boot above her fingers, and used her free hand to brush frost from Bran's belly.

"Not so much further," he said in reassurance. The skin of his face had begun to go numb. His breath steamed in the morning air. Swallowing a cough, he urged Bran forward.

Around two more turns of one hill, down a stony grade, up a low curve of land—and abruptly the scenery reversed, and snow covered more grass than stone.

"Ah," Mal breathed, through wind-battered lips. "There. Evidence of civilization."

"What is that?" Curious, she sighted along the line of his finger.

"A shepherd's hut. In good weather a man might live out here, on the skin of the Downs, with his herd."

"Good weather?" Siobahn scoffed. She eyed the sagging building doubtfully. "Didn't his lordship say the woman who found the Kingsmen was a shepherdess?"

"He did say she found the bodies penned in a field with her sheep," Mal allowed.

Just as the cold became unbearable, they turned the last corner, passed along an outcropping of smooth rock, and stumbled upon the edge of the village. The snow came now in thick waves. Mal could see little but the faint flicker of light ahead.

He thought he could smell the grease of cook fires, but he couldn't be sure. The wind and wet dulled his senses.

"There," Siobahn said. "A path."

"I don't see it." He could find nothing past the tip of his nose, and he could no longer feel his feet.

"Pass me the reins. I'll lead."

Mal tossed the reins over Bran's head. Siobahn snatched the loop of leather. Bran moved on without hesitation.

Mal tucked his gloved fists in his armpits, and tried to

squint ahead through the snow. Almost immediately his head began to pound with the effort.

He felt the tilt as they slipped down a slight grade, then heard the sharp strike of hooves on cobblestone. The sound echoed. Several times he thought he caught the ghosts of buildings through the storm.

Siobahn led Bran on past muffled lamplight. Mal heard voices beyond the fall of snow, but he couldn't make out words, couldn't be sure he heard true sound at all.

Then light bloomed, and the drift of snow eased.

"A tavern," Siobahn said. As though she had conjured it, a building materialized in the light. She tossed back the reins.

The sign above the door was red beneath a rime of ice. The door itself looked thick, and was scarred by weather or age. Here the scent of grease was very strong. As Mal slid from the saddle, his stomach woke and began to growl.

He pushed back his hood, letting snow fall on his hair. He stripped the gloves from his hands and tried to stamp the knots from his legs.

A shadow broke from the side of the building, and transformed into a boy.

Thin beneath a ragged fur cloak, the child flashed a toothy grin, and pointed his chin at Bran. The boy looked no older than ten summers, but something in his scrawny face spoke of an old man's humor.

"Stable your horse?"

Mal nodded, and reached for his saddlebags. As he stretched over Bran's hindquarters, the tavern door banged open, expelling a group of very loud men. The yellow gem on Mal's finger sparked.

The boy gasped and swore. Mal turned, ready for trouble, but the men had disappeared into the snow, all unknowing. When he looked sideways at the boy, the child looked frightened rather than angry.

"How much?" Mal asked.

The boy's eyes widened. "My lord?"

"How much?" Mal repeated without inflection. "To stable my horse?"

"Oh." The boy summoned his courage. He extended a grubby hand. "Four marks, my lord."

Mal picked six from the pouch at his belt. He let the coins drop, one after another, into the boy's palm. "Give him grain."

"Aye, my lord." The boy secreted the marks beneath his cloak. He took Bran's bridle with some hesitation. Shooting one last look at the ring on Mal's hand, the lad whispered to Bran, and led the horse away around the building.

The tavern door burst open again. An elderly woman wrapped in boiled wool staggered out onto the cobblestones. She tossed Mal an incurious glance, then lurched away into the storm.

Mal looked after her fading form. Then, brushing snow from his hair, he pushed through the heavy door and into the building.

Almost immediately, smoke clung to his form and clogged his throat. Swallowing a gasp, he blinked. Outdone by the tickle in his lungs, coughed.

The common room was packed, several large tables filled end to end, thick-hewn chairs positioned leg to leg. A large fire burned on a hearth at one end of the room.

Mal heard the splatter of grease, and the hiss of cooking meat.

He wiped watering eyes, peering around the room.

A hand fell heavy on his shoulder, squeezing.

"Lord Vocent?"

Mal turned, startled. He looked up into a thick and craggy face.

The woman loomed over Mal. Her smile of greeting seemed forced.

"We didn't expect you this far north," she said. "We hoped your business would be concluded in the keep."

Mal shook his head. He coughed again.

"You'll be wanting a seat," the woman continued, squeezing his shoulder further as she spoke. "Close to the fire. You're soaked through. Foolish to travel on a day such as this one. Something to eat?"

Mal noted the stained apron around her waist, and the kerchief over her abundant gray hair.

"You're the innkeep?"

She nodded, gruff. "They call me the Widow. The tavern is mine, and the inn upstairs, although we haven't had need to use a room for many seasons. Would you be wanting one?"

"Overnight, please. Maybe longer."

"Aye. You'll be snowed in a day or two. We'll make it work, we will," she said. "Come and sit down, and I'll bring you a mug of ale. Or cider?"

"Cider," Mal decided. He followed her ample form between tables.

The Widow directed him to the far edges of the room,

away from the rest of her patrons, seating him at a small square table. He wondered if she was setting him in shadow on purpose.

The fire burned at his back, crackling flames warm as summer. He swallowed a mouthful of smoke, and choked through clenched teeth.

The Widow's smile grew wider.

"You'll get used to it. The smoke will dry you out, warm your bones. Breath easy, and you'll get used to it." She patted his arm, seemingly intent on touching the tooled leather over his skin. "I'll bring you that cider, and a sausage. Sit and breathe."

Mal should have been annoyed, but the fire sucked moisture from his skin, and the smell of supper cooking tempted his stomach. He slouched back in his chair, idly running his fingers over the notched edge of the table, and let the smoke ruin his clothes.

The sausage came seared red and black, and longer than Mal's hand. The Widow dropped it on the table with a thump that had the meat bouncing in its trencher. Grease splattered. Mal leaned away from the table. He waited as the woman shoved a brimming tankard after his meal.

"Sausage and cider," she said with pride. "Both spiced. Eat."

Still more amused than irritated, he tried the sausage and found it delicious. The Widow laughed aloud at his expression.

"It's the smoke that does it," she explained, smug. "I have the wood carried in from below, special. Costs me most of a summer's earnings, but it's worth it." She swiped grease from the surface of the table with a corner of her apron.

"A room?" he asked, noting that the toothy grin she wore didn't quite reach her eyes.

"I'll have the boys sweep one out. Twelve marks a night. I imagine you can afford it."

Mal nodded. He tried the cider. Like liquid honey, the drink coated his throat, and then burned its way to his belly. The tankard was surprisingly clean, the bone handle polished.

Pleased, he took another sip.

"Avani's own recipe," the Widow said, as though divulging a secret.

Mal looked up. He caught the shrewd twist of the woman's mouth before her smile returned.

"She'll be along shortly, Lord Vocent. We've sent Liam out to fetch her back. So sit and eat, and dry out all that lovely dark hair." She wiped again at the table, then stilled, pinned by something she glimpsed on his face.

"Thank you," he said, very politely. "There's nothing more I need."

"Aye." The Widow took a breath, and her sturdy frame shuddered. But as she turned from the table she threw one last sharp grin over her shoulder. "Breathing easier now, eh?"

Mal watched the woman weave her way back through the forest of benches and chairs. He noticed as he did that the common room had almost emptied. The smoke stung his eyes. He bent over his meal.

The firelight made shadows dance around his corner. A

single spirit lingered near the front door. The ghost wore woodsman's togs and puffed contentedly on an immaterial pipe as it paced between living customers, blue eyes flashing. Mal ignored it in favor of his meal. For a while he was left in peace. He finished the sausage, and most of the cider. Lulled by the buzz of low voices, he let his eyes droop shut.

Mal waited. The tavern door banged occasionally open and shut, as lone patrons passed in and out of the cold.

He knew the moment she entered the room, recognized a change in the timbre of the voices, a certain anticipation. He sat as he was, listening to the scrape of the Widow's boots as she shoved her way across the commons.

"Lord Vocent!" the woman called, voice shrill.

Mal didn't respond. Tucked away in his corner, he lifted the tankard and sipped cider. By the time he had drained away the last of the wonderful drink, the Widow stood in front of this table.

"My lord!" she huffed. "Here is Avani."

The whine in the woman's tone snuffed the last of Mal's patience. He didn't understand her bluff mannerisms, or appreciate her loud charm. He thought he understood the sullen glaze behind her gawking, and he didn't like it at all.

Weary, he moved his left hand so the flames in the hearth bounced off the facets of the jewel on his finger. He pasted a hard smile on his own face. He looked up, and felt the table tremble when the Widow started.

"My lord," she repeated, more quietly. "Avani is here."

"Thank you," Mal replied. "Please bring us more cider."

"Aye," the Widow said. She bustled quickly away.

"Well, then, you have a way about you, no doubt. What did you do to frighten her so?"

The voice was sweet and liquid as the cider. Mal turned his head, picking a silhouette from the swirl of smoke.

Broken, he thought at first. Horribly malformed, a crooked spine, one shoulder noticeably higher than the other. Mal felt a shock of sorrow and pity, a shiver of sympathy in the pit of his stomach.

When she stepped from the smoke, the flash of relief was so strong he choked on a breath of thick air.

The woman was straight as his sword, keen edged and beautiful. She was small and very lean, and Mal recognized the whittling of hard work and too little to eat.

Her skin was brown, her hair long and black and loose. She wore an ugly cape of patchwork fur above an overlong tunic and torn trousers. In the firelight the lump on her shoulder became a large crow, a bird as dark as the woman's skin, and as sleek and graceful as her hands.

She moved those hands as she spoke, weaving a constant and gentle dance in the air with her fingers. Bangles of beaten gold chimed on both of her wrists, their glimmer almost hidden by the loose sleeves of the tunic she wore.

"I am told the vocent is more powerful than the king himself," she said, smiling slightly. Her voice was lightly accented, syllables fluid. "But I didn't believe a man existed who might cow the Widow."

She had eyes that were large and lovely, wide and slanted above sharp cheekbones. Her smile plucked at Mal's heart and made him uneasy.

He swallowed and gestured at the chair across from his own.

"Sit," he said. "You're hungry. What will you have?"

She shook her head as she slipped into the chair. The crow left her shoulder for the timbers above.

"He doesn't like the Widow, either," the woman said, still smiling. "I think he's afraid he'll end up in one of her pies."

"Can't say as I blame the bird." Her thin wrists and sharp elbows made him want to feed her, to put flesh on fragile bones. "Tell me what you'll have. Not a pie."

She laughed. "Cider will do."

"And a sausage," he decided, looking over the back of his chair for the Widow. "The sausages are really quite delicious."

"Lord Vocent," the woman said. She reached across the table, not quite touching his arm.

He turned back around, and arched a brow.

"I haven't much time," she explained. "The day is nearly half past. The sheep need to be turned." She shifted in her chair. The firelight brightened her hair to jet. "So. You have questions?"

"I do," he said, but he was unable to look away from the slant of her eyes. He didn't speak again until the Widow dropped two tankards of cider on the table.

Chapter Three

"A SAUSAGE," HE said then, looking not at the Widow but at Avani. "For the lady. Two."

Avani didn't know whether to be flattered or insulted. So she settled instead on irritated, and opened her mouth on a retort. But the Widow interrupted.

"The *lady*," she snorted, her contempt obvious, "doesn't eat my sausages. She finds the meat too greasy."

Avani sighed, and showed her teeth. "A bowl of stew, please. Just a small bowl."

"And some bread," the man across the table added. "Butter."

"Butter!" The Widow looked properly put out. In truth, Avani knew, the woman was gleefully totting up marks. "That will cost you—"

"Butter," the vocent said, eyes cold.

"Aye." The Widow spread a sickly smile across her face, then hurried away.

Avani picked up her cider. Letting the steam off the liquid warm her nose, she regarded her companion over the rim of the tankard.

"We could use you here," she decided. "The Widow needs a keeper."

"She's harmless."

"Perhaps." Avani took a sip of her drink, and found it a trifle too sweet. "Be wary, she has a longing for nice things. She'd kill you for the decoration in your tunic if she thought she could get away with it. Hennish leather, is it?"

His eyes gleamed. They were very green, green as good grass in the spring.

"Hennish," he agreed. "You know it?"

"Fabric is my business. But I know a thing or two about tanning," she replied. She couldn't help thinking that, really, the man was lovely.

Soft, burnished hair, as varied as the coals on the hearth, fell in waves just past his shoulders. His face was beautiful as a girl's, made even more beguiling by a hint of tragedy about the mouth.

Only a slight dent in the chin saved the man from being too pretty.

A vocent is more powerful than the king himself, Liam had warned as he pulled her through the snow. *And this vocent is the last of his kind. The last magus in all the world.*

She had assumed the boy exaggerated. Now she wasn't so sure.

Everything about the man spoke of money and privilege. The leather he wore, the large jewel on his hand, the very set of his mouth and shoulders. This was a man who was used to being obeyed.

"My lord," she began, intending to send him on his way. She had nothing to give such a man.

But he shook his head and lifted a long finger.

"Mal."

"What?" She blinked.

"I have a name." His lips curved. "Mal. Or Malachi, if you prefer. Malachi Doyle."

Avani frowned in disbelief. "Doyle? You weren't born a flatlander. You haven't the coloring."

"No. It seems we have something in common."

When she didn't respond, he wrapped his hands around his tankard. He leaned forward across the table until she could feel the strength of his stare.

"My foster father was a flatlander. Gerald Doyle. I took his name after he died. He was a good man, I owed him that respect."

"And now you are titled Lord Vocent."

"For many years," he agreed, surprising her. She thought he looked very young, and had imagined he was new to his post.

"And you?" he asked. "Your name?"

"Surely you heard the Widow."

"I want to hear you say it," he insisted, surprising her again.

"Avani," she relented.

"Avani," he repeated, mimicking her accent almost perfectly. "Wonderful."

In spite of herself, she laughed. "You're the first to say so."

"Born on one of the islands?" he guessed.

"Yes." She peered across the commons, and changed the subject. "Here comes your food."

"The food is for you," he corrected, but didn't press.

The magus waited silently as the Widow set bread, and butter, and stew on the table. He appeared to be unaware of the poisonous looks the Widow sent Avani, but once the innkeep bustled away, his pretty eyes narrowed.

"She doesn't like you very much."

"She doesn't like the raven. Black birds are bad luck. She thinks I'm a witch, or a demon."

He glanced up into the eves, but Avani knew he couldn't see Jacob.

"And are you?" he asked, mild.

Avani shook her head. She started in on the stew. Her empty stomach twisted painfully at the first taste.

"Jacob adopted me," she said around a second mouthful. "The Widow doesn't understand."

"Jacob." He peered around the common room.

"You won't find him until he's ready. He doesn't like strangers. My lord . . ."

"Mal."

"*My lord*." She gritted her teeth. "As I said, the day is passing, my sheep need to be turned. You've come a long way. I'm sorry, but I think you've made a mistake. I have nothing that might help you, or your king."

"Try the bread," he said. "And the butter. You need fattening."

Pride sparked. Avani forced herself to push the half-finished bowl of stew away. She started to rise.

His hand snapped out, clamped around her wrist, and held her against the table. His fingers were gentle, but the force behind his grip was implacable.

"Sit down," he ordered, mild. "Finish the stew, and the bread. Then, after you've eaten every last crumb, you and I will step out into this very nasty weather, and turn your precious sheep. And perhaps, while we care for yon wee beasties, you'll think of something that might be of interest to me, or to my king."

Avani thought to jerk away, and storm from the room. She moved slightly. His hand tightened. Behind the twinkle in his eye, and the curve of his tragic mouth, she sensed ice.

For a moment, she felt fear.

Reluctantly, Avani dropped back into her chair. She pulled the bowl of stew across the tabletop.

He let her eat in silence, simply sat back and watched. The flame off the hearth turned his skin a deeper bronze.

When the bowl was empty, and she had wolfed down the final bit of bread and licked the last of the butter from her fingers, Avani inclined her head.

"Very good," he said, as though complimenting a child. He stood up, dug around beneath his cloak, and tossed several coins onto the table. "Bundle up, and we'll go."

She almost laughed aloud at that, but instead obediently wrapped her cape around her shoulders. She wondered if he noticed the holes in her tunic and trousers, or the worn sheepskin on her feet.

What would it feel like, she mused, *to wear real leather boots?*

Mal put his hand on her back, and firmly steered her through the common room. The Widow looked up as they pushed past patrons, but kept her silence.

Unhindered, they slipped from the tavern and into the chill afternoon.

The fall of snow had tapered off. Avani thought she could see blue on the horizon. Drifts were knee high, but someone had cleared a neat path along the cobblestones. Probably Liam, she thought, looking around for the lad.

"There down the road," Mal said, as though he'd read her mind. "A friend of yours?"

She found the skinny lad across the cobblestones, and lifted her hand in a wave.

"He belongs to the Widow, but I like to keep an eye on him."

"He's looking after my horse."

Avani shrugged. She started along Liam's path. The cobbles were slippery, and she stepped carefully. Mal followed at her heels. She heard him suck in a deep breath of fresh air.

"I can still taste smoke."

Avani kept her eyes on her feet. "The Widow's is the only tavern in Stonehill. She does well."

"She said the cider was your own recipe."

Then she did look over her shoulder, and caught his dry expression.

"My mother's recipe," she said. "But the Widow makes it too sweet."

"Then you'll have to brew a mugful," he returned, "and correct my palate."

She almost laughed again. "You are very sure of yourself."

"Yes," he said, unembarrassed. Then, "Where are your sheep?"

"I live across the village, on the edge of the Downs. The herd is there. Do you really know how to turn sheep?"

"I learned," he said. "A long time ago, after I was made foster."

She saw the pain in his eyes, and turned away. But he touched her elbow.

"Is that your bird?"

She looked into the sky, and whistled. "*Ai!* Jacob!"

The raven circled and dove, fetching up on her shoulder with a dramatic flap of his wings. He turned his head side to side, eyeing Mal, and muttering deep in his throat.

"Admirable. Does he always come at your call?" Mal asked, regarding Jacob doubtfully.

"He is my partner," Avani answered simply. She waited as Jacob settled his feathers. Then she walked on.

She led Mal through Stonehill, across snowbound fields to her own corner of land. As they walked, she glanced several times over Jacob's head at the man, trying to read his face.

He seemed vaguely interested in the village, and in her little house when it appeared over the hill, but for the most part his face was still, his mouth without expression.

When they reached the pen, she loosed Jacob and clamored over the fence. Mal paused, leaning his elbows on the nearest sturdy post, and studied her mud-encrusted herd.

"The smell is exactly as I remember," he said, wry. "They look healthy enough."

"The best wool around," Avani boasted, proud of her hard work. "People come from all across the Downs for my cloth."

"Indeed." He didn't sound as if he believed her.

"I trade it through the keep, as well," she said, defensive. "His lordship takes a cut, but he gets me what I want."

"Blackwater?" This time his disbelief was tangible.

"He's a great head for figures," Avani scolded, annoyed. She started across the pen.

Mal hopped the rails and came after.

"I'm astounded. The man looked too frightened to do anyone any good."

"You're a cold one," she retorted. "Certainly his lordship would be frightened. He'd four murdered men in his keep, and a man more powerful than the king"—here she mocked without care—"come to poke the corpses."

He stepped around her, blocking her path. When she scowled up into his face, she saw that his eyes had gone to green ice.

"*Murdered* men," he repeated. "Are you guessing, or do you know?"

"Goddess take you. They were torn to pieces!"

"Are you guessing," he asked again, chill as the snow at their feet. "Or do you know?"

"I know!" she admitted, furious. Shrugging off his gaze, she dodged the reach of his hand, and kicked through the snow to her sheep.

Mal followed in silence. When she whistled at the

sheep, turning them from one end of the pen to the other, chasing them across the slope, he stepped into the work with the ease of old skill.

It took her half the time with his aid. When the last of the animals had found a new place to stand in the thin sunshine, Avani was surprised to discover she had energy left over.

She turned to thank the man, and found him watching Jacob.

"What is he doing?"

Avani frowned, and glared at the raven, but she didn't have the heart to lie. Not with the sheep turned and time still remaining in her afternoon.

"The men were found there, on that patch of grass."

"He's scenting their blood?"

"You might say that." Avani crossed to the center of the pen, knowing he would follow.

She crouched on the frozen ground where the men had died, and crossed her arms, keeping away from the raven. She didn't want Jacob to draw her in, not here, not with this man looking on.

"Tell me," Mal said. His shadow fell across the grass.

"They were here," she said. "Side by side. Ripped apart. Split open. Skin flayed from bone. What more do you need?"

"You said they were murdered. How do you know?"

"I saw it." She sighed. "There was a darkness, it tasted of deep places. It came upon them, and they had no chance. Whatever it was, it ripped them apart."

"You were here?" His voice was harsh.

She found some humor in the idea. "And alive to tell about it? No. When your Kingsmen were murdered, when Thom was murdered, I was safe in my home. Mulling cider, mixing dyes. I didn't sleep well, that night. But I didn't hear anything, or see anything. Not until the next morning."

"Blackwater said you had a fit. Suffered visions."

Avani thought she could still send him away. It wouldn't be easy, but he would go.

Yet as she frowned up at him, saw the mud stains on his expensive trousers, and the tear in his leather sleeve where one of the ewes had scored him with a hoof, she softened.

"Come into my home," she said, straightening. "And I'll fix you a mugful of cider to correct that palate."

Mal followed her obediently back across the field. He watched the swing of her hair against her spine. Like a black curtain of silk, it fell to the curve of her lower spine. He wondered if she left it loose for warmth.

Certainly the clothes she wore provided little protection. Mal noted the way she shuddered in the cold. He doubted the frayed boots she wore were any shield at all from the wet.

"You tell me your business is fabrics," he said, "yet take little care with yourself."

Her shoulders stiffened. Mal hid a grin.

Why, he wondered, *did he feel the need to prod at her temper? Why did he feel her quick flares of irritation so satisfying?*

"It's my business," Avani muttered, as she climbed between fence rails. "Not a vanity. The money I make goes directly back into the land, into the sheep. Dyes and loom, and rent."

"Rent?"

She waited as he scaled the fence.

"You wouldn't be thinking I own this land?" she said, politely scornful. "I pay your king good coin for the use."

"Of course. I'm sure His Majesty would be touched by your sacrifice." Mal gave her ugly cape a pointed look.

Flushing, Avani whirled around. She stomped up the slope; the raven swooped overhead. Mal followed more slowly, content to enjoy the grace of her temper.

Grass and snow cracked beneath his feet. The temperature was dropping again. Mal supposed dark came early in the hills.

Avani's home was little larger than a shed. The graystone foundation was buckling, and the old wood siding almost as dark as the rock. The roof was pitched, and mostly free of snow. Mal found himself hoping, for her sake, that the tiny building didn't leak.

Avani knocked mud and ice from her boots before stepping through the front door. Mal paused to do the same.

When he followed across the threshold, he stopped and stared, amazed.

Avani's home was warm, as warm as Stonehill's tavern. The floors and walls were covered by carpets and tapestries; the ceiling was hung with more samples.

Each color was more striking than the next. Mal studied one length of wool, and then the next, and another, unable to stop. He wanted to see more, wanted to touch. He reached out and ran fingers down the closest tapestry.

The wool was rough but finely woven. The colored patterns drew Mal in, and he found himself lost in the shapes.

Here, he realized, was real skill. He'd found a crafter talented enough to weave for Renault.

He released the fabric, intending to praise.

Avani stood on a pile of rugs, arms crossed over her breast, chin held high. He realized she expected derision.

The vulnerability he saw in the stubborn set of her mouth tightened something in his chest.

In the end Mal said nothing. He only inclined his head, and crossed the small room to a pile of bright cushions.

"May I sit?"

Avani grunted. She paced away to poke at a small wood-burning stove. Mal sank into the cushions. The raven perched on a rafter and buried his beak under a wing.

"He likes to keep an eye on guests," Avani said, as she fanned flames to life. "Don't let him fool you."

As Avani puttered, Mal took off his cloak and shed his gloves. He examined the tear in his sleeve.

"I'm afraid it's ruined." She sounded honestly regretful. "Hennish is impossible to mend properly."

"It was ruined the moment I stepped into the tavern," he replied, unconcerned. "Smoke that thick will cling forever."

"Fresh air and lavender," Avani said. She crumbled leaves into a pot of boiling water.

"I beg your pardon?"

"Hang it out in fresh air, and then pack it in dried lavender for a sevenday. It will take the stink right out."

"I'll remember." He spread the cloak over his knees.

Avani crossed back over her rugs. She handed Mal a mug of hot cider.

As she bent to pass the drink, the ends of her hair brushed the inside of his wrist. Mal's heart jumped in response. He took a deep, steadying breath, inhaling spice, then realized the scent he enjoyed was more the women than the cider.

Avani sat cross-legged at his feet. Mal edged back on his pillows, away from the woman, and forced his treacherous mind to business.

He took a swallow of cider, then bowed his head in homage.

"You're right," he said. "The Widow brews it too sweet. This is beyond description." He took another drink, widening his eyes in appreciation.

Avani scoffed, but pleasure flickered in her smile. A smear of mud darkened her brow. Mal almost reached across to thumb the dirt away. Instead, he balanced his mug on his knee, and examined the ring on his finger until his thoughts were again of his duty.

"Tell me," he said at last.

Avani sat quietly, hands clasped and still in her lap. Golden bangles slipped down around her arms, encircling her wrists.

"For my people," she explained slowly, "dreams and visions are not unusual. We don't fear them. We treat them as they are; a gift of the Goddess, messages from our ancestors. A lucky few of us are strong in that gift, and are trained up from the cradle to interpret and teach."

"You've had that training?" Mal guessed.

Avani's hands twisted in her lap, and her bangles sang softly.

"The gift was strong in my family," she said. "In my mother, and in her brothers, and their father. I had some schooling, yes."

Mal set the mug of cider on the floor. He knew better, but still he clasped her nervous hands in his own.

"What did you see?"

"I told you, did I not? Shadows, and rot, and the taste of deep earth. Old blood."

She paused, as if searching memories. "Violence, rage. Tearing, rending, hunger. They tried to save themselves, but it happened too quickly. Your Kingsmen had no hope of escape. Neither poor Thom, out alone on the Downs. Split open from breast to groin as he was."

Mal's grip tightened. "You saw him."

"*Ai*, I found him, didn't I?" Avani looked at Mal in surprise. "You didn't know that bit. They didn't tell you the entire story."

"I didn't know." He should have.

"He was the same," she said. "They murdered him."

"They?"

"More than three," she sighed, "less than seven. I think."

Mal shook his head in frustration. "It shouldn't be so difficult."

Avani took her hands back, lifting her chin. "I won't apologize. I've given you what I can. One of my brothers might have seen beyond the shadows, conjured for you their kind, their number, even counted the hairs on their bodies. I was very young when I was forced to leave my home, there is much of my birthright I will never know."

"You're shouting," Mal pointed out, calm. He picked up the cider, and took a slow swallow. He considered her dark, slanted eyes and the shape of her cheekbones. "Which of the Sunken Islands were you from?" he hazarded.

Avani glanced away. Mal had forgotten the raven. He started when the bird hissed.

"Jacob," Avani cautioned. She rolled her shoulders in a shrug.

"You said you grew up on the coast." She said, "You would have heard the stories."

"I imagine the entire land has heard tales of that cataclysm," Mal said. "But, yes. I helped collect the dead from the beaches. It's not something a man will ever forget."

"It's called the Horn, now. Some of the highest pinnacles still break the sea. Pinnacles not even the strongest of us could scale."

"I'm sorry. Your family?"

Avani shook her head. "All lost. There are a handful of my people left to confirm your horror stories, and that is thanks to your king and his fleet." She shrugged again. "I am the youngest survivor, I think, but not the last of my kind. We make what life we can in the flatlands, away from the water.

"I was quite young when the island fell, not fully trained, hardly full grown. I have trouble with visions. Often they come too quickly, and overwhelm. Dreams are easier." She hesitated. "I dreamed, that night, of strangers from the south."

"South."

Avani scratched her elbow. "South, and west, I think. I couldn't see their faces, but they smelled of the sea and sang songs of the Low Port."

"South and west is Wilhaiim," Mal murmured. "His Majesty's capitol. The Kingsmen."

"I'm sorry," she said. "There is nothing else."

Mal heard the hesitation in her voice, and wondered. He knew he could force the rest from her, make her speak, share every secret. Renault would expect it of him.

He didn't want to hurt her.

So instead he adjusted his cloak around his shoulders, climbed from the mountain of cushions, and returned his empty mug to her stove.

"I thank you." He bowed politely.

Avani appeared abashed and then, he thought, ashamed. "If I think of anything else—" she began.

"I'll come back," he agreed easily. "Perhaps tomorrow, on my way down the hills, just in case you dream again in the night."

Her brow wrinkled, but she kept her smile pleasant. "I do not expect that will happen. You may find yourself snowed in, tomorrow dawn."

"So the Widow suggested."

When they stepped from the house, he discovered it was indeed storming again. The sun was banished, the afternoon passed to evening.

"Good night," he said, bowing again.

"Good night," she replied, the raven watching over her shoulder.

Mal left her there. He found his way through snowfall to the tavern, where once inside he was given a late supper and a mostly clean room.

He recognized one of Avani's rugs warming the floor by the bed. The rug was patterned in red and black. Mal spent a long while admiring the artistry before he undressed for sleep.

The sagging bed was covered with a spread of more wool. He slipped between threadbare sheets. He fell asleep thinking of her dancing hands. He dreamed he was wrapped in her hair.

HE WOKE FRANTIC, thoroughly aroused. His heart pounded in his throat, and Siobahn was whispering into his ear.

"Wake up!" She hissed, "Get up! They've come!"

"Who?" He was already on his feet, lacing his trousers and pulling on his tunic.

"Your shepherdess's monsters." She stood by the window, peering past curtains into the night. "Dirt and shadows, rending and rot."

"You can feel them?"

Mal fastened his cloak. He slung his sword around his hip and, reassured by the weight, he crossed to her side and looked out over the top of her head.

The building across the cobblestone street was burning. The clapboard had already fallen; stone was crumbling to ruin, melting snow. Ash drifted on the night. Down into the village he could make out a second fire, and a third.

But the cobblestones below were deserted.

"Where are the people?"

"Dead or dying," she said, without remorse. "You are alive only because they did not know you were up here, and I kept it that way. But now they're searching."

Mal felt the tang of blood in his mouth. He realized he'd bitten the inside of his cheek. "Why didn't you wake me sooner?"

Siobhan's skirt rustled. "So you might die with the rest? No. I won't have you throwing your life away in this forsaken place. But—"

"What?" Mal felt the wildness rising in his throat, felt sweat bead on his brow. He could hear the building across the street groaning as it fell into the snow.

Siobahn looked at him with bright blue eyes. "They haven't come for you. As I said, I've kept you safe. The Kingsmen are gone."

Mal studied her face. Rage disappeared. Dread rose.

"Avani."

"Mayhap," his bride agreed slowly. "There is something—"

Mal didn't wait for Siobahn to finish. He broke her grip, and burst from the room. The corridor was empty. He could smell the Widow's greasy food.

"Mal!" Siobahn ran in his wake, slippers whispering on the floor. "Be careful!"

He took the tavern steps two at a time, forgetting silence in his fear.

The common room was quiet, the fire gone out. Mal stood on the last step, waiting for his eyes to adjust. He smelled death.

"Malachi." Siobahn stood on the stair behind him.

"Are we alone?" Although he guessed from the stillness in the room that they were.

"This building is empty. We are alone except for the dead."

"A light, then," he ordered.

Siobahn spoke a word, and light flared without source, chasing back the gloom. The stone on Mal's finger flashed.

He choked back a curse, and stepped slowly across the ruined commons. Siobahn followed, pressed against his back, skirts trailing in blood.

Gore painted the walls, the tables, and the massive chairs. Streams of blood dripped from the hearth. More of the liquid pooled on the floor, and ran in slow rivulets through the rushes.

Mal stood among the slaughtered. He counted five dead men and six women. Eleven corpses in all, each slit down the middle, many torn limb from limb.

The Widow lay abandoned in front of the door, both arms severed, her neck twisted at an impossible angle. Siobahn's light made the woman's eyes glitter.

Sword drawn, Mal stepped over the Widow's corpse. Beyond the tavern the world was on fire. More bodies lay in a tangle just outside the door. Blood dripped into the snow and onto the cobblestones, where it reflected flames.

Mal started down the road, intent on his destination.

Siobahn grabbed his arm. She tugged him around in a circle.

"Listen!"

Mal closed his eyes, willing his heart to still. At first

he heard only the moans of the dying village, the hiss of flames. Then he heard the sharp clop of hooves on cobblestones.

"Bran," Siobahn whispered. She vanished.

It was Bran, saddled up and tacked out. Avani's skinny lad perched high on the horse's back. The boy's thin face was very pale.

Bran stopped in front of Mal, ducked his head and snorted. The boy stared down, glassy-eyed.

"My lord," he said. "The stable is on fire."

Mal sheathed his sword. He swung up onto the horse, settling behind the lad.

"So it is. Do you have a name, child?"

"Liam," the boy muttered. He seemed unable to look away from the flames across the street.

"Liam," Mal repeated. "Do you know the way to Avani's house?"

"Aye, my lord." The boy brushed a trembling arm across his nose, wiping away snot and tears.

"Good. You'll show us the way, in case I've forgotten. Pay attention, now."

"Aye." Liam pulled his gaze from the burning buildings, and centered his stare between Bran's ears.

"Fine lad," Mal said. He reached up, gave the boy's shoulder a gentle squeeze, and then kicked Bran ahead through flame and blood.

"Have a care," Siobahn warned. Her breath was sweet and cool on his cheek. "I cannot protect you and the child both."

Mal only shook his head, and urged his horse to speed.

Chapter Four

THE BOY SHIVERED against Mal's chest. He clutched Bran's mane tightly in both hands. Mal doubted Liam saw much at all between the horse's ears.

A blessing, because Stonehill's fall had been a thing of nightmares.

The fire burned most fiercely at the center of the village. Buildings were already skeletons, their remains black and smoking. Snow had melted away completely in the great heat. Many of the cobblestones along the street had cracked clear through.

Bodies were thick on the ground. Dismembered corpses lay in grotesque piles against smoking buildings, or flung out across the street. Most of the dead were badly burned, flesh blistered.

Mal tried not to notice individual faces in the carnage.

Wind gusted, sending up a cloud of sparks. Bran spooked, nearly unseating Liam. The boy whimpered, his gaze suddenly riveted on the stream of gore beneath the horse's hooves.

Mal wrapped an arm around Liam's shoulders, drawing him close, squeezing until he regained the lad's attention.

"Just over the hill, now," he promised. "Am I right?"

"Aye, my lord." Liam straightened. "Just down the hill."

"Is there a way around?" Mal guided Bran past a bloodied corpse. "A way to come up behind the house, unseen?"

Liam regarded Mal doubtfully.

"The Downs are bare, my lord," he replied. "There's is no way to cross the fields unseen."

"Mmmm." Mal stared across the top of the boy's head, searching the horizon. "Then we must be glad the moon has set." But he worried even the cloak of night wouldn't be of help.

Mal pressed Bran on, leaving cobblestones behind, until they could no longer hear the crackle of flame. Over his shoulder the smoldering village turned the hills yellow and orange.

Away from the heat of the pyre, snow rose in drifts to Bran's hocks. When the horse stumbled, Mal pulled him up.

"Here," he decided.

With the fire at his back, the night ahead was dark as pitch. Mal couldn't see Avani's house, but he thought the building was just over the next hump of land.

He knotted the reins on Bran's neck and jumped from the saddle. Once he found his footing in the snow, Mal reached up for the lad.

Liam shuddered, jerking away.

"Nay!" The boy's teeth clicked audibly.

"You can't stay here." Mal frowned. He gripped Liam's leg. "My horse can't outrun or outwit whatever curse has taken your village. He's a good companion, but only a horse in the end. Come with me. I'll keep you safe, lad."

Liam huddled against Bran's neck. Mal tried not to swear. Time was trickling away; he could feel its loss in his bones. Siobahn's panic itched at the back of his skull.

Then the wind groaned, bringing with it the shrill scream of a sheep, and Liam all but fell into Mal's arms.

"Good lad," Mal said. He set the boy on his feet. He loosed his cloak and swung it around Liam's thin shoulders, then tugged the hood up and over the lad's head, hiding his face.

The boy's expression was wary, but there was something of awe on his face as he fingered Mal's heavy cloak. "My lord?"

"It will keep you warm, and it's dark enough to shield you from unfriendly eyes. Keep the hood up."

Liam nodded once, then seemed to collapse in on himself, huddling beneath tooled folds.

"Good."

Mal checked his sword. He touched Bran's flanks one last time.

"Make haste," Siobahn said. "They are here."

"Aye," Mal muttered, imitating the boy's inflection. "Come," he said. "Keep quiet."

They slipped over the snow, moving slowly up the slope.

Away from the village the night was dark enough to get lost in. Mal walked carefully, using Siobahn's eyes as his own. He kept one on the boy's shoulder, steadying. The other gripped his sword, and kept it loose in its sheath.

Mal's heart began to pound. His mouth watered. He forgot cold and fear. He thought only of the hunt, and the hunt was good. When an inhuman cry scraped over the Downs, his mouth stretched into a grin of anticipation.

Liam tripped and almost broke free of Mal's hand. He paused to drag the boy up against his thigh.

"Just a sheep, Liam."

He remembered the screams from his own boyhood, remembered the thick smell of slaughter on his foster father's plantation. Mal could scent it now: blood and sweat and urine, mixing on the wind.

Mal clamped a hand around Liam's wrist, and pulled the boy on. At last they topped the rise. Past a fist of stone, Mal looked down into the village pen and across the roof of Avani's house.

The field was trampled, pitted with muddy holes. Blood looked black where it streaked Avani's sturdy fence. The sheep had been torn apart, every ewe and ram and winter lamb. Their remains still steamed, a ghastly stretch of gut and sinew.

"Too late!" Siobahn's grief was a sigh between his ears. "Malachi, be careful!"

Mal didn't listen. Rage boiled in his veins. He whirled, leaping down the hill toward Avani's home, dragging Liam in his wake.

It was Liam who saved him. The child's choked cry of terror had Mal spinning, sword drawn. He knocked the boy down into the snow and stood over his small form, ready to defend, eager for the kill.

At first, in his fury, he didn't understand. The looming Kingsmen wore faces he had only recently searched for answers. One, he remembered as a brother.

They stood before him, blocking his path. Piers, and Stonehill's lord, and two others who had served Renault faithfully to their deaths.

The corpses were days old, and rotting. Three of the four were missing limbs. Yet Mal saw the men whole, ghostly bodies more solid than the shells of ruined flesh.

Their faces were slack; in their eyes burned a familiar blue fire.

They stood in a precise row on the hill, waiting. They left no visible tracks in the snow.

Mal tasted mud. He spat.

Then the dead men lurched forward, and he raised his sword.

AVANI HEARD A shriek in the night, and knew that, this time, the sound was human.

Hidden in her little cellar, crouched with Jacob at the foot of her Goddess, she'd listened as each of her sheep had been slaughtered, listened to the sharp calls and coughs as death took her animals.

This last cry was different. A thin wail ripped from a tortured throat, it was full of grief and too high to belong to a man.

A woman, Avani thought. *Or a child*.

She jumped from her rug. Jacob stopped her with a

hiss. The bird pecked at her hands, keeping them from the latch on the cellar door.

"Stop!" Avani scolded. "No child belongs on the Downs tonight!"

Jacob bit. A quick flash of his beak, and blood burst across Avani's knuckles.

She drew breath in a gasp, more startled than hurt. Jacob had never struck at her before, never purposefully unleashed claws or beak against her skin.

"Very well." Sucking blood from her hand, she sank down again.

Just as her knees touched the rug, shadows entered her home. Avani could smell the sudden wave of rot and earth. She could hear footsteps. Her heart beat hard, leaping high in her chest.

The floor began to vibrate, a slight thrumming that made the Goddess rattle on her pedestal. Jacob hissed and sneezed, and paced in front of the door.

The thrum spread from the floor through Avani's knees and up her thighs. Her bones began to hurt. She wanted to bolt up, to run from the cellar, but she couldn't move.

Instead she shut her eyes and chewed her tongue.

Fetid air crept under the cellar door, wreathing the room. Avani tried to slow her breathing, but a gritty film still managed to coat her tongue and make her lips tingle.

The cellar door rattled on its hinges. Jacob hissed again. Avani tried to think only of the Goddess. Instead she found herself imagining death on the other side of the door.

Silently, she begged her ancestors for courage.

How long she remained on her knees, how long the floor rattled and the shadows stalked through her home, Avani never knew. Tears of fright ran down her face and into her mouth, and then dried on her chin before the floor finally stopped shaking.

The cellar jerked one last time, violently throwing the Goddess from her pedestal. Then everything stilled.

The house fell silent. Avani opened her eyes, but couldn't stand. Wobbling on hands and knees, she crawled across the rug and picked up the idol. Trembling, she brushed the statue clean before she returned it to its place of honor.

The door rattled and burst open. Avani twisted around on her knees.

Jacob flashed across the room, screaming.

"Blood of the Virgin King!" The shadow in the doorway snarled back, "What in all the hells . . ."

"Jacob!" Avani staggered to her feet and threw herself forward, snatching beak and claw from Mal's face.

"Avani!" Another dark form jumped across the room, and attached itself to her side.

She felt skin and bones and smiled. "Liam!"

The boy clung for a moment, then reluctantly stepped away. "Avani, are you safe?"

"Yes," Avani said. She drew a breath. "They were in the house."

"They're gone," Mal said from his place in the doorway. The set of his shoulders reminded Avani of Jacob. If the man had feathers, she thought, they would be ruffled.

"For now," he added. "Can you bring a light?"

Liam reached again to touch Avani, as if for reassurance. "My lord's hurt."

"You're injured?" Avani's head stopped swimming. "Where?"

"Can you bring a light?" he asked again.

"The stove," Avani said. "There are matchsticks on the stove."

But there weren't. The inside of her home had been destroyed; rugs and pillows and stove and pots all torn or smashed or battered.

She couldn't imagine the force it would take to dent her iron cook pots. Struck motionless, she stood at the center of the mess, and tried to make sense of the havoc.

"I'm not sure," she said. She peered around, unable to gather her scattered wits. "I mean, I—"

"Never mind," Mal said from her back. He murmured a quiet word, and daylight bloomed in the center of her ruined home.

The fine hairs on the back of Avani's neck rose.

She turned, forgetting the damage to her home, and looked past Liam, past Mal, into a pair of burning blue eyes.

The skin on her forearms prickled. Gritting her teeth, she pushed past Mal, but the man reached out and pulled her up.

"Siobhan," he said, a stern warning.

Those blue eyes flashed at Avani. Then the tiny red-headed woman disappeared. The unnatural light remained.

Avani shifted her fury to Mal.

"Not now," he said, soft. "Right now, I need your aid."

She took a breath, found calm, and looked him over.

The magus was covered in blood. It dripped from his hair, and ran from his fingers. A new tear split his pretty tunic from collarbone to ribs.

Avani saw more blood beneath the tear, and also flesh, and the glisten of muscle and bone.

"Sit down!" She snapped. "Liam, help my lord find a place to sit. *Ai*, how will I boil water?"

"The matches are there," Mal said, unruffled. He pointed. Avani saw her matchsticks beneath a shredded pillow.

"Sit!" she ordered again. She grabbed the matches and reached for a cook pot.

She remembered water, and looked doubtfully at the night beyond her hanging blankets.

"It's safe to go out," Mal said. "But don't linger."

Avani shot the man a look. He stared back without expression. Avani hurried from the house, Jacob diving after.

Outside the night was very quiet. Snow dusted Avani's face. She had to break ice over the well to get at water. She filled the cook pot quickly, refusing to look at the silent pen.

She could smell blood in the air, but Jacob seemed calm, so she kept her pace measured as she walked back from the well, determined not to spill a drop of water.

When she ducked back into the unnatural light, she discovered Mal had made a seat of pillows and ruined blankets. He sat on folded knees, spine stiff.

A sword lay unsheathed on his thighs. The blade was red to the hilt, but he seemed in no hurry to wipe it clean.

Avani carried the cook pot to her stove. She fumbled with the matchsticks until she managed to coax a flame. Then she hung her pot from a tripod above the fire, silently urging the water to boil quickly.

Liam popped up from behind a swathe of wool. He eyed the wavering flame with some concern.

"Don't worry. It will heat." Avani turned to soothe the boy. As she did, she caught a flash of blue out of the corner of her eye.

Mal's red haired woman had reappeared. She knelt at his side, one slender hand curled on his muddied forearm, and spoke quietly into his ear. If Mal heard her, he gave no sign. The man's face had lost all color; his lips were drawn tight.

Avani had to clench her teeth to keep from swearing. The man had lied to her, Goddess damn him.

"Here." She yanked a thick woolen blanket from a peg on the wall, and handed it to Liam. "Give this to my lord. See that he uses it."

Avani watched carefully while Liam did as she asked. If the lad saw Mal's ghostly companion, he gave her no notice. He brushed past her and tucked the blanket around the vocent's shoulders, careful not to touch the sword.

Avani stared into her cook-pot until the water began to boil. Then she summoned Liam once more.

"Go with Jacob," she said, "and settle down for the rest of the night in my cellar."

She saw the beginnings of protest, and shook her head firmly. "It's the safest room in my house. Jacob will watch over you. I need to tend my lord's wounds, and I don't need you getting in my way, understand?"

"But—"

"Go!" She scraped a lock of dirty hair from the lad's equally dirty forehead. "The Goddess will keep you safe. I'll be in myself soon enough."

Liam went, dragging his feet over her rugs. Jacob stalked after, claws catching in fabric.

When Avani was sure the boy and the raven were settled in her cellar, she removed the boiling water from flame, set the pot carefully away from the dangers of temper, and rounded on her remaining guests.

"You." She looked directly at the pretty woman in her expensive gown. "Get out of my home."

Burning blue eyes widened. Mal started as if waking. He frowned.

"Avani."

She growled. "Don't. You sound just like the lad. This is my home, I give the orders, and no person argues." Hands on hips, Avani inclined her head. "Woman, get out!"

Mal's companion murmured one last sentence, then vanished. The light in Avani's house flickered. For an instant the room was dark as the night outside. When the light came up again, Mal glared from his throne of ruined cushions.

"You've made her angry."

"So I have." Avani collected the water and two of the thinnest blankets she could lay hands on.

She set the steaming pot at Mal's feet, then began tearing the blankets into strips and squares.

"I won't have you hurting her," he warned.

"Take off your tunic," Avani ordered. She wet a square of wool, burning the tips of her fingers.

Mal didn't move. The muscles in his jaw bunched.

"Siobahn is dear to my heart," he said, biting off one word at a time.

She wanted to fling the pot of scalding water across his patrician face.

"I'm no simpleton! You've brought your curse into my home, into my village. Your *bhut*, your geist! I'll have no such ghoul in my house!"

Mal bent forward. He pressed the palms of his hands against the flat of his blade.

"The shadows on the hill," he said. "They had nothing to do with us. Ghosts, aye, wielding swords as solid and deadly as my own. Do you know the amount of power such a conjuring would take?"

"No." Avani stripped the blanket from his shoulders and then the leather tunic from his chest. "Nor do I care." The leather came away in sticky fragments.

Mal swore violently.

"Hurts, does it?" Avani smiled thinly. "The wound is deep, and dirty."

She pressed her wet cloth against Mal's flesh. He flinched, muffling a gasp.

"Stonehill is destroyed," he managed as she cleaned the grit from his wound.

"I know." She made herself speak as though it didn't matter. As if her heart didn't break at the thought.

She forced her hands steady as she bandaged his wound. When she stretched forward to dab at Jacob's marks on his face, he caught her wrist.

"And your sheep."

Avani knelt on the floor and met the brilliance of his stare.

"Then it's time Jacob and I move on. Maybe the keep will take us until the season eases."

Thick lashes fell over his eyes. He looked away, releasing her hand.

"What is it?"

"You'll find no refuge at the keep," Mal said. He squeezed the bridge of his nose.

"You know that, *ai*?" Impatient, she brushed his hand from his nose, and wiped at blood. He flinched again, but didn't pull away.

"Siobahn says they've come hunting you."

"Hunting me?" Avani forced a laugh. "And why would that be?"

"I don't know. Why don't you tell me?"

Avani rocked back on her heels. Under the blood she'd cleaned away, the magus was corpse white. His ruined tunic and notched sword spoke of savage battle. She could tell by the set of his shoulders that he was in pain.

"Siobahn," she echoed. The syllables were awkward, a flatlander name. "She is your *bhut?* Your spirit?"

His eyebrows rose, mocking.

"Our customs differ, Avani. Your beliefs are not my own. Siobahn is harmless. What interests me," he admitted, "is that you see her. Is that a common island practice? Talking to ghosts?"

"Your *bhut* is a powerful curse. A person would have to be half-witted and blind to ignore her."

"You may be overstating," Mal replied. "But that

changes little. Siobahn says you're endangered. Tell me why."

"Ask your pretty spirit."

"You've banned her from your home. Not many people could manage to do that."

Avani snorted her contempt. Mal studied her, then nodded slightly.

She saw the moment when his attention left the room. His head cocked, his shoulders unclenched, and his breathing slowed.

Avani had seen the same ritual as a child in her great uncle's garden, when he'd used the bones of forgotten ancestors to commune with the Goddess. She'd been frightened then; she refused to be frightened again.

Angrily, she gathered strips of torn wool, and rolled them into quick, neat bundles.

"You wear it around your neck," Mal said. She saw his awareness had returned. "The thing they want."

Avani showed him her teeth.

"Give it to me," the vocent commanded. He held out one hand.

Avani wanted to refuse. The man, beautiful as he was, had no business ordering her about.

But the scratches on his face were beginning to puff, and beneath the aura of command he still held himself like it hurt to breathe. He'd saved her life, and Liam's, simply because he could.

Sighing, Avani relented. She drew it from beneath her tunic, the thing she had hidden so carefully from the Mal's prying eyes. She wouldn't have bothered with the deception, if she'd known of his meddling spirit. Very little escaped a *bhut*'s notice.

She'd knotted it on a cord of wool, and wrapped it with a scrap of silk to keep the point form scoring her breast. She pulled the cord over her head, and tugged the silk away.

The bronze key, hardly longer than Avani's middle finger, spun back and forth at the end of the cord, dangling.

Mal took the necklace by the length of cord. He didn't touch the key.

"Where did you find this?"

"On Thom." Avani watched the talisman spin. Miniscule etchings covered every inch of the stem and bit. The tip was knife-sharp. "Under Thom," she corrected. "Jacob dug it free. What is it?"

"I don't know," he admitted. "It's very old. Why did you hide it?"

"I don't know," Avani echoed. "It doesn't belong out in this world. It needs . . . protecting."

"You need protecting," Mal said. "Because of this. It stinks of death."

"You're wrong." Before he could protest, Avani snatched the cord back, and tucked the key hastily into her tunic. "It's kept me safe."

"Kept you safe?" His laugh rasped. "Your village is burnt to the ground, your herd slaughtered, and your home ransacked. The Downs are littered with the corpses of your friends. And those corpses are *walking*!"

"I'm still alive," Avani pointed out. "Unhurt, untouched. Maybe it's another of the Goddess's gifts."

"Has she given you many?" Mal scoffed.

"*Ai!*" He tried her patience, and he was cursed. But he'd come across the Downs to save her, and she recognized the concern beneath his mockery. So she answered truthfully when she would have preferred a lie.

"No," she said. "But Jacob found it, and I'd best not give it up. Certainly not to you."

He expelled a slow breath. "Then keep it under your shirt. Tomorrow morn, as soon as the sun rises, you'll leave this place."

"Oh, *ai*?"

"*Ai*," he mocked. "You, and that talisman, and the boy. Pack for the cold, but pack lightly."

"And where are we going, then?"

"With me," Mal replied. "To Wilhaiim. To see His Majesty."

He stumped her, but only for an instant.

"No," Avani said, and made to rise.

The vocent moved, and held her down with one hand, pinning her in place just as he had at the Widow's table.

"You'll come with me," he said, "or I'll tie you to my horse."

"Your horse!" Avani struggled under the weight of his grip. "Any horse in Stonehill will be dead, gutted like my sheep!"

"Not necessarily," he said, cold as the night. "Be ready. At dawn. You, and the lad."

He released her then, and turned away, settling carefully until he lay prone on the rug, weapon at his side. Avani stayed on her knees, indignant.

Mal closed his eyes.

Only as she watched his breathing slow did Avani real-
ize that he'd spread himself very precisely in front of her
door.

She cursed him silently, then rose. She carried her cook
pot back to the stove.

"Avani."

She'd thought he was asleep. Surprised, she almost
spilled tepid water.

"Dress yourself well," Mal said without opening his
eyes. "You no longer have any reason to skimp on your
own clothing. The journey will be long, and much of it
cold. A ragged tunic and worn sheepskin boots won't keep
you from the freeze."

This time she swore aloud, in the language of her
mother. She swore as she set the cook pot on the stove,
swore as she dug through the ruins of her home until she
found a blanket and pillow for Liam, continued to swear
as she kicked skewed rugs flat.

She stopped only when she reached the cellar door, and
then only because she didn't want to wake the lad.

Avani spread the blanket over Liam, and lay down
on the floor at the foot of her Goddess. Jacob squatted
hunched in a dark corner. Even the unnatural magus-
light that had turned her home into day couldn't warm
the cellar.

She squeezed her eyes shut and tried to sleep.

Chapter Five

MAL WOKE IN a tangle of wool. His lips were numb, the tip of his nose aching. Choking back a groan, he rolled onto his side, and tried to free himself from a nest of blankets and cushions.

His mage-light had faded away as he slept. The gray wash of early morning crept across Avani's curtains. Mal couldn't see any sign of his hostess or the lad.

He started to sit up, and almost cried aloud as a spike of heat tore across his ribs. He gasped and lay back again, and felt his heart flutter in his breast.

"The blade was poisoned," Siobahn said.

Mal waited until he was sure the contents of his stomach wouldn't rise past his throat. Then he turned his head. Siobahn knelt at his side, her gown spread across Avani's bright floor.

"*Agraine*," Mal said. "Piers. It was on his blade."

"*Agraine* is a vocent's tool." Siobahn licked her lips. "How —?"

"I haven't a guess." Drawing on Siobahn's strength, Mal slowly climbed to his knees, and then his feet. "The recipe is carefully guarded."

The room whirled about his head. He shuddered. The chill of the season seemed to have settled in his bones.

He wound a blanket around his torso, hoping to control the shaking in his arms. Dried blood coated his forearms like a second skin. The room tilted again, then righted itself.

"What will you do?" Siobahn asked, rising to grip his elbow.

"Wash," Mal replied, succinct. He shook her from his arm, and made his way carefully out into the dawn.

The sun hadn't yet filled the horizon, but just above the Downs the sky was silver. More snow had fallen overnight. The land around Avani's house looked fresh and new. Even the scent of slaughter had frozen away.

Mal crouched on Avani's front steps. He scooped up handfuls of clean snow and used it to scour his flesh clean. His skin numbed. He used the snow to wash gore from his boots, and to scrub his hair clean.

By the time Mal finished, his skin was turning blue, but he was free of the stink of battle. He stood tall on the stoop, wrapped in Avani's blanket, and looked out over the Downs.

The dead sheep in their pen were little more than snow-covered humps. In the distance smoke still blew over the swell of the land. Mal squinted up and down the stretch of snow, but nowhere did he see the remains of the four Kingsmen he'd chopped down in the night.

Just as a streak of pink shot over the horizon, herald-ing the dawn, footsteps crunched in the snow. Avani came around the side of the house, the bird drifting overhead.

The woman had tied back her hair, gathering the thick mass into a tight braid. She carried a roll of fabric on her shoulders.

She wore a tunic of thick virgin wool. Her new trousers were blue, and fit her better than the last pair. A hooded cloak, also of virgin wool, hung from her shoulders and just brushed the ground.

The new clothes and the gold at her wrists turned Avani into a woman of means. Only the tattered boots on her feet spoke of her true station.

When she caught him staring at her boots she scowled.

"I'm a weaver, not a tanner. These will have to do. Unless you think it's safe to go back into the village?"

"No," Mal said, sharp. "Those will do. Are you packed?"

"Close enough." She eyed the blanket on his back and his own bloodstained trousers. "How is the wound?"

Siobahn made a small sound, but Mal silenced her with a flick of his eyes. If Avani caught the exchange, or even noticed his bride, she gave no sign.

"Fine." Mal nodded at her bundle. "For me?"

"For Liam. You'll have to choose your own. I didn't bother to guess your needs." She cocked an elbow, point-ing back the way she'd come. "There is a shed behind the house. I had meant to trade its contents through the keep, but now, what use?" She shrugged. "Take what you need."

Mal nodded his thanks, and began a ginger shuffle through the snow, Siobahn fussing like a mother hen.

Mal could feel Avani's stare between his shoulder blades, but she didn't speak again until he was nearly around the house and out of sight.

"Your horse," she said. "I found him grazing up by the pen. I brushed him down and tethered him out back."

"Bran is a hardy animal," Mal said without breaking stride.

"You knew he'd be waiting," Avani accused. "You knew he was safe."

"I made sure of it," Mal said. "I'd be a pitiful magus indeed if I couldn't manage one simple warding charm."

But she'd already turned her back. Mal watched her stomp up the stoop and into the house.

When he was sure he was alone again, he stopped to rest, pressing folded arms against his ribs. He'd managed to dull the pain of his wound to a low scream, but his stomach bubbled restlessly, and the horizon seemed to waver in and out of focus.

"Will you be able to ride?" Siobahn demanded.

"Avani will ride. And the lad. Her boots won't hold up two days, and Liam doesn't have the reserves. That boy is more skeleton than life."

"Don't be a fool, Malachi." Siobahn's delicate features flushed. "You can't survive the journey on foot!"

"And perhaps not on horseback," he pointed out. "Although I'm made of sterner stuff than most would guess."

"Mal."

"Hush, Siobahn. Come and help me pick suitable woolens."

MAL LED HIS companions away from Stonehill before pink dawn turned orange. Liam rode high on Bran's withers, dressed in a new tunic and wrapped in Mal's cloak.

Avani sat behind the boy, a stained canvas bag slung across her back.

Mal walked at Bran's nose. He'd chosen trousers, tunic, and hooded cape from Avani's shed. The undyed wool heated his body and lifted his mood. Finally warm, he had the strength and courage of ten good men.

His sword, wiped clean, hung comfortably at his side. The raging poison in his veins had dulled to a low throb.

Siobahn had disappeared again. He thought she was avoiding Avani. He would have been amused if he wasn't worried.

At Mal's urging, Avani had gathered the scant food she had in her home and packed it away in her sack. He munched on a wedge of stale bread as he walked, glad of the nourishment. What else Avani might have in her sack, Mal wouldn't guess at.

As they pushed through drifts of snow, Mal considered the four reanimated corpses he'd disemboweled on the hills, and the key he knew still hung around Avani's neck.

The key he didn't recognize; the carvings on its surface were unfamiliar. But the poison on dead Piers's blade could only have come from Wilhaiim.

Siobahn murmured, and Mal turned Bran's nose, altering their course, avoiding a danger only his bride could sense. Avani rode silently, Liam dozing under her cloak. The sky stayed clear until midday. Then clouds began to gather, and Mal could smell snow in the air.

They left the Downs late in the eve, just as sleet gathered in whirlwinds and rushed from the sky. Mal called a halt at the edge of the River Mors, beneath the scant shelter of molting trees, and started making camp. Avani helped quietly, moving with quick competence, coaxing a fire from found wood, and setting salted bacon above the embers to warm.

Mal had just enough energy left to help Liam untack the horse. Then he sat heavily in the leaves before the fire, tucking his new cape close about his chin. His ribs stung fiercely, and his head pulsed with each heartbeat.

He closed his eyes and dozed.

HE WOKE ABRUPTLY.

"My lord?" Avani shook him again. Mal lifted a hand in dazed protest.

"Will you eat?" She set a strip of warm bacon in his hand, then a hard biscuit.

She propped a small tin cup in the leaves at his knee.

Mal blinked, thinking perhaps he was still asleep. Then he smiled.

"How did you manage?" he asked, swallowing hot cider gratefully.

"I have some journey skill."

Chill brought a pink glow to her dusky skin; wind and sleet had loosened strands of hair around her brow. "We spent many seasons traveling before I settled in Stonehill."

"We?"

Avani nodded. "We weren't many. Stonehill was too high, the air too thin, for any but myself. They went on."

"Stubborn." Mal stared across the fire. Sleet dripped through branches and made the embers hiss. Liam perched on a rock an arm's length from the fire, munching on a biscuit.

"Eh?"

"I said, you were stubborn. Not necessarily a bad thing."

Avani opened her mouth, and then snapped it shut. Mal almost laughed. Her eyes slitted. She thumped his knee with a fist.

Mal grunted as lightning arced through his bones, but Avani didn't notice.

"Eat," she said. "And while you eat, tell me your plan."

He did laugh, then; a short, unexpected bark from the depths of his gut.

"There is no plan," he said. "In the morning, we move on. And we move on each morn until we reach Wilhaiim. If we're lucky, we'll reach Wilhaiim unharmed. And Renault will have some answers."

"Renault?"

"His Majesty."

"You are vocent. You are more powerful than the king," Liam said around a mouthful of biscuit.

Mal smiled a little. "His Majesty is a very wise man, and learned."

Avani set her elbows on her thighs, and her chin in her hands. "What has learning to do with it?"

"This." Before Avani could twitch, Mal reached across air and plucked the key from beneath her tunic by its cord.

"This," he repeated, "is trouble. I don't recognize it. His Majesty may, or may not. But most certainly he commands a great library, which may house the resources I need."

"Resources you don't have."

Visibly annoyed, Avani bent backward against the pressure of his grip until he was forced to release the necklace or snap the cord.

She tucked the little talisman quickly again beneath her shirt.

"They are His Majesty's to employ," Mal agreed.

He squeezed the hard bread in his hand, no longer hungry. He set it aside.

"Before the sun rises, I'll go down to the keep and see what might be salvaged."

"You think it's fallen."

"I know so." Mal didn't elaborate. "But I may find food, other things we need. Good boots for your feet."

"I won't wear a dead man's boots."

"Oh?"

Avani shook her head. "I won't use a dead man's belongings. It's unlucky."

"Very well." Mal didn't bother to point out she wore a dead man's trinket around her neck. "I'll leave you with my sword."

"I have a knife." Avani touched her side.

"That's a cleaver. Fine for hacking gristle, but a bit short on reach."

She lifted her chin. "And what will you have, if you leave us your blade?"

"I'll have Siobhan."

"That one's of little use to any but herself," Avani scoffed. "I'll stay here. You'll take your sword. I have no use for such a weapon." She flashed him a quick grin. "I'd cut off my foot, more like than not."

"Stubborn," Mal said again, but relented. "Run, if trouble comes. Before you rely on the cleaver."

"Finish the bread and meat," Avani returned. "Don't let it go to waste. And wake me before you start for the keep."

"As you wish." Mal downed the last of his cider.

Avani rose and wandered away. She crouched at Liam's side. Mal couldn't hear what she said to the lad, but Liam nodded and smiled.

"She's an arrogant wench," Siobahn said from where she leaned against a weathered tree.

"She won't want to see you here," Mal cautioned.

Siobahn's expression hardened. "We're no longer guests in her house. I shall do as I wish."

"So you always have," Mal conceded.

With supreme effort, he finished his supper, then curled on the ground in his cape. The last thing he saw, before sleep took him, was the petulance on Siobahn's face as she scowled across the fire at Avani's slender form.

SIOBAHN LED THE way as they forded the river. Cold made the water sluggish and low, baring sand that in spring would be buried under the rush.

Mal crossed a step behind Siobahn, striding from rock to rock. His fuzzy head made it hard to balance, but he felt more awake than he had the day before—stronger, revived by the crisp, early hour.

The pain in his bones had receded overnight. His heart beat now for the hunt.

Mors Keep was outwardly quiet, still in the morning.. Mal studied the tower as they approached, but he could see nothing amiss. The river licked gently at the old water wheel. He sniffed the air, but it tasted clean.

"Nothing," Siobahn said. "They've moved on."

Mal kept his hand on the pommel of his sword. Side by side, they inched their way up the bank. When they reached the old portcullis, they found it open.

"Now?" Mal asked.

Siobahn stood on tiptoe in front of the gate, head tilted to one side as though listening.

"Still nothing," she said. "It's empty."

Mal ducked under the portcullis. Siobahn lifted her skirts and followed.

Wind blew in and around the bailey, lifting a fine wet sand. The tower and the temple gleamed beneath a growing layer of ice. Mal saw no indications of life.

"Temple first," he decided.

The temple was empty, the bier clean. The rushes scattered beneath were beginning to mold.

"Nothing left to tell the tale," Siobahn said.

Mal leaned his elbows on the bier, frowning at the pitted surface. The table was clean; even the stone's natural pores were scoured free of dirt. There was nothing left of Piers or his unfortunate companions.

"By the hells!"

Mal kicked a clump of rushes, then whirled. He paced up and down the building, searching every dim corner. Siobahn stood by the bier and watched. She grimaced when he scowled up at the eaves and cursed again.

"There is nothing here," she said. "You're wasting time. Come. You've done your duty by Renault. Now look after yourself, and move on."

"Blackwater will have winter supplies set away in the tower." Irritable, Mal brushed past her. "We'll have need of anything we can take."

The tower door rattled at his kick. It swung open, unbarred. Beyond, the inside of the tower was black as night.

Mal blinked hard, but the shadows remained. He felt the back of his neck begin to itch.

"Siobahn?"

"I don't know," she admitted, peering around his elbow.

"Spelled," Mal decided.

"And expertly done, to last so long," she agreed. "The darkness lingers, but I think we are alone."

Before Mal could protest, she darted around his side and through the door. He drew his sword and followed, conjuring mage-light with a word.

The tower was as he remembered, little more than a dining room and a staircase to the rooms above. Blackwater had set a small plank table before the single hearth. Mal had broken bread upon it before his journey to the Downs.

Chased by his light, shadows clung to the walls and crawled up the staircase. Mal set a palm against the table. The plank was cold and dry.

"Does the man have a pantry?" Siobahn wondered.

"There." Mal nodded. He followed her to the small alcove.

"Stale bread." He groped through the shelves. "A jug

of ale, thank the saints, and a wedge of ham more green than brown . . ."

He paused as his gloved fingers encountered something unfamiliar. He stuck his nose into the alcove.

"Odd," said Mal. "It looks like a brick of clay. Siobahn, what do you suppose—"

He picked up the molded soil, and his light went out.

Mal heard her shrieks before he understood. He dropped the brick, and the food, roaring in anger.

He lunged into the darkness, swinging his sword at an enemy he couldn't see. His howls of rage mingled with Siobahn's screams.

"Siobahn!" He bellowed.

He couldn't find her in his head. He felt panic rising. Something brushed his shoulder. He spun, striking blindly.

"Siobahn! Where are you?"

Abruptly she was back. Mal's mage-light blazed like the sun.

He saw blood, fresh gouts of it. It pooled on the table, ran over the dead coals in the hearth, and dripped from his sword.

Blackwater lay in a broken heap at the center of it. His lordship lay on his back on the table, mouth open, unmoving. His head was nearly severed from his neck, his hands and torso slashed and still bleeding.

"Siobahn," Mal whispered.

She didn't reply, but he felt her again, hiding in the back of his skull.

Blackwater's body quivered. The man's bowels let go, a

last flex of muscles. The reek of blood and feces made Mal choke. Pressing a forearm over his nose, he strode quickly from the tower.

In the small courtyard, rain dripped. Halfway across the bailey, Mal staggered. Pain raked through his chest and bit at his lungs.

Coughing, he bent over and vomited into the dirt. His hands were red with blood.

Gasping, Mal wiped ineffectually at his tunic, then stumbled on. His struggling lungs whistled. Three steps and agony sparked again. Blinded, he felt the world spin, felt his sword drop from fumbling fingers, felt his body tilt.

Then he went down, into the mud.

AVANI SAT ON a tree root, knife clutched in her hand. Mal had been gone too long. She could feel the ache of trouble at the back of her teeth. Jacob rustled and chuffed in the branches above.

Something had gone wrong.

As soon as the sun hit mid sky, she would wake Liam and go in search of the vocent. She wasn't sure how she would convince the lad to stay safely behind.

He slept soundly beside the remains of the fire, wrapped in Mal's long cloak. He hadn't stirred once in the last hour. Avani envied him his ease.

Wind dropped more rain from the heavens. Jacob complained loudly.

"Be silent," she scolded. "Do you want trouble to find us?"

But the raven only hissed again, and left his perch. Calling angrily, he flapped into the sky.

"Quiet!" The command came from behind Avani, and crackled like the branches of Jacob's tree.

Avani spun, knife readied, and looked into furious blue eyes.

"Keep the bird quiet!" Siobahn hissed, "Or do you wish to die today?"

"Where's my lord?" Avani gritted. She fought the temptation to prick Siobahn with her knife. She wasn't sure the blade would make itself felt.

"Here." He sounded gruff, and hoarse. He leaned against the tree trunk behind Siobahn.

Avani took a step in his direction. She stopped.

"You're covered in blood! What happened?"

Mal waved a negligent hand, but his shoulder slipped against the bark of the tree. He would have fallen, if Avani hadn't dropped her knife and hurried forward.

"Thank you." He leaned on her shoulder.

Mal drew a shallow breath. Avani noticed suddenly how drawn and hollow his cheeks had become.

"Pick up your knife," he said, although he didn't move to step away from her support. "Wake the lad. We have to move on."

"What happened?" Avani demanded. Mud from his tunic stained her own.

"A mistake," he muttered. He wouldn't meet her stare.

"A trap," Siobahn said. "Hurry."

Mal started forward. With Avani's help, he made it

around the trunk of the old tree and into camp. Avani heard the rattle in his lungs.

He tripped over Avani's sack, and when he lurched sideways, Avani couldn't hold him upright.

The man crashed face-first into the leaves. Liam bolted out of his blankets with a cry. Avani fell to her knees on the ground, and pawed at Mal's limp form, frightened.

"My lord!"

Only Siobahn remained unfazed.

"Poison," she said. "*Agraine*. I can't keep it at bay much longer. He's dying."

Chapter Six

AT FIRST AVANI assumed Mal had fainted. Then she real-ized it was the fall that had stunned him. He rolled onto his side, gasping. Avani managed to prop him upright be-tween her sack and a tree root.

"Get him water," Siobahn ordered.

"His wound has broken open," Avani said. She fum-bled in her sack for fresh bandages.

"Leave it!" the *bhut* snapped.

She stood at Avani's shoulder, but her head was turned away, her ghostly eyes focused on the distance.

"The blood isn't his own. His lordship's wound is heal-ing. It's a poison that takes him down. Ease his throat with water, and get him on the horse. Hurry!"

Shocked, Avani dug further into her sack. She held her tin flask to Mal's lips, almost spilling the contents down his chin.

He swallowed the water gratefully.

"Thank you." His smile was grim, but awareness had returned to his green eyes. "Now the horse."

Mal couldn't quite find his feet. Liam helped Avani hold the magus steady. When the boy saw Avani's intentions, he hesitated.

"Bran isn't saddled—"

"Then do it," Avani growled. "Quickly!"

"Don't bite the boy," Mal murmured. "Any conversation he witnessed was very one-sided. He's probably decided you're mad."

Avani scowled in Siobahn's direction. The spirit didn't appear to notice.

Liam returned in a rush, Bran in tow. He held the horse steady as Mal pulled himself into the saddle. The vocent coughed; a wet, hacking spasm that left his face white.

"Get the boy mounted," Siobahn said. "And gather your sack."

Avani hesitated, held fast by Mal's obvious agony.

Siobahn reached out and gripped Avani's arm, fingernails biting.

"Do you think we can shelter in this clearing indefinitely? Move!"

Avani balled her fist, intending to knock the spirit away. Jacob fell from the sky, screaming rage. Liam covered his ears.

"Too late!" Siobahn said, and was gone.

Avani froze. Bran stamped a hoof. Jacob dove again, and flapped his great black wings above the clearing.

"Avani," Mal said, gentle.

It was enough. She sprang forward, grabbing Liam, and tossing him into the saddle.

"Take the reins. You're in charge. Direct the horse."

"Where?" Liam's fingers slipped on the reins.

"West," Mal wheezed. He lay half slumped against the boy.

"West," Avani repeated. She grabbed Liam's thigh and squeezed. "Go."

Liam nodded, eyes wide, and turned Bran's head away from the sun.

Avani slapped the horse across the tail. Bran jumped, then bolted way through the trees, scattering rock and mud.

Swearing quietly in her mother's tongue, Avani found her knife in a drift of leaves, shoved what she could into her sack, and ran after.

Bran was quick. Avani was soon left behind. Chased by every imagined horror, she ran away from the river, away from the keep. Only the sun at her back kept her from loosing direction.

Her fingers cramped around her knife, but the air was softer below the Downs, and she ran a fair distance before her legs became leaden.

Eventually she was forced to slow to a trot, and then a walk. At last she drew to a reluctant halt. Pausing in the shade of a thorny evergreen, she strained her ears and senses.

She heard nothing. Jacob circled high overhead, lazy. She began to feel foolish. She slid her knife back into her belt and searched for sign of Bran. The sun was over her shoulder and sinking again when she found the first hoofprint. After that, the trail was easy enough to follow.

"He's having trouble controlling the horse," she realized. "Little wonder. The child has no muscle on his bones."

The ground began to slope. A stagnant creek muddled back and forth between clumps of reeds and marsh flower. Avani picked her way carefully through vegetation, following Bran's prints.

The creek widened and grew to a small tributary. The horse's trail ran in a straight line along the bank. Avani stopped to drink, and to refill her flask.

The water tasted sweet and clean. The sun began to warm her skin through wool. She unclasped her cloak, rolled the fabric into a tight ball, and shoved it into her sack.

Several paces later the river plunged into a dense snarl of thicket. Avani was forced to abandon the bank and pick her way through the water. By the time the vegetation eased to grass, she was wet and miserable.

The grass grew high, waving. She couldn't see the horse's trail, and was forced to use Jacob's eyes for guidance.

She followed the river around a wide bend, paused. Then she continued on, stomping past the geist standing in the grass.

Siobahn padded after.

"I must give you some credit," the *bhut* said, innocent. "I imagined you down with a cramped gut several lengths back."

Avani lifted her chin and looked forward, studiously ignoring her companion.

"They fetched up just down that hill." Siobahn lifted her gown, stepping daintily over a pile of cracked rock. "In a bramble clearing. The horse simply stopped. That was a wise thing you did, sending Malachi ahead to safety."

"Oh, *ai*?"

Avani stopped. She regarded the other woman. "You spurred me to it. I've seen no danger, then or since. Only a wounded man sore in need of rest. You'd risk his life to be rid of me?"

Siobahn's eyes burned blue. "The keep was set with a trap. Its jaws closed neatly over Mal's head, and he killed a man." She ran a hand through her tangled hair. "The spell was very strong. Once it struck, he wouldn't see me, hear me. He cut down Blackwater as thoughtlessly as one would gut a fish."

Avani kept the unease she felt from her face. "So you panicked, and set us all running like sheep before the wolf."

"I was frightened," Siobahn admitted. "I've never felt such a spell. But I'm no fool, either. Whatever magic was in that tower did not want to let him go."

"Is it chasing him, or is it chasing me?" Avani touched the loop of cord at her throat. "Your tales are fickle, trickster. You cry warning, and then disappear."

"You know not of what you speak." Siobahn turned and continued walking. "*You* mean nothing. It's Malachi I intend to see safely home."

"You speak of him as though he is your own."

"Because he is." The spirit walked straight through a clump of spiny thicket. "I am his wife."

Avani felt a shock of fear and anger. Before she quite realized it, she had her knife in her hand.

"The dead have no claim on the living!"

Siobahn halted. She stood very still and regarded the weapon in Avani's hand. Then she smiled, insolent.

"What do you know of the living and the dead, child?" She turned, staring down the slope. "They're waiting for you. The boy is frightened. I've slowed the poison as best I can, but Wilhaiim is still a sennight away. If Malachi dies, I'll see you in His Majesty's stocks."

"I won't let him die," Avani said, and meant it.

She scrambled over the slope, thorns scratching at her legs.

"Avani!" Siobahn called after.

The spirit gave Avani's name a musical inflection. When Avani looked back, Siobahn stood on the edge of the hill. The sun lined her slight figure in gold.

"You have as little claim on him as I." The expression in Siobahn's flickering eyes made her delicate features ugly.

At the foot of the slope the edges of a forest grew. Avani could see birds high on evergreen branches. Most had red and yellow plumage; a few were more black even than Jacob. She stood for a moment, admiring their colors, then hurried on.

She realized quickly that she hadn't walked into a lone cluster of tree and bramble. The woods thickened and pressed close. The tall evergreens were only the guardians of a sprawling forest.

Jacob led her onward into the depths, gliding from branch to branch. Without the raven's help Avani would have been lost. There was no path to follow, no trail of broken vegetation.

Eventually the evergreens spread into a wide clearing. There she found Bran. Liam slouched against the horse's shoulder, watching the trees with anxious eyes.

When he saw Avani, he let out a muffled whoop of relief.

"I see you managed to stop him," said Avani. She ruffled the lad's hair, glad to find him safe.

"He stopped on his own," Liam said. "As soon as he reached the trees. He's a good horse. I think he was hungry. I think he likes those red flowers."

"As well he might," Avani said. She looked past the grazing horse.

Mal sat cross-legged at the base of a giant evergreen. A splash of filtered daylight brightened his hair and gave his cheeks false color. When Avani looked in his direction, the worry lines on his brow softened.

"You found us."

He was hoarse from coughing. Avani didn't let her concern show. She drew instead on irritation, flashing a scowl.

"No thanks to your hound."

"My hound?" He awarded her bluster with the wry smile she had come to enjoy.

"If it barks like a hound, and stinks like a hound, then dog it is." But the shadows beneath his eyes had her relenting enough to add: "I left her up on the hill, sniffing for trouble."

"She'll find us when she's ready," Mal said. "Do you need rest?"

Avani didn't, but she could see the man did.

Seven days' steady ride, she thought, then sternly pushed worry aside.

"An hour's rest might do me good," she said, glancing up through interwoven branches at the sky.

"An hour, then," Mal agreed. He closed his eyes.

While Mal slept, Avani checked Bran for stones. Finding the horse sound, she tended Liam, feeding him a strip of dried meat and several swallows of water.

Jacob landed on her shoulder, and took a piece of jerky from her hand.

"You did well," she told Liam. "Half a day's ride west, and you kept your seat."

"I rode some before," the lad replied, wrinkling his nose. "Still, my backside throbs like the Widow tanned it."

Avani laughed. The lad brightened. The arrogant tilt of his smile reminded Avani of her own childhood. She straightened the heavy cloak around his shoulders.

"A bit too large, *ai*?" The cloak dragged in waves around the boy's feet.

Liam shrugged. He ran a grubby hand along the grain of the leather. "His lordship gave it to me. To keep, he said."

"So he did," Avani schooled her face. "But you don't want to trip over it in the night, or in the middle of battle. Would you like me to hem it for you?"

"Will you?" He eyed her doubtfully.

"Of course. I've a strong needle and thread in my sack."

Avani settled down on the mossy forest floor, and spread her sack on her lap. Liam unclasped his treasure. The cloak pooled over Avani's legs.

Siobahn walked into the clearing just as Avani finished hemming.

The *bhut* knelt at Mal's side. She woke the man with a murmur.

Avani watched the vocent rouse, then glanced sideways at Liam. The lad was frowning in Mal's direction, nose wrinkled.

"What do you see?" Avani stuffed her needle back into her sack. She passed the lad his considerably shortened cloak.

"Nothing," Liam muttered. "But I know it's there. I hear him talk to it."

"What do you mean?" Avani followed Liam's stare.

"The dead thing he orders about. His familiar."

"Familiar," Avani repeated the word with interest.

"It's like a tool," Liam explained. "The Widow said every magus has one. I didn't know she meant a dead thing." The boy shuddered.

"You needn't worry," Avani smiled at the lad. "Jacob and I will keep an eye on it."

"Jacob?" Liam dragged his suspicious stare from Mal. He craned his neck, seeking the raven.

"Jacob's fearless." Avani stood up, brushing needles from her clothes. "Once he even bit the Widow on the nose."

Liam laughed, then sobered. "I saw the Widow, laid out across her own floor. Her woolens were all over blood."

"I know." Avani touched a hand to his cheek. "Are you ready to go on, then?"

Liam nodded. Avani gave the boy another swallow of water. Then she boosted him onto Bran's back.

She looked around and found Mal at her side. His eyes were bright, his spine straight. Avani wondered if Siobahn had a hand in his renewed strength.

"Can you make it?" She nodded at Bran.

"Most certainly." He launched himself into the saddle.

"When you're tired of walking," Mal said from Bran's back, looking down his nose. "We'll switch."

Avani only nodded. Taking the reins from Liam, she shouldered her pack more comfortably, and led Bran on through the trees.

They traveled until nightfall. Avani walked the entire way. Mal dozed in the saddle. As the hours stretched, Avani thought she could see the man's strength seeping away again.

He muttered in his sleep. Liam used most of his own energy trying to keep the man still. By dusk the boy looked as drawn as the vocent.

Siobahn kept out of sight. Avani didn't miss her company. Jacob seemed in high spirits; he spent the afternoon chasing brightly colored birds, laughing raucously after their retreat.

They made camp just after dusk on a stretch of dirt near singing water. The evergreens were too thick for much undergrowth, but the red flowers Bran seemed so fond of were plentiful. The sound of rushing water soothed Avani's aching head.

Mal all but fell from Bran's back. Avani and Liam helped him to a bed of needles beneath an ancient tree. He muttered his thanks, choking on the words, and then coughed until he was breathless.

Avani helped Liam untack Bran, then showed the lad how to build a fire. He flushed with pride when he managed to draw flames from a handful of timber.

Together they roasted three of the little journey potatoes she'd secreted in her sack. She warmed the last of her cider, adding an extra handful of spices for luck. Jacob brought her a tiny red-breasted corpse, but she wasn't yet hungry enough to touch the offering.

Liam ate hungrily, burning his fingers on potato skin, and slurping cider. Mal was harder to tempt. He took drink eagerly, but he abandoned the potato after a few listless pokes.

"Will I have to coax you to eat every night?" She demanded. "Because I haven't the patience."

He blinked. Then he scowled. Avani only scowled back.

"Eat," she said. "Don't waste my food."

Mal nibbled at the potato, but soon lost interest again. He stared instead at the bangles around her wrists.

"True gold?" he asked.

The grate of his voice made Avani flinch. She passed him the remains of her own cider, hoping the liquid would ease his raw throat.

"Gold was plentiful on the islands," she said in answer. "A woman's wealth is in her jewelry."

"Not so very different from flatland dowry. Here, a woman's wealth is in her land." Mal touched one of her bangles. "Land is practical. Gold is prettier."

"And less likely to be seized by your king." Avani nudged his finger away. "Eat."

Mal frowned at the potato, then down at his empty tin cup. "If you'll bring me something more to drink."

"The cider is gone."

"A pity," he said. "Water will do."

So Avani took the little tin cup to the edge of the creek. Water ran like ice over her fingers, waking the blood in her veins. She filled the cup, then set it on the bank. Squatting, she splashed water across her face.

Above the forest canopy a moon rode high in the sky, unfettered by clouds. Silver light brightened the creek. Avani sat for a moment, enjoying the sight.

At last she picked up the cup and stood. She started to turn away from the rush of water, then paused. Across the creek, several strides back into the trees, something glinted silver.

It was the gleam of moonlight reflected on metal.

Avani felt a jolt of fear. She wheeled around, spilling water on her trousers, and tripped over Jacob.

The raven crouched at her feet, wings spread, beak open wide. Avani hit the bank on hands and knees.

Jacob's calling sounded like laughter. Avani scrabbled, but something heavy fell between her shoulder blades, and pressed her face down into the carpet of needles. She struggled, trying to breath, but inhaled only dirt. Choking, she tried to wiggle free, but the forest floor clogged her nose and mouth.

Then the forest receded, and her world went dark.

Chapter Seven

AVANI FELL FROM the moon onto stone; a great expanse of gray rock, seamed, and cracked, and smelling of mildew.

Moss grew in mounds over the stone. The stone scraped through Avani's trousers as she landed. The moss burst into puffs of dust beneath her knees. Her elbow struck a glancing blow, stinging.

The fall left her stunned and breathless. She lay for a moment on her back, gasping in the earthy perfume of old land.

Eventually she rolled over. Rubbing bruised hands on her tunic, she sat up. The sky above her head was molten silver, filled almost entirely with a fat farmers' moon. Avani struggled to her knees.

The stone she'd landed on appeared to be a marker. A square slab as long as one man and as wide as two, it was surrounded by bare, loamy ground. More slabs marched across the earth into the distance; an impossible, endless distance that made Avani dizzy.

She jumped from the slab. Her boots sank into soft earth.

Avani had heard tales of the old flatlander graveyards, but she'd never before seen one for herself. The island people burned their dead; to lie beneath the ground with grubs and roots tugging at your bones was an unimaginable horror.

Flatlanders, Avani knew, preferred to rest in the ground, and wait for their god to bring their bodies whole and alive again from the soil.

Avani found the very thought gruesome. And although the vast graveyard was peaceful, and the air had the warmth of late spring, she shivered.

The farmers' moon shone as bright as a silver sun, limning wildflowers that grew from the clay. The flowers were as plentiful as the graves.

There were flatlander symbols carved into the slab. Avani, who had spent her first winter on the Downs learning to read, traced the symbols with a thumb.

"Everin, son of the Aug."

Everin's tomb had broken her fall. The graven date had worn away, as though rubbed back into the stone by many fingers.

Avani walked on. Most of the gigantic markers were old and pitted, many unreadable, several unmarked. As she wound through their ranks, Avani counted.

Very quickly their great number overwhelmed, and she lost count. The moon hung fixed in the sky. Only Avani's footprints in the loam kept her from wandering, lost, in circles.

She saw no end to the regimented rows of stones.

When she grew tired, she found a slab cleaner than most and sat, drawing her knees up under her chin. Someone had left flowers on the grave. The woven wreaths were dried, now, the petals falling, but Avani could smell old roses.

She brushed petals away and read the engraving.

"Andrew, son of Rodger."

A cluster of spring flowers grew in the soil at the head of the slab, nearly hidden. The buds were closed for the night, pink in the moonlight.

Avani couldn't help herself. She lay on her belly, stretching over the edge of the stone, reaching. The flowers bobbed in a breeze she couldn't feel. As soon as her fingers closed around tender stems, the silver sky shattered and fell down around her ears.

She came to on the bank of the creek, one hand drifting in icy water. Hard fingers gripped her chin.

There were needles in Avani's mouth. She spat them free.

"Be still."

Her captor gripped a naked sword. His boots were wet; he'd crossed the water to reach her. His hair and his beard were caked with dirt, his eyes narrow slashes of yellow.

He wore more leather than wool, and he stank of loamy graveyard.

Avani shouted and came up swinging. Her fist connected solidly with the man's nose. He rocked back a step.

Avani managed to free her knife from her belt. She yelled again, and swung.

Quick and lithe as a serpent, he knocked her back onto the ground.

Jacob fell out of the trees, screaming. The raven's claws scored the man's scalp. He yelped in surprise, slapping. Jacob wheeled.

"Call him off!" Avani's captor growled. "Call the bird off or I'll be forced to spear him through!"

"You couldn't!" Avani spat again.

"I can." He ducked Jacob's spread toes. "And I will." He hefted his sword by the hilt, taking aim.

"Jacob!" she cried. "Jacob, stop!"

The bird landed again on the bank beneath the trees. Wings spread wide, he danced from side to side, hissing.

"Better," the man allowed. When Avani twitched, he adjusted his weapon. "Stay where you are. I've frightened you. Sit until you're calm again."

Avani glared. Her side hurt where he'd struck her. She'd lost her knife somewhere in the needles.

The stranger took one step closer, and squatted.

"I'm no bandit," he said. "And I've not come to kill you. I saw you were ill, floundering in the dirt like a fish."

"Not ill," Avani said. "And not alone."

"I know," he admitted. "I've tracked you from the keep."

She jumped up, smashing headfirst into his throat. He rolled over backward. She tumbled with him, and they tussled in the needles.

Light flared; a bright flash of red in the silver wash of

moonlight. Avani couldn't move. An unseen hand held her in place. The stranger lay motionless at her side, his beard in the mud, his sword flung away from his outstretched hand.

"By all the hells." Mal swore from beneath the trees. He coughed. "You're loud enough to wake the dead."

The weight in Avani's bones eased. She sat up slowly.

"Are you all right?" Mal asked, brows quirked.

Biting the inside of her cheek, Avani rubbed her nose. The stranger's fist had connected at least once.

"Well enough," she decided. "I didn't need your help."

Mal padded across the needles, Siobahn at his side.

"You might have brawled him to death, if we hadn't interfered," he agreed, mild. "Who is he?"

Still rubbing her nose, Avani looked down at the stranger. Mal's force of will held him to the dirt, but his yellow eyes were wide and aware.

"I don't know. He came from the other side of the creek."

"You saw him approach and didn't give warning?" Siobahn asked.

Avani opened her mouth on anger, then closed it again. "Where's Liam?"

"Guarding Bran and our fire," Mal said. "The lad's fine."

"There might be others—" She started up the hill, but Mal blocked her way.

"I don't think so," he said. "Let the boy be. He's learning manhood."

Avani shook off his hand. She almost walked on just

to prove she could, but in the end curiosity won out. She crossed her arms over her chest, scowling.

Mal bent, and studied the bearded man with interest. Siobahn set her fingers on the vocent's left shoulder, protecting.

"He's angry," the spirit said. "Prideful. But he seems harmless enough. He's full of the woods—ancient trees and clear water. And he has the yellow eyes of a desert mongrel."

"Moss and loam," Avani said before she thought.

Mal looked at her. His eyes narrowed to emerald slits. To Avani's horror, she felt herself blush. She turned her face away.

"Get up," he said, and straightened.

The stranger bolted from the dirt. He couldn't quite gain his feet on the first try. He staggered, falling down onto his knees. Then he found his balance and managed to stay upright, although his legs shook.

"My thanks," he said, breathing hard. He glanced at Mal, and then over the vocent's shoulder.

Avani realized with a start that the man looked directly at Siobahn. But then his attention shifted back to Mal, and she was no longer sure.

"Lord Vocent," he said, smiling slightly. "You are far from the city."

"Traveling," Mal replied. He coughed. "And you?"

"The same." The man's grin grew wolfish beneath his beard. "Traveling. Looking for a late supper. A handful of berries, or an unlucky fish."

"He said he's tracked us from the keep," Avani warned.

"So I did. From the keep, up into Stonehill, and back again. I almost gave you up when I found the slaughter on the Downs, but then I found your campsite on the Mors. And didn't His Majesty say Malachi Doyle had a knack for outrunning trouble? His Majesty is correct, although I might say you've been very lucky. There's little left of Stonehill, and the keep stinks of murder." His stare settled on Mal's stained tunic.

"We've had a time of it," Mal said.

"Aye. Heading home with the tale, are you?"

Mal's lips curled. "Indeed."

The stranger shrugged. Something in his stance made Avani think the man had only then relaxed.

"I've a message," he said. "From His Majesty."

Expressionless, Mal held out one gloved hand. The courier rummaged beneath his leather jerkin, and pulled forth a small scroll. Standing calmly in the light of the moon, Mal broke the king's seal. He unrolled the bit of paper, and read.

The message must have been brief, because he quickly rerolled the scroll and attached it to his belt.

"You've a name?" he demanded.

"Everin," the bearded man replied. "After the Virgin King. There's at least one in every village, aye?"

Mal smiled, but Avani felt her heart jump. Blood rushed from her cheeks to her toes. She must have made a sound, because Everin reached out and gripped her elbow.

"Milady is ill," he said, gruffly concerned. "She nearly drowned herself in the creek before I pulled her face from the water. Senseless as a babe, she was."

Mal's smile disappeared.

"I'm only tired," Avani protested. "I slipped in the mud. And then yon bearded fool tripped over me."

"You're bleeding," Mal said. He raised a finger to his cheek.

She touched her own face, and discovered that he was right.

"I'll tend to it," she said. "After I check on Liam."

She started over the needles, plucked up her knife, and then stopped to free her tin cup from the edge of the creek.

"Avani," Mal murmured. "This isn't finished."

She supposed he wasn't speaking of the courier. She refused to look back over her shoulder.

He didn't speak again, but she could feel him watching her all the way up the bank. As soon as the evergreens closed at her back, relief freed her stuttering heart, and she could breathe easily again.

Liam was happy enough to see her. He seemed calm and unafraid as he tended his little fire. Perhaps the boy did need some growing up. The Widow had kept the lad on a tight leash, and allowed him little freedom.

Avani ruffled Liam's hair. He grinned and ducked away.

"WILL YOU COME and sup, then?" Mal asked Renault's courier. "We haven't much, but you're welcome to share what there is."

Everin's teeth gleamed in his beard. "I will, thank you."

He bent neatly and retrieved his dropped sword.

Mal nodded, and left the creek. "When will you return to Wilhaiim?"

"I'm no Kingsman," Everin said. "My mother had a fondness for the legendary son of Aug, and so she gave me his name, but I've little in common with lords or monarchs. Begging your pardon, of course, m'lord."

"Renault didn't pick a man from the street and make him his messenger."

"No," Everin agreed. "It was a favor I did him. As his particular concern is my own, as well."

"Oh?" Mal stopped at the edge of the clearing.

"I expect you knew my father well." The bearded man's smile nearly split his face. "Andrew Lorimer. They say he picked you out of the farms and made you his squire. My lord."

Mal felt a flash of pain that had nothing to do with the wound in his side or the poison in his veins.

"He was very dear to me."

"So His Majesty promised." The man wouldn't stop smiling. "Like a father to you, he said. As you've gone white as a frightened maiden at his name, I'll believe it."

Mal took a slow breath. "Andrew is dead."

"I know it," Everin replied. "Your king found me in my grief, weeping over my sire's new-made marker." Thoughtfully, the man plucked at his beard. "The tears were a surprise, and unlooked for. Andrew may have taken *you* in, my lord, but he left *us* when I was a babe. Couldn't change what he was, could he?"

"I'm sorry."

"I never blamed him," said Everin. "Not even for my

mother's sake. He lived a long life, and served your king. In the end it killed him."

Mal touched Renault's scroll. "Murder."

"An old poison, His Majesty's tonsured priests said."

"And I didn't see it." That galled him.

"His Majesty thought mayhap you suspected."

"No," Mal remembered Andrew's last convulsions. "I assumed his time had simply come. He'd been ill on and off for many seasons. He was in his last years."

"Will you speak to his shade, ask the truth of him?"

Mal thought he heard longing in the man's tone, but when he opened his eyes he saw only curiosity.

"It isn't so easy as that," he replied with some sympathy. "The body would have to be dug from the ground, and even then . . ." He shook his head.

"Likely that is why His Majesty wishes your immediate return."

Mal arched a brow. "Did you read the scroll, then?"

"Was the seal broken? Nay! I've merely become adept at reading faces. Yours is harder than most, I admit, but I'm not blind. You're worried."

"I am." Amused in spite of himself, Mal rubbed a hand over his face. "Come and eat, will you?"

"Certainly," Everin said. He followed Mal under the trees, polite as any lord.

They sat together on the edge of the fire, across from Avani and Liam. Everin tucked into his small supper with ill-concealed greed. He murmured happily over the spices Avani stirred into his mug of heated creek water.

To Mal's surprise, Liam took to the courier immediately. The lad laughed at Everin's coarse jokes, and giggled helplessly whenever the man glowered across the flames.

When the moon began to set, Avani chased Liam away to bed, and then began to scoop needles into a nest of her own. Mal watched her idly, admiring the way the firelight sharpened her cheekbones. Her braid was coming loose, the silken strands of her hair twisting into curls.

"She's got a strong right fist," Everin said. He rubbed at his purpling chin. "For a pretty little thing."

Mal coughed. He climbed carefully to his feet. "Stay with us tonight, if you like. We ride early in the morn."

"The morning is nearly here," Everin pointed out. "But I'll stay. And perhaps ride on with you, for a time."

"You're welcome, of course." Mal said. He left the man to his hot tea.

WRAPPED IN HER cape, Avani was cuddled in a hollow of needles like a child in a cradle. Her dark eyes were wide and wary as Mal approached. The raven slept on a branch overhead.

He sat slowly at her side.

"Tell me," he ordered.

"What is there to say?" She scowled a little. "The man surprised me. One breath I was drawing water from the creek, and the next, vision caught in the dirt. I can't always control it, *ai*."

Mal winced a little, remembering the keep tower and the stain of innocent blood on his blade. "The visions were attached to Everin?"

"Or the man came with the visions." She curled deeper into her nest, shivering.

Mal found himself reaching for her hand. Avani let him touch her fingers, very briefly, before she pulled away.

"Will you tell me what you saw?"

"No," she said.

Mal laughed, a true laugh. Real mirth rose from his gut and grabbed him by the throat. The violence of the emotion made him choke and wheeze, but even the pain in his lungs was worth the merriment.

"Are you all right?" Avani sat up. She gripped his shoulders with both hands.

Mal nodded, fighting for breath. "It's been a long time since anyone has refused me anything. You're not afraid of me, or of what I might do."

"I'm not." Avani cautioned, "And neither, I think, is your new friend."

"He's the son of my father," Mal said, between gasps of air.

"What?"

"No matter." He inhaled cautiously, and then again. "Please. Tell me what you saw."

Avani lay back in her cape. She stared up through the branches.

"A flatland graveyard," she said at last. "Running on forever. Slabs of old stone. The sky was silver, the ground sticky. It was springtime. There were flowers growing beneath his grave."

"Whose grave?"

"Everin, son of the Aug."

Mal frowned.

"You see," said Avani. "The man and the visions muddle."

"You're untrained," Mal agreed. "Dangerous. What happens the next time you fall senseless into a river and no one is about to pull you free?"

"I am as I am." She shrugged, and yawned a little.

"You could be far more." Mal realized, as he spoke the words, that it was true. And that truth surprised him.

She shrugged again, then eyed him narrowly.

"You said you'd tell me," said Avani. "What it meant to be vocent."

He had, but still he sighed.

"Hunter, assassin, inquisitor, magus," he said. "Beloved of the monarch, and ever his dog. Vengeance in human form, but also keeper of the peace, guardian of the throne."

"There are rewards," he continued when she frowned. "Hennish leather, for one. More land than I will ever need. Respect, fear. His Majesty's favor. Wealth and status for one's family."

"Do you have one?" asked Avani.

"A family?" Mal shook his head. "No."

"A wife?" she challenged.

"I did," he met her stare with his own. "I don't speak of it, not even to one as stubborn as you." He touched her swelling nose. "Does it hurt?"

"Burns like fire." She shifted, the bangles on her wrists chiming.

"But not broken," he decided, pressing gently until she gasped. "I've some salve that will help."

"No. The Goddess looks after her own. And punishes those with too much pride."

Mal smiled. "Too much pride, is it?"

"Or stupidity. The man is built like your horse." She yawned once more. "Won't you rest?"

"That depends. Do you have anything more to tell me?"

Avani shook her head.

"Very well," he allowed. "Sleep."

"And you?"

"I will."

He meant to stand, and find a spot closer to the fire, a warmer place for his own bed, but he found his strength depleted. Weary and aching, he imagined he could feel the poison running in his veins, reaching for his very heart.

Worn through, he settled where he was, at Avani's side. He pressed his cheek to the pungent carpet of needles, and closed his eyes.

AVANI DREAMED OF the flatlander graveyard. She knew it was a dream, and not a vision, because she couldn't find the Goddess anywhere in her head.

She floundered for a while in the dream, chased through the graveyard by old childhood terrors. Rain fell, in warm torrents.

Water rose from the earth, creeping up over her ankles and then her knees. Old bones rose on the waves, too many to count.

Avani clamored out of the flood and onto a slab, trying to escape the water.

She looked down between her feet and discovered the grave she stood upon was Mal's. Water lapped over the edge of the stone, washing against the tips of her boots.

Avani shivered, and knew she would drown.

Then a shadow fell across the water. She looked up, startled.

Everin stood at her side. His beard grew thick, and there were as many strands of white in the tangle as there were of gold. He wore mail instead of leather. Rain dripped from the edge of his drawn sword.

"What have you done?" he demanded.

Avani couldn't speak. The water was still rising; she could no longer see her feet. Floating bones bobbed against her thighs.

"What have you done!" This time it was a howl.

His mailed hand closed around her throat. She struggled, but he lifted her into the air, as easily as if she were nothing. Shaking his head sadly, the bearded man tossed her into the water.

Avani screamed.

Water and bones closed over her head, and she sank.

Chapter Eight

AVANI OPENED HER eyes to sunlight, and to the drift of falling needles across her chest. Everin's face was in her own, his hand on her shoulder.

For a breath she was back in her dream; the man's beard was long and lined with silver, his yellow eyes filmed with sorrow. Then she blinked, and the wisp of dream unraveled.

Everin smiled, showing white teeth. "Good morn. And a pleasant one it is, warmer than the last."

Avani sat up. Her nose throbbed. She rubbed it, groaning.

"The sun's well up," Everin said. "It's past time to be about."

The man spoke true. Avani could see the wink of afternoon sun past the sheltering forest.

"We've slept so long?" She scrambled to her feet, alarmed. "Why didn't my lord—"

"Your magus won't wake," Everin interrupted, still smiling. His hand found his way to Avani's shoulders, and held her still.

"Hush," he warned. "You'll frighten the boy."

Avani looked across the clearing. Liam stood beneath the trees, readying Bran for saddle and bridle. As Avani watched, Bran's tail flicked impatiently, and Liam laughed, patting the horse on the nose.

"Let the lad do his job," Everin said. "There's no need to spook him just yet. Nor you. Come."

Although the day was the warmest Avani had seen in many sunrises, the campfire still burned. Someone had revived the ashes and coaxed the flames high. They crackled merrily, giving off smoke and heat, and illuminating Mal's drawn face.

The vocent lay on his side at the fire's edge, dangerously close to the flames.

Avani broke from Everin's grip, and crouched at Mal's side. When she saw the steady rise and fall of his chest, she expelled relief in a whoosh of air.

"Aye, he's alive," said Everin. "And not yet close to death. But he won't wake, and this sleep is not natural." He reached down a calloused hand, and gave Mal a quick shake. "I moved him closer to the fire, hoping the warmth would help."

"But it didn't." Avani set her own hand against Mal's brow. His skin was smooth and dry, and very cold.

She set her fingers against his lips, waiting for the faint puff of breath. When it came, the gentle stir of air felt as warm as the flickering fire.

"Is it a spell?" she wondered. She touched her thumb to Mal's lower lip. The skin there was soft.

Everin considered Avani from beneath bushy brows. "More likely the sleep a magus takes when his body is deeply rent."

Avani shook her head, remembering the man's presence in her dream. "Are you a magus, then, to know of such things?"

Everin laughed. "Nay. But the vocent, by his very nature, is. And I've heard a tale or three in my youth."

"He said nothing of such a sleep last night." Avani bent over Mal. His eyelids flickered. "He's dreaming."

"Mayhap." Everin lifted one shoulder. "It's only a sleep, albeit one too deep for waking."

Avani didn't know what to believe. She brushed hair from her eyes, and glanced around the trees. Jacob watched from above, but Avani didn't see Siobhan anywhere.

"Lost something?" the big man asked, smile wide.

"Why," Avani replied, "are you still here?"

He answered easily," You need me, I think."

Avani started to argue, but Everin stopped her retort with a shake of his head.

"Do you know the road to Wilhaiim, black eyes?"

"No."

"Well, then."

His confidence nettled. "My lord—"

"His lordship," Everin interrupted with some emphasis, "won't be up and about for some time. Certainly not soon enough to help you, or himself."

Avani's protest died. Everin's yellow eyes had turned hard over his smile.

"It's a poison in his body, is it? *Agraine?*"

Avani reached for her knife, but Everin ignored her.

"A deadly poison, that. He's lucky he's the strength to fight it off. Even so, the body won't last forever, not with *agraine* in the blood."

"What do you know of it?" Avani demanded.

"I've seen it once before. He hasn't much time left to waste. Put your little blade away and gather your things."

"And why should we trust you?" Liam asked.

He'd approached Everin from behind. The lad held Mal's long sword in his own two small hands, determined and frightened all at once.

Everin stood very still.

"Don't fuss, now," he said. "I mean you no harm. I promised the king I'd bring his vocent home, and that's the truth of it. Alive, because that's how His Majesty prefers it. The scroll's there, on his lordship's belt. Read it if you like."

Liam looked at Avani. She glanced up at Jacob. The raven opened his beak, and then closed it again, unconcerned.

"Go stand by there, away from the horse, until I say otherwise," she said. "Liam, step away."

The lad edged backward, Mal's sword wavering in his hands. Everin bowed his head and retreated.

"I can't read," Liam whispered.

"I can." Avani untied the scroll, scanning it quickly. "How did you get his sword, lad? He's not been without it once."

"The dead thing," Liam said in a small voice. "Dropped

it right in front of Bran. From nowhere. And I knew what it meant me to do. I couldn't let him hurt you. Or my lord, neither."

Avani pulled the boy close. She hugged him hard.

"He won't," she promised. "You and I, we're too smart for that. Now. Come and help me."

It took all of her strength, and Liam's, to boost Mal into the saddle. Everin watched, expressionless, as she used her last bit of cord to tie the vocent to the saddle. Bran danced uneasily until Liam soothed the horse with a low whistle.

"He doesn't like it."

"A horse like that wants a live rider," Everin said. "That's a fine horse, not bred to be a pack animal. Well, lass, have you decided, or must I stand here till the snows come?"

"They're not far behind," Avani replied. "You'll come, but you'll walk ahead, and quietly, or I'll give Jacob leave to have your eyes."

Everin's smile reappeared. "As you wish. But the road to Wilhaiim is long, and I've a mind to change your heart before we see the city walls."

THE REST OF the afternoon passed slowly. The trees pressed in. Ferns grew out of the forest floor, many as tall as Liam. When Avani touched a frond, she found it damp. The dew clung to her fingers and smelled sweet.

The air grew warm, and Avani shed her cape. Liam wouldn't loosen his beloved cloak. Everin seemed untroubled by the heat. The big man walked as though he knew the land, and just as Avani thought the forest had swallowed them forever, he brought them through the brush to a trail.

"King's Highway," he said.

"It's little more than a goat path," Avani argued. She stared doubtfully along the sandy path.

"We're days yet from Wilhaiim." Everin smiled over his shoulder. "This is merely a small branch of the greater highway."

Avani didn't reply. She walked on at Bran's side, her hand on the horse's neck. Jacob rode on her shoulder. Liam trailed in her footprints. Mal lay quietly, stretched limp as a dead man across Bran's back.

His lifeless slump frightened Avani. She stopped often to check for breath.

She saw no sign at all of the *bhut*.

They followed the path until night fell, then they stopped and made camp on the road. Everin coaxed a small fire while Liam cared for Bran.

Avani did her best to tend Mal. When she dribbled water from her flask between his lips, he swallowed, and that gave her hope. There were blisters growing on his wrists where her cord had rubbed at his flesh. She cleaned the ulcers as best as she could.

He muttered when she sluiced water over the blisters, but still he didn't wake. She wrapped him in his cloak and sat by his side until Everin banked the fire. Then she bedded down at his side and stared at the darkness until morning.

Everin roused Avani before dawn. Mal had turned over

in the night, but he didn't stir, even when they bundled him onto the horse. Avani winced when Everin lashed the cord again around his wrists.

They journeyed on, munching berries and tubers as they walked. The path curved back and forth through the forest, sometimes almost disappearing between the growth of wild fern. They traveled in silence. Even Everin's wide smile seemed diminished in the sticky air.

On the eve of their third day on the King's Highway, the evergreens began to thin. The ferns slowly vanished; thickets and brambles grew up in their place. Slender trees with white trunks and red leaves grew alongside the widening road. The air grew cooler, and dry.

"We've nearly reached the edge," Everin said, pleased.

Liam brightened. The lad stared around with renewed interest. Avani didn't respond. She saw only more trees, and the bite of cold was newly unpleasant after the warmth of deep forest.

Then, just before nightfall, they rounded a bend in the path and the sandy trail widened further, becoming cobblestone beneath dirt.

"As you see," Everin said, bowing low. "Civilization starts here, at the very edge of the monarch's scarlet woods."

"Where civilization begins," Avani retorted, "is not for any man to decide."

And yet, when they bedded down for the night at the edge of a still blue pool, Avani slept better than she had since Mal's collapse. Even the vocent's breathing seemed eased, although his lips were parched, cracked. He no longer swallowed the little water she tried to coax into him.

Late in the afternoon of the fifth day, they left the red trees behind. The King's Highway grew until it was wide enough for ten men to walk abreast. The cobbles were worn smooth beneath the soles of Avani's boots.

"An old road," she said, noting wheel ruts worn into the stones.

"Aye," Everin agreed. "And well used. In the summer the highway teems with farmers, merchants, outlaws for hire, even families of good stead. They all flock to Wilhaiim in the warmer months. In the winter," he tugged at his beard, "fewer make the journey. When the rains come, life is easier at the hearth."

Avani tilted her chin toward the sky. The horizon was blue, free of fog or cloud. She saw no sign of rain, but when she looked from side to side, she saw that the rolling hills to either side of the highway were more mud than grass. A myriad of tiny streams bisected the land.

Everin cleared his throat.

"You'll meet the rain soon enough," he said, yellow eyes bright. "Don't go looking to invite it down."

Avani ignored the man, turning her attention to Liam instead. The lad, although more than half grown, seemed to have a babe's penchant for falling into puddles. He jumped every stream he could find, and several times she had to save him from an untimely submersion.

Jacob bobbed his head, muttering disgust, and took to the air.

Not long after, the clouds rolled in, chased by a cold

wind. The heavens opened up, and rain sluiced in great waterfalls from the sky. As if in response, Mal began to cough. Great, wracking spasms shook his body, and nearly felled the man from Bran's back.

His blisters oozed, turning the cords binding his wrists to red. More red stained his mouth. Alarmed, Avani refused to travel on. They found scant shelter beneath a rocky overhang several lengths from the highway.

Squatting in the mud, sodden hair stuck to her cheeks and to her nose, Avani examined Mal with her hands and her eyes. Everin knelt at her side, watching with concern. Liam huddled, the vocent's head on his lap, and looked at Avani with desperate eyes.

"He's feverish," Avani admitted. She tried to swallow back the lump in her throat. Mal's skin burned her chilled fingers.

Everin pulled a leather flask from his belt, and tried to tip the contents down Mal's throat. Mal choked, and wheezed. The water spilled back out between his lips, mixed with a goodly amount of blood.

"Stop it!" Liam cried. He knocked the flask from Everin's hand. "You're making it worse."

"Hush." Avani tossed her pack at Everin. "Pour your water into the tin cup, add a pinch of the herb you'll find in a little white pouch, and heat it over the fire. Just enough to make the water bubble, understand?"

Everin nodded.

"More of your teas?" Liam wondered.

"It may ease his cough." Avani gave the boy a smile full of assurance she didn't feel.

She waited until Liam responded with his own crooked grin. Then she unlaced Mal's tunic, pulled old bandages free, and muttered.

"What is it?" Everin asked from the fire.

"His wound is healing." Avani rubbed her nose with the back of her hand. The bangles looped on her arm belled. "No infection."

"A magus heals quickly," Liam suggested hopefully. Avani wasn't sure she liked the gleam of superstitious awe in his eye.

Avani studied Mal's face. She saw his skull beneath the skin. She touched one of his limp hands, and felt more bone than muscle.

"He looks more skeleton, less man," she said. Liam flinched. She sighed.

"I'm sorry." She stroked a muddy hand over the lad's hair. "I don't want the man to die, either."

"He won't," said Everin. He passed Avani the steaming tin cup. "He's burning away reserves, fighting the poison, but we're nearly knocking at Wilhaiim's gates."

The hot tin made Avani's hand sting, but she didn't look away from Everin's cool stare. "You don't intend to tie him back up on the horse. The ride's killing him as quickly as the poison."

"I haven't got the man this far, only to let him die outside His Majesty's walls."

"He needs rest," Avani argued. "Flat on the ground. Without a horse's spine bouncing beneath his breast."

Everin spread his hands. "Aye. Until the sun climbs to the middle of the sky. Then we move on."

Avani looked beyond the crop of stone to the fall of rain. "What sun?"

Everin glared. "I will know. You have only a short while, black eyes. Make him as comfortable as you can. I intend to present him at the throne alive, even if he draws his last breath at Renault's feet."

"Renault," Avani echoed softly. "Does every man call the flatlander king by his given name, then?"

Everin's lids drooped. He started to speak, but Mal's sudden fit of coughing split the air and bounced off rock. Liam shivered. Everin grunted.

"Ease the man with your tea," he ordered. "We've little time to spare." He rose to his feet, knees popping audibly, and moved closer to the fire.

Avani bent over Mal. She massaged his chest until the coughing eased. She cleaned fresh blood from his mouth, then pressed the cup against his lips. He swallowed automatically, and some of the mixture stayed down.

Avani waited until the bubbling in Mal's throat seemed to ease. Then she assessed Liam.

"Get some sleep," she suggested. "We all need the rest."

Liam made a face. "It's cold. And wet."

"So it is," she agreed. "That didn't stop you from splashing about, earlier. Pretend you're a mudhog, *ai*?"

Liam grumbled. He stretched out on Mal's cloak, closing his eyes.

Avani loosened her own cape, and tucked it around Mal. She curled at his side, her ear on his breast, and listened to the steady thump of his heart.

No flatlander graveyard, this time. She dreamed of

a garden, a beautiful pocket of spring, grass growing as thick as a rug, and brilliant flowers climbing invisible walls. She saw marble benches, and glistening fountains, and rolling hedges sporting violet berries.

Mal sat at ease on the rough-hewn edge of a three-tiered fountain. He wore silk, dyed the lightest of blues, and a sun Avani couldn't see turned his hair to shining ebony.

He watched as she approached, one hand flat along the lip of the fountain, the other cupped loosely on his thigh.

"Avani," he said, and smiled sweetly as he never had before. "You're covered in mud and . . . grass?"

Frowning, Avani brushed bits of wet grass from her tunic. "It's the rains. They've soaked everything."

He laughed. "I've no place for mud and rain in my dreams."

"No dream, this."

Mal's eyes narrowed to green slits. "I've the skill to tell dream from vision."

"My vision, your fever dream." Avani tucked her fists in her armpits. The garden sun had dried the mud to a crust. Flakes of dirt fell from her trousers. "But what does it mean?"

Mal rose from his perch. He glanced around with new awareness.

"This garden, I remember. Siobahn's mother tends it. Siobahn and I were married here, not so long ago. I wore"—he glanced down at himself—"blue. But not the silk of lords. Where . . ." He looked around. "Where is Siobahn?"

"What—" Avani returned. The sun beat down across her brow, spawning a fierce headache. "What is in your hand?"

Mal blinked, distracted, and his hand opened. A loop of wool caught on his fingers, knotted. And dangling from the end, a tiny bronze key.

"My talisman!" Avani groped at her throat, and found the necklace gone.

"I don't understand." Mal squinted at Avani. "Where's Siobhan?"

"Hush." She reached out to soothe him as she had Liam, knowing instinctively that fever turned his dream opaque as mist. "You're ill."

Her hand bumped his own, and the loop of wool fell free. The key spun to the grass; the end sunk tip first into the earth. Avani bent to retrieve it, but couldn't seem to connect.

Mal began to shake. Where the bronze point split soil, smoke rose in a slow coil. Avani realized that it wasn't the sun that made her head pound, but something more.

"My lord!" She cried a warning, but Mal was gone.

The fountain had disappeared, the garden dissolved, but the key remained.

AVANI SAT UP in the mud, blinking the remnants of the vision from her eyes. Mal tossed at her side, muttering. The fire flickered. She could hear the patter of rain beyond their shelter.

She spread her fingers across her throat. The necklace was gone.

"Avani!" Everin materialized in the gloom.

"What is it?" She blinked. "I dreamed."

Everin shot her a quick look. He set his hand across her mouth. His flesh tasted of salt.

"Quiet." The words were more a growl than a whisper. "They've brought down the horse."

She shot to her feet. "Where's Liam?"

"Out in the rain. The lad went after the animal before I could stop him. He took the vocent's sword."

"What?" Avani jerked from under his hand. "You let him go?"

"Aye," he said, and she heard regret. "Or else who would guard the magus?"

Avani took a step toward the fall of rain, but Everin yanked her back.

"Where are your wits? Do you seek your own death? The bird went with him."

Avani ducked away. She slipped on a spot of muck, and suddenly she was free of the outcropping, and cold rain bathed her face.

"Avani!"

"No!" she spat. She turned resolutely to the rain. "I have to find Liam." Terror threatened to push her back, but she set one foot in front of another, and took two real strides into the storm.

"Damn you, black eyes!" Everin swore. He leapt after. Avani caught the glint of steel in the wash of rain as the man freed his sword.

She dug for her own little knife, and held the weapon in a numb hand.

"Go back," she cried. "Go back and watch after my lord!"

"Not likely," Everin replied. He steadied her when she slipped again.

"Hells," he swore. The word sounded very raw.

She followed his bleak gaze and saw that she had stepped once again into slaughter. Blood mixed with mud stained her boots. A gleaming length of gray gut snaked away into the rain.

Just beyond, Avani saw the body of Mal's gentle horse.

"Goddess," she breathed, and had to gulp back bile.

"Have a care," Everin muttered. He steered her around the gore. The man's yellow eyes seemed to burn through the fall of rain.

"Liam!" Avani choked. She spun away. "Liam!"

"Have a care!" Everin shouted, but his warning came too late.

Shadows grew up into the storm. Avani dodged, and slipped, and went down. The ground scraped, and she tasted her own blood.

Everin shouted again. Avani rolled over, trying to wipe mud and rain from her eyes. She thought she heard Jacob scream. The world blurred, then cleared.

Six distinct shadows loomed. She scrambled backward, yelling, and kicked out.

She connected with something solid. Remembering her knife, she slashed wildly, but the weapon was knocked from her hand. She gasped, clutching numb fingers to her chest.

Rain ran across her face. Avani climbed to her knees, slipped once more, and went down. A loop of Bran's gut tangled her feet.

Then the tallest of the shadows slid forward, and grabbed Avani around the throat.

Chapter Nine

MAL WOKE TO warmth, and to agony.

The warmth was almost a comfort. It wrapped around chilled limbs, dulling the blade of ice that was his spine.

The agony was unbearable. It burned in his lungs, turning every breath to fire, and it sank claws into his heart.

He gasped, and opened his eyes wide, and looked up into Renault's set face.

"Malachi," the king urged. He sounded very far away. "Lie still."

Mal couldn't obey. His body twisted of its own accord. Muscles jittered and stretched as he tried to escape the blazing pain in his chest. His back arched in visceral protest, and he groaned.

"Vocent, let be!" Mal could no longer see Renault, but the royal command rang between his ears. "Let be before your body breaks."

Mal responded automatically. There was nothing of

brotherly concern left in Renault's tone. Mal had been schooled well to his office; he belonged to the king heart and soul, mind and body.

A royal command couldn't be ignored.

His mind worked before his body noticed. Reaching down to the very foundation of his core, Mal sectioned off pain, and locked it away, dividing his body for the moment from scraping agony.

He went limp. Fluid bubbled in his throat, sour, but he managed to take a breath.

"Better," said His Majesty.

Mal tried to open his eyes, but his lids were heavy and dry. He licked his lips, and tasted old blood.

"But not yet enough." The king's hand closed about Mal's wrist, fingers cool and strong. "You need healing. The *agraine* is nearly finished with you. There isn't any time left. Do you understand?"

Mal couldn't find the strength to answer. He wanted, very suddenly and very strongly, to see Renault's face.

"Malachi?" Renault's hand clenched. "Do you hear me? Siobahn must let the priests through. She's blocking, they can't touch you. Mal! Are you listening?"

Mal tried. He concentrated, but he couldn't find the sense in the words. Siobahn's name brought a brief niggle of worry, but even that slid away.

WHEN HE SURFACED a second time, the pain in his chest had numbed to ice. His heart fluttered like a bird behind his ribs.

He found, to his immense surprise, that he could move. He rolled over, propping himself on an elbow, and looked around.

The great high bed was his own. He was in his old suite. The space was bright and airy, familiar. The hanging tapestries he had chosen himself, for their verdant greens and blue.

Siobahn had helped him tack the fabrics to the walls, so many years past.

The dark outside the windowpanes said nighttime, and the streaks of wet across the panes told of a rainy season well under way. Lamps were lit; fat white candles sheathed in colored glass. Mal had carried those lamps from his foster father's estate, and kept the pretty things more out of sentiment than practicality.

Their rainbow flickering warmed the room. Mal eased back against a bolster pillow. He struggled to pull the heavy velvet coverlet up over his chest.

"Green for the bed, *ai*? I expected more black."

For some reason her voice made his already uneasy heart trip. He coughed, a great hacking wheeze, and then another, and another. When the spasm finally eased, he was breathless.

Mal wiped shaking fingers across his mouth, and blinked tears of exertion from his eyes. He frowned across the room. He hadn't seen her there, hadn't sensed her, and that was more troubling than the ice in his lungs.

She moved from her seat in the great leather chair he kept by the largest of the windows. Lamplight tinted her dusky skin rose as she stepped onto the sleeping dais.

"The walls are finely done," she said. "And the bed fit for a king. You need only a rug or two across the floor to keep the chill from the stones."

"Avani," he said, ignoring a prick of temper. "What are you doing here?"

"Watching you sleep," she said, as though it were the most natural thing in the world. "Waiting to see if you would wake."

Wind and rain rattled the windowpanes. The bank of lamps flickered. Light caught in Avani's dark eyes and gathered around the edges, turning them lambent. Mesmerized, Mal watched as the glitter of gold overflowed the woman's lashes.

Embarrassed, he looked away.

The raven fluttered under the bed canopy. Jacob paced up the length of bedding and back again, head cocked to one side, mumbling. The bird reminded Mal of a petulant old man.

He watched the raven pace until he had his emotions back under control, then dared a glance at Avani.

Her eyes were dry, her face still and calm. Light sparkled at her wrists, where true gold jingled.

"You look weary," Mal ventured, because she did. When he looked further, he saw that her wool tunic was stiff with dried mud, her trousers torn. More mud crusted her chin, and her nose was swollen and bruised.

He thought he saw tufts of winter grass tangled in her hair.

"What happened?" He asked, then had to stifle another fit of coughing.

"You don't remember?"

"I remember the bearded mongrel, and the message he carried. I remember rain, and cold, and . . ." He hesitated, searching. "Dreams. Of Andrew, and of Siobahn, and once, of you."

"That was more than a dream," she said with the assurance he remembered from the fevered garden. "The Goddess spoke, a warning."

Mal frowned at the pacing raven. He shook his head.

"I was there, *ai*?" Avani insisted. "You were dreaming, and I fell into it. You had my key, in your hand."

"I dropped it," Mal whispered, remembering. "It stung my hand. And pierced the earth."

"And now it's gone." Avani brought her fingers to her throat. "I woke, and it was gone, and we were hunted again."

Mal sat forward. The coverlet pooled in his lap. Pain throbbed, but he ignored it.

"What happened?" he repeated, sharp.

If Avani heard the sting of his tongue, she pretended not to. She watched the dance of light in the lamps.

"A bear," she said. "It was only a bear. A great, shaggy, black bear. Big as Everin. Or as close as to make no difference."

"A bear?" Mal watched her face. The thin, nervous line of her mouth worried him.

"It was raining, wasn't it?" Avani said, "We took shelter. I fell asleep, and walked in your dream. And I didn't wake until too late, until it had already started on Bran."

Mal felt a pang of grief. He pushed it away. "The horse?"

"He's dead," she said. Once again his lamps high-lighted her sorrow. "I'm sorry. He was dead before we realized. Torn apart. Liam tried to stop it, but he's just a boy."

She broke off, swallowing hard.

Mal caught one of her hands in his own. "Is the boy all right?"

She laughed then, amazed. "He killed it. With your sword. He had some help. Your monarch's Kingsmen finally found us. But Liam finished it, with your sword. Cut the monster's liver right out, mostly by accident. The blade's far too heavy for him."

"Good lad. Well done. And where is our hero now?"

Her mouth twitched. "Asleep. His Majesty gave us a nice suite of rooms. I'm afraid he still has your sword."

"He can keep it, if he likes," Mal said. He sighed. "Poor Bran."

"The Kingsmen said the bear was water-mad, and far out of territory. There were six of them, six great men, and it took all of their arrows, and a skinny boy with a man's sword to bring it down."

"You were frightened," Mal realized. "I'm sorry."

"The dream was a warning," she said. "Delivered too late."

Mal didn't reply. He sat cross-legged under velvet, Avani's hand still pressed in his own, and listened to his heart flutter. She looked into his face, exasperated.

"Don't you see? That bear wasn't water-mad. It was another trap, *ai*? That animal was sent after us. I could taste the shadows in the air. At first, I thought it was in your Kingsmen. But then the bear went down, and the light left its eyes, and I knew."

"Are you saying the poor thing was enscrolled?"

"Enscrolled. Like the rotting men on the Downs, with poison on their blades. Like the keep, and your sword that cut through an innocent man."

He shot her a look. Avani wrinkled her nose, winced when it throbbed.

"Siobahn told me," she admitted. "And why not? It seems I'm the only one with sense."

"Are you sure about the bear?" he asked.

"I am. Are you ready to believe me?"

"I saw the walking dead on the Downs," he relented. After a moment of thought, he lay back again on his pillow. "The key?"

"Gone. I searched. Through the mud and rain. It melted, smoked away to nothing, in the Goddess's vision. Perhaps it did the same in waking life. Or perhaps whatever was in the bear stole it away."

Mal nodded. He closed his eyes, then drew a long breath.

"What is it?"

He heard her concern, but didn't open his eyes. The bed shifted as she rearranged the coverlet. He could feel the warmth of her breath on his brow.

"I'm tired," he said, enjoying the cool black shelter behind his eyelids.

"You're dying," Avani returned, blunt.

That opened his eyes. He stared. She glared back.

"Your king says the poison's put holes in your lungs, and started on your heart. He says you've only hours left."

"So he's sent you to keep me company as I fade? How very comforting."

Her black eyes flashed, and the corners of her mouth pulled downward.

"You burn like the sun when you're angry," Mal said before thinking. He had the satisfaction of seeing her flush.

"He can save you," she said as though he hadn't spoken.

"I'm relieved."

"But only if the *bhut* will get her claws out of your mind."

That gave Mal pause. He slitted his eyes, watching her narrowly. "What do you mean?"

"Can't you feel her? Even *I* can feel her. She's walled you away from everyone who intends to help. Gone mad. Or simply too jealous to do you good. The priests can't help you, Malachi. Not unless she lets you go."

He frowned. For the first time since he woke, he took a moment to reach for Siobahn.

"I can't feel her," he said, suddenly afraid.

"You're the only one in the room who can't. Isn't she driving poor Jacob mad?" Avani said, bitterly. "Haven't I warned you? They're nothing but endless trouble, *bhut*. Spoiled children, always wanting the wrong thing. She's carrying you to your grave, whether she plans it or not."

"I can't turn her otherwise if I can't feel her," Mal said through clenched teeth.

"I know." Avani seemed almost repentant. She brushed a hand against his cheek. Her touch burned, and he flinched.

"Ice cold, you are. Death is rooting in your body. Will you let me help?"

"You?" He snorted. "You, Avani?"

"Let me try. I may have no flatland training, but the Goddess walks at my side."

"I don't believe in your Goddess."

"Let me help," Avani said. It was as close to a plea as he had heard her utter.

"You'll tear her apart."

"If I could," she said. "But I'm not that strong. I'm no vocent."

"What will you do, then?" He was wary as the child he'd named her.

"This," she said, moving before he could change his mind.

The hand on his cheek slid to cup his brow.

A jolt of power flared across his spine, and melted the ice in his lungs. Pain came rushing back, and he yelled. His cry echoed, mingling with the thumping of his strained heart.

The room swirled away, draining through his mind to nothing.

IT WAS THE garden again, with bubbling fountains, and the sweet-tart scent of spring flowers. He sat on the edge of the same fountain, fingers clenched on a lip of granite. He wore wedding blue, but his hands were empty, and the spray off the fountain didn't touch his skin.

Avani sat on the grass at his feet.

His bride waited in the shade of a flowering elm, and watched them both.

"Coward," Avani accused. "Will you kill him so carelessly?"

Mal opened his mouth and found he couldn't speak. He was rooted to the stone, unable to move, frozen in place by the strength of Avani's untrained mind.

He struggled briefly against the bonds, but his own power was weakened by poison, and he couldn't break free.

Siobahn stalked into the garden, her gown drifting on gentle breezes. She was as clean and beautiful as Avani was filthy. Her smile was bitter.

"Let him go!" Avani ordered.

"They'll kill him."

"You'll kill him. Stupid spirit. Let him go, the king's priests will heal him."

Siobahn shook her head. Bright curls bounced on her shoulders. "It's only another trap. They'll take his mind, and his body."

"Use your head. There's no danger here."

"Clay, and ash, and blood and bone," moaned Siobahn.

A bangled hand flashed out. Avani slapped the spirit. Her blow was solid, her aim good, and Siobahn stumbled. She tripped over the hem of her gown, crumbling to the grass.

Mal wanted to curse, but his mouth was sealed tight.

Avani stood over Siobahn, her shadow across the spirit's bowed head. Siobahn pressed a dainty fist to her cheek, rubbing away a handprint.

"Won't you listen?" Avani challenged, "Or must I force sense into your silly head?"

"Interfering bitch," Siobahn snapped. Mal felt his eyes try to widen in astonishment.

"So. And is that the problem?" Avani wondered. She looked into Siobahn's red face. "Are you keeping him from danger, or are you keeping him from *me*?"

"One and the same," whispered Siobahn. "One and the same."

"Has death addled your brain, stupid ghostie? I won't harm him. I won't take him from you, Siobahn. But you have to let him go, or he will die."

Siobahn sat in a huddle on the grass and sulked.

"Or is it that you want him dead?" asked Avani, suspicious. "Dead and sleeping in the ground with your own bones?"

"No!" Siobahn's temper blazed. "No. He must live."

"Then let him go."

"I can't."

"You're a child."

"Aye," Siobahn hissed. "So I was, and so I am. But I won't let any harm come to him."

"Can't you see? The harm is here, in this garden, where you keep his center locked away. I should have seen it, last time. This prison is full of your cloying sweetness."

"He's safe here!"

"And didn't I just say he's dying?"

"Mal—" Siobahn begged, turning toward his frozen form.

"No." Avani grabbed Siobahn by the sleeve, and shook the spirit until her teeth chattered. "My lord loves you," she said. "Even I, fool that I am, can see it. He'll waste away here in your garden if you ask it of him. Don't ask. Let him go."

Siobahn drew in, curled around the folds of her gown, and her eyes gleamed feral blue. "If you promise."

Mal's heart bumped uneasily. Avani stilled, watching the spirit.

"What is it you ask, *bhut*?"

"Promise me," demanded Siobahn, high and clear. "Give up your claim. Stop interfering."

Mal didn't understand, but Avani obviously did. She glared down at Siobahn, and the heat of her rage might have shriveled a lesser spirit. Mal felt the surge of raw power, and was amazed.

Siobahn didn't flinch. "Promise me!"

"Spirits have no claim on the living."

"This one does," Siobahn said. She bared her teeth. "You can't understand flatland ways, island witch. Leave us be."

Avani's brows drew together. "And you will let him go."

"Aye." Siobahn smiled. "I will let him free, and Renault will see him healed, and he will live."

"Very well," Avani conceded after a long stretch of silence.

"Promise," Siobahn pressed. "You must promise."

Avani blew through her nose, a sound of disgust. "I promise. Before the Goddess who judges all, I give you my word."

Siobahn's smile grew wide. The spirit laughed. Her laughter echoed off the granite fountain, and warmed his bones. Then he felt something rip, and he was free, the garden frayed to dull pieces.

WHEN MAL CAME to himself a third time, dawn warmed the room through storm-streaked windows, and the smell of guttered candle was in the air.

He opened his eyes slowly, and discovered that he couldn't breathe without gasping.

"Vocent." Renault bent over the bed. "We've been waiting for you to grace our presence."

Mal had to swallow twice before he could speak, and even then his voice was almost without sound. "Have you brought the shriver then, Your Majesty?"

Renault snorted, but his beard was wet with tears. "Nay. Merely an army of priests, brother."

"Let them do their best, then."

"So be it." Renault almost smiled. "First, you must drink."

The king's gaze shifted slightly, and Mal's own eyes followed. Avani stood at Renault's side. She held a silver chalice, the stem clutched between both hands, and her knuckles were white against the metal.

"More tea?" Mal breathed, amused.

Renault gave a bark of laughter. "Wine, and herbs. The witch said it would make your body sleep, and your mind willing. The priests do not disagree."

Mal slanted Avani a look. "Your herbs?"

"They're better in cider," Avani replied, somber. "But the wine will do."

He lifted a heavy hand, beckoned. "Bring it here. Help me drink."

She brushed past Renault, and stretched over the bed, tipping the chalice carefully. Mal swallowed as best he could, but coughed much of the liquid back onto the priceless velvet. The wine was bitter, but the herb tasted of summer.

When the chalice was empty, Avani straightened.

"You've still mud on your chin," Mal whispered. "Hasn't His Majesty offered hot water for bathing?"

"I offered," Renault said. "She wouldn't take it. Nor food nor sleep nor clothes not torn to threads."

Avani only folded her hands again about the chalice stem.

"See that she gets them all," Mal said. The herbs were beginning to work in his veins. He could feel his blood growing sluggish, and the pressure in his heart eased. "And boots, Renault. She's been walking days with nothing but sheep's thin hide to protect her feet."

Renault made a sound that might have been a laugh.

Mal heard the tread of many boots in the corridor outside his rooms, and knew that once again he listened with Siobahn's senses. He reached for the spirit, and found her hovering at the very edge of consciousness.

Renault's troop of priests burst through the door. They were great hairy men of the north, yellow eyed, trained from childhood in the ways of healing a king. Mal knew their smell and the gentle touch of their hands.

They stripped away velvet, and bared his naked body to the chill of the room.

Mal was grateful for the dulling properties of Avani's herbs. His mind drifted at a distance; he felt no interest in fear or embarrassment. He let the priests poke and probe, and he spoke not one word of protest when they brought the pain back.

"Sleep, Mal," Renault said. "You've done well. Sleep, and when you wake, it will be to health."

Mal turned his head to the wall. He shut his eyes, and when he slept, he was free of dreams.

Chapter Ten

RENAULT LED AVANI down a long corridor to the set of rooms he'd made her own. When she might have protested, the king only frowned beneath his close beard.

"There is no space for you and I in such a task," he said, standing in the hall before the door to Avani's room.

The king was a slight man, little taller than Avani, but of sturdy frame. He wore Hennish leather, dyed in the red and black of his house, and a circlet of true gold about his brow.

His eyes were the color of mud, but they were quick and bright, and sparkled at Avani's temper.

"Leave the working to the priests, yes?" He reached past Avani and shoved open the heavy door. "Sleep. Wash the stains of travel from your body. I've had water prepared."

Avani looked through the door and saw that he spoke true. A half casket of water sat in one corner of the room.

Steam rose in a spiral to the rafters. Flames crackled merrily in a hearth that was long as Avani was tall. Someone had set a platter of meat and cheese on the room's round wooden table.

"The flask holds wine," His Majesty said. "The tin, spring water."

Avani gazed past the table at the bed. The sleeping dais was a smaller twin to Mal's, but it was the bundle of clothing on the woolen coverlet that made her gasp.

"*Salwar!*" She hurried across flagstones to examine the bundle.

A *salwar* it was, the island coat with stiff collar and loose sleeves, and pleats of tailored fabric that fell just beyond the knee. Matching trousers were folded on the bed beneath the coat, and soft island slippers set neatly to one side.

Avani touched the fabric reverently. It was island silk, white as snow, and the embroidery on the collar and sleeves was of the gold thread she remembered from childhood.

"A bit light for winter," Renault admitted. "But we thought you'd find it acceptable."

"Island silk." Still clutching the *salwar*, she turned in time to catch the king's quick smile. "By the Goddess, how?"

"There is a merchant," Renault explained. "Island born, I understand. He sells his work at the Fair, winter and summer. His jewels do better than the silks, but he makes a good living. Perhaps you would like to meet him?"

Avani looked at the *salwar*, and nodded, mute.

"Later, then." His Majesty sounded pleased. "Once

you've eaten and rested. Once we know that Malachi is sound. Then I'll have someone guide you down to the Fair."

He took a step into the room, and directed Avani's attention to the foot of the bed. "There are boots, as you can see. We imagined slippers wouldn't do in the rainy weather."

The boots were black leather, oiled and shiny. Avani touched the leather with one trembling finger as she blinked back an emotion she didn't understand.

"You're welcome," Renault said. "Will you bathe?"

She nodded. "Will you send for me when you hear?"

"Aye," the king answered. "As soon as."

She nodded again, hugging silk to her chest. Wilhaiim's king bowed once, ever so slightly. Then he left the room, shutting the door gently at his back.

"Avani?"

Liam stuck his head around the far corner of the bed. His eyes were puffy, his cheeks flushed. Avani smiled, and walked around the bed.

"All is well," she soothed. "Go back to sleep. I'll wake you when it's time for supper."

The lad yawned. He lay back on the squire's pallet a servant had earlier unrolled along side the dais. Avani stood, watching until she was sure Liam had fallen back into sleep. Then she set the *salwar* carefully back on the bed. She went to investigate the steaming water.

The casket was as wide as her hips, and tall as her middle. The water was still hot.

"This will scald me clean," she said to Jacob. The raven

glanced up from his spot on the windowsill, then went back to his preening.

The wood of the casket was rough against her bare skin, but the heated water eased muscle aches and bruises. Avani soon found herself dozing.

She dropped into a half sleep. When she woke again the water was cool, the fire burning low in the hearth. Jacob perched on the edge of the casket, feathers ruffled. He croaked.

"I'm awake," she said, groaning when she tried to rise. Muscles had stiffened again, and goose bumps prickled her flesh.

She climbed from the casket, shedding water, and plucked a fluffy cloth from the hearth. Wrapped in the warm fabric, she rekindled the fire until the flames leapt high and Jacob was satisfied, then padded over to check on Liam.

The boy still slept, curled knees to chin. Mal's sword lay in its scabbard at his side. Avani readjusted the cloak he used as a blanket, then climbed onto the dais in search of her new clothes.

The trousers bagged some about her waist, but their length was perfect. The coat hit in all the right places. She blessed the tailor for his skill. She remembered her own faded *salwar* from childhood; many had first been her mother's, later cut down to fit Avani. They were lost, now, at the bottom of an angry sea.

Avani found a length of thick gold thread coiled neatly in one of the slippers. She wove the thread through her hair, fingers remembering the complicated island braid, an intricate, age-old pattern that was said to please the Goddess.

When the braid was finished, she tied off the length of thread, smiling.

"I'd trade two good rugs for a mirror," she told Jacob, laughing at her vanity.

She picked up the pretty embroidered slippers, decided with some reluctance to yield to practicality, and set them aside again. The leather boots were a near perfect fit. The leather was soft. She tucked the cuffs of her trousers into the tops.

Feeling much refreshed, and made almost giddy by the feel of island silk against her flesh, Avani sat at the round table, and tucked into supper.

The meat was salty, the wedge of cheese thick as her arm. She ate her fill, and fed the raven when he came to beg. Then she took the flask of wine to the hearth and waited for Liam to wake.

Renault found her there still, long after dark, the flask empty.

"My lady," he eyed her up and down. "You look . . ."

"Out of place?" Avani suggested, tongue well oiled by the sweet wine.

"Not at all. But one sees so few of your people, and rarely in traditional dress."

"There are few of us left," Avani replied without bitterness. She rose to welcome the king. "Liam is still asleep."

Renault glanced at the boy. "He'll sleep on through the night."

Avani snorted. "I'd prefer if he woke long enough to eat."

"He's a lad. He'll sleep for hours and wake starving. Come with me."

"It's done?" She sprang to her feet.

"Aye," Renault said. "And done well. He'll have to spend much of the winter indoors, if not in bed. His lungs may never be the same. But he'll do, if he gives his body the time it requires."

"And will he?"

Renault laughed. "Unlikely. But you'll keep an eye on him."

"I'd not thought to winter here."

"Oh? And where will you go?" The king smiled slightly.

Avani shrugged. "I thought perhaps north."

"The mountains will soon be impassible. You're safe here."

"For now," Avani returned. "Until whatever killed your Lord Andrew decides to dip poison in my drink."

Renault's brows slanted. "Whatever, you say?"

"What or who," Avani allowed. "Little matter to me."

"How," the king asked, "did you know about Andrew?"

"My lord dreamed, fever dreams. He often spoke aloud in his sleep."

"And you listened."

She wouldn't be cowed. "I was there to hear."

He shifted, shoulders set. She could see him dismissing the subject. A king, she supposed, could afford to pick and choose his interests.

"Come," he ordered once more. "I'll take you to him."

She allowed Renault to lead her from the room, and back through twisting corridors. This time she counted paces and doors. She didn't intend to wander lost every time she wished to visit Mal in his sickbed.

Jacob rode on Avani's shoulder, bobbing his head.

Mal's suite was dark, rainbow lamps snuffed. Avani could hear the wash of rain across windowpanes. The flagstones were winter cold even through her new boots.

One fat yellow candle burned on a small table beside the high bed. A man sat on his knees in the faint light of the single flame. He was clothed in rough brown robes, and wore his beard long. His skull was shaved down to the flesh.

"My Masterhealer will keep watch through the night," Renault said, indicating the man with a flick of his hand.

Avani frowned. "You said he was whole."

"See for yourself."

She stepped onto the dais, edging past the priest. The robed man seemed oblivious, lost in the glow of the candle.

Mal lay on his stomach underneath the coverlet, one arm thrown wide. He appeared to be sleeping peacefully. Some of the color had returned to his face.

"Like the boy, he'll rest for many hours yet," Renault murmured. "Are you reassured?"

Avani didn't reply. She bent over the great bed, and listened to Mal's lungs.

"He's breathing comfortably," the king said.

"The poison is gone?" she asked.

"We pulled its fangs," said the priest, stirring. He stared at Jacob with some curiosity. "His heart, at least, is saved."

"And his lungs?" Avani worried.

The priest bowed his head. "We did our best, my lady."

"Your best is incomparable," the king said. "Now is not the time for modesty."

"Yes, Your Majesty." The man blinked at Avani. "There should be no reason to worry. His lordship is young and strong." He paused. "The bird is your familiar?"

Jacob had left Avani's shoulder and was exploring the room, hopping from floor to table and back again.

"The bird is my friend," Avani corrected. She watched with some bemusement as Jacob plucked a small silver brooch from a table.

The raven marched across the flagstones, then fluttered onto the bed. He settled himself on the bedclothes. Poking absently at the bit of silver, Jacob watched Mal with a black, beady eye.

"Your friend can stay," the priest decided, deadpan. "Since he seems to have made himself at home."

"This room is ice cold," Avani complained. "Why not kindle a fire? The hearth is large enough to heat six homes."

The priest frowned. "His lordship needs rest, undisturbed by light or the snap of flames."

Renault made a sound that might have been a laugh. "A little warmth would not be amiss, Masterhealer. I'll send a page to tend the fire."

The priest glared in Avani's direction. The king sketched a sign in the air over Mal, and then preceded Avani from the room.

The air in the hall seemed close after the chill in the sickroom. Avani eyed the king sideways.

"You will see about the fire?"

The royal beard twitched. "I will. Are you satisfied?"

Avani nodded. "I am." She lingered outside Mal's door. A candle flickered in a sconce on the wall. The hot wax smelled pungently of honey.

"The sign you drew over his lordship's bed, was it a warding?"

"Of sorts." Renault leaned against a tapestried wall, relaxed as a youth.

"A spell?"

"I'm no magus," he said, obviously entertained by her question. "And no priest. There is little magic left in this land, and I have not a drop of it in my blood."

"Royal blood." Avani considered the king's face. He was handsome in a broad, solid manner. Where Mal was long and lean, Renault was sturdy, immovable.

"Royal blood," Renault agreed. "And a temple man. The sign I drew was for Malachi's protection. An invoking of the saints."

"Flatland saints, and flatland kings. I know very little of either."

"You will learn," the king replied, unfazed. "But not tonight. It grows late. Malachi sleeps, and so should you."

As if in response, a yawn suddenly cracked Avani's jaw. She lifted a hand to cover it, bangles belling, and Renault smiled.

"Shall I escort you back to your rooms?"

Avani found herself smiling back. She shook her head. "I remember the way. My thanks."

"*My* thanks," the king replied. "You brought my brother home."

He laughed silently at Avani's startled expression, then moved away from the wall and left her alone in the corridor. He walked at ease as a man in his beloved home.

Avani yawned again. She started back along the forty-seven strides to her own door.

Liam still snored, sprawled like a pup over Mal's cloak. Avani rekindled the fading fire, broke an edge from the remaining cheese, and nibbled as she pulled off her boots.

Barefoot on the flagstones, she snagged her sack from its place on the floor, and dumped the contents over the foot of the bed.

She'd wrapped the idol in a cocoon of wool and silk, and buried it at the very bottom of the sack. Now she unwrapped it carefully, muttering a low chant of welcome and blessing as she did so. The statue's golden skin glittered in the firelight.

Avani set the Goddess gently on the edge of the hearth. At the idol's feet she placed the tin bowl she used for her offerings, as well as the small candle she sometimes lit for worship.

She left the candle unlit, but sank to her knees on the flagstones, and said a quick prayer of thanks. She unbound her braid, coiled the golden thread, and dropped it into the bowl, an offering for her ancestors.

A SHARP KNOCK on the suite's heavy door roused her from muzzy dreams. The fire had gone out, and the dim light of early dawn fell through the room's narrow windows. Liam stirred on the floor, and sat up.

He blinked owlishly at Avani, then at the door.

"What is it?"

Her clothes were across the room. Liam watched her with sleepy anticipation. Swearing under her breath, she wound bedclothes around her naked body and hitched from bed to door. The fabric caught at her feet, and her curses rose an octave.

She set a smile over gritted teeth, and flung open the door.

The woman on the other side of her door gasped, then began to laugh. Her face was as open and innocent as her laugh. Avani found her irritation softening in a reluctant echo of real mirth.

"I've come too early," the woman said. "I'm sorry. My curiosity got the best of me, as usual."

"Oh, *ai*?" Avani brushed a tangle of hair from her brow. The woman in the doorway had hair of gilt, light as true gold, and eyes nearly as green as Mal's.

She was small and delicate, and she made Avani in her wrappings feel clumsy.

"Renault promised me you were an adventure," she said, still smiling. "I had to come and see for myself."

"Did you then?" Avani supposed she looked and sounded like a fool.

"I'm sorry." She held out a graceful hand. "My name is Kate. I am the king's mistress."

Avani managed to keep from gaping, but she had to swallow twice to do so.

"Would you like to come in?" she tried.

"Thank you, no." Kate shook her head. "I'll return, in an hour's time. You'll be dressed then?"

Feeling witless, Avani nodded.

"Good. Dress for the rain." Kate clapped her hands. "I nearly forgot. I've a gift, from Renault, who claims your cape is destitute."

A small red-cheeked page poked his head around the door. Avani flushed from toes to ears. The page set a small bundle on the threshold, and then popped back out of sight.

"I'm to take you to the Fair," said the king's mistress. "For breakfast, and some shopping. You, and your squire. You'll be ready?"

"Aye," Liam promised, because Avani couldn't seem to find her voice. "In an hour."

Kate curtsied, plain woolen skirts dusting the floor. Then she reached out and pulled the door shut, leaving Avani to stare at the bound planks and brass latch.

"What did she bring you?" Liam asked. He scrambled from the floor and swooped down onto the bundle.

He unrolled the package, and gasped: a cloak of white virgin wool, lined with soft black fur and fancifully embroidered.

"It's beautiful," Avani breathed.

"Not so different from the cloak you gave Thom last saint's day," Liam pointed out. "But the gold thread is pretty."

"It matches. His Majesty gifted me with *salwar*, yestereve. The cloak matches."

"Kings always have gifts to give," Liam said, unimpressed. "What did he bring me?"

That made Avani snort. "Nothing, as you were asleep, and you already have a very pretty cloak of your own, and a very pretty sword. Mal says you may keep it."

Liam's eyes sparkled. "Will he teach me how to use it?"

"For other than the slaying of bears?" Avani ruffled the lad's hair. "Someone will have to. But you've got growing to do, yet. There is cheese and meat on the table. Go and feed yourself while I dress."

"And then to the Fair?"

"And then to the Fair."

WHEN THE KING's mistress knocked again on the door, they were both presentable, Avani in her *salwar* and cloak and boots, her sack over her shoulder, and Liam, freshly scrubbed.

Kate smiled, and held out her hands in greeting, palms toward the ceiling. Avani took the delicate fingers and squeezed back. Liam bowed, blushing.

"It is raining hard, and it will likely be cold," Kate said. "But the Fair will already be bustling at this hour, and so close to the Winter Ceilidh there are always treasures to be found."

Avani thought of her empty money pouch, but nodded gamely. Kate reached across to take Liam's elbow.

"His Majesty has awarded you a stipend," she said. "For your bravery. While you are in Wilhaiim, the king's money is your own."

Avani shook her head in protest, but Kate raised her finger in an echo of Renault's imperiousness. "It is His Majesty's pleasure, believe me. You have brought his brother-in-name back to the city, alive. Renault gives thanks as he knows how; you must accept."

Still Avani would have refused, but the steel beneath Kate's smile convinced her otherwise.

"Come," said Kate, tugging Liam from the room. "There is so much to see and a third of the day gone already."

WILHAIIM'S FAIR SPROUTED up at the very base of the palace. Kate led Avani and Liam through many winding halls and down steep stairways before at last they made fresh air.

The king's mistress was correct; rain fell in heavy sheets. Laughing, Kate pulled them ten more steps through the downpour, and suddenly the rain stopped.

Avani looked up and saw that they stood beneath oiled canvas. A patchwork tent stretched over the Fair, a multicolored roof over a bustling bazaar. The canvas let in a little light and some wet, but the cold and damp was much lessened.

"Look!" Liam pulled on the edge of Avani's cloak. "Look, Avani!"

Wilhaiim's Fair was a miniature kingdom in itself, a realm of merchants and traders, a village of stalls and tents, ribbons and pennants. The noise was unbelievable. Merchants shouted their wares while patrons cried lively bargain. The air smelled of spice, and smoke, and roast meat and vegetables, and—

"Cider!" Liam cried, "Look, Avani, real cider!"

He loosed himself from Kate's grip, and dashed between two stalls. Avani followed after, Kate at her side.

The lad fetched up alongside a sagging tent. Huge pots boiled and steamed beneath yellow canvas. A fat man used a dipper to ladle liquid from pot to mug. A line snaked around in front of the tent.

Avani saw women in good wool, and women in torn burlap skirts, men who looked like lords, and men who were obviously laborers, all standing in line awaiting their drinks.

"He does well in the winter," Kate said into Avani's ear. "But, truthfully, his cider is rather bland."

Bland or no, Liam wanted cider, so they stood in line. If people recognized the king's mistress, they gave no sign, although they stared unashamedly at Avani, and pointed at the skinny lad in the rich cloak.

When they had mugs warming their hands, they moved on from stall to stall. Avani sipped her drink as they walked. Kate chattered on. The woman knew every merchant by name, and had an eye for quality.

Liam stopped to admire a set of tiny carved knights, each painted in Wilhaiim's red-and-black livery. Kate bought the little figures for him. When the boy found a pair of boots that fit, the king's mistress snapped them up, bargaining the merchant down to an acceptable price. And, as they strolled, she bought Liam an endless stream of pastries and sweets and more cider to quench his youthful thirst.

Once, as Liam admired a well-tooled belt, the king's mistress glanced back at Avani and shook her head playfully.

Avani soon became lost among the tents. The press of people was somehow reassuring. She was warm beneath her new cloak, and comfortable in Kate's friendliness, and pleased by Liam's fun.

When the crowd parted and Everin made his way through fruit mongers to her side, she discovered she was glad to see him.

"Shopping, black eyes?" he asked.

"At His Majesty's pleasure," she replied, looking him up and down.

He wore the same battered jerkin. His hair and beard were wet. She smelled the rain on him, and also ale.

He laughed when she wrinkled her nose at his breath.

"As I have been drinking away my reward. His Majesty is generous, aye?"

"You haven't yet moved on." She made it a statement rather than a question.

"Not yet. You look well. New clothes, new boots, new cloak. And your hair loose about your shoulders." He made as if to touch the drape of her hair, then paused. "Have you never cut it?"

"Not often," Avani said. "And only when the Goddess wills."

"You bound it back on the road."

"I shall again. I thought I might find some suitable ribbon here."

He did touch her hair, then, a daring wriggle of his

fingers against the crown of her head before he set his fists at his belt. "May I come along?"

"We have an escort."

His teeth showed white in his beard. "Lady Kate. The king's mistress and I are newly fast friends."

So it seemed, for when Kate caught sight of the big man, she laughed and embraced him in welcome. Liam was also pleased to see their traveling companion.. Avani wondered when the boy's distrust had faded.

When they walked on, Everin and Kate led the way, Liam edged between the two, Avani trailing in their wake.

She found the island merchant at the very edge of the Fair, sitting under a stall of fringed purple. He glimpsed her coming, stood and bowed in welcome, and blessed her in the name of the Goddess.

"It looks well on you, lady," he said, meaning the *salwar*.

"It is a wonder," she replied.

The man was small and withered, his black hair shaved in mourning. He saw the blink of her eyes, and tapped his counter with one brown hand.

"My wife passed in the spring," he explained. "I've had no one to mourn properly with me."

Spring was long past, the man's sorrow heavy on his brow.

"I will mourn with you," Avani offered.

He accepted without surprise. "In three days' time? His Majesty told me of your arrival. I prepared the wine."

"In three days' time," agreed Avani. "I will meet you here?"

"At dawn," the merchant said, very earnest.

"Oh, *ai*. At dawn. I remember."

The man bobbed his thanks, then he seemed to come to himself. He spread his wares across the counter, arranging fabric and jewelry with deft skill. Kate bent over the counter and exclaimed in delight.

Everin appeared uninterested, but after a moment his blunt thumb found a knot of color.

"Thread for your hair, black eyes," he said.

The strands were more cord than ribbon, cousin to the thin gold braid she'd given to the Goddess. They lay together in a rainbow tangle; red, and black, and green, and more gold, and white, and a blue deeper than the sky.

Avani bought a length of each.

"Avani," Kate said from where she examined a display of jewelry. "This would suit you well."

She held up a long string of beads; carved rubies the color of blood, and a clasp of true gold.

"They are pretty," Avani agreed. The stones were warm against her fingertips.

Kate set the necklace about Avani's neck and fastened the clasp.

"Wonderful!" Kate clapped her palms together with a child's delight. "Take them."

Avani did, if only to please the king's mistress. But it was the spindle she found shoved to the back of the tent that was the real gift.

"Old," the merchant said. "And in disrepair. It belonged to my wife. And there is a loom. And some raw island silk, very precious."

"There was a merchant selling unworked wool," Liam said.

"Many such merchants," Kate agreed, eyeing Avani with new interest. "Do you weave?"

"Weave and spin, and dye and sew," said Avani, stroking the spindle. "And a bit of handiwork here and there. This, I could repair."

"Then it is yours," said the merchant. "And the loom. Gifts to keep you busy during the long winter."

Avani couldn't refuse.

"Goddess bless you." She touched the spindle again, imagining the tapestries she could weave with island silk.

"And you," the merchant said. "My name is Deval."

"Deval." She smiled. "I will see you in three days' time, here, at dawn."

He smiled back, patting Avani's shoulder with his wrinkled brown fingers. She felt a flash of warmth when he smiled his friendship, and knew that in this strange kingdom of flatland merchants, the Goddess had given her another gift.

Chapter Eleven

THE RAVEN PERCHED in a pool of sunlight, sorting through the jewels of Mal's office.

The jewels belonged in a small wooden chest, and the small wooden chest belonged on Mal's breakfast table, but Jacob had knocked the chest to the floor, and now silver and precious stones littered the ground.

Jacob appeared to be sorting the mess into an order only he understood. As far as Mal could tell, the piles were random and changeable.

"Mind, each one of those pretties belongs to His Majesty," he warned the raven. "Lose even one and I'll spend the rest of my natural life working to repay the debt."

Jacob didn't even look his way.

Mal sat up slowly, setting his spine against the bed's carved headboard. A fire burned in the hearth, warming the room, and he was grateful. He could see the rime of frost along the outside of his windows, and knew the rain hadn't gone far.

He pulled the edge of the coverlet up to his chin, and took inventory. He felt well, better even than well. His head was clear, his stomach empty.

The bowl he kept on the mantel was newly filled with fresh fruit. Mal could smell the tart perfume of Renault's favorite winter apples. His mouth watered, and his gut growled ferociously.

He slid from the bed and discovered he was naked. Yelping at the smart of bare stone against his feet, he hopped across the room to the ancient wardrobe he used for the least formal of his clothes.

Halfway there his head began to spin, his heart to pound, and his muscles to cramp.

He'd been in bed too long. His vision fogged, but he forced his body the rest of the way to the wardrobe, and didn't stop until he'd found an old robe and wrapped it around his indignant flesh.

By then he was dripping with sweat and could barely see. Cursing, he stumbled the rest of the way to his chair, dropping with a sigh into the leather embrace.

Jacob squawked in irritation. The bird flapped from the floor, leaving his sorted treasures behind. He perched on the back of Mal's chair, muttering.

Mal sat, listening to the slick rustle of Jacob's feathers. He nearly fell asleep again, but his thoughts wouldn't let him rest. Questions circled in his head, stalking answers, routing few.

Mal shifted. Siobahn stood over Jacob's mess, considering the scattered jewels without expression.

"You are yourself again," she said when she noticed

Mal's regard. "Dreaming of revenge, anticipating the hunt."

"There is something murderous loose in this land," he said. "Would you have me do nothing?"

"You are fretting more over Andrew's death than the corpses on the Downs."

"One and the same, I think. The *agraine* is no coincidence. Renault sees it. I should have caught it earlier; perhaps much of this savagery would have been avoided."

"You were grieving."

"The king's vocent can't afford grief. Andrew would never have let any sorrow cloud his judgment."

"You are still young."

"Not," he said, "so young as that."

Siobahn pursed her lips in a pout. "What will you do?"

Mal set his elbow on one chair arm, and his chin on his hand. He considered his bride in silence. She watched him back with inhuman blue eyes.

"You're angry," she accused.

He studied her face, remembering how volatile she was. His wife for all of three years, little more than a child then, and not changed now, half a decade later.

"Not angry," Mal corrected. "Just wary. I don't want to upset you, Siobahn."

She came to kneel on the floor at his feet, her skirts pooling in sunlight. Jacob tilted his head from side to side, watching.

"I was afraid," she said. "I thought it was another trap. The poison clouded your senses, made my own unreliable.

You are all I have, and I thought . . ." She trailed off, and shook her head violently.

"Even after so many years spent in His Majesty's service, we have much to learn." Mal leaned forward, pressing his brow to her own. "And so we will continue on, and if we are lucky, make less grievous mistakes."

She snuffled a little, then smiled bravely. "You're not angry."

"I told you," he said. He brushed his fingers through her brilliant curls.

She wiped the back of her fingers across her mouth, rested her chin on his knee, and scowled at Jacob with some of her usual temper.

"That creature has been here every hour of every day you slept."

"And how many days have I slept?" He couldn't remember.

"Four."

"No wonder my stomach is gnawing at my ribs." Mal looked hopefully across the room at the bowl of apples.

Siobahn stood. She plucked an apple from the mantel and tossed it into Mal's lap.

"She left it here to watch over you, I think."

"The bird?" Mal asked, amused. He bit into the fruit, closing his eyes in bliss.

"No more a bird than I am a living woman," Siobahn said. She glared at Jacob. The raven looked back with the bland disinterest of his kind.

Mal grunted, enjoying his apple. He licked juice from his hand.

"Beyond all expectation, she is magus," he said, remembering the bright flash of Avani's power.

"A hedge witch," Siobahn scoffed. "And who is left to train her? You?"

"And you," he returned. "Perhaps. With Andrew gone, I am the last. She would be worth her weight in true gold."

"She won't want any part of it," Siobahn argued.

"We'll see," Mal said. He finished his apple in silence.

When he'd swallowed the last of the succulent fruit, his stomach was cheered, but his body was beginning to protest. Weary, he let Siobahn lead him from the chair.

She stripped him of his robe and tucked him between the sheets. Then she unleashed a lick of energy that set the flames in the hearth to roaring, and another that sent Mal spiraling down into unconsciousness.

The next morning Mal dressed in the uniform of his office: trousers and tunic, all in black, and the hooded cloak that spoke most eloquently of his office. The clothing, new and finely made, had appeared in his rooms overnight.

Renault's doing, Mal knew. He accepted the gift as his due, ready once more to serve the king.

The sky stormed again. Rain fell, and wind rattled the windows. Mal sat at his writing desk, back to the gloomy weather, and shuffled through scrolls in the glow of lantern light. Jacob sat atop the bed canopy, dozing.

The king found them there, together, at midday, the man chewing halfheartedly on a wing of roast turkey, the bird asleep..

"You need more than meat and apples to bring back

your strength," Renault said. He eyed Mal with some amusement. "Come and sup in the hall."

Mouth full, Mal shook his head. He cocked his ringed finger at the pile of parchment. Lamplight turned the yellow stone in its setting to deep orange.

"You may be up and about and working for me again," Renault said, unsurprised. "But you're still thin, Lord Vocent. Come and sup."

"Tomorrow," Mal replied.

"Avani will be there tonight," said the king. "No doubt she'd like to see her pet again."

"She left it here as nursemaid. The bird's content, and so am I. If she wants to see it, she will come." He paused, glancing up at Jacob. "She's well?"

"She's found a friend in the Fair." Renault smiled beneath his beard. "An island man. She spends little time in the palace, I think. Except, of course, to baby her lad."

"She's too protective. That boy needs to be uprooted and allowed to grow in his own soil."

"I'll leave that to you," the king decided. "You know the woman far better than I."

"She's stubborn."

"As are you," Renault pointed out. "Convince her to let the boy into my service. You need a page. He'd find a good home here."

Mal arched a brow, then relented with a dip of his head. "I'll mention the possibility."

"Do so." Renault pulled a piece of parchment from Mal's desk. "Andrew's hand," he said, reading.

"I've gathered together his journal."

Renault's brow furrowed. "A vocent's journal belongs to his king."

Mal met Renault's stare, steady beneath the flame of royal temper. His Majesty exhaled.

"Have you found anything of interest?"

"Nothing," Mal answered. "Yet. But I have only just begun."

Renault touched his fingers to his beard. He looked over Mal's head, and out the windows. "Whatever killer is running wild in my kingdom, whatever man or beast took my Andrew, you will find me answers."

"I will. I want to unearth Andrew's body."

Renault flinched visibly. When he looked at Mal, his eyes were wild. Alarmed, Mal rose halfway in his chair, but the king shook his head. Renault mastered himself quickly. With a royal disregard for embarrassment, he brushed the drip of sorrow from his eyes.

"Is it necessary?"

"Yes."

Renault puffed out a breath. "Are you strong enough?"

"We haven't time to waste."

"When?"

Mal said, "Two days' time. Before the Winter Ceilidh. With luck, the weather will ease."

The king's laughter was bittersweet. "You've lived too long among us to foster that dream. It will rain until we drown, and then the sun will come and bake us brown until next winter."

Mal regarded his monarch with affection.

"Your Majesty," he said gently, "leave me to work. I'll send word when it's time to visit our dead."

Renault looked as though he wished to argue. But he nodded.

"I'll have your supper sent up," he decided. "Something hot, and filling, before you fall to dust before our eyes. You're too frail a man to do this king much good."

Mal quirked one mocking brow, but Renault only laughed.

WHEN HIS EYES grew tired of Andrew's handwriting, he went in search of Avani. The bird rode on his shoulder, heavy and warm against his ear.

Renault had put the woman in the smallest of the state suites. The rooms were only a short distance away, but Mal was out of breath by the time he reached Avani's door.

He had to stand several moments longer in the hall before the door rattled and opened.

"My lord," Avani said, surprised. "What are you doing?"

"May I come in?" he asked, shocked into formality. The woman standing in front of him was much changed from the traveling companion he recalled.

She stepped back, and let him into her rooms. The suite smelled of spice and smoke. A fire burned on a hearth half as large as his own.

Mal's eye came to rest first on the loom set up in the far corner, against one narrow window, and then on the idol gleaming on the edge of the hearth.

"Lovely," he said, and now he was not looking at the glittering statue, but at her dusky face.

She might have flushed, he wasn't sure. She turned on her heel, and stalked across the room. Mal followed. He could see that she had been sitting before the fire on a patterned rug so new the fabric still smelled of dye. A silver goblet steamed on a small table, and a thin leather volume lay open on the rug, waiting.

Jacob left Mal's shoulder. The bird settled next to the idol.

"Troublemaker," Avani scolded. "Where have you been?"

"Playing nursemaid," Mal said. He plucked the book from the rug, and examined the neatly lettered spine. "Ra'Vadin?"

Avani faced down his surprise, annoyed and then amused. "You assumed I haven't any letter learning."

"No." He set the book back in its place. "But, philosophy?"

"Your scholars tell me the Virgin King adored the man. I thought that I'd see what he had to say."

"And?"

Avani shrugged. "He's a flatlander."

"And?" Mal repeated.

Avani shrugged again. "He thinks in straight lines. But some of his ideas are interesting."

Mal choked. "The Virgin King's beloved philosopher, and you pronounce him merely 'interesting.'"

She settled cross-legged on the rug. Mal stood against the fire, his shadow across Avani's knees. He studied the woman carefully.

She was still more bone than flesh, but she was clean,

and looked content. The wretched cape was gone. Instead she wore trousers and a coat of silk in black and red. Her feet were bare, the nails of her toes enameled and shiny, black as ebony, edged in gold.

More gold gleamed in her hair; thread braided in elaborate coils.

She was exotic, foreign, and yet somehow familiar. Her black eyes were luminous.

Mal crouched on his heels, and found his hand reaching to touch. But Avani slid away, the string of rubies around her neck glinting in the light.

"A gift," she explained when he raised a brow. "From His Majesty. This *salwar*, as well, and others. And the book, and a knife for Liam."

Mal crossed his arms over his chest. "His Majesty believes in rewarding service well done. You rescued the kingdom's last vocent from extinction. That, indeed, was very well done."

Avani kept silent. Mal slanted a glance, and saw that she frowned.

"I sound bitter." He chased dark thoughts away. "But I'm only embarrassed. It should not have happened."

"Sit," she replied, tart, and patted the rug. Her bangles rang. "You look more dead than alive, yet."

"It's the black," he explained, but sat obediently.

"It is . . . stark," she agreed, grinning. "Why black?"

"Tradition. And a color that looks well on you."

She snorted. "*Ai*, a compliment. Thank you, my lord."

"Mal."

She laughed. Then she picked up the steaming goblet,

and sipped mulled wine. When she held the drink up in offering, Mal shook his head.

"There is cider, if you like. Deval had the correct spices. I've replenished my stores."

"Deval?"

"An island man. A friend. He made this *salwar*. The necklace is his handiwork, also."

"Ah. Renault mentioned your new friend."

Avani didn't reply. Mal gazed around the room again, noting the platter of meat on the battered table. A bright scarf lay across the foot of the bed. His eye came to rest on the squire's pallet unrolled beneath the dais.

"How is Liam?"

"Eager," said Avani. "He's out at the barracks with Everin, playing with your gift."

"My gift."

"The sword."

"That sword is too big for a boy to use properly. Surely Everin knows better."

"Little matter." Avani shook her head. "Liam will use no other. You are his hero, my lord."

"The boy will hurt himself! He needs . . ." Mal rubbed a thumb across his chin. "He needs schooling. Renault has offered to take the boy into service. It would be the wisest thing."

"Liam is no nobleman's son. He's an orphan, of farm stock. What would he do in a king's service?"

"Grow," replied Mal. "And, no doubt, prosper. Liam needs a home, Avani. This is as good as any, better than most."

"His home is with me now."

Mal felt a twinge of disappointment. He looked down at the vocent's ring on his finger. "You're moving on, are you?"

She hesitated. "I haven't decided. Wilhaiim is no more my home than Liam's."

"Make it your home," he suggested.

She bit her lip in indecision.

"At least stay through winter," he urged. "Let the lad train with the other pages. When spring comes, then you can reconsider the matter."

"I'll think on it," Avani agreed slowly. She met his gaze. "And you?"

"Wilhaiim has been my home for many years."

"Because you've made it so." She guessed his unspoken thought. "And what happened on the Downs? Will you go back to your life here and forget the blood on the hills?"

He sighed. Deciding he wanted wine after all, he took up the goblet from the hearth. The hot drink was tart on his tongue, sweet as the winter apples.

"Tomorrow, or the day after, I will raise Andrew."

Avani's chin came up. Her eyes narrowed.

"His Majesty does not find the idea pleasing, either," Mal allowed. "But he has agreed."

"Why do you want to disturb a dead man?"

His smile was wry. "It is the core of my office, Avani. The dead talk to me. Sometimes, they give me strength. In this way, I serve my king."

She looked down at her hands, thinking. When she glanced up again, her face was smooth, expressionless.

"You've an unnatural skill."

"Not so different from your own," he said, gentle. "It serves me well."

"An abomination." She drank from the goblet. "The dead are meant to rest."

Mal shifted on the rug, gathering resolve. "I want you to be there, when I raise Andrew."

"No." She shook her head. "Why?"

"I think you know. You've been at the center of this. And you may note something I miss. After all," the bitterness flooded back, "I haven't been at my best."

"You were poison pricked," she protested.

Her defense made him grin, but he quickly sobered. "Even before. I should have seen Andrew's death was murder. Stonehill might have been saved."

"No."

"Will you argue with me?" He set his fists on his knees.

"No." But she sighed. "If you believe you need me there when you talk to your dead man, I will come, but there will be no joy, nor approbation, in it."

"There is no joy in it for me, either. Thank you."

She nodded. She didn't rise when Mal got to his feet. He found himself at a loss.

"Are you well?" he asked, at last.

She nodded, then smiled, a flash of white teeth in a dark face. "Very. Thank you. And, Malachi?"

He started at her casual use of his given name, staring like a fool. "Yes?"

"Eat something," she said, sounding testy as a priest. "Your king worries you'll waste away to naught. And he has much greater things to fret over. So do I. Eat something."

Mal felt a blush rise to his cheeks, and found himself callow.

"I will." He made for the door with all the dignity he could muster.

He thought he heard her laughter as he shut the door on the suite. He didn't notice until he was down the hall that she'd sent the raven after.

"Hells," he said. Jacob stared back with equal indignation.

Mal couldn't help himself; he laughed out loud as he went in search of supper.

ANDREW'S STONE WAS freshly hewn, strike marks still sharp.

Mal stood in the mud, and ran a finger over the striated surface. The burial slab hadn't yet been finished when he'd left for Stonehill; he hadn't been given a chance to say good-bye.

"Andrew, son of Rodger," he read, tracing the letters.

Someone had left a clutch of roses on the stone. Red and white buds, they were the flowers of the Ceilidh, the flowers used to decorate the palace, the flowers given to loved ones. The roses were tradition, a symbol of rebirth.

Mal wished he'd thought to bring a similar token.

He disentangled a stem from the bouquet. He touched the flower to his lips, and then set the single bloom on the stone beneath Andrew's name.

"The king's mistress brought the flowers."

Mal straightened and turned. Everin stood in the drizzle, watching.

"Kate has a good heart," Mal replied. "I didn't hear you approach."

"Apologies, my lord." Everin showed his teeth. "I never meant to startle."

Mal brushed the damp from his palms, and pulled black gloves back over his fingers. He moved deliberately, watching the other man. Several persistent shades lingered about the graveyard, haunting the hallowed ground. They gathered close, moths drawn to the light of the living. Mal ignored the spirits. Everin appeared oblivious.

The big man shifted, crossing thick arms. "I didn't expect to find another here."

"He was my friend," Mal said simply. He wouldn't let himself be put out by Everin's manner.

"More than that," the bearded man returned. "I saw that you loved him, that night in the forest. The two of your were very close."

"He trained me to my office."

"He thought of you as his heir," said Everin. "According to His Majesty's eldest squire, Andrew wanted to give you his name and properties."

A spatter of rain wet Mal's cheek. He wiped it away with a corner of his cloak.

"Do you want an apology?" he asked, at last. "I never knew the man had left a family, let alone a son."

"And now that you do?"

Mal looked down at the tomb, then at Everin. "It

changes nothing. I loved the man then, I still do. He will always have my respect."

Everin growled, and scuffed through the mud. He glared down at Andrew's stone. "Curse the old man. I loved him, too. And I can't find it in my heart to forgive him. Not yet."

"Perhaps if you understood better what drove him," Mal suggested. "If you looked a little through his life, instead of digging through my own."

The big man inhaled sharply, and then chuckled; a deep, rolling sound of reluctant mirth. The graveyard ghosts grinned and giggled in helpless reaction. "Mayhap."

"Andrew will always be dear to my heart. But you are his blood."

"Blood," Everin murmured. "And was it a poison in the blood that killed him? The same *agraine*?"

"So His Majesty believes," said Mal. "So, now, do I."

"Murder." Everin clenched a fist. "What of vengeance?"

Mal hesitated. "I plan to raise him tomorrow afternoon."

The man narrowed yellow eyes. "His shade?"

Mal nodded. "You spoke of it, in the woods. I rejected the idea, then." He shrugged. "Andrew's been dead for many weeks, and I am not at my best, but perhaps this is the surest way to thresh out the information you seek."

Everin bowed his head. Mal thought he saw the other man shudder.

"Tomorrow afternoon, you say? I will attend."

Mal drew a breath to argue, then changed his mind. "As you wish. It will be here, tomorrow, just after the nooning hour."

"Aye," replied Everin, grin in place. "The rainiest half of the day, no doubt. I'll be here, waiting. Waiting to greet my father's shade."

On an impulse, Mal reached out a gloved hand.

"You saved my life," he said. "I won't forget it."

Everin blinked, but he clasped Mal's hand in his own great paw.

"See that you don't," he said, smirking.

The bearded man walked away as he had come, silent and cat-quick.

Mal shook his head, bemused. Then he looked back down at Andrew's stone.

"I am afraid," he admitted softly. "And I need you."

There was no answer, not even from the lingering haunts. Mal hadn't expected one. His mind was quiet, his power tightly reigned. But his heart longed for what discipline couldn't allow; a loosening of power, an hour or two alone in the company of an old and beloved friend.

Temptation was very strong. The ring on his finger gleamed yellow in response. Tomorrow, when he called Andrew forth from the dead, it would be as vocent, and not as bereft son. There would be no room in duty for pleasure or grief.

Mal touched the stone a last time. Then he rose to his feet, and left Andrew to the mud.

Chapter Twelve

AVANI WORE LIAM's cloak to Andrew's grave.

The lad was reluctant to give his treasure up, even for a short while, but overnight drizzle had turned to solid rain, and Avani wouldn't ruin Kate's gift in the mud. She left Liam sulking by the fire with Jacob. The raven had returned to her rooms sometime in the long hours before dawn.

Outside the palace Wilhaiim was gray and wet. Mal's stark black suited Avani's sour mood. The new hem that fit Liam so well swooshed mightily around her boot heels. She pulled the hood over her face, puffing smoky breath into the miserable weather, and scowled at the sky.

The flatlander graveyard had turned to a thick stew. Mud slurped greedily at Avani's feet. Stone slabs gleamed wetly. Avani sloshed on until she sighted a small group huddled together against the downpour.

The tallest of the four stepped forward in greeting.

Everin, wrapped head to toe in wool, beard dripping. He smiled, but his smile was wide and too bright.

"At least it isn't snow, aye, black eyes?" His breath puffed between his lips.

"Not yet," she replied, doubtful.

Through the rain she picked out Mal, standing at the head of Andrew's marker, bundled in a twin of the cloak she wore. He looked her way, green eyes brilliant in a pale face.

Renault stood across from Mal. The king's face was set, still. Kate stood at his side, dressed in boys' trousers and a furred cape, her dainty hands encased in leather gloves. She lifted a hand in greeting.

"Come," Everin said.

He flung one long arm around Avani's shoulders, pressing her close against his side. She let him pull her through the muck to Andrew's grave.

"Your raven?" Mal asked when she joined the somber circle. He didn't look up from Andrew's grave, and his question sounded remote.

"He wouldn't come," Avani said. "He's tired of the rain."

"Ah," the magus did glance up then, but Avani could tell that his mind was very far away.

Something stretched unseen between them. She imagined she could feel his very center thinning, feeling about, searching.

Avani shuddered and looked up into the sky.

Everin shifted against her side. Mal spread his hands over Andrew's grave. The yellow ring on his finger glimmered.

Avani had expected a ceremony, a wailing of prayer or an invoking of flatland gods. Instead, Mal murmured a few low unintelligible syllables. His power was a visible thing, now, a faint glow and a flicker of warmth. A yellow and green nimbus coated his form; the shifting colors made Avani yearn for something she didn't quite understand.

She took a step forward, but Everin held her back. She struggled, but his grip remained firm.

"Let him finish," he warned.

His words were meaningless against the lure of Mal's power. Avani pulled. Then the vocent spoke a last word, and the warmth of his colors turned brittle, thickening to black.

The sudden change shocked Avani's system. She almost shouted aloud with loss. Mal straightened. Across the grave slab rain took shape and turned into a man.

"It is done," Everin muttered.

Breathing hard, Avani watched as the vocent's power became a line, a braided swoop of cold black, insubstantial as smoke. The line poured from Mal's center, tying man and spirit together. She could feel the Mal's very self feeding the dead thing that was Andrew, giving the dead man form.

She cried a warning, but when she looked around the circle for help, she realized that they were blind to the flow of magic. They saw their vocent sweating in the rain, a dead man standing on a grave, and nothing at all of power or price.

She bit her tongue until it bled. She huddled against Everin, glad of his bulk.

It took all of ten breaths for Andrew's spirit to fully coalesce.

A tall man with a straight spine and wild, grizzled hair, he stood firm on his stone, squinting through the fall of rain. He seemed very human, and very solid. Only the flare of unearthly blue in his eyes hinted otherwise.

"Your Majesty," he said. He stepped down from the slab and into the mud. His feet were bare and white. The muck splashed around his ankles.

Avani stole a quick peek at Mal. He waited, hands locked behind his back. Avani could yet see the black power storming about the man, and the flow of life that rushed in a coil from live vocent to dead. She wondered how he could stand it. She wanted to run through the rain, and shake him until the line of power broke.

"There," Everin said into her ear. "Look."

She turned her head, following Andrew's progress. The spirit stopped before Renault. He knelt in the mud. The simple robes he wore remained clean as his feet had not.

"No, my friend," Renault said. "Rise." He drew Andrew upright.

"You look well," Andrew said, surprising Avani with dry humor. "And also your love. Your beauty outlasts even this foul torrent, Lady Katherine."

Kate faced the spirit without fear. Avani thought she glimpsed tears brimming on the woman's cheeks. The king's mistress cupped Andrew's face, and drew one slender finger over solid flesh to the dead man's lips.

"You are missed, Lord Vocent," she said. "Greatly missed."

Andrew smiled. "Missed so that you call me back on a day such as this, wet enough to rot the dead in the earth while they sleep?"

The man rebuked Renault, Avani realized. Dead and gone, no more than an echo reanimated by Mal's strength, the man dared rebuke his king. He spoke gently, but the scold was clear.

Renault swallowed. Avani noted the flash of quick anger across his brow. Then the king drew himself up.

"Attend me, Andrew," he said, monarch to vocent. "There is trouble in Wilhaiim."

"Trouble?" Andrew mused. He moved very slightly, glancing over his shoulder and along the thread of power that bound him to Mal. "Trouble my heir cannot handle?"

Mal didn't move or speak. Everin stiffened. Then, with the clumsiness of one maddened by grief or wine, he stumbled to Andrew's side, dragging Avani after.

"*I* am your heir!" he growled. Avani could smell the rage on his body. She was reminded of the bear Liam had cut down.

"Let me go!" She twisted in his grasp. "Everin, let me go!"

Everin ignored Avani. "I am your heir. Have you truly forgotten?"

"Lord Everin," Renault lifted a hand as if to blunt the man's emotion.

"So it's a lord I am now, aye?" Everin scoffed, yellow eyes fixed on the dead man. "Born a sand farmer and a peasant, son of a peasant, and now that he is vocent, and dead, I am made lord?"

Avani saw Renault's mouth go flat. She thought the king would order Everin away, but Kate murmured, and the monarch stilled.

Andrew studied Everin with vague interest. At last the dead man sighed, and the light in his eyes flickered.

"Emilie's boy, are you then?"

"Aye," Everin grunted through bared teeth. "Emilie's get. And she misses you still, every day of her life, while she waits for death."

"I am sorry," Andrew said, very simply, remote as Mal could sometimes be.

Everin spat in the mud.

"Your mother understood why I left," said Andrew. "She had no regrets, then. And I regretted it each day after."

"But you never came back!"

"How could I?" the spirit asked. "When by that time I saw ghosts every moment, waking or sleeping, and the power within me burned till I was half mad? I needed guidance, help."

"You found it," Everin said. "And then you used it to climb high, become near the richest man in the city, as close to the gods as any mortal might reach, and still you didn't come back."

"I was no longer the father you knew." He studied Everin. "I sent money."

"Aye, enough to buy me a sword and leathers, and a place in a sand lord's army. Enough to buy my mother a cow, and a goat, and half a haunch of meat every season. And when, a grown man, I found the courage to come after—you'd gone on."

Everin shuddered. He released Avani all at once.

"I'm sorry," repeated Andrew, after a stretch in which the only sound Avani could hear was the harsh rasp of Mal's breathing. "Are you still called after the Virgin King?"

"Aye," Everin said, reluctantly.

"No doubt your mother continues to keep a candle burning in the Son of Aug's shrine, no matter the day or the weather?"

"Aye," replied Everin, softly. "No matter the weather. She dips the candles by hand, and pays dearly for the wax."

"As she did before you were born. I regret, more for your sake and less for Emilie's, that I didn't remember to come home once before I died."

Andrew's dead eyes drifted from his son's grief, over Avani, and then on to Renault.

"You called me here, Majesty," the spirit said. "What is the trouble that disturbs your kingdom?"

Renault regarded Andrew. "Murder. Poison. *Agraine*. Men torn apart on the eastern Downs, villages burned away to nothing. Death in the wake of shadows."

Andrew lifted a thin hand to his chin. He gazed across the graveyard, blue eyes flickering. "*Agraine*, you say? A specialized poison."

"It ran in your veins," the king said. "Or so we believe."

"Ah," Andrew breathed out. "Now I understand. You want to unearth my mortal flesh. Or what remains of it."

The king didn't flinch. "Aye. But I won't do so without your permission, Andrew."

"And will my putrid guts solve your mystery, and banish the trouble from your kingdom?"

Another rebuke, Avani thought, but the king refused to hear.

"Mayhap. Mal believes we must try."

Andrew looked over his shoulder again. He eyed his motionless heir, then slid his blue eyes over the circle of faces, lingering long on Everin's scowl, and passing once more over Avani as if she did not exist.

"Very well," the spirit conceded. "You have my permission. Remove this heavy stone, dig down into my new grave, unearth what of my body remains, and pray long that the god forgives my disinterred soul." The flames in his eyes sparked bright. "But remember this, my liege, your worries go far beyond the misuses of *agraine*. And I predict there will be other deaths. Closer to your heart, even, than my own passing."

Renault scowled. "What is it you know?"

But the spirit remained silent. Andrew stared once more out over the graveyard, his brow puckered. Suddenly, he turned back and frowned at the king.

"There!" he whispered. "Do you hear them?"

Puzzled, Renault shook his head, but Avani gasped. The sound was very slight, a vibration only, but the thrumming spread through the mud, and soon the ground seemed to jump beneath her feet.

Andrew staggered. In respond, Mal took a step forward.

"What is it?" Kate cried, gripping Renault's arm.

Overhead, the sky turned white, and the rain began to slacken.

Everin reached beneath his cloak for his sword. The

ground trembled at a higher pitch, and Avani's ears began to ring. Mal appeared at her side. She looked up into his face, and saw the strain in the hollows of his cheeks.

"They come," he said. "Even here, they come."

His hands were empty; no sword hung at his belt. Avani feared he hadn't the strength to wield a blade.

She pulled her own little knife free. Mal's attention remained focused on Andrew. She followed his gaze to the spirit, and chewed on her tongue.

The blue light in Andrew's eyes had died to black. The dead vocent's lips stretched in a rigid grin. His fingers moved restlessly against his robes. Mal groaned suddenly, and stumbled.

Avani smelled rot, and knew that danger had arrived.

Whatever stood in Andrew's stead sucked at Mal's diminished strength, pulling power from the vocent's center with brittle joy. Mal fought, but the *agraine* had left him weak. Avani could see the force of his life seeping away, strung on a shining braided coil.

Avani thought she heard Siobahn's voice lifted in rage. Mal flailed. Everin moved at Avani's side, but she was nearly blinded by the pulse of Mal's fear, and the world threatened to dissolve into tangled confusion.

She gripped the hilt of her little knife and threw herself across the grave at Andrew. Renault ran at her side, weapon in hand. Her own blade stuck in Andrew's foot, drawing blood. She heard the spirit howl.

Andrew kicked hard, knocking Avani aside. She found herself sprawled across the tomb, looking up into the spirit's empty eyes.

It smiled down at her, showing sharp white teeth. She heard Mal hiss. She wished for Jacob, said a heartfelt prayer to her Goddess, and opened herself to the living vocent.

Instinctively, Mal seized what she offered. Her senses rebelled, her head spun. She could feel his skill drawing on her reserves until her very bones felt hollow.

The Goddess laughed.

And then Avani was one with the vocent; she looked out from his eyes and tasted his rage. Mal had regained his feet. Her innate magics bolstered his heart and mind, and made him strong.

She felt his amazement as her own, and his sorrow as he struck back at the creature that had been Andrew, and behind it all she felt his raw desire for the hunt, for the chase and the battle and the finish. She reveled with him.

Andrew drew back, shrinking from Mal's onslaught. As Avani watched through Mal's eyes, the spirit glanced down at her own motionless body.

"What have you done?" the thing that wasn't Andrew demanded. "What have you done?"

Then Everin's sword came flashing down, and cleaved the spirit in half. But it wasn't mortal steel that chased the rot away. It was Mal's newfound strength, and the brilliant pattern he wove with Avani.

The spirit frayed and was torn away to nothing.

Mal flung Avani from his mind, and the part of her that was power was thrown from his center, and fell in a spiral back into her own body.

The shock of return was cold and hard. Pain raced

through Avani's spine. She yelled, and opened eyes that felt wrong, eyes that saw only a fraction of the world.

She stared up into the sky, gasping.

Kate's face filled the horizon. Her gentle hands brushed hair from Avani's face.

"Avani," she murmured. "Where are you hurt?"

Avani wanted to weep away the anguish in her heart, the agony of abandonment, the pain of separation. Instead, she opened her eyes very wide to keep the tears back.

"Jacob," she said. "I want Jacob."

Kate nodded, and helped Avani out of the mud.

LATER, AS AVANI picked at the bowl of cooked oats Kate insisted she eat, she remembered her little knife. The weapon was gone, lost in the mud of the graveyard.

She set the bowl of oats in front of Jacob. She sighed.

"*Ai*, Thom gave me that blade. I'm not losing it."

Jacob poked at the oats with his beak. Avani grunted. She pulled on her still wet boots and tromped to the door. She wasn't eager to leave her cozy room, but she refused to be cowed by the uncomfortable thought of returning to the graveyard.

Opening the door with an angry jerk of the latch, she found Mal standing in the hall. He looked so at a loss in his surprise that she wanted to laugh, but found instead tears stinging her eyes.

"I'm going out," Avani said, gruff.

"I see," he replied. When she scowled, he cocked a brow.

"You're blocking my door," she pointed out.

Mal stepped past her into the room, instead of moving aside as she'd expected. He shut the door with a firm hand. Avani balled her fists at her side, and fought down rising temper.

"You look awful," he said. "Have you eaten?"

"Some."

"Touch of colic? It happened to me, often, the first few times. Spent hours doubled over the chamber pot."

"The first few times?" Avani echoed.

"The first few times I tangled in Andrew's power," Mal explained. "It's irresistible, and it's painful, and it's a shock to the body and mind. With training, you'll soon learn enough to keep it from happening again."

"What happened was no accident," Avani choked out. "It was purpose, my lord. I saved your hide."

Mal paced across the room. He stared down at Jacob, at the bowl of oats. Jacob stretched his wings long, then refolded them across his back.

"It was dangerous," Mal said to the bird. "It could have killed you. You have strong talent, Avani. To manage . . . *that* . . . so easily, and without instruction." He turned on his heel, earnest. "You need that instruction. You need training, schooling, to keep yourself safe and prevent similar mistakes. An untrained magus is a disaster waiting to happen."

"I saved you." Avani followed Mal to the table. She stood almost on the toes of his boots, seething. Mal didn't flinch. "That thing was drawing at your very life. You couldn't stop it. You've grown used to it, letting the *bhut* feed upon you every day. You couldn't save yourself!"

Mal's mouth thinned. Treacherous tears leaked down the side of Avani's nose. She dashed them away.

"And I thank you," Mal replied, stiff. "But you mustn't attempt such a thing again. I won't see you killed for lack of education."

"You're arrogant," Avani accused.

To her surprise he jerked as if he'd been struck. He walked to her small window, and stared through the glass to the courtyard far below.

"Where is Liam?" he asked.

"Sparring. Practicing. With the other pages."

Mal turned from the window, visibly pleased. "You've given him into service?"

"*Ai*, it wasn't my choice, was it? It's what he wanted, for now." She shrugged a little. "Soon you'll have the lad sleeping on your own floor, as I understand His Majesty intends Liam for the vocent."

"Renault said as much," he admitted. "Liam will do well."

"He loves you, my lord," Avani said.

"He's young." Mal studied Avani's face. "The young fall easily to dreams of heroes."

"Arrogant *and* patronizing," Avani said. But she couldn't keep her lips from curling at the corners.

Mal snorted. He ran a hand over his face, then through his hair.

"Perhaps we can start over again," he suggested. "I came in fact not to discuss yesterday, but to ask you out on an errand."

Avani blinked suspiciously. "An errand?"

"Indeed." Mal took a step forward, and bowed formally, suddenly whimsical. "His Majesty has given me the day free." He waved one hand, sketching in the air from his top to bottom, and for the first time Avani realized the man was relieved of his stark black.

He wore wool and silk, in deep greens that matched his eyes.

"For the first time in many years," he said, "I find I wish to spend a day as plain Malachi Doyle, and forget my office."

"Oh?" Avani said, more suspicious.

"Day after next is Winter Ceilidh." Mal left the window. He stood in front of Avani, head bent.

The top of her own head came almost to his chin. Idly, he stroked a wayward lock of hair from her brow. His touch shocked Avani to her core. She shivered, remembering the sweet thrill of his essence entwined with her own.

He tucked his hands behind his back.

"I know you feel less than hale," he said, steadily. "But I find I yet need a few Ceilidh gifts—for Kate, and for Liam. And a wreath." He seemed as eager as a lad. "I haven't had a Ceilidh wreath of my own for half ten years. Will you come?"

"Where?" asked Avani, though if he'd said to the Goddess's own pit, she would not have denied him.

"The Fair, of course." Mal cajoled, "Come, will you?"

"Why?"

"Because"—and he bent close, until she could smell the scent of apples on his breath—"you and I, we need to discuss what happened in the graveyard. But not now, and not yet. For now, let us just *be*. Yes?"

"Yes," Avani agreed, heart singing.

She grabbed her wrap and her bangles. As an afterthought she added the string of rubies.

"I need a knife." As she smiled into Mal's face, she realized her grogginess had fled. "I lost mine in the mud."

"That was a cleaver," Mal corrected. "I will buy you a knife."

"Perhaps. My lord?" she asked, as he secured the door.

"Yes?" He turned, attentive.

"Did you dig him up, last night?"

"Yes," he said. "Renault, and Everin, and I. He's waiting now, waiting in my coldroom And he'll wait until after the Ceilidh."

"You're frightened," she realized.

"I am. But Andrew's body, and my own unease, will keep. Come." He took her elbow. "Now you've agreed to be my Fair companion, surely you'll wait a moment while I stop by my rooms for my cloak."

"The black?" Avani was determined to match his light mood.

"I have only four winter cloaks," Mal said, deadpan. "And each is black."

Avani laughed at him then. Her smile didn't falter, even when Siobahn stepped from the air and accompanied them silently down the hall.

Chapter Thirteen

Mal spent the Winter Ceilidh as a member of the court.

He stood patiently by Renault's side as the king led the rites. The temple was damp, the old stone walls dripping. Even the bright tapestries decorating pew and altar didn't keep gloom at bay. Wind snuck through the cracks, snuffing an occasional candle. The smell of greenery and the freshly culled boughs hanging in swaths from the beams did little to bolster Mal's tepid enthusiasm.

He'd always been uneasy in flatland temples. The peaked buildings and the dour-faced priests guarding the altar reminded Mal of boyhood, and the memories were far from pleasant.

He crossed his arms over his tunic, rocking on his heels, and tried to focus on Renault's intonations. But he'd heard the rites too many times before. He knew the tale of the Virgin King's succession by heart. His mind refused to settle.

Mal let his gaze drift over the congregation, noting faces. He knew every person in the temple, from the littlest squire crouched on the stone floor at the back of the pews and trying very hard not to doze, to the eldest lord, white mustached and wrinkled, expression fierce with anticipation.

That one wouldn't last many winters more. Mal would be sad to see him go. He wondered if the old man heard his own funeral rites in the poetry of the Ceilidh.

Mal turned his head slightly, and found Liam. The lad wore the plain brown uniform of the king's pages. He sat on the floor behind the last of the pews. The boy was bright and alert; he smiled a little as one of his restless young companions poked him in the ribs.

Several rows up from the lad, on one of the foremost benches, Mal found Avani. Her presence surprised him.

To his right, the king's mistress shifted minutely. She touched a finger to Mal's sleeve.

"I wondered," she murmured, a whisper of sound beneath the king's louder intonation, "when you would spot the girl."

Mal snorted. "She's little younger than yourself, Katherine."

Kate leaned into Mal's side. "Avani said the flatland ceremony interested her. But I think her curiosity ran in another direction."

"Oh?"

"I believe she wanted to see just what part His Majesty's implacable vocent played in the Ceilidh rites."

"He stands between the king and the royal shrew, and

pretends rapture while he mouthes the sacred lines and imagines the elders of the court stripped to the skin of their finery."

Kate lifted a hand to hide her smile. To Mal's left, Renault faltered over a syllable, and then continued resolutely on.

"Stop," Kate scolded. "If you make His Majesty miss a line again this year, he'll have your sorry hide for boots."

The king finished a cant and paused, expectant. Mal turned to the altar, lifted the Virgin King's tattered red shroud from its place of honor. He laid the shroud carefully across Renault's forearms. Renault touched a corner of the fabric to his lips in benediction, then launched into the next verse.

Mal listened to His Majesty's soothing tones. At his side, Kate shivered. Mal thought he could hear her teeth chatter.

"Cold, Katherine?" Casually, he unclasped his cape, setting it carefully about her shoulders.

Kate swore under her breath. Color bloomed on the tip of her nose.

"Now they're all watching us."

"There's no good reason for the king's beloved to stand up here and freeze," answered Mal, unimpressed. "I seem to be giving out a multitude of cloaks, lately."

He paused, glancing again over the congregation. "Where did she get the gown?"

"What?" Kate blinked, then slowly smiled. "Oh. It's one of my own. I had it altered for the occasion. I thought the color would suit her. Red as Ceilidh berries against her skin. Do you like it?"

Mal grunted.

"Renault's invited her to the King's Celebration, of course. You will come, Mal? You've been away too long, and Renault spent an entire season choosing your Ceilidh gift. You know how he is with presents. He's expecting you. You'll come?"

"Katherine," Mal said, gently. "There's no need to play matchmaker."

Kate sighed. She tugged his sleeve again.

"Siobahn has been gone for a long time, Malachi."

He took her hand from his sleeve, squeezing her fingers once before letting go.

"She's been dead a very long time," he agreed. He turned his gaze up into the temple rafters. Pine boughs swayed in a swirl of winter air. "I love her still."

THE RITES CAME to a close at sundown.

Mal freed himself from the crowd, intending to duck back into his suite and change clothes before Renault's feast. Formality vanished with the sun. The Ceilidh was for celebration and hilarity, and for happy remembrances.

The fire on his hearth had gone out, most of the palace servants too busy with the Ceilidh preparations to tend the vocent's embers.

Siobahn stood between two jeweled lamps, the wreath he and Avani had picked out at the Fair very green on the wall above her bright curls.

Mal smiled. He crouched before the hearth, gathering tinder. He reached for a candle, but Siobahn set fire in the wood before Mal could lift the taper from its sconce.

"Thank you," he said, and rose. His knees cracked. He'd been standing in one place for too long.

"You've lost your cloak again," Siobahn said, crossing to his side.

"I lent it to Kate." He bent to kiss her brow. "I expected to see you in the crowd."

"No," she said. And then, "The wreath smells lovely."

She smiled, but he thought her expression was wary. "It smells fresh, of life, full of promise."

"You're worrying," Mal said. "Stop. Tomorrow, we will fret again. Today is Ceilidh."

"A celebration for the living," she said. "Will you feast with the king?"

"He expects me. Unless you'd rather I stay?"

Siobahn waved a small hand. "You're no longer so ill that you can hide. Go."

Mal heard her bitterness. He gathered her close, soothing. She felt solid, and warm, and soft. His heart, and his body, responded to the feel of her.

He was skewered by a sharp pang of loss, more vivid than any he'd allowed himself to experience before.

"I won't stay long," he promised. "I'll dine, and duck out, and then we'll sit together and wait for the sun to rise."

She backed away from his embrace, but her expression had softened.

"I'll wait," she said, and slipped back to her place between the lamps, bathed in multicolored light.

AVANI WASN'T PREPARED for the crowd outside the king's chambers.

She recognized most of the faces from inside the flatland temple, and there were many new. She supposed most of the court and many of the lesser peerage had been invited to dine with the king this Ceilidh.

Usually a crowd put Avani at ease, as the crush of people provided her an opportunity to blend and hide from unwelcome attention, but this eve the milling bodies set her heart racing.

The chamber doors were still closed. The doors were guarded by two tall men in red-and-black livery. His Majesty's guests lingered in the corridor, packed wall to wall. They chatted with an animation Avani hadn't expected.

When she closed her eyes, the buzz of voices echoed in her ears, and she inhaled the stink of bodies too closely pressed. Her stomach protested. She opened her eyes again, backing slowly along the hall until she stood at the very edge of the crowd.

Avani eased against a tapestry. She leaned into the shadows of a guttering wall sconce, watching faces.

She'd rarely experienced such a gathering of people.

From her place against the wall she studied eyes, and hair, and statures. Eventually the wide range of fabrics drew her attention. She noted several new colors, and unusual lengths in hem and trouser.

Embroidery was plentiful, but the court wore very little jewelry. The bangles on her own wrists, and the rubies at her breast, and the tiny true gold hoops she wore in her lobes seemed opulent.

She fingered an earring, marveling over the differences in cultures. She thought then of Stonehill, and the villagers' struggle to make a living off the land, as far away from court intrigue and luxury as possible. Little good that retreat had done them in the end, slaughtered like her sheep on the Downs. She doubted Wilhaiim's reigning families would care to hear the details of Stonehill's fall. She wondered if they would change their mind if they knew they were no safer here, at the center of civilization.

When the great chamber doors swung suddenly open, silent on oiled hinges, Avani jumped, heart pounding. For an instant she thought she could smell the soil-and-rot perfume of danger. There were shadows on the walls, creeping close. Then the crowd began slowly to trickle over the threshold, and Avani gasped, and came back to herself. The hall was bright and festive once again, the air clear.

She clenched her fists, driving her nails into her palms to clear her head. Then Avani arranged herself behind a large woman in a brilliant purple gown, and allowed herself to be nudged forward.

The flow of people compacted, stopping briefly. Avani stood on her toes, trying to see over heads, but flatlanders were tall, and she could glimpse little beyond shoulders and elbows. She bounced a little on the balls of her feet, exasperated, and then found herself meeting a pair of eyes at her own level.

The man was very short, his face broad, and his grin wide. He gripped Avani's shoulder, steadying her lurch.

"Careful," he cautioned, flatland accent as thick as his fingers. "Not yet used to the fancy shoes, aye?"

Avani glanced down at the tiny, heeled slippers she'd borrowed from Kate, and then up again into twinkling gray eyes. She smiled.

"I'm more used to boots and trousers," she admitted. He wore a Kingsman's badge on his collar.

His white hair was long, his face weather lined, and his amusement made the shuffling crowd seem suddenly more bearable.

"The gown is lovely on you," he said, guiding her forward with one hand. "You look like royal blood, you do."

Avani laughed. The Kingsman smiled.

"There," he said. "Better now? I thought for sure you would topple across my feet. Not good with crowds, are we? Do you need air? I can clear a path to safety, if you like."

Avani shook her head. "His Majesty expects me. He promised me a seat at his side."

The man cocked his head. "A place at the king's side? Are you royal blood in truth?"

Avani wondered if he was blind to her island coloring.

"His Majesty's latest favorite," she said. "I brought his vocent home, alive."

"Ah." The man's eyes lit with unabashed interest. "The weaver. I've seen your work, my lady. It's a wonderful talent you have."

Avani was surprised. "You know my work?"

"Aye. Kate introduced me just last week to the rug you finished for her study. The colors are beautiful. I'd love one for my own floor, only a little larger. Do you work for hire?"

Avani blinked. "I do."

"Good." The man beamed. "I see we've almost reached the royal chambers. Perhaps we can discuss pattern and color while we sup? That is, if you don't already have a dinner partner?"

"No. I mean"—Avani felt her cheeks heat—"I have no one."

The Kingsman took her hand with elegant grace. He led her between the great doors and into the king's hall.

"Wonderful," he said as they walked. "My dear, you have just made my eve that much brighter."

Two of the king's outer chambers had been decorated for the Ceilidh, set with long tables and upholstered benches. Pine boughs and red berries brightened the otherwise austere rooms. Tapestries had been pulled back from tall windows, allowing guests a view of winter weather. Fires burned in three large round pits in the floor.

The Kingsman ushered Avani without hesitation through the first chamber and into the second. Here the wide table was decorated with live trees and white birds in silver cages. A single fire roared in a single pit, sending lazy sparks into the air.

Renault sat at the head of the table, a wreath of winter greenery on the wall over his head. The king wore robes as red as Avani's gown, and a thin silver circlet across his brow. A group of equally colorful lords surrounded the king's chair, sipping wine from silver goblets.

"The king's table is always the wildest on Ceilidh night," Avani's companion said. "And although a seat at His Majesty's side is a great honor, I think we might be safer at the other end of the table." He smiled. "I am sure he will understand."

Avani nodded. The Kingsman guided her across the room, past lord and lady and ill-washed laborer. He set her at the end of the table, on a padded bench. He collapsed at her side, found her a tankard of sweet wine, and a trencher heaped high with bits of lamb.

"Though you're too polite to ask"—he awarded her another bright smile—"my name is Peter Shean. My wife and I have just moved into our first home. Rugs are something we need, desperately, as are wall tapestries, and coverlets. I've rarely seen such fine work as your own, Lady Avani."

"You know my name." Avani tore a piece of bread from her trencher. "And you've seen the rug I worked for Lady Kate."

"And you're curious as to how." He chuckled. "Katherine is my littlest sister, you see, and has always held the key to my heart. She was proud of her new rug, and of her new friend the island witch who saved Mal Doyle. She has a soft spot for that one, and has since they schooled as youths under the king's watchful eye."

"Schooled together?" echoed Avani.

"Mal as vocent, of course, and Kate in the ranks of the temple acolytes.. Or didn't you know?"

"No," Avani admitted. She tried the lamb and found it peppery, and pleasant to the taste.

"They were both very young," Peter continued. "Malachi newly married and not yet ready to work at Andrew's side. Kate was a friend to Mal's Siobahn. And a shoulder for the poor man to cry on after Siobahn's death."

"How did she die, then?"

Peter's forehead wrinkled, sun lines turning to furrows. "It's not a story I like to repeat, aye? Not one for me to tell. You understand?"

Avani did. She tried to hide her disappointment. She sipped more of the sweet wine and scanned the room. The fabrics on the wall next to her seat were lovely, the threads hardly faded.

Ceilidh tapestries, she thought, noting the theme of berries and winter scenes.

The last tapestry was larger than the others. Embroidered at the very center of the snow scene a man stood, a youth with startling green eyes and long black hair. He was dressed as a peasant but the seamstress had used gold thread to pick out the lute on his hip.

"The skald who birthed our celebration," Kate said, appearing at Avani's shoulder. "They called him Eric the Gold, for the gilt on his lute. That tapestry is one of my favorites. The fabric is very old, but Renault's family kept it carefully through the generations."

Avani looked up, and returned Kate's grin.

"A bright Ceilidh to you, Avani, and to you, brother," said the king's mistress. She wore a gown the color of fresh pine needles, and red berries in her hair. "I see you've discovered the one quiet spot at His Majesty's table."

"Aye." Peter reached up, plucking a sprig of berries from his sister's hair. With the ease of an old acquaintance, he stuck the sprig behind Avani's ear.

"Matches the gown perfectly," he explained. "Your taste is impeccable, Katie."

"I've always thought so. Come and see me before you run away for the night, Avani. I've been showing off your work, and you've got a line of eager suitors waiting to court your loom."

Peter laughed at Avani's expression. "I've placed my order first, remember, my lady!"

Avani shook her head. Kate ran a finger over Avani's string of rubies, then looked out over the crowd.

"There's Everin. He looks a tad muddled. I'm off to his rescue. Remember, Avani, come and see me before you disappear. And you, brother."

She darted away in a flurry of skirts. Peter coughed in amusement.

"Katie never changes," he said fondly.

"She's lovely." Avani looked down into her tankard, and found the wine gone.

"That she is." Peter stretched across the table, plucked up a loose wineskin, and refilled Avani's tankard.

"Now," he said, a gleam in his eye. "About that rug . . ."

Avani smiled, and relaxed, and let herself be guided into a discussion of dyes and wool.

SHE DIDN'T SEE Mal until much later in the night, after the sleet outside the windows had turned to snow. By then the wine had gone to her head, and Peter's company had sparked her humor, but her bones were growing tired and she couldn't seem to stop yawning.

Kate's brother was a gallant man, and determined to escort Avani safely through the palace to her rooms. Because his arm about her waist was steady, and because she enjoyed the way he made her laugh, Avani decided to be gracious.

She leaned on his shoulder. He steered her through courtiers toward the door. Someone at the king's table began to sing Ceilidh poetry, an octave too high and badly off key. Peter's heartfelt groan made Avani giggle.

"Lord Brendan," the little man sighed theatrically. "Every year we suffer through his rendition of 'Snow and Cedar.' Often more than once."

"Like a goose," Avani whispered back, trying not to trip on the hem of her borrowed dress. The sweet wine made her head spin, and her face felt very hot.

"What?" Peter paused in reach of the great double doors, blinking.

"He sounds like a goose!" she said. "Like a goose spread on the huntsman's arrow!"

Peter choked. He began to laugh. Avani felt a grin split her face, and snorted.

Wheezing in his mirth, Peter took his hand from Avani's waist, grabbed at her fingers, and tugged her hastily around a very large man in a sweaty leather jerkin.

Avani dodged the big man's elbow. She stumbled straight into Mal.

She froze. Peter returned quickly to her side. Mal rocked back on his heels. The goblet of wine in his fist shivered, almost spilling across his shirt. As it was, the liquid sloshed along the rim, dribbling across Mal's knuckles.

"Avani," he said, smile dry. "Have a care. This bit of fabric I'm wearing probably cost Renault a season's worth of tithes."

Deftly, he set his goblet in the hand of a passing servant. He brought his knuckles to his mouth, sucking sticky wine from flesh.

"Mal," Peter said, surprised and pleased. "I didn't see you in the crowd. A blessed Ceilidh to you, my friend."

Mal's face was very grave, but Avani caught the gleam of amusement in his green eyes. "And to you, Peter. Fleeing the celebration so soon?"

Peter flushed. "My lady grew weary."

"The moon is long set," Avani pointed out.

"The king's celebration runs until dawn," Mal returned. "Often much longer. Flatlanders are loath to let the Ceilidh pass into New Year."

Avani felt a flash of annoyance. The man's lips were curling, as though he contemplated a secret bit of mirth.

"Lord Peter has kindly offered to escort me home." Chin high, she turned to brush past the magus, and instead tripped over Peter's booted foot.

Mal's hand snapped out, hauling her up and back. "Be careful."

"Let me go."

He released her wrist at once, and set his hands carefully behind his back.

"How much wine have you had?" The curve of his lips deepened and began to resemble a grin.

"It's the slippers!" Avani snapped. "Kate's toes must be twice as long as my own."

Peter snorted. Mal coughed. She widened her eyes, trying to keep the room in focus, and peered at Peter.

"I'm ready."

"Ready?"

"To go!" she huffed, shooting a venomous glance Mal's way. Then she paused. "Is that linen?"

Expression very bland, Mal set graceful fingers on the fabric of his shirt. "And I feared you'd never notice. A bit light for the cold, I know, but Ceilidh gifts should be appreciated."

Avani studied the shirt, red as her own gown. It looked light and soft as feathers. She resisted the urge to touch.

"From the king?"

"As I said," replied Mal. Avani was certain she saw the man wink at Peter.

"He dresses you like a concubine," she said. "But at least he has the sense to stay away from black."

"Renault has always been considered a wise king," Mal agreed, deadpan. Peter snorted again.

Avani turned to Kate's brother, firmly taking his arm. "I'm weary," she reminded him pointedly.

Peter patted her hand. He bowed once to Mal. "Blessings upon you, Lord Vocent."

Mal dipped his head, silent. Avani could feel his stare on her back all the way across the room and beyond, into the corridor.

As soon as they were past the doors, she heaved a sigh.

"Relieved?" Peter asked. He patted her hand again.

Avani stopped and looked back at the great doors. The two liveried men standing on either side of the king's chamber gazed back impassively.

"Was he trying to be foolish?" she asked.

"Perhaps he was just trying to make you smile."

"Why?"

"Why not?" Peter shrugged. "You're a pretty thing, Avani, and even our vocent is allowed a flirtation or two."

"The man's heart is shackled to his dead wife."

"Mm." Peter set his hand at the small of Avani's back, propelling her down the corridor. "Come along. I'm feeling lucky, tonight, and hoping I might get a peek at your loom."

Mortified, Avani stared into the man's face. This time his teasing was plain, and she laughed back.

"Wait," she said. Pausing in the light of a sconce, she kicked off first one slipper, and then the second.

"*Ai*," she moaned in relief. "*Now* we can go."

Chuckling, Peter collected the discarded slippers. He draped an arm about Avani's shoulders. "Onward, my lady?"

"Onward!" Avani agreed, realizing with satisfaction that she had found a second friend in Wilhaiim.

MAL ROSE LATE on the first day of the new year, rested and pleasantly at ease.

He'd spend the Ceilidh celebrating with friends as dear as family, then returned to his rooms in time to see out the dawn with Siobahn.

Snow had fallen steadily overnight; drifts lay in mountains against the palace walls. But the sky was a clear blue, and for the moment the nasty winter wind Mal had come to expect was gone.

He dressed quickly. He brushed sleep knots from his

hair with his fingers, then breakfasted on fruit, sitting in the light that fell through his windows.

As he devoured a winter apple, Siobahn tended to the guttered sconces, then came to stand at his side.

"A bright New Year," she said.

Mal passed her a slice of apple, in fun. Without blinking, she made it disappear.

"And now the Ceilidh is over, and the next year begun?" she asked.

"Now," he said, swallowing a mouthful of tart fruit, "the hunter hunts."

"Ah!" Siobahn's unnatural eyes darkened. "You have an idea."

"Several." Mal tossed her the ravaged apple core. He climbed to his feet.

"Where are you going?"

"To see Avani."

Siobahn scowled. Mal sighed. He reached out and knuckled the tip of her nose.

"You are my bride, always. Don't fret. You will never lose me. Certainly not to Avani. After all," he plucked his cape from the foot of the bed, "have you not a promise?"

"Yours?"

"No." He turned, and let her see the irritation on his face. "Did you think I would forget, Siobahn? That I would wake, the dream lost? I am magus. I remember. Avani gave her promise, quieted your jealousy, and in so doing saved my life. She keeps her promises; even I can see the truth of that. Don't fret, my dear, Avani will never let herself want me."

"And you?" Siobahn cried. "Malachi? Do you want the island witch?"

But he was already gone, out the door, and he didn't respond. Her distress sounded too much like an accusation, and the ache in his heart felt too much like guilt.

Even so, Mal found himself standing again in the hall outside Avani's door.

He knocked five times, and was about to give up when at last the door opened.

Mal couldn't help himself. He laughed aloud.

Rumpled, hair falling into wild tangles over her face, still dressed in Kate's gown, Avani squinted over the threshold, scowling. Jacob crouched on her shoulder, beady eyes sharp. Behind Avani, the suite looked very dark and cold.

"Bright New Year," said Mal easily. He smiled when she winced. "Just up, are we?"

She put a hand to her head, groaning. "Why must you always pop in when I'm ill?"

"That bad?" He slid past her and into the room before she realized what he was about.

"Goddess take you, Malachi. What do you want, now?"

"I'll settle for a kind word and a smile. This chamber is freezing, Avani. Shall I light the fire?"

She growled, brushing a snarl of hair from her eyes. Because her sulky temper made his blood sing, he ignored etiquette and used a lick of power to start the flames in her hearth.

"Show-off."

But she moved across the room and leaned into the warmth.

The Goddess glittered in reflected firelight. For the first time Mal noticed the small tin bowl at the idol's feet, and the handful of yellow powder in the bowl itself.

"Turmeric," she said, noting his puzzled frown. "You interrupted my own celebration."

He raised his brows. "You were celebrating in the dark?"

"The windows are light enough."

Mal knelt on the hearth and, without seeking permission, dipped a finger into the powder. Avani didn't move. Mal brought a yellow stained finger to his nose, and sniffed.

"Ginger?"

Avani shrugged. "It is a similar root. It's been a long time since I've had any proper turmeric with which to welcome the new year. Deval had a supply."

Mal stuck his finger in his mouth. He made a face at the taste.

"*Ai*," Avani scolded. "It's not for eating plain." She sighed. "My lord. What do you want?"

He straightened. "To see how you fared after last night's bout with His Majesty's wine. I see you survived the tussle. Did Peter?"

Mal glanced around the room, gestures exaggerated.

Avani rolled her eyes. "He didn't even ask to come in. He dropped me at the door and absconded with Lady Kate's slippers."

"I see you still have the gown," he pointed out, bland.

She growled. Then her frown cracked, and she laughed, a quick burst of mirth. She brushed again at her hair, the bangles on her wrists chiming.

"I've never swallowed so much sweet wine in my life," she admitted. "And never again."

"Don't make rash promises," Mal cautioned, grinning. "I've brought you a gift. A Ceilidh gift. A day late, but . . ." He shrugged.

Her eyes widened. "I didn't think, I don't have anything for you."

"No matter." Still smiling, he dug into the folds of his cloak, and passed Avani a small square of bronze.

"What is it?" She studied the metal.

"A chit. A merchant's chit," he explained. "I've ordered the king's blacksmith to forge a sword for you, Avani. It takes a bit of time. He promised me it would be done in the next se'enday. You present him with the chit," Mal tilted his chin at the bronze, "and he will give you the sword."

Avani didn't look up from the chit in her hand. "A sword."

"You're quick with the knife, I admit. But I think a sword might do you better. One forged correctly, one that fits you. The king's blacksmith has a fine eye. He was watching you very closely last night, at the celebration, and believes he knows your measure."

Avani gaped in surprise. Mal had to fight back a laugh. "Big sweaty man in a leather jerkin."

"Oh. I nearly ran him down."

"Before you almost ruined my linen shirt, yes. But you impressed him."

"I don't want a sword."

"You need one."

"I have no use for such a weapon."

"Every vocent needs a sword."

She gasped. Jacob bobbed. Quick as a cat, Avani hurled the chit at Mal's chest. He caught the bit of metal neatly.

"I'm no vocent!" she bit the words out. "And never will I be!"

"Avani."

"Get out!" She stormed from the hearth, yanking open the door. Jacob's bobbing became an agitated dance.

"Avani."

"Goddess take you, Mal! Get. Out."

He crossed to her side, took her shoulders in his hands, dislodging Jacob.

"You need training, woman. Or you'll loose yourself in your power. Will you be so foolish as to let it kill you?"

"I have lived twenty summers. It hasn't killed me yet."

"So." He gripped her shoulder blades. "Will you tell me it's always been this strong? Have the visions always come so easily, the dreams solid? Have you always been able to throw yourself into another's mind?"

"No." She took a heaving breath. "It doesn't matter."

"Ah." He forced his fingers to unclench. He backed away. "You're afraid. You hide it well, but you're terrified. And so you should be."

"Turning vocent is not the only answer, not my answer! My people have lived for generations without kings or—

a"—and she spat into the corridor—"pretentious uniforms of black Hennish leather."

"This is the only flatland answer," Mal replied. "Mayhap the only answer left. Your island is gone, Avani. Your people and their learning, gone. You have no one else to turn to."

"Deval—"

He cut her off with a wave of his hand. "If your Deval can jump into my head and bolster my power, I'll give up my office and camp in the mud with the laborers."

"You're arrogant!"

"So you've said. And I am also right. You know it, Avani. You need help." Trying to soothe, he set his hand on the tangle of her hair. "I can help you."

She jerked away, slamming the door shut on the hall. "The rest of the palace doesn't need to hear your foolishness."

"Someone has to listen. I'd hoped you would."

"Or what? You'll seek audience with your brother the king? So he might have me dragged off, forced into service?"

"Do you think I would do that?"

"*Ai*, and haven't you said it before? You're the last living vocent, your kingdom is in need of at least one more. *You* need *me!*"

"You're wrong," he said quietly. "I'd let you go if I thought it right, if I thought it safe, if I thought you'd manage to survive on your own until the next season. The office is not one I'd willingly lay on another. But your strength is growing in leaps and bounds. I can see it, I can feel it. You won't be able to control it much longer. People will notice. No flatlander king will tolerate a magus wandering about unbound. You need my help, Avani. Let me give it to you."

She hesitated, gripping the folds of Kate's gown between her fists. For a moment he dared hope he'd won.

"Can't you help me without making me your king's?"

"No," he said.

She hissed. "Why must I serve a flatland king?"

He shrugged, feigning calm.

"It's the way of things, Avani. A magus is too powerful, a magus must be restrained at all times by his king. Any who goes renegade, who refuses the word of his king, is hunted down and killed. It's the way of the world, to watch closely that which is too powerful to trust. Thus the office of Lord Vocent, and the vows and binding that come with the honor."

"And who watches over the king?" Avani shook the hem of her gown so violently her bangles rattled without harmony.

"His people, his queen, perhaps even his vocents."

"There are other kings . . ."

"Three others," agreed Mal. "And all desperate for a vocent. You needn't stay here. Once you have your power under rein, you may serve any monarch you wish. But I am the only man alive who can show you *how* to control your power, *how* to keep it safe."

She looked into his eyes, and then away. Mal watched her shoulders slump.

"Have I convinced you?" he asked, when her silence stretched too long.

"No. Yes. *Ai*, how can I say?" She looked at him again, and he saw the tears on her cheeks.

Mal took a breath. "What are you doing, this morning? Come with me, let me show you my life, let me show you it's not quite so bad as you assume."

"I have appointments." The sullen inflection she put on the word nearly made him smile.

"Appointments?"

"With two lords and six ladies. All wanting to meet my loom. Lady Kate has been finding me patrons."

"You'll meet with them later," Mal decided. "Eager customers will always wait. You won't lose even one."

She brushed the tears from her face. The temper he so enjoyed returned to the set of her mouth.

"I promised Deval I'd meet him, this day. We're going to celebrate the New Year together, between nooning and sunset."

"It's after noon."

"Don't I know it?" She sniffed. "The wine fuzzed my head and I slept too late. And now you've stalled me longer. He'll be wondering where I've got to." She paced barefoot across the floor to a trunk alongside her bed, and hauled up the lid. "I need to hurry. I need to dress."

"I'll come with you."

She turned, a silken coat in her hands, and stared. "What?"

"It's only fair, *ai*?" he mocked her accent gently. "If I'm tossing a new life at you, I might as well see where you're starting from. Perhaps I can ease the shock."

She shook her head. Mal wouldn't give up.

"Let me come with you, Avani. Introduce me to your Deval. Mayhap," he cocked a brow, tried to look innocent, "mayhap he will like me."

"He'd be one of the few," Avani returned. "Leave. I have to get dressed."

"I'll turn my back."

She hissed again and then, all at once, gave in. "Goddess help me. Turn your back, my lord, and shut your mouth."

Obediently, he moved to look out the windows. Sunlight bounced off snow. Jacob landed on his shoulder, pinching. Mal peered out over the palace gardens, then blinked up into the clear blue sky, dazzled by the sun.

Chapter Fourteen

DEVAL LIVED IN a small hut built against the palace walls, not far from the shadow of the Fair. The hut was brick and stone and straw, with a spread of burlap over the roof to keep the rain and snow out. A thick black pipe sprouted from the burlap, and vented soft white smoke into the air.

Deval's hut was one of many, a single home in a make-shift village. The squat buildings had sprouted up alongside the Fair, as laborers and merchants began to spend more time in Wilhaiim, as the Fair became a way of life, a way to prosperity and riches.

During the winter rains, when the Fair was at its lowest peak, many of the brick huts remained empty.

But Deval's small shelter had become a home. Mal assumed the islander lived against the palace walls year round. There were rugs on the floor, and on the brick walls. A sleeping pallet covered with worn cushions, a wooden chest with many drawers, and a carefully constructed cook fire at the very center of the single room.

Mal thought Deval's home resembled Avani's abandoned cottage. He decided the abundance of bright color was an island affection.

Deval was weathered. His skin was dusky and wrinkled, his head shaven. He wore a coat and trousers similar to Avani's. His feet were bare, his toenails enameled red. He wore a bit of true gold in the lobe of his left ear, and his eyes were lined in kohl.

If the man was surprised to see Wilhaiim's vocent, he didn't let the emotion show. He took Mal's hands between his own slender fingers, bowing very correctly.

Avani said something in the island tongue, a language of fluid sounds and quick lilts. Deval smiled, nodding, and released Mal's hands.

"Welcome, my lord," the islander said. "Come and sit."

Avani moved with an ease that proved she was at home in the hut. Mal couldn't guess how much time she'd spent in the island man's company, but he could see immediately that the two were very close.

He followed Avani to the edge of the cook fire, and settled into a pile of cushions at her side. It was then he noticed the tiny altar set up to one side of the flames.

Little more than a worn wooden trunk covered with a collection of scarves, the altar served as a pedestal for a tiny silver statue.

This idol was not the same goddess Avani kept on her own hearth. This statue had the beaked head of a bird and four long arms. The idol's ankles were crossed, tiny toes curled.

Mal couldn't tell whether the creature was supposed to be male or female, god or goddess.

"*Cre'an*," Deval said. His bright black eyes reminded Mal of Jacob. "The god who keeps my ancestors."

"It's not the same." Mal glanced at Avani.

She made a face, obviously impatient. "There is the Goddess, and below her, the household gods, the *jhi*."

"There are flatland cults which teach a similar doctrine," Mal replied, unperturbed. "I have never had much time for religion."

"It is not simply religion," the island man said. "It is also tradition. A way of life. The household *jhi* take an active interest in a family's daily life."

"Theists believe only the purest of souls are lucky enough to touch the face of their god. Unfortunately there are very few pure souls in Wilhaiim." Mal shook his head. "The rest are damned, according to temple doctrine."

"Even the damned have wisdom to dispense," returned Deval. "Although, certainly, each generation has its lost souls, souls who remain unfinished or broken before they can reach the Goddess's embrace. Lost children, *bhut*."

Mal started.

"Deval," Avani murmured, but the man only showed crooked teeth in a grin.

"These are not necessarily our enemies," he said. "Often they appear useful. But in fact they are always trouble. Their hunger is never satisfied. A man would be wise to steer clear."

Mal's hackles rose. Deval leaned forward, black eyes bright, as though he could see Siobahn where she hid at the back of Mal's skull.

"Avani has no *jhi* on her hearth," Mal said.

The man's smile grew.

"Avani's *jhi* rides on her shoulder," he said. "It was the way of some families; a sign of great favor."

Mal looked at Avani.

"Jacob," she said.

Mal glanced from Avani to Deval.

"I don't believe in divinity. The bird is a bird. The idol a handy focus. I believe only in the power a man is born to."

"And yet you are a magus. A magus who uses the spirits to serve his king."

"It's far more than that," Mal argued.

"Is it?" Deval leaned forward across cushions. "Tell me—"

But Avani interrupted. "Deval. The day grows late and I have much to do."

The island man started to protest. Avani spoke again, sharply, in the language of her people. Deval bowed his head.

"I am sorry," he said. "Our weaver is right. Will you stay a moment longer, while Avani and I welcome the new year?"

Mal found himself nodding. For some reason, his throat hurt.

He could hear Siobahn whispering uneasily in his skull.

"The bird is a bird," Mal said as they left Deval's hut. "And that man thinks I am a fool."

"Not exactly." Avani ran a finger over her braided hair, refusing to meet his eyes.

"If not a fool, then certainly loathsome."

Avani shrugged. She kicked a little at the slush as they walked.

"Did your Andrew hold with the *bhut*?"

"He was a strong magus. He spoke to the dead with ease. They flocked about him, an entourage of souls." He scowled a little. "It's part of what we do, Avani. We see past this world into others."

"Did he ever speak to you about Siobahn?"

"They were dear friends."

Avani met his gaze at last. Mal saw that she was troubled.

"*Ai*, well, mayhap you are right, and it is only a difference in cultures."

"I know I am correct." Mal tapped his fingers on his thigh. "You are young yet, and your friend is old and stubborn."

"Deval is not old!"

Mal heard a tremor in her voice. He touched her shoulder in reassurance.

"He is old, but he is healthy, solid as the earth. What were the words he said, when you made a paste of the ginger powder?"

"Turmeric. He spoke a welcome to the new year, and to ask the blessing of the Goddess. I did the same, this morning, before you interrupted."

"You truly believe," Mal realized.

"Of course. The Goddess is here, in my heart, and in

my gut." Avani thumped her stomach with a fist. "It is the way of my people. It is faith. Haven't you any at all?"

Mal looked down into her face, and recognized the bright curiosity in her eyes. He wondered what she hoped he might say.

He shook his head, silently squeezing her shoulder. "Avani. I have no use for faith of any kind. In all my learning I have seen many unusual things, and heard a multitude of unusual tales, but never have I seen any hint of true divinity. And I think I would have."

Her brow wrinkled.

"Perhaps," she said, "you haven't been paying attention."

LATER IN THE day Mal took Avani to his coldroom. Hidden in the depths of the palace, not far from the king's dungeons, the little cell Mal used as his workroom was more closet than laboratory.

There was just enough room between stone walls for a scarred table, a set of stacked brick shelves, and the high stand that held his journal. The walls were white with frost. Long ago, Mal had grown used to the dry cold, but Avani began to shiver as soon as he unlocked the door.

"One of Wilhaiim's first vocents spelled the walls to cold," he explained, watching carefully as Avani examined the room. "Although in the winter, the spell is hardly needed."

"And the light?" Avani asked. She glanced up at the ceiling, at the bright glow that emanated from the stone and threw the room into stark relief.

"Another old spell."

"Why not candles?" Avani pointed to the empty sconces on the walls. The fixtures were rusting, and encased in an outer skin of frost.

"The room is kept cold for a reason," he replied, bleakly amused. "Come."

He led her into the center of the room. He stopped in front of the table, waiting.

He saw the moment her eyes adjusted to the light, saw the moment when she realized just what the table held.

Avani blanched, wrinkling her nose. She closed her eyes, turning her face away from the table, breathing shallowly. Mal wondered if she would vomit. Then, after several quick breaths, she opened her eyes again and looked back down at the table.

Slowly, the disgust on her features melted away. Mal was foolishly proud of her control.

"There's no smell," she said. She swallowed audibly.

"Another cant," Mal explained. "The room is rife with them. Congratulations. Most guests empty their stomachs very quickly across the floor."

Avani shot him a quick stare. "Do you have many? Guests in this place?"

"Often." Mal pumped the spigot on an old well a past occupant had drilled down into one corner of the room. He scrubbed his hands beneath the icy stream. "Sometimes a witness, or a family member. Sometimes, Renault. He's learned to control his innards."

Avani was looking again at the table. Mal thought he saw more curiosity than revulsion on her face. "Is it marble?"

"Aye. Very old. Put this on." He passed her a leather apron, and pulled its twin over his own head. "Wash your hands under the spigot."

He waited as she tied the strings of the apron, and as she washed her hands. Avani's breath puffed like smoke in the chill room. Mal's did not.

When Avani's hands were clean and dry, he took her elbow and set her firmly back at the table, positioning her at his side.

"The room is kept cold so the body will remain mostly unchanged." He looked down at Andrew's ravaged face. "This one has been in the ground for half a season. The rot and worm work is started, but the face is still recognizable."

"Goddess," Avani whispered, shuddering.

"Look carefully, deeply," Mal ordered, making it a challenge. "Tell me what you see."

Avani scowled. "If this is what makes a vocent—"

"*This*," Mal interrupted, "is where you show me how you use those island wits, or whether you are lacking. Tell me what you see."

She glared. He knew she'd already noted Siobahn in the corner of the room by his journal. He knew that she wouldn't allow herself to be cowed while Siobahn watched. Still, he held his breath.

When Avani clenched her fists, narrowing her eyes, and bent over the body, he had to hide a smile.

"The table is indeed very old," she said at last. "And notched by one blade or many. Many," she decided, "as the damage is not uniform. There are grooves along the edges, and at the center, and the surface is slanted . . ." She trailed off.

"Drainage," said Mal. "Some corpses are more fresh than others. When I work, I keep a basin at the foot. Good. Now, the body."

Avani sighed. She deliberately turned her back on Siobahn. She peered down at Andrew's deflated limbs. Mal noted she avoided looking at the dead man's face.

"He's dressed," she said. "Boots, tunic, trousers, cape, leather jerkin. There's a sheath at his belt, no sword. Not a vocent's uniform."

"A lord's," agreed Mal. "You're surprised?"

"He wore robes, there in the graveyard."

"My doing. Robes are the simplest way to clothe a summoned spirit."

"A summoned spirit," Avani repeated. "And if he'd walked on his own accord, what garments might he have chosen?"

Mal shrugged. "Does it matter?"

"Perhaps. The pretty gown yonder *bhut* wears so proudly? Is that your doing or her choice?"

Siobahn shifted minutely, but said nothing.

"Her choice," Mal said, amusement fled. "Why?"

"I only wondered. Often the Goddess will present her self in different forms, to drive a point home."

"Sometimes I think a spirit will simply choose the last form they remember."

Avani grunted. She frowned down at Andrew.

"What else do you see? Look deeply."

"Flesh that is mostly dissolved. Worm work." Her mouth

twisted in disgust. "His eyes are gone, as is most of the skin on his face. His fingers are dried, dark. Is it soil, or was he a man who knew the sun?" She didn't wait for a reply. "He wore a ring on his left hand, just one. It's gone, now."

"You know this?" Siobahn demanded. "Or are you guessing?" The spirit's tone was as frosty as the room.

Mal saw Avani hesitate, but she replied readily enough. "I can still see it, a phantom yellow stone, gleaming on his finger. My lord wears one similar."

"A vocent's seal," Mal said.

"Where has Andrew's gone?"

"When a vocent dies, he is stripped of his office. His ring returns to his king, to await the next initiate. Renault will have it."

Avani hummed slightly, but said nothing.

"Your wits are keen today," he said. "The ring was important to him. Its shade lingers, for those of us with eyes to see. What else?"

"I never knew the man," argued Avani.

Mal cut her off with a shake of his head. "Look," he urged.

Avani stood still, silently studying the dead magus.

"He's been cut open," she said at last. "There is a long scar on his throat, and two more behind his ears."

"And more beneath his clothing. The priests cut him open after death, looking for poison."

"*Agraine*," Avani remembered. "Did they find it?"

"The Masterhealer believes they did," said Mal. "But now it's our turn to see what these beloved bones might hide. Help me strip his clothes. Try not to touch his flesh."

Avani went to work without visible reluctance. Her fingers were deft, and very gentle, chapped purple by the cold. Mal felt an irrational surge of pride.

They folded the ruined clothes, setting the fabric in a pile on the floor alongside Andrew's boots. Mal drew a metal basin from its place under the table and propped it beneath the slant of the drains.

There would be no blood from this body, but Mal had learned early that corpses were often more liquid than solid, even when they had been interred in winter ground.

Siobahn drifted close. She stood at Andrew's head, watching. Avani wouldn't look in the spirit's direction.

Mal reached for his journal, pulled the stand close, and passed Avani his old stylus.

"A good vocent begins his daily log at the top of the next blank page in his book, thusly." He took Avani's hand, setting it on an open page. "He begins with the date, top rightmost corner."

At Avani's shuttered stare, he cocked a brow. "I want you to take down my dictation, you understand?"

"You think I have the lettering?" She lifted her own brows.

"You can read. Every successful merchant can scribe the royal lingua," Mal said easily. "And you hold the stylus like a seasoned scholar. Am I wrong?"

"I can scribe." She was annoyed he'd guessed correctly. Mal grinned.

"Good," he said. "Do I need to lower the stand?"

"I can reach," she said, offended. She stood on her toes

against the stand, set the bottle of ink at her elbow, and positioned the stylus over his book.

"Begin," she said, with all the dignity of a monarch.

Siobahn scoffed. Avani kept her gaze on the parchment. Mal swallowed a laugh, and then began his examination.

Avani took his dictation with an ease that spoke of skill. Mal noted she spent more time watching the way he touched the body than worrying about her letters. He paused once to walk around to her side. Her hand was neat and her scribing accurate.

"Lovely," he said. "I might have guessed."

She only pursed her lips. "And how do you do it when you haven't an unwilling guest? One hand on the body, the other on your book?"

"Siobahn scribes for me," he replied, and was surprised at the lurch of his heart when he caught the flash of anger over her face.

"I might have guessed," Avani mocked. She swiveled her chin, looking for the first time at the spirit. Siobahn stared back, blue eyes burning.

Mal walked back to his table. The priests had done a neat job. The seams split neatly under his knife. Most of Andrew's entrails had been removed, but temple custom demanded the heart be left intact under the corpse's breastbone.

The organ had deteriorated. Putrid liquid ran through Mal's fingers. He scooped a handful of the mess into a bowl, added a bit of flesh trimmed from Andrew's rib cage, and stirred the contents with his blade.

He set knife and bowl aside, and used an old needle and a length of temple-blessed thread to sew the body shut.

"Put his clothes back on, please, as best you can." He smiled at Avani, then moved to wash his hands beneath the spigot. "Use the needle and thread if you need to mend any of the fabric."

"That's all?" Avani set the stylus down. She gathered up Andrew's tunic.

"In this case. I needed a sample of tissue. Lungs, or heart, the two spots in the body *agraine* attacks. His lungs have been removed. His heart remains, although somewhat less than it was."

"Corpse magic," Avani said, trying to piece the tunic around Andrew's cold shoulders. "Necromancy."

"Science," Mal corrected.

"An unnecessary violation. The man's body should be left alone."

"You saw what happened when I summoned his spirit. Sometimes simple is best."

Avani shuddered. "What will you do with the poor man's juices?" She pointed at the tin bowl.

"An easy cant and a drop of lye will bring any *agraine* to the top of the mixture."

"Lye is for sheep dip."

"*Agraine* is a vocent's poison, rare and delicate. One of its ingredients responds to lye. An old vocent's trick, the use of lye to test for poison."

"And will a drop of lye tell you who poisoned the man?"

Mal bit back a surge of irritation. "No."

"Or how the concoction got on a dead man's sword and poisoned yourself?"

"No." Back to Avani, Mal bent over the bowl. He crumbled a thimbleful of lye into the liquid. Siobahn drifted to his side and peered intently into the cup.

"So what good . . ." Avani argued. Then she stopped. "Mal?"

He turned at the surprise in her voice. "What is it?"

She blinked at him. "There's something in his boot."

"I beg your pardon?"

"There is something," Avani repeated, holding up the boot, "in his left shoe."

"What is it?" He jiggled the tin bowl, set it in Siobahn's waiting hands, and returned to the table.

"I don't know." Avani's forehead creased. She peered into the boot. She stuck her fingers into the mouth of the shoe, and upended the sole. "It looks like a sphere. It's cold soft, like—" She stopped again.

"Wait!" Mal crossed the rest of the stone floor in a bound, reaching for Avani's arm. "Don't!"

But he was too late. Avani's body twitched, then went rigid. The boot fell from her grasp, tipping under the table. Siobahn cried out. And Mal couldn't look away from the ball of frozen clay Avani held in her fist.

"Drop it! Avani, let it go!"

She didn't see him. Her eyes were glazed, her spine stiff. As Mal watched, horrified, her mouth began to work. Her teeth clicked together, frantic, and spittle flew.

"Hells!" He worked at her hand, trying to free the soil from her grip. "Siobahn!"

"I can't reach her," the spirit said. "I can't get past it."

Avani's chattering teeth were cutting into her own mouth, tearing into her lower lip. Blood tinted her spittle pink. Mal thought he could hear her scream, deep in the back of her throat. He couldn't pry her fingers from the clay.

"Blood of the saints!" he swore aloud. Then he curled his fingers into a fist, and struck Avani across the chin.

She collapsed, falling heavily on the floor. Her body shook. Her fingers fisted, then relaxed. The ball of clay, crushed by the violence of her grip, spiraled across the floor and fetched up against a table leg.

"Don't touch it!" he spat at Siobahn.

He knelt at Avani's side. Her eyes were still open, still empty. Blood trickled from her mouth, oozing from the tears in her lip. Her body was limp, relaxed, her breathing slow.

Mal gripped her chin between his hands, and tried to wipe some of the blood from her mouth with the edge of his tunic. He called her name.

"She won't hear you," Siobahn said. "She's too far gone."

"Where?" Her blood stained his already grimy fingertips.

"I can't find her." Siobahn's eyes slitted like a cat's. She stared at nothing. "There is a thread of power. I can see it through the spell, but . . ."

Mal didn't pause to think. He stole Siobahn's senses, used them as his own. His urgency made him rough, and he heard her gasp, but she gave him what he sought.

The spell was dark, constructed of shadows and earth. It wrapped around Avani's face like a mask, trailing in dark threads to the abandoned clay. The room that had seemed so clean a breath ago stank of rot and dank vegetation.

He found the crack in the spell, and a tiny flicker of light buried in the shadows. Avani's essence, struggling against the trap, unable to beat the smothering darkness back.

Mal dove after the tiny flicker. He heard the Siobahn's cry of warning and ignored it. He slipped through the crack in the shadows, and sent his own strength spiraling after Avani.

He found her, locked in a spell-cast nightmare. She was wild with terror, staring at a ceiling Mal didn't recognize, trapped in a body that was not her own. That body was close to death, breathing its last, and Avani was frantic, unable to escape the vision.

Avani!

She was lost in the struggle to survive, caught in the pulse of a heart faltering. There was pain, but it was distant, muted by approaching death.

Avani!

He encircled the tiny flicker that was her core with a tendril of himself. Then he reached back, stretching through the hole in the spell, groping for Siobahn.

His bride met him, a rope of burning blue energy, and served as his anchor. He held on to Siobahn, and he held on to Avani, and he pulled.

He was clumsy, his power wild, and he knew it scalded at both ends. But he was strong, and Siobahn solid. And the spell was weakening, the body in the vision nearly dead.

The other heart stilled, and Avani began to drift. Mal could see it, could feel it, up and away from the bloody floor, a soul caught in death's net.

Terrified, he strained again, determined to drag Avani free. He wrapped a second tendril of power around her flicker, tugging.

The spell unraveled all at once. Avani came free in his grasp. Together, they spun back along his line of power, through the unraveling coil of earth and shadow.

As they spun, Mal looked one last time through Avani's eyes, at the vision that might have killed her, and at last he recognized the trap.

He took a sharp breath, and found himself kneeling on the stone floor of the coldroom, arms splayed, one hand on Avani's brow, the other braced on the frigid floor, clay crushed beneath his palm.

Avani stirred. Her eyes rolled open, then drifted shut. Her body jerked. Her fingers fell open, limp.

Frightened, Mal grasped at her wrist, feeling for a pulse. Her blood still warmed her veins, and her pulse was shallow yet steady.

"She but sleeps," Siobahn said gently. She stood over Mal, the bowl still cradled in her hands.

"It was the slaughter in Stonehill's tavern." Mal ran shaking fingers through his hair. "The spell trapped her in the body of one of the dying. The remembered death nearly took her."

"It was an illusion." Siobahn said, "Weeks have passed since Stonehill burned."

"An illusion. One so real it nearly took her life."

He gathered Avani's lax body to his breast, and rose slowly on cramping legs. "She needs a priest."

"She's well," Siobahn insisted. "If you would calm enough to *look*, you would see."

"I'm taking her to the priests. Clean up here. Don't"—he took a breath, glanced at the pile of crumbled clay—"don't touch it."

Siobahn nodded. Mal searched her unnatural eyes, looking for reassurance. He found warmth, and love, but nothing of fear.

She moved, gown rustling, and his gaze was drawn to the bowl in her hands.

Her lips quirked slightly on something that might have been a smile.

"*Agraine*," she said, answering his silent question. "The film rose very quickly."

Mal nodded, once. Then he carried Avani from his coldroom, leaving Siobahn and Andrew behind.

Chapter Fifteen

AVANI SPENT THE next two sennight's trying to forget the trap she'd sprung in Mal's coldroom.

Denial was easily managed, as her hours were filled from dawn to dusk, and often after. Mal kept himself absent from her days. Avani suspected the man was hiding, although she wasn't sure from what. When she remembered waking in his arms in the Masterhealer's quarters, and the strain she'd seen then on his face, Avani grew angry.

He had no right to regret a danger he hadn't foreseen. Avani had never been coddled, not even as a child, and she didn't intend to let Mal start now.

So she told herself she was glad of his absence, and she did her best to stay away from his quarters, and if she looked for him on those handful of days when she supped with the king and court, she told herself it was only mild curiosity.

She wondered what he was doing, and whether he'd

found *agraine* in Andrew's heart, and if he had, what did it mean?

When she remembered the coldroom and the frozen bit of clay, she suffered from vicious headaches. Even the old leather apron she'd worn from the priest's rooms made her temples throb.

Eventually she grabbed the abandoned apron from its place on the back of her single chair, balled it up, and thrust it under her bed. Liam no longer slept in her rooms, so only Jacob remained to see her consign the garment to the dust under the bed frame.

Avani wouldn't feel guilty. If Mal needed his butcher's garment, no doubt he would come to retrieve it. She couldn't help it if the man was hiding out, as afraid as she to face what had happened in the frigid depths of his coldroom.

She missed Liam terribly, and started spending much of her free time in the pages' yard, practicing alongside the lads, trying to learn the way of her new sword. The king's blacksmith had crafted her a beautiful weapon, and she loved it. Simple and deadly, the sword fit in her hand easily, and she had no trouble hefting its weight.

She could almost forgive Mal his meddling when she held his gift in her hand and battled imagined foes.

Often, when she braved the cold for the joy of practice, she found Everin in the pages' yard with the boys. She wasn't sure exactly what purpose he served there, but the pages seemed to like and respect the man. The armswoman, a solid woman with a loud voice, appeared to enjoy his company, as well.

Avani knew Everin watched her sparring avidly. He teased her often over her temper, but spoke little of her skill, until one day he stopped her mid-strike, dismissing the boy she'd chosen to partner.

"That sword is a lady," he said, peering at her through bushy eyebrows. "You handle her as though she has a whore's stamina."

Avani fumed. "If you have something to say, man, say it plain."

Sheathing his sword, Everin stepped behind Avani. He set his right hand on her own, pressing her fingers against the hilt of her blade.

"You are too free with her," he explained. "You need to be sparing, jealous. Swing her too wide, or too often, and you'll find yourself open, and your guts across your toes."

Avani grimaced. "The armswoman has said nothing."

She felt the big man's ribs quiver as he chuckled. "She's afraid of you, black eyes. She's giving you basic training, but will be little more help than that."

Avani squirmed in his grip, and looked up into his face. "Afraid of me?"

"Aye, haven't you heard? They're calling you the king's witch, Avani. Many suppose you're vocent in training."

"I'm not!"

"Oh, aye? And yet you spend your days in his company, and your time in his lair."

"I haven't seen the Lord Vocent in a score of days."

"Regretting it, are you?" Everin snorted.

Avani showed her teeth. Everin laughed, and took her sword, and nodded at the crooked log bench that had been set up on the edge of the yard, beneath the sheltering branches of an ancient evergreen.

"Come and sit," he said. "And we'll cheer yon Liam on for a stretch more. He needs the encouragement, if the snow burns on his knees are any indication."

Reluctantly, Avani followed. "He's nearly made page. The armswoman says soon he'll be ready to take on service."

"Aye, though it will be a long time yet before he's ready to squire."

Everin sat on the edge of the lopsided bench. Avani sank down at his side. The bearded man turned her sword over and over again in his hands, although his eyes were on Liam as the boy battled a brother in the falling snow.

"By spring he'll have enough skill to make the vocent proud," Everin mused. "He's the makings of a good page, and maybe someday he'll wake and find himself a Kingsman. Would he like that?"

"He worships His Majesty, and he adores Mal. *Ai*, and he's become fast friends with many of the other lads. I think he'll be happy here. It's a far leap from life as a stable boy in Stonehill. Here, at the very least, he gets a full meal and a clean bed."

"So you've warmed to the idea," Everin said, pleased.

"I have," Avani admitted. "He's happy."

"And you?" Everin turned from the yard. He studied Avani.

"I've lords and ladies beating at my door for a rug or three. I've made a friend, here and there. His Majesty seems a fair man."

"But you're not happy."

She inhaled, then shrugged. "I don't belong here. The same lords and ladies who desire my fabrics look askance when I sup with the king. I'm a foreigner. I always will be. Flatlander ways are uncomfortable."

"You may grow to understand them better."

"I may," she agreed. "If I stayed until I was an old woman, and abandoned my *salwar*, and my braid, and put away the Goddess who graces my hearth. Then, perhaps. And perhaps not."

"So you will, what? Find another village at the heart of another rock mountain, and set up shop? Tend sheep until you grow old and wither to nothing?"

Avani eyed the man. She didn't see any pity on his face.

"It's the way I chose years ago," she said. "Why abandon it now, just because a man with a pretty face promises me power, and wealth, and the way to a king's ear?"

"Ah." Everin puffed his breath into the cold air. "So he does want to make you vocent."

Avani sat straighter as Liam whacked his partner a solid blow across the thigh with the flat of his blade. "Oh, *ai*! Fine work, Liam!"

Still watching the lad, she sighed. "He says he wants to save me."

"You don't look as though you need saving." Everin shifted on the log. His knee brushed her own. "You'll never find your island again, Avani."

"I know it. My home is gone." And her heart wanted to break. "Does that mean I should abandon the ways of my people?"

"Were your people shepherds, Avani?"

"Weavers."

"Weavers, and warriors, and politicians, and merchants, and princes, and wisewomen," Everin retorted. "And one or two witches. Magi. I've been studying up on the islands, black eyes."

"Why?"

Everin's smile split his beard. "Because I like you, and because I wondered, and because I could see that you were frightened."

"I'm not frightened."

"You are. And you have need to be. Something wicked roams this kingdom, and you've become entangled. You needn't stay and fight. You can run and hide yourself in another tiny village, and hope to live out your years untroubled. Or you can stay here, become vocent, and skulk around, keeping counsel with the king. But," he balanced her sword between his thumb and forefinger, "there are other options."

"Other options?" Avani echoed, puzzled.

"Yes." Everin leaned close, yellow eyes glinting. He started to speak, but Avani suddenly started in her seat, and set her hand on his arm.

"Wait."

The vocent slipped through the yard, a slender man in elegant black. Siobahn dogged his footsteps. Avani held her breath, heart pounding, but Mal didn't so much as glance in her direction.

He crossed the yard, eating up snowy ground with quick strides. He stopped beside Liam, squeezing the boy's shoulder, and bent to speak in his ear.

Liam smiled. He nodded, and set aside his wooden sword.

Together, Avani and Everin looked after as Mal led the boy from the yard and into the palace.

"Well," Everin murmured when the two had disappeared. "The lad is advancing quickly."

Avani couldn't help herself; her lips curled in a grin. "He has friends in the court."

Everin snorted.

Avani forced Mal from her thoughts. She turned to study her companion. "You said, once, that you'd seen *agraine* at work," she said. "Where?"

He frowned. Avani thought the yellow gaze went cold.

"In the desert guard," he replied. "One of the 'scripts stumbled into the middle of an assassination gone bad. He was pricked with an arrow meant for another. The arrow was poisoned. It killed him very slowly."

"And it was *agraine*?"

"Aye."

"But *agraine* is a vocent's poison, used only in kings' business."

"Mayhap the assassin was a vocent in peasant's clothing." Everin regarded her steadily. "Carrying out royal orders. I know naught. I was a youth, and remember only how the 'script died, and the lord's fury."

Avani stared back. "And was it in the desert lord's army you became acquainted with the ways of the magi?"

Everin nodded pleasantly, but his eyes were still flat and cool. Avani shivered. She stood abruptly, and held out her hand for her sword.

"Going in?" the bearded man asked.

"Nay," replied Avani. "I've more practicing to do, if I'm to make this whore act the lady."

He laughed, as she'd hoped, but her goose bumps didn't ease. And he sat on the bench and watched her, all through the afternoon, until Avani grew tired of swordsmanship and went in search of her loom.

LATER IN THE evening, after a quiet supper at her hearth, Avani sought out the king's mistress.

She found Kate in Renault's chambers, sorting herbs before a fire much warmer than Avani's own. Kate sat on a cushion on the floor, the herbs divided into piles at her feet. Peter slouched in a brocade chair at her side. Sister leaned on brother's legs, apparently comfortable, and the king was nowhere to be seen.

"Welcome!" Kate cried, obviously delighted to see Avani. She didn't rise from her seat, but held out delicate fingers in greeting.

"I've been missing you," she said. "And longing to leave the palace. Shall we go Fairing tomorrow, if the snow lets up, and Peter says it will for certain!"

Her brother laughed, winking at Avani. "And Peter is always right, so promise this child you will go shopping with her, otherwise she will force me along instead."

Avani laughed. She dropped to the floor at Kate's feet and examined the gathering of herbs.

"Renault's bootman is suffering from the gripe," Kate explained. "He has a fondness for too much ale and too little rye. I thought perhaps dandelion." She set her hand on a tiny mountain of leaves. "And peppermint."

"All the man needs is a good whack about the shoulders and a nice, long dry spell," Peter retorted. He shifted in his chair, dislodging his sister, and stretched his stockinged feet toward the fire.

"You have yarrow, and rosemary," Avani said with pleasure. "I haven't found a good patch of yarrow since before the leaves around the river turned to orange."

"You're welcome to take some," offered Kate. "The root is indispensable."

Avani studied the king's mistress. "Lord Peter said you trained with the healers."

"The priests, yes." Kate blushed a little. "When I was a girl I dreamed of being Wilhaiim's Masterhealer."

"And then His Majesty swept Katie off her feet, and the herbs were all but forgotten," Peter teased.

"I miss it, somewhat," Kate admitted. "But not often. And there is always a bootman longing for succor."

Avani hesitated, fingering the yarrow. Then she gathered her courage.

"I apologize, my lady, my lord. But I need to know. How did Siobahn meet her end?"

Katie stilled. Peter scowled.

"It's not our story to tell," he muttered, looking away into the fire.

"You've said that once before," returned Avani. "And then, I had to agree. Now, *ai*, it's true, I've changed my mind."

"Why?" asked Kate.

"There is something amiss. That ghostie is more unnatural than any *bhut* I've yet heard of. She keeps secrets, my lady. She keeps secrets from my lord."

"Secrets?" Peter echoed. "From Mal?" He stared hard at the back of his sister's head.

"Have you seen her?" Avani asked, blunt.

"I knew Siobahn when she lived," Kate said. "Neither Peter, nor myself, nor any other but the vocent has the skill to treat with the dead. We might never have known she still walked but for Andrew."

"I can see her," Avani said. "And so can Everin."

"Everin?"

Avani nodded. "The man gazes straight at Siobahn, when he thinks no one is looking, and she returns his regard, and neither the man nor the spirit admits their communion."

"'Communion'?" Peter blinked owlishly. "A strong word, that. Perhaps the man has some inborn talent."

"It's possible," Avani allowed. "But when I first glimpsed Siobahn, she was furious. She wanted me blind to her. And this man looks her up and down. She doesn't flinch, she doesn't protest, and she doesn't say a word to my lord."

"How do you know?" Kate challenged gently.

"I *know*," Avani said. "I touched his mind the night of Andrew's summoning. My lord has no idea. That *bhut* is keeping secrets."

"Everin is a good man," Kate mused.

"You like him," murmured Peter, "simply because he has a beard and a strong arm."

"Hush," Kate scolded without heat.

"I don't understand Everin," Avani said. "But the spirit is trouble. More and more, I think she is dangerous."

Kate bent over her herbs. Peter stared up at the ceiling. The fire crackled, and outside the king's large windows, snow fell in silent swirls.

"Siobahn was never good for Mal," Kate said at last. She didn't look up from her herbs. "But she loved him, and he loved her, and eventually we learned to care for her in our own way."

Avani waited. Peter frowned and studied the rafters intently.

"Peter never really liked her," continued Kate. "But he won't tell you so. Renault adored her, and still does. Sometimes, he talks to her as though he knows she stands at Malachi's side, even though he is as blind to her as I."

"How did she die?" Avani pressed.

Kate ran dandelion stems between her fingers. "It was an arranged marriage; they were both babes. Mal's family, as well as Siobahn's, was from one of the small coastal villages. Those villages were settled by refugees from the Black Coast, you remember, and even today their customs differ greatly from the flatland ideal. Mal was to marry Siobahn just after his fifteenth birthday, but something happened before their union was finalized—I know not what—and he was sent early to foster."

Kate shook her head. "Malachi's father is a sea lord, not a minor one, and was friend to Renault's sire. Renault arranged Mal's fostering to Gerald Doyle. He grew up on Doyle's flatland plantation, and learned the ways of Wilhaiim's own peerage. When he was in his second decade, Siobahn's family shipped her from the coast, and they were married. Very late to it, and I think both families were relieved the handfast was finally sealed."

Avani bit her lip. Kate shrugged very slightly.

"They lived a year on the plantation, and I believe they were happy. Then Mal began seeing his shades, and accidentally setting things afire. It nearly drove him mad. Gerald was no fool. He sent Mal to court, and Renault set him under Andrew's care. There were three vocents still in the palace, then. Three skilled magi."

Avani couldn't help herself. "No women?"

"No. Althought it's certainly not unheard of."

Kate set her dandelion down. She folded her hands in her skirts.

"Andrew set about schooling Mal, and it was a good thing. He found control. He threw himself into learning, and into the ways of a magus. Siobahn grew jealous. She was still so young, and far from home. She wouldn't spare the time Mal needed for himself. They argued and several times, I understand, nearly came to blows. But Mal wouldn't leave court. Eventually he took his vocent's vows."

"You said he loved her," Avani said.

"Aye," Peter huffed. "He loved her. But Mal has never been a fool. He couldn't give up on the training that kept him sane." He sighed. "They had an especially bitter fight one spring evening. Siobahn demanded he return her to the coast so she could start a new life. Mal refused, as usual. She waited until he was asleep, and then sliced her own throat open with a paring knife, did the same to her wrists."

"When Mal woke, she was long cold," Kate whispered.

"We feared it would drive him over the edge entirely," Peter confided. "Andrew was wild with worry. We thought for sure Mal would join her in death. He was desolate. We rarely saw either of them. We knew Mal wasn't eating, we knew he barely slept.

"And then, one day, he eased. His heart seemed to revive, and he started paying attention to the world again. Andrew promised Renault it was over, and that all would be well."

"Because she came back," Avani guessed.

"Aye," Peter said. He met her gaze, and Avani saw fury set on his mouth. "Because she came back."

Two DAYS LATER, in the early hours just after moonset when she could be sure most of the court was abed, Avani crept into the depths of the palace, seeking Andrew's cold-room.

She took Liam with her; stole the sleepy boy from his pallet in the pages' hall. She wanted the boy at her side because she knew how quickly the lads learned the ways and halls of the palace, but also because she didn't want to be alone in the dead vocent's laboratory. She'd been uneasy enough in Mal's workspace. She worried Andrew's cold-room would be even worse.

It took them much longer than Avani had hoped to find the room. Liam knew the way down to the mouth of the

dungeons, and from there Avani remembered the winding hall and steep stairway leading to Mal's coldroom, but
soon after they passed that door, they became lost.

She'd guessed Andrew's lair would be near Mal's, but
had no real reason to be sure. The drafty hall at the bottom
of the stair housed room after room, a long marching line
of ancient wooden doors, all closed, most of them locked
or wedged shut.

Avani paused in front of Mal's coldroom. She jiggled
the latch. The door was locked. She set her back against
the wood and frowned along the corridor.

"Which one?" Liam whispered. He followed her stare,
glancing from one door to the next. "There must be two
score rooms down here, at the least."

Avani regarded the lad. He wore a page's uniform and
thick woolens. He'd gained confidence; his shoulders were
straight and proud beneath his tunic. He'd gained weight,
as well, and his hands and neck were no longer quite so
thin.

The sight of him made her heart swell. She tousled his
hair in affection.

He dodged her hand with casual ease, making a face.
"Avani. Which *one*?"

She folded her hands beneath the warmth of her cloak.
"I've no idea. I'd hoped you might know."

"I don't." Liam sighed. "Andrew's old page serves His
Majesty now. He's too snooty to speak to the likes of me."

Avani grunted. She turned around again, studying
Mal's door.

"They all look the same," she admitted, disappointed.

Liam blinked around her elbow. "You thought you'd be able to tell?"

"Mal said his room was full of spells." Avani shrugged. "Spells to bring light, spells to keep it cold, spells to keep the air fresh. I thought there might be some sign on the door, a rune, or a mark . . ."

"I don't think magi use runes," said Liam. "Not like the priests. Ralph says a vocent uses black magic, and the healers, white."

"*Ai*? And who is Ralph?"

The lad's pale cheeks turned ruddy in the light of the guttering sconces. "He's a squire. He serves the Masterhealer."

"Ah. Perhaps he's a bit biased?"

"Nay!" Liam replied. He blushed further. "Mayhap."

Avani pursed her lips. She frowned at Mal's door. Still embarrassed, Liam ducked his head, poking idly at the door with one foot.

All at once he stilled.

"Avani?"

"Mmm?"

"Avani, it *is* different. Look, here. Look at the latch."

Avani considered the latch in question. "It's bronze."

"Aye. But *look*. There are *two* keyholes."

"So there are." Avani dragged a finger slowly over the two holes. "I remember. My lord used two keys."

"And look! This door here, and that one there—only the one keyhole each!"

"Well done, lad!"

"And that one and that one have only the one. They all have just the one, on this side of the hall!"

"Well, then," Avani said. "Let's find another with two."

They searched quickly. Three of the fifteen doors had two keyholes set in bronze plates. Two of those three opened onto unlocked, empty rooms but for shelves and spigot. But the old spells were still there; the ceilings gleamed and frost covered the walls.

"Coldrooms." Avani shivered. "Empty."

"For how long?" Liam wondered.

"I don't know. No dust. Try the last."

"It's locked," the lad reminded her.

Avani tested the latch. It was stuck tight.

"I'll open it." Liam rummaged in his tunic. He pulled free a small felt wallet, unwinding the fabric to reveal a set of picks.

"Where did you get those?"

"They belonged to the Widow," Liam answered. "She said she kept them on hand for emergencies."

"Imagine that. Can you use them?"

Liam nodded. "I'm good," he said. "The Widow used to say I've fine picking hands."

"Well. Get to it."

Avani watched as the boy struggled with the keyholes. When Liam began to sweat, she was sure they'd been foiled. Just as she thought he'd given up, the first latch clicked, and Liam let out a muted whoop of joy.

"Didn't I say?"

"Good lad," said Avani. "Try the next."

The second latch gave more quickly. Grinning, Liam secreted the picks again beneath his tunic. Avani reached over his shoulder, pushing the door open with her knuckles.

The room looked as dark as a cave until they stepped over the threshold. Then the ceiling glimmered slowly to life. Avani stood still, her hand on Liam's belt, until her eyes adjusted and she could see clearly in the gentle illumination.

Liam gasped. Avani scrubbed her hand over her nose.

"Goddess," she swore. "Has no one thought to clean up in the man's absence?"

"Is it his?" Liam wondered. "Is this Lord Andrew's coldroom?"

"I'd bet my last spool of thread it is. Come with me." She grasped his belt more firmly. "Don't touch anything."

Together, they edged further into the room.

It was a much bigger space than the closet Mal employed. Almost as large as Avani's suite, the room extended straight back from the door. The walls were brick, patchy with ice. There was a square hole in a corner of the ceiling; not a window, Avani decided, but some sort of shaft.

She stood under the hole, peering up into blackness, and couldn't see where it led. She thought she felt a draft of night air, but wasn't sure.

Three of the walls were lined with shelves, and every shelf was weighted with books. The fourth wall held an iron sink, bristling with spigots and basins.

Avani tried the pumps. Cold water ran down from the spigots, then swirled away through the basins into real drains.

The single shelf above the sink held a collection of wooden boxes. Avani couldn't reach the shelf, but she did see a footstool hidden away under one of the basins.

"Look, Avani," Liam broke the silence. "A dead man."

Avani turned to the long table at the center of the room, and saw bones. She edged closer. Liam followed.

The bones were laid out carefully on the marble table. The skeleton appeared complete, from skull to finger bones to small slippered feet.

"Not a man," corrected Avani, looking at the slippers. "A woman. A lady."

The bones were clean, the skull hairless. A necklace of yellow diamonds encircled the bony throat. Rings glittered on the jointed fingers.

The skeleton wore tattered and yellowed pantaloons, lacy underclothes that might once have been virgin white. All that remained of the woman's gown was a piece of torn and purpling satin attached to the skeleton's right arm

Avani chewed her tongue. She reached out, quickly pulling a string of pearls from the skeleton's wrist. Then she detached the small flag of satin from the corpse's forearm..

"What are you doing?" Liam hissed when Avani stuck the ring and fabric into the pocket of her *salwar*.

"Research," Avani replied calmly. "Now, where's the man's journal?"

She found a wooden stand, complete with stylus and ink pot, but no book. A small pile of leather-bound tomes sloped at one end of a low shelf. When Avani pointed, Liam ran to pull the first one down.

He tossed the slim volume to Avani. She opened it reluctantly.

"Not a journal," she said, relieved and disappointed. "A

treatise on Wilhaiim's colonies. But . . ." She felt a sudden bloom of triumph. "It has his name in it. Andrew, son of Rodger."

"This is his room, then!" Liam grinned, triumphant.

Avani set the book down. She crossed to the shelf and opened the next book. It, also, was inscribed with the dead vocent's curling hand.

"*Ai*," she agreed. "Andrew's coldroom."

"Why haven't they cleaned it out? The books, and the bones?"

"I don't know." Avani piled the slim volumes carefully back on their shelf. "I don't believe anyone has been down here since the man's death." She straightened, rubbing her hands on her thighs. "Help me find his journal. It'll be a big, thick book. Bound in leather, like these. My lord's was bound in black hide."

They searched for a long while, but found nothing. At last Avani gave up.

"We've examined every tome. It's not here."

"Likely His Majesty has it," Liam decided. "Ralph says everything that is a vocent's belongs first to his king, from his heart to hose."

Avani scowled.

"What about those?" Liam pointed above the sink, at the little wooden boxes, each adorned with a delicate filigreed keyhole. They'd found them locked, and Avani knew he wanted to try his hand again with the picks.

"They're too small to hide a journal." Avani smiled when the lad pulled a face. "We've used up our luck; it will be dawn soon. Let them be, for now."

"For now? Do you mean we'll be coming back?"

"I suspect my lord will soon have you far too busy for adventure."

Liam scuffed a booted foot on the stone floor, sulking a little. His eyes gleamed in the false light as he took one last look at the shelf.

"What's that? There, on the shelf, overhanging the basin. It looks a like a long maggot." He grimaced.

Avani laughed. "It's only thread, lad." She fingered the end, pulling. "Cat gut. Used for sewing up corpses, most like." The thread snagged on the shelf, dragging.

She tugged again, and the thread came free, and something fell into her hand.

"What is it?" Liam nudged close. "It's pretty, but too small to use on meat or man."

Avani stared at the tiny bronze key in her hand, glinting against her thumb.

Chapter Sixteen

MAL WORKED WITH the sun at his back, and tried to pretend that spring was close.

The winter light through the windowpanes shone as yellow as summer where it fell across his desk. The blocks of sunlight warmed his shoulders beneath his shirt.

He thought briefly of napping, there in his old chair. He couldn't remember when it was he'd last slept. Instead he made himself sort again through the papers on his desk.

His hands looked strong and brown against fading parchment. The ring on his finger sparkled. Mal peered into the gem, frowning idly.

A rap on the door of his suite made him start. He glanced across the room. Renault was off speaking to a gathering of tenant farmers, and few others at court dared disturb the vocent in his suite.

The door shook again, as though the hand without promised violence. Mal rose from his chair.

"Your island witch," Siobahn said from the windows. "She feels . . . frightened." Her unnatural eyes gleamed with something other than sympathy.

"Come," Mal called. He stood in front of his desk.

Jacob swooped into the room, arcing from door to the back of Mal's chair. The raven settled, croaking softly. His nails scored the leather. His beady eyes reflected Siobahn's disapproving stare.

Siobahn glared at the bird as if she hoped to consign it to the hells by force of will alone.

Avani followed Jacob into the room. She set her back against the door.

"Welcome," Mal left his desk. Avani only looked at him, expressionless.

"I'm glad to see you," he continued. "It's been at least a sennight since we spoke. I've missed you."

"Oh, *ai*?" She moved from the door, walking to his desk, and absently fingering the silver ink pot that had belonged to Gerald.

"Yes." He took the pot from her hand. "What's wrong? Has something happened?"

At last he had her attention. She glanced askance, from beneath a fringe of dark lashes.

"Longer than a sennight. You've been hiding," she accused.

"I've been working," Mal corrected. He studied her carefully. He didn't like the shadows under her eyes. "What have you been about?"

"Wandering the palace. Spending the king's money at the Fair. Weaving, all hours of the night. Supping at court.

And practicing, in the pages' yard so I might learn to appreciate your gift."

Mal smiled. "Lane tells me you've improved dramatically."

"The armswoman?" Avani picked up the ink pot again. Then set it down. "She's a whirlwind, that one. But I've picked most of my learning from Everin, and from Liam. The lad's a quick hand."

"He has great promise," agreed Mal, hoping to please. "He's catching on quickly. And he has an endless supply of patience for my foibles."

"He would need it." She considered Mal with an intensity he didn't understand.

"Avani, what it is?" he asked, worried.

"We broke into Andrew's coldroom."

Siobahn's gown rustled. Mal felt the spirit bristle. His pulse raced at her anger, began to pound behind his temples.

"What did you say?"

"*Ai*, you heard me. Liam yields a picklock as skillfully as a blade. Don't punish the boy, my lord. It was my idea, he did it for me."

"I guessed as much already. Hells take you, Avani, what were you thinking?"

She collapsed into his chair beneath Jacob's half-spread wings. Her cheeks were flushed, and even through his temper Mal noted the raw places on her lower lip where she'd bitten through to blood in his own coldroom.

She wore one of her *salwar*. The silk was light blue, the color of the winter sky, the color of coastal weddings. She wore her chain of rubies on her breast, and matching studs in her ears.

She looked lovely, and desirable, and tired, and fragile, and dangerous all at once. He almost forgot his anger for the fear in her eyes.

"Avani!" He wanted to shake her, but he only gripped her shoulders, forcing her attention.

"I've been nosing about," she allowed after a heartbeat. She shrugged off his grip. "I wondered about your Andrew, and decided the best way to understand the man was to visit his workroom. Did you know"—she peered up at Mal, nose wrinkled—"that the room hasn't been tended to? There were bones lying on his table."

"Bones?" Mal shook his head. "Not a client. A client's bones would have been missed. Mayhap private research." He spread his hands. "Andrew's coldroom and his suite have been left undisturbed. Renault preferred it that way.'"

"A waste." Avani tapped a finger on the edge of his desk. "His coldroom is at least three times as large as your own lair."

Mal grunted. He reached down to still her hand.

"I like the size of my 'lair.' Avani, let it be. Andrew is not yours to explore."

Avoiding his touch, she picked up a piece of parchment, and then set it down again. "If you are the last vocent, the last magus in Wilhaiim, what of the priests?"

"The priests?"

"They sing the spells of healing."

"Ah." Mal squatted on his heels so he could look Avani in the eye. He caught her wandering hands and held them firmly between his own, ignoring Siobahn's pang of jealousy. "That is book learning. The priests have the temple lore. It has nothing to do with innate skill. It is herbs, and cants, and the proper words in the proper order."

Her fingers twitched against his palms, but this time she didn't pull away.

"The vision I had in your coldroom . . ."

"A trap," he said quickly. "It was a trap, meant for me. It was in the clay."

"Who set it?"

He sighed and stood, releasing her fingers.

"*Someone* must have set it," Avani pressed. "Do your priests have such spells?

"No," Siobahn said. She drifted close. "That was strong magic, not book learning."

"Well then." Avani sprang from the chair, restless. "It was one of the Widow's serving girls, in the vision, *ai*?" She dodged Mal, and paced in front of the windows. "She lay on the floor, bleeding, and she opened her eyes, and they were mine own, and I felt the jittering of her heart, as she died. As she died."

"Avani." Her energy frightened him. "I was there, remember? I pulled you free."

She swung around until they stood almost eye-to-eye. "I remember. The shadows bent close, did you see? The shadows bent close, as she died, and the shadows were but a guise, the murderers casters of spells, as solid as you and I."

Mal stiffened.

"No!" Siobahn said, "Stupid witch. You're wrong."

"I remembered," Avani said slowly. "I'd tried to push

it away. But I remembered, in Andrew's workroom. I remembered."

"You saw through the shadows?" Mal watched Avani closely.

"I saw," she answered. "I saw hands wielding power. I heard voices, calling death from the wind."

Mal said nothing. Avani's stare sharpened.

"You knew," she accused.

"I guessed. Neither Siobahn nor I could grope beyond the shadows to the truth of it. You're strong, Avani. Very strong."

"It's impossible," insisted Siobahn.

"And the *agraine* on the swords?" Avani mocked, "A poison my lord himself says only a vocent knows?"

Mal turned his back on both women, and stared out his windows. The sun had reached the top of the sky, but the snow on the rough palace walls had yet to warm.

"What are you implying?" Siobahn moved between Mal and Avani.

"I think that's clear. I found this"—she dropped something onto his desk—"in Andrew's coldroom."

Mal didn't move from the windows. He could see the bronze key quite clearly through Siobahn's eyes.

"It's the same," said Avani. "The same as Jacob and I found on the Downs, beneath Thom. The same."

"Andrew didn't kill those men," Mal said patiently. He buried his clenched fists in his armpits. "Andrew himself was murdered."

"And many days before Renault's men met their end in your village, witch."

Avani stood tall beneath Siobahn's fury. She glared at the spirit, but she spoke to Mal.

"When, exactly? Are you sure?"

He knew what she wanted. He couldn't give it to her. He turned way from the glass.

"Three days dead before I left for the keep," he said quietly. "It wasn't Andrew."

She gazed at him with wide, dark eyes. He wanted, sorely, to take her with his mind, to plunder her heart, to wipe the doubt from her face and remind her who he was.

It would be easy, and it would be sweet.

"Leave," he said instead.

"Malachi." Avani did what he refused to allow himself. He felt a tendril reaching, trying to entangle, seeking. Siobahn hissed and leapt, intending to knock Avani to the ground.

Mal banished the spirit with a word. Avani's untrained intrusion was just as easily turned at the gates of his mind.

"Leave," he repeated, cold. "Now. Before Siobahn comes back. I won't stop her a second time."

Avani moved. Mal slammed his hand down over the little bronze key before she could take it back.

"I'll keep it."

"Goddess take you, Mal!"

He forced back anger and hurt. "Avani, trust me. I need time to think. Now, just go."

Avani's eyes sparked, catching sunlight. Then she whirled and was gone, the door rattling in the wall with the force of her temper.

Only Jacob remained, watching from the back of Mal's chair, unblinking.

"THE BRONZE IS very old. The tip unusually sharp," Renault said, scuffing the key gently across one knuckle. "It's not been kept in particularly good condition."

He sat on the edge of his graystone chair, the mantle of kingship about his shoulders, the circlet of his rank set lightly on his head.

Mal stood two deep stairs below the throne, his forehead on a level with Renault's knees. They were alone in the hall, but for the two soldiers who served as the king's morning guard. The early audiences had ended, and it would be hours before the next began.

"The scrolling is unfamiliar."

Renault cupped the talisman in his palm. He set his hand on his knee.

"Old, certainly. I believe you'll find most of the marring is age."

"The markings are exact, I'm sure of it. I had a good look at its twin, before Avani lost it."

"Lost it, did she?" The king lifted his brows. "And this one, she found in Andrew's laboratory?"

Mal nodded once. "Apparently she's taken to jimmying locks. I don't know what she hoped to find."

Renault's beard twitched. "Not this, I think."

"She was frightened," agreed Mal. "And angry. She more than half believes I've been out on the Downs murdering the innocent."

Renault considered his vocent. "Does it matter what she believes?"

"Yes," Mal replied simply.

"Ah." Renault handed back the key. "Find out how it ended up in Andrew's coldroom."

"There's a chance he simply picked it up at the Fair, or purchased it on his travels. The decoration would have appealed to his taste."

"There's a chance," the king drawled, "but you know I don't believe in coincidences. Have you found nothing in his writings?"

Mal hesitated. "He mentions the Downs only once. Nothing at all of Stonehill. Only the keep, and the river. He expressed interest in the composition of the water, and its effect on the scarlet woods."

Renault smiled slightly. "Very well. Keep looking."

Mal slipped the key beneath his tunic. He felt the weight of his king's gaze and looked up, cocking a brow in query.

"There's gossip about," Renault said.

"Gossip?"

"Aye." The king shifted one his chair. He pushed the mantle irritably from his shoulders. "Have you caught me a magus, Mal?"

"She doesn't want the office."

"Is it true?"

"Aye."

"What she wants matters as little to me as what she believes. Convince her."

"I've tried." Mal couldn't keep his jaw from bunching.

"Try harder, brother. I won't have her slip through our fingers only to be plucked by another. The old laws are plain."

Mal shifted on his step. Then he nodded, bowed once, and left the throne room.

MAL FOUND HIMSELF pacing the palace corridors. His hand returned again and again to the talisman secreted in his tunic. Eventually he abandoned the stifling walls for the lure of the Fair.

He found, to his surprise, that the weather had eased. The afternoon was warm; icicles melted and dripped from the great canvas shelter.

The Fair bustled. Both customers and merchants seemed in good spirits, affected, Mal thought, by the early thaw.

Mal wandered idly, stopping here and there to examine anything of beauty or interest. Time slipped away, until at last he stood lingering beneath one edge of the canvas, a wrapped parcel tucked beneath each arm.

Past the edge of the canvas he could see the red gleam of sundown. He knew it was past time to return to work, but his boots seemed rooted in the mud.

"Enjoying the colors?"

Mal didn't turn. "And the solitude."

Everin laughed. The big man hopped over a puddle to stand at Mal's side.

"Shopping?"

"Thinking."

"With your money pouch, I see." Everin chuckled again. "You look lonely, my lord."

Mal watched the sunset flare and die.

"One man's loneliness is another's respite," he replied.

Everin wouldn't be put off.

"Come and sup with me," he said. "Share an ale or three. It helps with the thinking, I've found."

Mal was surprised to find the idea appealed. "Where?"

"There." Everin tilted his thumb along an outward aisle. "There's a tent there, run by a retired tavern wench. She serves lamb on the bone, and ale so thick you can float a coin on the foam."

Mal smiled. "That I've time to see."

"Come then," Everin's yellow eyes sparked. "I'll treat you the first round."

He turned on his heel. Mal followed after, juggling packages, looking forward to a long-overdue evening of relaxation in his cups. But as they crossed from one aisle to the next, the back of his neck prickled warning.

Mal swiveled mid-stride, glancing over his shoulder.

A pair of dark, kohl-rimmed eyes met his own.

Avani's friend, Mal realized. Deval. The little man stood alongside a sausage maker's stall, watching Mal with undisguised interest.

Mal gazed back. Deval didn't flinch.

"What is it?" Everin called. "Are you coming?"

"Yes." Mal replied. He walked on, deliberately turning away from the island man.

Even so, he felt Deval's stare until he followed Everin into the tavern's smoky tent.

MUCH LATER, MAL stood alone in the hall outside Avani's rooms.

He wondered how he kept ending up at her door. He didn't dare look the answer in the face.

His stomach was heavy with spiced lamb, and he knew he was well into his cups, but his mood was light. He didn't intend to knock, or linger. He meant to set his packages outside her door, where she would find them in the morning.

He placed his hand against her door and stood, simply breathing.

It didn't occur to him that, late as it was, the woman might still be up and about. Or that she'd round the corner and catch him leaning unsteadily against her door, crushed packages at his feet.

She slid around his side and stood at his elbow. She frightened him so badly that the flames in the wall sconces flared high and spat green sparks.

"Fool," Avani accused when the candles had calmed and she was assured he hadn't set anything afire. "What are you doing?"

Mal refused to be embarrassed. He laced his fingers behind his back, trying to find some semblance of dignity. "Heading on to bed."

"Your bed is several turns of the corridor back," she pointed out. She eyed the wrapped packages. "What are those?"

The candles flickered again. This time the flames took on a purple hue. Mal didn't twitch.

"For you," he said, gracious.

"Gifts?" She scowled.

"Aye," Mal replied. He waved a hand. "Open them, at your leisure. I'm off to sleep."

She stalled him, stepping neatly into his path.

"You sound thick as a farm boy. What happened to your pretty court accent?" Her nose wrinkled. "You're sauced."

"Better sauced than a murderer," he returned, and had the distant pleasure of seeing her flinch. "It's very late. Where've you been?"

"Not breaking into any coldrooms, if that's what you're thinking," she snapped.

Mal only stared.

She hesitated, rolling her shoulders.

"Kate and Peter and I went out. A group of mummers played the in Royal Gardens, Kate's favorites."

"The gardens or the mummers?"

"The mummers. What are you thinking?"

He wasn't entirely sure.

"Everin said I looked lonely," he explained.

"I'm to blame Everin for this? You're callow as a lad." She dodged his elbow, and opened her door. "Come in."

"Nay," he began. "I'm just off to bed—"

"Come *in*." She dragged him over the threshold, nodding at her single chair. "Sit."

He did, reluctantly, and watched as Avani kindled a fire on the hearth. The flames reflected off the idol as they grew. Mal couldn't look away from the Goddess's face.

"Are you ill?" Avani demanded.

She set his parcels inside the door. Jacob appeared from nowhere and began to poke at the paper wrappings.

Mal shook his head. He winced as the room tilted.

"Have you eaten?"

"Spiced lamb. Heaps o' it. Everin sups like a wild boar."

Avani grimaced. "You'll be bringing it all back up before morning."

Mal stiffened, insulted. "I can hold my drink."

Avani made a sound. When Mal glanced up, wary, he saw that her mouth had softened. She shook her head.

"You look wretched. Here, let me make you tea. It will help settle the head and stomach."

"You've a tea for everything."

"I do."

He didn't protest because he enjoyed watching her move. Her hands were quick and efficient as she warmed a pan of water on the hearth, then stirred a sprinkle of dried leaves into the depths. When the water rose to boiling, she sifted the mixture through a tiny square of fabric and into a mug.

She handed Mal the steaming mug.

"Drink."

He took a swallow and found it pleasant. "Thank you."

She gathered his parcels, shooing Jacob off a bit of string. The raven complained loudly. Mal watched doubt war with curiosity across her face.

"Am I to open them?"

"Aye," Mal said over the rim of his mug.

Avani settled cross-legged in front of the fire. Croaking, Jacob hopped after, determined to have his prize.

"There's a woman at the Fair," Mal said, amused. "She does all o' the wrappings, for a price."

"She does a fine job. Look at the primroses on the paper. Jacob, off!"

Mal grinned into his tea as she folded the wrapping carefully back. She examined the first gift suspiciously.

"A stylus?"

He nodded. "And a matching ink pot. You'll want to select the ink yourself, I imagine."

Watching him, she fingered the stylus. "Is it ebony? It's lovely."

"Open the other."

She did, more quickly than the first. When she saw the book beneath the wrappings, she stilled.

"Do you know what 'tis?" he inquired softly.

Avani flicked him a glance. "A journal, bound in black, tooled like your own."

"Exactly like my own. This was to be my next volume, the tanner had the order last season. Now he has a second order in, and this one will be yours."

It wasn't gratitude he saw in her eyes, but he hadn't expected it.

"I thought a full suit o' Hennish might be too presumptuous."

"And these are not?"

Mal let the heat from his tea warm his hands.

"Think on it," was all he said.

Avani shook her head, but when she set the stylus and journal on the rug, he saw the care she took.

"I was looking for Andrew's journal," she admitted. "We couldn't find it."

"Because I have it. And have had it since his death. I thought you realized."

"*You* have it."

Mal watched as she struggled with an emotion he couldn't place.

"Why?" she demanded.

"For answers, aye? I'm looking for answers. Exactly as you are, it seems."

"Have you found any?"

"Nay." He sipped his drink. "I've found nothing un-usual." He set the mug at his feet, and leaned his elbows on his knees. "Avani. Do you truly believe I killed them?"

He was distantly surprised to find that his next breath hung on her answer.

She avoided his stare by watching Jacob kill his cap-tured string.

"If I did you wouldn't be drinking my tea," she admit-ted, low. "*Ai*, my lord, I'm frightened."

"Malachi. I know you can say it. I've heard you."

Avani looked at him, mute.

He abandoned the chair and settled on the floor at her side. On impulse, he slipped the yellow ring from his finger and set it in her hand.

She looked down her nose at the gem.

"It's warm," she said.

"From my hand. There's no magic in the gem itself, Avani. It's merely another a badge of rank."

She held the ring up to the firelight, watching the facets

twinkle. "Liam believes you use it to command armies of bloodthirsty ghouls."

"His Majesty prefers his soldiers live and thirsting for ale," Mal returned, dry. "The ring is a symbol. I swore an oath upon it, before I took up Andrew's office. I wear it as a promise to Renault. I am his protector."

"And his assassin."

"When it's called for. It's been a long time since he's had need o' such. I didn't kill those Kingsmen, Avani, nor the innocents in Stonehill. I *know* you feel the truth o' that."

She shifted her shoulders. "And Andrew? He tried to kill us in your flatland graveyard."

"You said yourself that thing was no' Andrew."

"What was it, then?" She didn't hide her fear. "I dream of them, now, over and over. But I can't see their faces." She held out his ring. "Malachi. I'm afraid. Something is terribly wrong."

"Let me help you." He couldn't stop himself. His hand caught hers before it could retreat. He linked their fingers around the yellow ring.

She froze, eyes narrowed, lips parted. He closed his own eyes, shutting out the eddy in the room that even strong tea couldn't banish.

He could hear the puff of Avani's quick breath. He could smell the faint salt on her skin. Past the black barrier of his lids he could see the flare of her power as easily as if his eyes were wide.

He could taste it on his own tongue; delicious as spring, bitter as ash. Unschooled, her power called to him, and his own responded.

It was the ale, or the lazy weight of too much lamb in his stomach, or the loneliness that Everin had sensed, or something more, the crack in his discipline that had grown to a fissure since Andrew's death.

He forgot resistance, he let go his training. Mal dropped the walls Andrew had so diligently helped him craft, and he let her in.

They twined about each other, a dance of minds, a give and take that bolstered one and then the other, and set his body humming. Mal gasped at the sheer rush of it, and opened his eyes. He saw double, he saw thrice. He was himself, and he was Avani, and to a lesser extent, he was Jacob.

He strained forward, touching his lips to Avani's throat, just below the curve of her jaw. He heard her gasp, and her racing heart was his own, his urgency in her blood.

"Avani." Mal fisted his hands in her hair, watched himself through her own eyes. She wanted him. Their combined desire drove him to near bursting. "Hells, Avani!"

He was free, he was *complete*, and it didn't matter that he broke every law that had been trained into him. He was whole, and he burned with it.

Avani pulled away, retreating all at once, leaving Mal reeling. Her sudden absence was a black wound, and his power shivered at the loss.

He exhaled, and righted himself slowly. He met Avani's baleful glare.

"If you apologize," she said, low, "I will knock you flat."

"No." Mal shook his head. He sounded raw even to his own ears.

"You said, last time, *ai*, you said it was wrong."

"It is." The yellow ring was still in his hand, digging into his flesh. He pushed it back over his knuckle, into place. "Very wrong."

"Why?"

"I think you know." He could taste blood on his tongue, his own. The salt of her skin lingered on his lips.

"I could feel you," she whispered. "Not just your body, although that—*ai*—that was also lovely. I could feel your power, I could see your heart. You and I—"

"Yes," he agreed quietly.

She sat motionless in front of the fire, as much a statue as her Goddess. The firelight touched her hair, and her brow, and the panic in her dark eyes.

"Very wrong, you said," she repeated.

He pinched his yellow ring between thumb and forefinger, twisting. "If Andrew were here, alive, he'd have me cast from the office. Shackled for my protection. For *your* protection. As it is," he shook his head, and wondered why fear was so slow in coming, "Renault must never find out."

She trembled a little, but her mouth was set, determined.

He kept his hands away from her. Shock had cleared the wine from his head. He rose to his feet.

"I'll see myself out."

"Yes."

He cleared his throat. "Remember. A vocent always begins her daily journal at the top of the next blank page in the book. She begins with the date, top right-hand corner. And whatever she scribes belongs to her king."

Avani choked out a sound that might have been a laugh. She didn't follow him from the firelight to the door. He stepped out into the corridor, alone.

HIS HANDS WERE still shaking when he reached his own rooms, but he'd managed to mute longing to a low hum. Avani's flame lingered in his mind, tempting. Together they had been unimaginably strong, perfect.

Alone, he was less than he had been.

Mal shoved through the door and into his suite. The room was warm. A fire burned in the hearth, and the rainbow lanterns were lit. Dawn was not so very far away. Liam snored softly on a pallet at the foot of Mal's bed. The boy smiled as he slept.

Mal shut the door quietly. The lanterns flickered, and his attention narrowed.

Siobahn met his startled gaze, blue eyes wide and frightened.

She hadn't been expecting him, Mal realized, hadn't known he was outside the door, and how was that possible?

There was guilt on her mouth. She held the bronze talisman between two fingers. The little key began to quiver when Mal frowned.

"What," he demanded softly, "are you doing?"

He thought she would set the key back down on his desk, rise from his chair, tinder explanations. He expected it of her.

Something had changed. He couldn't reach her mind,

couldn't touch her senses. Couldn't understand the growing terror he saw in her unnatural eyes.

She was closed to him. Worried, now, he took a step forward.

"Siobahn?" He held out a hand.

She vanished, without a word or a thought, without even a flicker of candlelight.

She was gone, the chair empty. She'd left him, and although he stretched to his very limits, he couldn't feel her.

Frightened, he sank into the empty chair, and stared blindly down at the papers strewn across his desk.

It was only then, as he blinked stupidly at the pages of Andrew's journal, that he realized Siobahn had taken the talisman with her.

Chapter Seventeen

MAL HAD GONE into hiding again.

This time, Avani didn't search him out.

She didn't need to.

He was still there, in her mind. She sensed him at the oddest times; while working at her loom, while bartering with a customer, while scrubbing dyes from her fingertips. She felt him, a quiet itch at the back of her skull, while kneeling in front of the Goddess, while she tossed in her bed at night, afraid to sleep, afraid to dream.

Avani was as aware of Mal as she was of Jacob. She always knew vaguely where the man was in the palace. She knew when he slept, when he worked. Her stomach hollowed when he missed a meal.

She thought that if she stretched just the tiniest bit, she would be able to see through his eyes, hear his thoughts.

She'd retreated from the caress of his power, but he

hadn't bothered to rebuild the walls. Somehow, for some reason, he'd left the connection open.

Avani didn't like it. Or, if she forced herself to be entirely honest, she liked it far too much.

She tried to gain back control, to shove him out. But she didn't seem to have the discipline, or the strength. She looked at the vocent's tools he'd left her, and thought that finally, the man was making his point.

She couldn't protect herself.

Avani almost went after him and demanded he leave her alone. But even the idea of seeing him again made her head swim, and her breath hitch. She refused to let him witness her unbalance.

When she woke in the deep of the night, troubled by dreams of the deep earth, Mal's presence in the back of her head was almost reassuring.

So Avani snuck about during the day, avoiding the vocent, avoiding the king. She even refused Kate's invitations, for fear her friend would see something of guilt on her face and report back to Renault. She'd witnessed the fear in Mal's green eyes when he'd spoken of punishment. Three days later, she felt the same blunt unease across their link.

She wondered if he was frightened for himself, or for the both of them.

Avani poured her restless energy into swordplay. She shared her breakfasts with Liam and the other boys in the yard. She took dinners in the barracks with Everin.

The bearded man spoke of enlisting as Kingsman. He

seemed relaxed, even happy, and in no hurry to leave the palace. He never mentioned Andrew.

SPRING CAME MIDWINTER. On an evening warmer than any she'd yet witnessed in Wilhaiim, Avani took a break from her sword, and decided instead to explore the king's extensive gardens.

She'd heard tell of the Broken Maze, built entirely of flowering holly, and of the Rose Spiral, and of the great pond where the black swans nested. Kate had often raved about the herb plot hidden at the center of the landscape. And Liam had come to her once with a tale of jeweled peahens.

So Avani packed an early supper of meat and cheese in her old sack, then set out in exploration.

Exercise felt good. Avani's legs welcomed the pace. Even in the winter the gardens were a feast for the eye. Man-sized hedges provided shelter and privacy. Avani soon lost herself behind the thorny walls.

Thin blocks of melting ice floated on the ponds. The swans slept on a small island bright with winter flowers.

Jacob found the herb garden. The raven dipped and dived overhead while Avani sat on a slope of brown grass above the plot, her back against a marble fountain run dry for the season.

She crossed her ankles and closed her eyes, and allowed the wind through Jacob's feathers to chase away Mal's distant irritation.

The brief touch of the sun on the top of her head felt delicious, and the hedges blocked any breeze.

She dozed there on the grass, elbows pillowed on her sack. She woke to a gentle murmur. Everin, talking to the raven. She opened her eyes, peering along the slope, and watched as the man scolded Jacob from beneath a red pine.

"What did he steal?" she asked, smiling a little. "The lice from your beard?"

"Nay," Everin replied. He grunted, shot the raven a last venomous look, and climbed the slope. "Napping, black eyes?"

Avani nodded. She looked the man over. He'd abandoned his leather jerkin and his oily tunic, and donned the garb of a lord: velvet and lace and a fur-lined cape. His beard had been neatly trimmed, and his hair snipped to some order. The pommel of his sword gleamed.

"I've an audience with His Majesty," he explained, although Avani hadn't asked. "But I saw you come in here, and followed."

"Why?"

"Kate says you found a trinket in Andrew's coldroom."

Avani sat up, trying to see the man's face through the glare of the sun. His expression was mild, but something in the way he held his shoulders made her uncomfortable.

"Yes."

"And a similar piece on the Downs?"

"Yes," said Avani, slowly. "Bits of scrolled bronze, in the form of a key."

"Where is it, now?"

"My lord has it, or His Majesty." Avani adjusted her

pack, and sat straighter. She wasn't sure she liked the way Everin loomed. "The first was stolen from me."

"What else did you find in his workroom?" demanded Everin.

"If any man has a right to Andrew's things," Avani replied, "it would be you. Go and look for yourself. Perhaps it will give you peace."

Everin's beard split. His teeth gleamed. "Oh, aye. I plan to clean out his rooms, with the king's permission. The laboratory is less appealing."

Avani brushed her hair from her face. "Are you afraid of a few bones, then?"

"Is that what you found?"

"Books, boxes, bones. More books than boxes and bones."

She rather hoped he would laugh, but his lips narrowed.

"Bones?"

"My lord supposed they were left over from the man's private research. A woman's skeleton, laid on his table. Old bones, clean, but the body was still garbed in satin and adorned with jewels."

"Jewels?" His yellow eyes lit.

Avani shifted, rummaging in her sack. She found the piece of satin and the bracelet of pearls at the bottom of her sack. She drew them into the light.

"I meant to show them to my lord," she admitted. "But by all rights they belong to you."

"Let me see." He held out one big hand.

She dropped her finds onto his palm. Everin examined

the bracelet first, scratching at the pearls with this thumb-nail. Then he studied the fabric.

"Grave-rotted," he said, disappointed.

"What did you expect?"

He shrugged and started to speak, but the sound of voices around the hedges interrupted. Avani froze, and her heart began to race.

Everin dropped the pearls and satin back into her lap, and turned, just as Kate and Mal rounded the last wall of hedge.

"Everin." Kate's pretty face glowed. "I've been looking for you. Malachi said he saw you duck this way. The king's waiting upon you."

Everin bowed to Kate, and to the vocent, and to Avani. The yellow gaze, as it touched Avani's face, held a warning she didn't understand.

She closed her fingers around the items in her lap, but too late.

Mal cocked a quizzical brow. Avani could feel the press of his curiosity in her own head.

"What have you there?" he asked.

"Nothing of import," Avani said, reaching for her sack.

Everin took Kate's arm, and led her away. The king's mistress looked over her shoulder at Avani, concerned.

"My lord?" Everin urged.

"In a moment," Mal said. He turned his back on the pair, stared hard at Avani.

"What is it?" he asked.

She could feel him slipping around the edges of her mind.

"Stop it!" she hissed. Jacob called from the top of the red pine.

Mal swayed, startled. Then his eyes narrowed. She saw lines about his mouth, and above his nose. She felt the temper snapping behind his sharp stare.

She refused to be cowed.

"I'm not one of your corpses, stripped to bone and waiting for examination. Stay out of my head."

"Avani. I haven't time to play games." He sounded very tired.

She remembered then that he was the king's hunter, and that he was Wilhaiim's justice. She felt his power gathering, and knew that he would take by force what he believed he needed, if she wouldn't give it up, if he thought he served Renault.

Everin and Kate had vanished around the edge of the maze. Avani moved her hand from her sack, and opened her fingers.

Mal looked down at the pearls, and at the square of satin. His expression didn't change. But his mind went black and angry, and in response she quivered.

"Where did you find those?" he asked quietly.

"On Andrew's table."

"You didn't tell me."

Avani looked away. "*Ai*, I meant to. I started to. But then . . . the key . . ." She shrugged, and wondered why she should feel guilt. "I forgot."

His mouth hardened. "I see. What did Everin want with them?"

"Just to look. He was curious." She hesitated, "By rights they are his."

"No," he spoke softly, but she could feel his rage pressing down in her skull, "by all rights, they belong to me. Stay out of it, Avani. Go back to your loom and leave the intrigue, real or imagined, to me."

The bitterness in his green eyes stunned her. For a heartbeat she sat still, unable to move. Then she surged to her feet, ready to fight.

But Mal was gone; she could hear his footsteps behind the hedges. His emotion gave her a headache.

"Goddess," she swore, and sank back into the grass. Jacob dropped from the tree and took the rotted fabric in his beak.

"Stop," Avani cursed again, in her mother's tongue.

She snatched the satin from Jacob, shoving it and the pearls into her sack. Then she lay flat on the hill and tried to press the pain from behind her nose.

It wasn't a dream, or a vision. Yet still she followed Mal, through tapestried corridors and drafty stone halls. Down, down into the depths of the palace, she rode in the back of his head.

His bootheels clicked as he launched himself along the ancient steps. His anger throbbed in the air.

On the landing before the king's dungeon, he paused, listening to the shrieks of the damned, some of whom owed their circumstances to his own tenacity. Then he strode on, clattering down the last curved stairway.

He carried a long dagger in his belt. The knife had been an anniversary gift from Siobahn so long ago, in celebration of one year's wedded bliss. The dagger was jeweled, more for decoration than use, but Mal wore it often at his belt, in remembrance.

Now, as he ran, he clutched the hilt in one hand, squeezing until his flesh ached. The pommel became slick against the heat of his palm, and the jewels bruised his flesh.

Along the final corridor the sconces had guttered out. Mal called a light and set it over his head. He passed his own laboratory, stopping before Andrew's door.

For a moment he felt real fear, and regret.

Then he pushed hesitation aside, and kicked the door open with the toe of his boot.

The locks were still jimmied open. The door swung wide.

Mal stepped over the threshold. He waited for the ceiling to light. The spell on the stones was very old and needed renewal. The clean-air cant was already beginning to unravel. He could smell mold and the tang of dried blood.

Andrew's coldroom was much as Mal remembered. The vocent had been a collector of the unusual, of objects beautiful and objects revolting. Boxes lay in piles on the shelves, and books sat in tilting stacks.

The old shaft in the ceiling, once used as a lift, was dark and silent. Mal stood under the gaping hole, but couldn't feel any shift in the air.

As he turned, examining the walls, forms flickered on the edges of his sight. Forgotten spirits watched Mal without expression, faces smooth, eyes burning blue. Mal ignored them.

The ghosts of victims who had spent their last uninterred hours on Andrew's table, they had made the room their home. A simple word of banishing might have sent them on their way, but Andrew had never bothered.

Mal was more scrupulous about his own workspace.

He set his palms on Andrew's table. The marble slab was empty, the surface clean. He saw no stains, no bones, no scraps of fabric or tarnished jewelry.

It had been clean when he had come many weeks earlier for Andrew's journal.

He might have dismissed Avani's tale as hysteria, if not for the bracelet she'd shown him.

He knew the bauble. He'd clasped the pearls around his wife's wrist on the day of their wedding, and she'd rarely been without it after. The bracelet had gone into the ground with her corpse. He knew, because he'd arranged her in the burial shroud himself.

Mal swore, bringing his fist down on Andrew's table. The ghosts in the room watched with gleaming eyes.

He cursed again, and then whirled, suddenly frenzied. Turning to the nearest set of shelves, he tore through the contents, searching blindly, tossing books and boxes aside. Volumes fell to the floor, pages tearing, spines cracking. Boxes split and opened, and bits of bone and parchment and feather and stone fell free.

He knocked over the stand that had once held Andrew's journal, and ran to the next set of shelves, sorting roughly through the dead vocent's collections. Still nothing. He ran his fingers over each of the basins. The sink was dry, the drains empty.

Nothing.

Mal shoved his fingers through his hair and howled. "Siobahn!"

His rage echoed from wall to wall, but there was no reply. The silent spirits flickered out, one by one, until Mal stood truly alone in the room. He shouted again, a wordless cry, and then struck out, attacking the last set of shelves with fist and boot.

The shelves were old. The wood sagged, then collapsed, raining boxes down on Mal's shoulders. He stood still and let the boxes fall around him, battering his flesh.

When the room was quiet and still again, he felt calmer. He knelt amongst the scattered boxes.

Mal recognized the leather containers. They were rare pieces of art, handcrafted by nomads on the westernmost coast. Renault had made a gift of the set to his most beloved vocent on Andrew's fortieth birthing-day. And so there were forty of the small boxes, a priceless collection, gathering dust.

Mal grabbed the nearest of the boxes, prying at the lid. The box was locked. The latch wouldn't budge under the force of his fingernail. He smashed it with the jeweled pommel of his dagger.

The box popped open, empty. He reached for the next, and found it locked. He smashed the latch. Again, empty. He moved on to the next.

Mal broke a score of the boxes before he found anything. The box was smaller than its brothers, the leather darker, soft with handling. When Mal smashed the lock, the box fell from his hand, falling upside down on the flagstones. Grains of fine dirt rolled from beneath the lid. Bits of ice sparkled amidst the kernels.

Mal jumped away from the small avalanche. When the slide of dirt had stopped, he stepped gingerly around the mess. Using the tip of his blade, he turned the box over.

The clay had been packed into brick form and dried. The fall of the box had dislodged the brick, and one corner had broken away, crumbling. The rest of the clay remained in form, an accusation, or a trap.

Mal stared at the thing for several long breaths. Then, careful not to touch any of the soil, he moved on to the next.

The next many boxes were empty. The thirty-seventh held a cache of true gold coin. Mal ignored tit. He split the next box, and tossed it away. His dagger wouldn't crack the thirty-ninth. He broke the box by pounding it repeatedly on the edge of Andrew's table.

The box ripped and broke apart. A ring fell from the velvet-lined depths. It rolled across the floor until it fetched up beneath the sink. Mal didn't notice. He saw only the ruins of the box in his hand, empty, and tossed it away.

In the garden, in the cold grass, Avani turned restlessly but didn't rouse.

Mal cracked the final box. Empty. He dropped it, and rubbed his temples. Then he straightened, knees cramping, and regarded the broken clay brick with revulsion.

He didn't dare touch the stuff. He'd learned in the keep that gloves provided little protection, but he couldn't leave the crumbled soil lying about. Spelled or otherwise, he knew it was dangerous.

Without Siobahn he felt crippled, half a man, groping through a haze.

Crossing the room, he dug one of Andrew's leather aprons from its place on a peg beneath the table. He grabbed a basin by one metal lip, then carried both basin and apron to the mess of boxes.

Crouching, Mal folded the apron twice. He dropped the creased leather over the brick.

He waited. Nothing happened.

Mal set the basin on its side. Holding his breath, he used the blade of his knife to push the apron and its contents across the floor and into the basin.

The clay brick lost several more grains and a few pieces of frost over the rough stone floor, but remained mostly intact. Mal turned the basin upright. The brick fell to the bottom with a heavy clunk.

He'd have to leave the scattering of dirt on the floor. He didn't dare touch it, not even with the sole of his boot.

He would have to find away to lock the door again.

Mal lifted the basin gingerly. Beneath Andrew's sink the yellow ring winked.

Avani fretted. She could see the facets in the gem clearly. She knew he mustn't leave the coldroom without the ring. She wanted to shout at him. She did shout at him, but he wouldn't hear.

Mal started from the room, basin balanced on one hand. He closed the door and spoke a locking cant, securing it.

Avani dropped through his skull and touched his center.

Mal stiffened, and shut his eyes in protest. Avani had a

moment to feel the gaps in his mind, the weakened walls, the disjointed edges of his power. When he opened his eyes again, she was Mal, bruised and weary.

Her power bolstered his, filled the gaps, rebuilt the walls, smoothed the edges. She fed him her strength, and the world brightened again. For a heartbeat, they rejoiced.

Then Mal stiffened further, remembering fear. He tried to cast her out, and failed. She clung, wrapping tendrils about his center.

Raging now, he struck at her again. This time he used the very energy she'd lent him, this time he routed her.

He flung her from his skull. His rage chased her back through the halls of the palace, across the sky, and into her body. He slammed her back into place and, as easily as if it didn't matter, broke their connection.

She sat up with a groan. For a moment she floundered, hurt and afraid. She poked with a finger of flame at the spot in her skull where his thread had been, and found the absence tender.

"Goddess take you, Mal." But she knew he didn't hear her.

AVANI CARRIED HER sack with her down into Andrew's room. She knew the way without hesitation, now. She didn't stop on the landing before the dungeon, but trudged on.

She knew she should be in bed, safely asleep, the hearth warming her toes. She also knew she couldn't leave the yellow ring to gather dust beneath Andrew's sink.

Mal had locked the door with a simple cant. Avani had seen the structure of the spell in his head, as he spoke it. She'd witnessed the pattern of it.

She unspoke the cant, her instincts good, her confidence growing. The latch quivered. The door swung free.

She waited for the ceiling to glow. Mal had torn the room apart. Dust and mold floated in the air. She saw no sign of the spirits.

Avani stepped carefully around the pile of broken leather boxes. She could see the glitter of clay and frost on the floor around the torn leather.

She could smell the trap in the air, as she hadn't before. She could smell the deep earth, and the threat of shadows.

She almost ran from the room. She had to force her feet along the floor, boots scuffing sullenly. She sank onto her hands and knees in front of the sink, peering into the darkness.

Her sack shifted on her shoulder and fell against her arm, knocking her ribs.

The yellow ring lay as she had seen it, gleaming, tiny motes of dust floating in the air around it.

Avani exhaled. The dust puffed into a miniature whirlwind. She groped under the sink and grabbed the ring. Metal and stone felt cold against her fingers. She crawled out from beneath the sink.

Avani sat on her knees, studying the thing. It looked exactly like the band Mal wore on his left hand: square gem in a true gold setting. It might have fit Avani's hand. She thought Andrew must have had slender fingers.

But Mal had said a vocent's ring went to his king after

death, to await the next initiate. Avani was certain that the yellow ring didn't belong in a leather box in an unused coldroom.

She shoved the ring in her sack to keep company with the pearl-and-silver bracelet that had been Siobahn's wedding trinket, walked carefully back around soil and leather, and left the room.

Chapter Eighteen

MAL LIVED IN a fog, listless, alone with the echoes in his skull.

Siobahn's loss pained him; the tear in his center where she should have been bled bitterness, wounding his core and weakening resolve. Siobahn had been his companion for most of his adult life, lover and then friend. She'd been half of him since he'd spoken his vows as vocent, except for the brief period of horror after her death, and then he'd been lost to sanity, little more than a mindless animal.

He wondered if he were close to madness once again. He spent almost all of his waking hours seeking Siobahn, and most of his nights dreaming of Avani's face.

He clung to his office, repeated over and over again his oath to the king, and sought his work as a distraction.

But he found himself pacing around Siobahn's grave when he should have been searching through Andrew's journal. A body waited on his table, a woman who perhaps had been murdered by her sister, but Mal couldn't face that duty.

Sometimes, when he sat at his desk, he thought he caught a glimpse of the small bronze key beneath a sheaf of parchment. He would scatter the pages across his desk, finding nothing.

The talisman was gone, vanished with Siobahn.

On the shortest night of winter, he gathered his courage and went to the graveyard with a trowel. He dug down into his wife's grave until the towel scraped against cloth.

Scrabbling in the mud, he hauled the burial sack from the ground, and ripped it open with the edge of his trowel. The sack was empty. Her bones were gone.

Then, some of his grief dulled and turned to ice. He went back to Andrew's journal, examining page after page. He forgot to eat, refused to sleep. Only the parchment and Andrew's slanted scribing held his interest.

He didn't see another living soul for two days. On the fourth day Jacob appeared in his suite. Mal didn't have the energy to chase the raven out.

On the fifth day, as Mal read yet again Andrew's description of the River Mors, the king came in search of his vocent.

Renault didn't bother to knock. He burst through Mal's door, strode across the floor, and set his fists on Mal's desk.

"Malachi," the king said. "Are you poisoned again? Do I need to call my priests?"

One end of his stylus pressed against his mouth, Mal blinked. He shook his head.

"Are you obsessed, then?" Renault demanded. "I understand there are now *two* corpses moldering in your laboratory."

Mal grunted at the implication. "The room keeps them from rot. You know that."

"Aye, and does the room also seek out the manner of their deaths? I have families waiting for justice, Lord Vocent. I can't summon their spirits or sort through their innards myself."

"I haven't forgotten. I'll tend to them in the morn."

Mal glanced down at Andrew's hand. He squinted, his attention caught by a word.

Renault reached over the desk, snatching the journal from beneath Mal's finger. Mal jerked, and reached for sarcasm, but the bite in Renault's eyes stopped him.

"Malachi. Attend me. Deep spring is coming. The kingdom's blood is beginning to thaw. With spring comes violence, and plague, and madness, you know so. You are the only vocent I have. Will you neglect your duties?"

"No."

"You are still young, brother. I understand this. But you cannot allow your attention to wander. Andrew—"

" —is dead," said Mal, "his murderer still loose."

"Even so." Renault plucked at his beard. "You cannot let the one case consume you. We both loved him. But your page tells me you haven't eaten more than bread and fruit in days, and that you bathe less than he would like."

Mal growled. "The boy is—"

" —correct," the king interrupted, wry. "You are far from yourself, Malachi. Is it the talisman that preys on your senses? Tell me, what have you learned?"

"Nothing. The key is gone."

Renault stilled. "Aye?"

Mal sighed. He rolled the end of his stylus between his fingers. "The thing was stolen, many nights ago."

"A thief? In my palace?" The king's suspicions grew to anger. "I hadn't heard of this."

"No one knows but I," Mal replied. "There was no thief. My wife took the bloody thing, Your Majesty, and vanished with it."

"Siobahn?" Renault's mouth went hard. "I don't understand."

"Neither do I."

Mal sprang from his chair, muscles knotted. He paced to the windows. Jacob, crouched on the sill, clacked his beak in warning.

"Tell me," demanded Renault.

"Twelve nights ago, Siobahn took the talisman and disappeared. I cannot touch her, I cannot summon her. I search for her endlessly, but she is gone. Gone." He clenched his fingers, pressed his fist against one pane.

"I will not believe this. Siobahn has loved you even from beyond the grave. She would not leave you willingly. Mayhap the thing was enscrolled, mayhap it stole her away."

"Mayhap," Mal allowed. "But there is more."

"Tell me," the king repeated. He walked around Mal's desk, dropping into the leather chair.

Jacob left the windowsill and perched above the king's head. Renault ignored the raven stoically.

"Avani found the talisman in Andrew's laboratory. She also found bones, laid out on Andrew's table. A woman's skeleton."

"You said nothing of bones."

Mal opened his fingers. He spread his palm against the glass. "I didn't know. She didn't say until it was far too late. The bones belonged to Siobahn, Renault. It was my wife's skeleton Avani found on that table."

"You're certain?"

Mal nodded. Renault waited, silent.

"I dug up her grave, to be sure." Mal turned from the windows. He looked straight at his king. "Her corpse was gone, and yet the grave itself apparently undisturbed."

"What does it mean?"

"She moved the bones herself. Sometimes, a spirit will do so. If its grave is flooded, or vandalized, or the bones stolen by another."

"But what reason would Siobahn have?"

"None," said Mal. "None that I can find. And I never had an inkling. I never guessed she could vanish so completely, that she had the strength of will. She's been keeping secrets from me, Renault."

"Avani believed so."

Mal's chest tightened. "Did she?"

"Aye." Renault regarded his vocent with sympathy. "She spoke to Kate of her suspicions."

Mal shrugged that off with a wave of one hand. "She has an islander's superstition."

Wisely, Renault left Mal's bitterness alone. The king rose to his feet.

"Renault," Mal asked. "What were those men doing on the Downs?"

"The Kingsmen? Chasing trouble."

"You'd heard word of trouble in Stonehill, then?"

"In Stonehill, nay. The three were part of a small troop Andrew ordered to the scarlet woods, in search of a chronic poacher."

"They had no reason to be up on the Downs, then."

"Unless the poacher made his home on the mountain? Nay."

Mal shook his head.

"You're doing your best, brother."

"Andrew would have had the first murder solved before Stonehill burned."

"Perhaps not," returned the king. "Step back, step away, attend to your other duties. Things have a way of resolving, in time. Siobahn loves you. She too will return, in time."

"If she can."

Renault sobered. "If she can. If she can't, you will find her."

Mal followed the king into the hall. Renault turned at the door.

"Lord Vocent? The lady corpse sleeping on your table was a very good friend to my mother. See that she is attended to. Immediately, if you will."

Mal bowed his head beneath the reprimand. Renault set a gentle hand on his shoulder, and squeezed. When Mal looked up again, the corridor stood empty.

He shut the door and went back to Andrew's journal.

MAL WAS LURKING in his coldroom, working on a bloated corpse, when Avani found him the next evening.

She'd spent most of the day searching for him, and had saved the coldroom for last.

He'd left the door propped open, perhaps to allow some of the chill to dissipate. Avani took this as an invitation. He barely glanced up when she stepped into the room.

"Do you ever weary," she asked, "of inhaling unwashed body and grease?"

He didn't look up from his work. "Unwelcome visitors weary me. The heightened senses came to me as a boy, when my power bloomed. I've grown used to the tangle of scents."

"Once I believed my sensitive nose was because of Jacob. But now I'm to believe it's just me, *ai*?"

"It is," he said, "just you. Part of your legacy, as a magus. Learn to deal with it. Or wear a string of garlic around your neck. That will block even the strongest of nature's scents."

Avani crossed to his side. The corpse on the table belonged to a man. The skull was smashed, jaw hanging from a few threads of muscle. He wore a laborer's uniform of dirty wool.

"Who is he?"

"A minor blacksmith. Killed for the coins he kept in a chest behind his forge."

"You know that from his body?"

"I know that from his shade," replied Mal. He tilted his chin slightly to the left.

The spirit was there, a round man, pleasant face intact,

eyes blue flame. He watched with distant interest as Mal dissected his body.

"You see him?" Mal asked.

"Did you summon him?"

"No. His spirit is strong in its desire for revenge."

Avani eyed the shade. "Do you know who killed him?"

Mal brought the tip of his knife along the corpse's jaw, severing muscle. The jawbone dropped from the dead man's skull, shedding bits of flesh.

"He told me. He was quite emphatic."

"Then why are you still butchering his body?"

"It's my job," Mal said. "I cannot make a ruling on a dead man's word alone."

"He's quiet, now," Avani said, watching the spirit.

"Likely you frighten him."

Avani heard the man's sarcasm and decided to ignore it. Stretching up on her toes, she grabbed his wrist, stilling the knife.

"You have no reason to blame me, Malachi."

"Don't I?" One brow arched, and his eyes burned green, nearly as brilliant as the spirit's.

"This"—she tapped the tip of one finger to her temple—"is as much your fault as it is mine."

He shook his head. He drew back, but not before she glimpsed the bittersweet twist of his lips. She edged closer as he retreated, peering up into his face. She could smell the leather of the apron he wore.

"Something's happened," she realized. "Something else. You're not angry, you're grieving. What is it?"

Her brown fingers looked pale against his black sleeve.

He stilled as though pinned by the weight of her hand. His eyes shimmered, and she could feel his resolve crumbling. Another moment, and he would drop the barrier he'd put up, let her see again into his center. She could scent him, taste him. And beneath the musky layer, his pounding grief.

He opened his mouth to speak, and was interrupted by a scuffle in the hall.

Avani felt his walls slam back into place. She staggered under the force of his refusal. She put a hand on the vocent's table to steady herself, and felt the brush of dead flesh against her wrist.

The touch of the corpse shocked her back to calm. Her head cleared. Her hand rested on the table against the severed jawbone. She pulled it away, wincing in disgust.

The blacksmith's shade had disappeared. Mal moved away from his table, and stood looking at the door.

A guard waited there, one of the king's own, liveried in red and black. Avani recognized the man and remembered his name: Jack. The jocular guard was one of Kate's favorites.

The man's face was free of all its usual mirth, his lips set, his cheeks ashen. He looked only at Mal, and his hand trembled on the pommel of his sword as he spoke.

"My lord. His Majesty needs you. There's been another murder."

Eyes on the guard, Mal began to strip off his apron. "Where?"

Jack's hand trembled further, but the man's voice was steady as he replied. "In the gardens, my lord. The herb plots."

Avani's head spun. She sank back against the table, clutching the battered edges for support. She was aware of Mal, as the man's breathing slowed to a near stop. She could feel the chill in his heart as if it were her own.

Perhaps it was her own, the terrible fear that brought tears to her eyes.

"Thank you," Mal said, dismissing the guard. The vocent walked calmly to his sink and began washing his hands under the spigot.

As she leaned against the table, Avani searched Mal's face. She saw no sign of the warm man she'd come to know. His expression was cold, withdrawn. Here was what it meant to be a vocent, she realized, as he dried his hands and set the black cloak about his shoulders.

This man cared only for duty, and for the hunt. He seemed no more alive than the corpse on his table. His face had gone smooth, shuttered. His eyes were shards of green ice.

"Come," he said, a command, and Avani's feet walked her across the room to his side.

He took her by the hand, his grip firm and impersonal, and led her from the room. He locked the door of his cold-room with the two bronze keys he kept on his belt, and then marched Avani at a steady pace down the hall.

"Shouldn't we . . . hurry?"

"Since Renault has sent for me, I imagine it is too late for hurry."

"*Ai.*" Avani swallowed. She felt grief rising through her shock. "Is it Kate?"

"Yes," Mal replied.

A SILVER SPRING moon bathed the Royal Gardens. Night-blooming flowers perfumed the air. Mal walked the paths without speaking, Avani at his bootheels.

Mal had stopped in his rooms to retrieve his sword and one of his rainbow lanterns. He carried the lantern in his right hand, unlit. The left rested on his sword. Avani wondered if he expected trouble.

They came together around a wide hedge and into the herb plots. Torches burned high over the rows of plants; guards lighting the night for their king. Avani counted ten Kingsmen and three robed priests.

Mal pushed through the crowd. Avani followed after, forgotten.

The king's mistress had been gathering herbs. Her basket lay on its side on the grass, leaves and stems scattered around its broken handle. The large silver fork Kate used to tend the plants was stuck tines down in the soil beneath a growth of rosemary.

There was blood on the fork, and blood on the rosemary.

The king sat on the grass, not far from the overturned basket. He, too, wore blood. It had dried on his tunic, and on his mantle, and a long smear ran across his brow. The torchlight bleached his face of color. He cradled Kate in his arms.

Mal walked through the grass. He crouched at Renault's side. Avani couldn't bring herself to follow. She stood rooted in place, beside an expressionless Kingsman, watching as Mal tried to comfort his king.

She waited on the hill, listening to the silence of the

gardens and the shuffle of frightened men, and she tried to pretend she had a vocent's control. Tried to pretend the wet on her cheeks wasn't the damp of tears. Tried to pretend the torn thing on Renault's lap wasn't Kate.

When Mal moved again, to light his rainbow lamp and examine the body, Avani looked away. She wrenched her gaze to the sky, to the brilliant moon.

"She's been dead for several hours," she heard the vocent say, very softly, to the king. And then she couldn't look even at the moon, and she shut her eyes.

She could smell the herbs, and the waking grass beneath her feet, and the iron tang of blood, and the reek of exposed organ. She could taste nothing of shadows, or of soil, or of danger.

She took a moment to search out Jacob, and found him perched in Mal's suite, watching over Liam as the lad snored on the floor.

Avani heard Mal murmur to the king. She opened her eyes. The Kingsman on her left had disappeared, and instead Peter stood there in the grass, his face ravaged..

"I missed her all evening," he said. "I couldn't find her anywhere. This was the last place I looked. It should have been the first."

Avani peered into his face, heartsick. "You found her?"

"Aye," he answered, turning to watch Mal examine the body. "I found her."

Avani followed Peter's gaze. Renault still cradled Kate's head in his lap. Her face was serene, untouched, marked only by spots of blood across her chin.

From the neck down, the king's mistress was unrecognizable, flayed to the bone, blood and sinew and dirt mixing over the herbs.

"Renault won't let her go," Peter said.

Avani glanced at the king's face, and saw that the little man spoke the truth. "He must have loved her very much."

Peter pulled his gaze from his sister's corpse. He looked into the sky, finding refuge in the moon as Avani had.

"She wasn't theist," he said absently. "And she wouldn't convert. The king's wife must share his faith. For years he begged her to consider, but Katherine was very stubborn. And then they seemed to reach a peace." He sighed, and brushed at last at his tears. "She wasn't Renault's queen, but the court loved her all the same."

Grief lodged in Avani's chest. She wrapped her arms about her ribs. She looked back across the plot at Mal. The vocent's hands were smeared with Kate's blood; she couldn't see his gloves beneath the gore.

He lifted Kate's foot, and a fragment of white bone came away in his grasp.

Avani spun away. The back of her throat burned, she couldn't swallow her tears. She stumbled a few steps away, but Peter stopped her.

"What's he doing?" he demanded roughly.

Gulping back bile, Avani stared. Mal had paused in his examination, the fragment of bone clutched between his fingers. As Avani watched, his mouth fell open and his body tensed.

Renault spoke, but Mal didn't respond. He went rigid, and his teeth began to click.

"A vision!" She grabbed Peter's hand, trying to push through bodies. "The man's having a vision!"

She saw Mal's eyes roll up into his head. She tried to reach him, but the Kingsmen, apparently frightened by the sight of their vocent helpless in the throws of a fit, pressed close around the king and the corpse and Mal, closing Avani out.

Frustrated, she pounded on the back of a towering guard, but the Kingsman ignored her.

Peter took her elbow.

"Come away," he urged, raw.

"But —"

"The priests will help him. There's no getting through now. Come back to the palace."

Avani shook her head, but he pulled her away, and led her protesting from the gardens. She cursed him all the way, but he kept silent, his hand firm.

When they reached the palace, he bowed stiffly.

"Go and sleep," he said. "No doubt you'll be sent for soon enough."

Avani doubted it. "Where are you going?"

"To the temple," he replied. "To mourn as I know how."

"Let me come with you."

He looked as if he wanted to argue, but then he sighed.

"If only because I fear, otherwise, you'd trot on back to Mal's side. And," he said sadly, "because you are a font of strength, island witch, and tonight your temper is an easement."

She would have laughed at him if her heart wasn't broken. She took his arm, and walked with him to his temple.

Mal found her there, near dawn. She knelt still at Peter's side, on the hard floor beneath the temple altar. She almost jumped when the vocent touched her.

Peter didn't stir. The man's eyes were shut, and his mouth moved in silent prayer.

Mal helped Avani to her feet, and then lent support as she wobbled on stiffened muscles from the temple. When they stood in fresh air, he released her elbow, and immediately she missed the warmth of his fingers.

"I'm riding out," he said, "as soon I'm packed."

"Where?"

Avani saw he didn't want to give her answer. Chewing at the inside of her mouth, she bent over and rubbed frozen kneecaps.

"To Stonehill," he said, just as she was about to give up on patience and shake the answer from him.

She stilled, hands on her thighs, and peered up through the drape of her hair. "Stonehill?"

He nodded, once. "I saw it. The tavern, burnt to a shell, bones spread on the charred floor. And in the middle of it all, stuck in a broken floorboard, your little key."

"My key."

He turned, eyes shining. "Siobahn stole it from me, Avani. She took it and vanished, and I think I will find her on the Downs."

At last she understood his rage, and his grief, and his desperation. "The *bhut* deserted you?"

Mal winced. "Avani."

"*Ai*, I'm sorry." She reached to soothe, but he sidestepped away.

"I'm going to Stonehill. Because that's where I believe

Kate's murderer has gone. Because the key is there. And because I need to find Siobahn."

Avani licked her lips, thinking. The man was tightly drawn, she could feel it. She didn't want to misstep and prick his anger further.

"You might have told me you had visions. Instead of scoffing at my own."

"I never scoffed," he said, mouth hard. "And until today, I didn't know visions."

"Your first?" she asked. She wanted to laugh, but couldn't find the humor.

"I thought at first it was the beginning of another trap," he admitted. "But there was nothing of danger remaining about her corpse."

"The Goddess spoke to you," Avani decided. "Congratulations."

Mal shot her a scowl. "The Goddess is your creation, Avani, not mine. Things have been . . . odd . . . since Siobahn left me."

"What things?"

He shrugged, and began to pace restlessly along the temple steps. "I see things I hadn't noticed before. And yet other senses I took for granted are gone. I can't touch them."

"Perhaps you're adjusting to the ghostie's absence. I would rejoice," she said, bland, "if you didn't look so helpless."

He snarled, and whirled, cloak flaring about his heels. Avani waited for him to shake her, but he wouldn't. He

clasped his hands behind his back, and cocked a disdain-
ful brow.

"I don't have time to spend arguing. I came only to tell
you I am riding out. Renault will make sure you're looked
after. You'll be safe until I return."

Her temper smarted. "You're not my keeper, my lord.
I've no need of looking after. I've learned how to use a
sword, and even I know better than to lock muscles at vision's onset. Still stings in the ankles, *ai*?"

Mal snarled again. He started down the ramp, away
from the temple. Avani almost let him go. Then she swore,
and ran after.

"My lord!"

He stopped, but didn't look around.

She slid to a halt at his side, and stood on tiptoes to
meet his stare. "Take care, my lord. Listen to your heart.
Stay away from shadows, and don't touch anything that
smells of the deep earth. And bears, stay away from bears.
Don't get yourself poisoned again. *Ai*." She sighed and
rubbed her chin. "*You* need the keeper."

He snorted, but his expression didn't soften. "Avani, if
you come after, I'll spell you to the nearest tree and leave
you. You're needed here, whether you see it or not. Promise me you'll do as I asked."

She cocked a brow, mirroring his own.

"Promise me," he insisted.

She pursed her lips, then nodded reluctantly. His
mouth curled, not quite a smile, and he touched a strand
of her hair with the tip of his finger.

"I'll be back before the trees decide to bloom."

"If you're not," she threatened, "then I will come after."

Mal's almost-smile vanished. He touched her hair one last time. Then he stepped onto the cobbled street and walked away into the dawn, leaving her behind.

Chapter Nineteen

MAL BORROWED A horse from Renault's stables.

The animal was spare of flesh, and quick, but not as steady as his lost Bran. The stallion started at every rustling leaf, and Mal had a rough ride out of Wilhaiim.

The battle of wills, man and equine, suited his temper. For most of the day he concentrated only on the simple pleasure of teaching the horse manners. By the time evening fell, the stallion was weary and lathered, but far more accommodating, and some of Mal's temper had eased.

He made his first camp under the canopy of the red forest. He fed and watered the horse, then ate his own dinner on new grass in front of a merry cook fire. Supper was dry hardtack and sausage. He drank sweet wine from a leather skin, and wished for Avani's spiced cider.

The stars came up, glimmering fitfully through branches. Mal rolled himself in his cloak. He lay down alongside the fire, and watched the heavens, chasing sleep.

He rose with the sun, and struggled with the stubborn horse through most of the morning. He stopped at midday on the bank of a winding creek, washed his face and hands, and dumped cold water down the back of his neck.

The stallion took advantage of the break, and began to graze, cropping up tender green shoots that poked through the forest floor. Mal sat on the bank of the creek, and let the animal eat.

The vision he'd seen over Kate's corpse lingered. At idle moments, if he turned his head too quickly or glanced too hastily from beneath his lashes, he would see the burnt floor of the Widow's tavern beneath his feet. He'd smell the blood and the smoke as he remembered it. In his mind's eye he saw blackened bones.

Avani was right. Mal had never known a vision, had never been schooled in how to handle their strength. He knew spirits and shades, he knew how to speak the language of the dead. He knew how to uncoil his power and send it forth to light a lamp or stop a man's heart.

But the vision had stunned him, left him sick and dizzy, and still it wouldn't let him be.

Without Siobahn to guide him, he felt useless as a lad, and unsure of the world about him.

The horse pulled a mouthful of grass from beneath Mal's boot, startling him from his thoughts. He saw the smoke-stained walls of Stonehill's tavern. Then he blinked, and shook his head, and the image disappeared, leaving only red trees.

He pulled the stallion from his breakfast and climbed

back into the saddle, and for the rest of the day he concentrated on keeping his head clear and the horse calm.

BY THE END of his second day in the saddle, Mal had decided he was being followed.

He could sense no danger in the air, no stink of the earth and rot he'd come to associate with murder.

His first thought was Avani. He would not have been at all surprised if the stubborn woman had broken her promise and come after.

Both his heart and his temper leapt at the possibility. He wanted her by his side, he wanted her gone from his life. He wanted to hold her, he wanted to shake her, he wanted her to fill the cracks that had opened in his center.

He blamed her for Siobahn's defection, though he knew better.

He rose after dark. Then he warmed a double portion of rations over his campfire, expecting Avani. When the stars rose and the woman still hadn't appeared, Mal began to grow uneasy.

He ate the double ration himself. Then he shut his eyes and sent tentacles of power spiraling through the woods.

Spirits gathered around the fire, drawn by his questing: an old woman who had gone to sleep in the red forest and never woken. A woodcutter, mortally gashed by his own axe. Three poachers, two men and a woman, each killed by a Kingsmen over a span of decades.

Mal banished the spirits with a murmured cant and

continued his search. He sensed nothing human in all of
the wood but himself.

He didn't know whether to be alarmed or relieved. He
wondered if she'd sent Jacob after him. He left a bit of
hardtack on the grass, hoping to lure the raven in, and
went to sleep with his hand on his sword.

When he woke, the hardtack remained, untouched.

Mal drank more sweet wine from the skin, then broke
camp. As soon as he was under way he felt it again: a presence shadowing, following. Once or twice he thought it
was close by, thought he could hear leaves crackle under
solid weight, but when he looked back or sent a questing
tendril, he found nothing.

More than a little unnerved, Mal gave the horse his
head. The trees flashed past. He ran the stallion as long as
the horse could stand, walked him cool, and then ran the
animal again.

The next few days passed without incident. Mal nearly
rode his horse into the ground. His own flesh showed the
bruises of hard riding. He dreamed at night of Siobahn,
and of Renault's stricken face over Kate's corpse.

During the day he thought only of the passing landscape.

He thought he'd lost his shadow.

Winter still held the Downs. He could see snow on
their peaks, and the Mors remained sluggish. But high
green grass grew along the river, and the sky was a warm
blue overhead.

Mal rode the horse to the gates of the keep and tethered it to a clump of weeds. He remembered leaving Bran

in the same spot. He gave his new companion a smart pat on the flank for good luck.

The portcullis was open, as he knew it would be. The snow in the bailey had melted.

Mal crossed the courtyard slowly, sword drawn. He inhaled, testing the air, and found it clean.

The temple roof sagged; the old building had barely survived winter. Mal edged through the cracked door. Molding straw littered the ground. Melting snow ran from a hole in the ceiling, over the altar, and into a puddle under the straw.

The candles in their votives had long since snuffed out.

Mal left the temple. He knew, as surely as if Siobahn had spoken, that the keep was free of any trap. Still, his heart pounded uncomfortably as he slipped into the tower.

Lord Blackwater rotted in the warmth of the changing seasons. Mal took shallow breaths, refusing to remember the dried gore on his hands.

Even with the door open to sunlight, the room remained dim. Mal started to speak, intending to ask Siobahn for light. He stopped, swallowed back grief, and spoke the cant himself. The ceiling bloomed. Mal stood beneath the glowing mage-light and looked around.

He'd been the last living creature in the tower. His footprints still marked the bloodstained earth. He recalled the dance of his feet as he'd fought off the grip of the spell.

Mal walked around the table to the pantry, leaving fresh prints alongside the aged ones.

The ham he'd dropped lay rotting in the dirt. A hand-span away, he found the scattered pile of clay.

The brick was no longer frozen. It had shattered when he'd dropped it, and now lay in loose piles in the pantry's shadow. Tiny green stems grew from the dark earth. Mal squatted. He touched a seedling with his thumb.

Nothing happened.

He stood, and was about to search through the rest of the pantry when the tower door scraped. Mal whirled, sword in hand.

He looked down into frightened gray eyes.

"Blood of the saints!" he swore. "Liam! Blessed Aug, I nearly severed your head from your neck!"

The boy trembled, then seemed to muster courage. Looking carefully away from the dead man on the hearth, he set his jaw.

"You left me, my lord." Liam sounded vastly insulted. "I'm your squire."

"Not yet, boyo." Growling, Mal sheathed his sword. "You're my page, and pages stay behind, especially when I've told them to. At least three times. Have you no sense?"

"I belong with you, my lord," Liam replied stubbornly, standing his ground, eyes wide.

Mal sighed. He looked the lad over. Liam had dressed wisely, in heavy tunic and trousers. His boots were coated with mud. The journey pack across his back was worn but well patched.

"I see you've given up my cloak."

Liam flushed. "I didn't want to draw attention, my lord."

"Canny of you." He noted the knife on the boy's belt. "And wise enough to know you can't yet handle the sword I gifted you."

Liam's mouth tightened, but he held to his dignity. "I brought it along, my lord, just in case. For luck, like. It's tied to my saddle."

"Your saddle?" Mal let his brows rise. "You've a horse?"

"Yes, my lord." Liam brightened. "A fine one. Come and see."

Mal followed the boy from the tower. Liam's horse stood calmly in the shelter of the bailey; a sturdy pony loaded with a second journey pack. Mal's own horse waited next to the pony, ears flicking.

"You've a horse," Mal repeated in disbelief.

"Everin helped me borrow him."

"Did he, then?"

"From His Majesty's stables," Liam said, unconcerned. "Everin said nobody would miss him. His name is Fox, and he belongs to a lad who's fostered out. Everin said Fox was lonely, and ready for an adventure."

Mal caught himself gaping. He snapped his jaw shut, and glowered down at the boy. "Avani will have my hide."

For the first time, Liam looked truly uneasy. "Avani doesn't know."

"She'll find out," promised Mal. "And if I dare show my face again in Wilhaiim, she'll skin me alive." Yet the image of Avani in a full rage somehow lightened Mal's heavy heart.

Liam stared up into Mal's face, obviously confused by his smile. "Will you send me back, my lord?"

Mal narrowed his eyes, regarding the boy. "You followed me all this way, did you?"

Liam dimpled. "I nearly caught you the once, my lord.

But then you let your horse run. He's faster than Fox. What's his name?"

"He hasn't earned one. Would you go back if I asked it of you?"

Liam hesitated. Then he shook his head.

"I thought not. Bloody hells." Mal rubbed a hand over his face, then gave in. "No, I won't send you back. Help me make camp, there's a lad. We'll stay in the bailey tonight."

Liam blinked. Then he whooped, and ran to unsaddle the pony. The lad's enthusiasm spooked Mal's horse. The stallion kicked out, tether broken, and danced along the courtyard on his toes.

Mal groaned, and went to collect his mount.

AVANI HADN'T MEANT to break her promise.

She'd planned to stay hidden away in the palace, keep busy with her loom and her dyes. She'd convinced herself not to worry. Although she wouldn't admit it to the man himself, she trusted Mal's good sense.

She'd almost decided Mal could easily handle whatever waited on the Downs.

Then she learned from Peter that Wilhaiim's king didn't know his vocent had left the city. She began to fret, just a little. The palace felt deserted. The court was quiet, mourning. Avani's own grief was a sour ball in her gut.

Lonely, she took Jacob with her to the yard in search of Liam. There she learned from the other lads that the boy had disappeared two days earlier.

She knew, then. Even so, she ran all the way to Mal's suite, and burst through the door.

The rooms were cold, dark, and empty. Liam had left his pallet rolled on the floor. His treasured black cloak lay in a neat bundle alongside.

She couldn't find his sword, or his knife, or the new boots Kate had purchased for him at the Fair.

Avani kicked the pallet once, savagely. Then she stomped across the room to Mal's desk. Collapsing into his chair, she set her elbows on her thighs and her chin in her hands, and glared out the windows.

Jacob left her shoulder for Mal's bed.

Avani sat motionless until long after dark, until Everin disturbed her quiet fear.

"When the lads said you'd come asking after Liam, I knew I'd find you here," he said from the door. "Aren't you cold?"

"He stole my boy away," she replied, savagely. "And didn't say a word to me about it."

Everin bent before Mal's hearth, fumbling for matchsticks. When he came up empty-handed, he set his back to the cold embers with a sigh.

"Liam went on his own, black eyes. He wouldn't be left behind. The boy has more courage than sense."

"*Ai.* I have the sense, so I'm left behind. Or I'm the coward."

"Mayhap." Everin scratched at his beard. "I can't think you'd want to see the place again."

"Neither would Liam."

"He loves the vocent."

Avani put her fists to her eyes, knuckling. "He'll never catch my lord. He'll get lost and starve, or fall into a ravine, or freeze."

"I found him a sturdy horse. He'll do."

"You found him a sturdy horse?" repeated Avani. She dropped her hands in disbelief. "*You* found him a sturdy horse?"

"Aye." Everin grinned. "I couldn't let him go off alone on foot."

"You knew!" Avani jumped up. "You knew, and you let him go!"

"I couldn't stop him."

"And you didn't tell me?" Avani stalked the big man, hands balled into fists.

"I'm telling you now, aye? The lads said you'd been looking for Liam, so I came right after, to find you." He dodged when Avani lunged, holding up his palms. "Don't smack me, black eyes. I'm here to help."

She paused, breathing hard. "Help?"

"I've two horses readied, and two sacks packed. Change your clothes, and we'll go."

"I'll go on my own." Avani crossed her arms, glaring.

Everin shook his head. "They've got a three-day start on you, lass. You'll never catch them now, not by the king's road. I know another way."

She wanted to hit him. "Another way?"

"Straight through. We'll catch them easily, if we hurry. Go and change your clothes. Something warm. We'll ride when you're ready."

"It's night out."

"So it is." Everin's teeth flashed. "Go and dress."

"I promised my lord I wouldn't chase after." She hated to admit that last hesitation.

Everin didn't blink. "You're chasing after the boy, Malachi. Now, hurry."

AVANI EXPECTED TO travel east, away from Wilhaiim. Instead, Everin led them south along the western edge of the city. They passed the westernmost gates of the city just as the moon rose in the sky. Past Wilhaiim, the King's Highway ran through sand dunes away toward the sea.

Everin rode in silence. Avani managed her mare with more ease than she'd expected, but Jacob complained from her shoulder whenever the animal jolted over broken cobblestones. Even so, he didn't leave his perch for the night sky.

Everin set his horse to a gentle pace. Avani quickly realized the man was in no great hurry. Just as the moon began its gentle descent, the highway narrowed. They climbed a low sand dune and down again into a small village.

"Whitcomb," Everin said as they rode off the highway onto village streets. "They grow the king's grapes on the hills behind the town. Whitcomb prospers on the court's thirst."

The homes along the streets were clapboard and brick, roofs sharply peaked. Torches burned alongside every door, smoking and sparking in the air.

"Why are we here?" Avani asked. She craned her neck.

The streets appeared deserted. She supposed the villagers lay asleep in their beds.

Smothering a yawn, she thought wistfully of her own linen sheets.

Everin didn't speak. Avani sighed, but didn't press.

They turned down a side street, walking their horses past more homes. The alley dead-ended in front of a fishmonger's shop.

Everin slid from his mount and tied his horse to a waiting post.

"Are you coming?"

Avani growled. She dropped from her saddle, dislodging Jacob in the process. The raven grumbled, and shot into the night.

"Where's he going?" Everin asked, as he tied Avani's horse beside his own.

"That one goes where he pleases. What are we doing here?"

Everin jerked a thumb at a house, then made for the door. Avani followed more slowly, her hand on her sword.

The door had been freshly whitewashed to match the clapboard house. Torchlight flickered on real glass windows.

Everin rapped loudly on one pane.

The latch rattled, and the door swung open. A young man slipped through. He wore a loose black tunic and linen trousers. His feet were bare, his toes long and pale.

The youth looked at Everin, then at Avani. Then he bowed once.

"Come in," he said, stepping back into the house.

Everin followed easily, Avani reluctantly. She wished Jacob hadn't disappeared.

The inside of the house spoke of wealth. The floors were polished wood. Tapestries hung on the walls, and porcelain lamps were set in every corner. The lamps burned singly and in groups, warming the air.

"This way," the young man said. He led them down a sloping hall.

In the lamplight Avani saw that the youth was bald, and beardless, his round eyes large and dark. She saw no razor shadow on his chin or skull. She wondered if he had been born hairless, or if he had plucked out each strand.

A second whitewashed door waited at the end of the hall. The youth held it open as first Everin and then Avani crossed the threshold.

Beyond the door the air went suddenly chill.

Avani's neck prickled. She stood in the square room. The floor was bare unpolished wood. The walls were equally bare, whitewashed. There were no lamps. The ceiling glowed.

Avani squeezed her fingers around the butt of her sword. The young man stepped into the room, shutting the door precisely.

Smiling at Avani, he spoke a pattern of words. The air in the room immediately warmed to comfortable.

"A magus," Avani accused.

Everin snorted. "Far more than that, black eyes." He waved one massive paw at the young man. "Show her, Faolan."

A hint of a smile brightened the youth's pale face. He

spread the collar of his black robe, baring his neck. A torque gleamed there, seamless bronze, near green with age.

Set into the bronze at the base of the young man's throat a familiar yellow gem glittered.

"Faolan is an acolyte," Everin said, smile flashing. "He holds our passage into the mountains."

Avani hissed. Faolan shrugged slightly, as if in apology, and extended one pale hand. Avani drew her sword.

Everin chuckled. Grasping her wrist, he kept Avani still.

"What are you doing?" he asked, still grinning.

Avani couldn't answer. Faolan's face was corpse white, and in the magus-light his dark eyes were empty. Avani squirmed, trying to escape Everin's grip.

She stumbled, falling into the acolyte. Faolan staggered. The light caught in his fingers and at the hollow of his throat, glittering in the yellow jewel, sending stark amber rainbows across the bare walls.

And Avani's head seemed to crack into equally bright shards of amber glass.

MAL AND LIAM found the first corpse at the very foot of the Downs.

Spread across the narrow road, the dead man had been nibbled upon by scavengers and maggots. The body was whole, except for a wound through the man's right side.

He'd been cut down by a sword, and bled his life away there on the road. Mal couldn't summon his shade.

"I don't recognize him," said Liam. The lad stared down his pony's neck at the corpse. His lips had gone white, and his eyes were very round, but his hands in the pony's mane were steady.

"Neither do I."

The dead man wore a peasant's uniform of trousers and smock. His toes were gnarled and frostbitten.

The next body was all but disintegrated, flesh and bone broken open on the rocks. When Mal touched the corpse, shadows seemed to gather about, and he tasted murder.

On the corpse's belt Mal found Renault's badge.

"A Kingsman," he murmured, wondering if Andrew had been sending his spies up into the Downs all winter long.

The third corpse was a Stonehiller, and a woman. She was badly burned, badly decayed, and lacked one leg. Her skeletal hand clutched a notched sword.

"I know *her*," Liam whispered. "Mistress Rourke. Henry's wife. She died in the fire, I saw her, dead on the cobblestones, blood in her mouth."

"Aye," Mal muttered absently. He frowned down at the corpse.

"What's she doing here, then?" Liam pressed. "With a sword? Mistress sold vegetables. She never held a sword in her life."

Mal only looked at the dried blood on the blade.

"What does it mean?" Liam seemed unable to turn away from the dead woman's charred face.

"I don't know."

Mal slid from the saddle. He knotted his reins, and loosened his sword in its sheath.

His eyes told him the Downs were quiet, but the senses Andrew had schooled told him differently.

"Keep your head up," he told the boy. They started again along the curving path. "If you see anything that moves, grab mane and gallop."

"I'm not leaving you," Liam said stubbornly.

Mal thought to argue, and then changed his mind. He couldn't make light of the lad's bravery, or the sudden flare of gratitude he felt.

"Well, then. In that case, thank you."

The boy shot Mal a puzzled glance, then he smiled bravely and turned those searching gray eyes back to the Downs.

Around the next bend they found four slaughtered Stonehillers. And around the next, two more.

After that, Mal stopped keeping count.

Chapter Twenty

THEY REACHED STONEHILL as the sun turned the sky red with setting.

Halfway across the Downs they'd turned the frightened horses loose, and so they came down into the village on foot. Filthy, covered with muck, they edged over blackened cobblestones, trying not to step on bone.

Mal summoned a light, a soft ball of white flame to keep dusk at bay. He kept his sword in hand, and one watchful eye on Liam.

The boy's stride was stiff and clumsy. His eyes had gone glassy, but he held his knife firmly. He kept his shoulder pressed against Mal's side.

Stonehill had been charred down to blocks of graystone. Empty foundations made gaping holes along the street. Mal could hear the soft drip of water over stone.

There had been some snow left on the Downs, blanketing the highest hills, but in Stonehill, even the sludge had melted away.

They had to stop once on the street, blocked by a stretch of skeleton. Mal stepped over a shattered skull. Liam followed after.

There were no ghosts in Stonehill. He'd seen no spirits on the Downs, no shades guarding abandoned corpses. And there were armies of corpses, fallen down among rock, or in hollows; peasants, Kingsmen, Stonehillers.

Mal thought the freshest had fallen only days earlier.

"What do you think killed them?" Liam asked, looking back at the skull. It was the first time he'd spoken since they'd left the nightmare on the Downs.

Mal gripped the boy's shoulder, steering him around a puddle. "I don't know. Nothing natural."

But Avani had said they'd felt human. Mal didn't want to believe it, couldn't believe it. He shuddered, and touched Liam again. The boy's hand was cold, clammy.

"Still with me?" Mal asked gently.

"Aye," the lad replied, squaring his small shoulders.

Crooked Creek Inn was gone, gutted by flames. As they stood together in front of the sagging frame, Mal sent his light close against the ruins. He could see spires of ravaged timber, and the great rock hearth the Widow had kept endlessly burning.

"What now?" Liam asked.

Mal hesitated. "I go in. And take a look."

"You can see from here," the lad pointed out, shrill.

"I need to go in, Liam. I'll be fine, there's no danger

there but the collapse of old wood. I want you to stay out here, right here, where you can see me. Understand?"

"I should go in with you." But he'd begun to shiver, and Mal knew the boy had reached his limit.

"I need you here, to keep watch," insisted Mal. "I'll leave you a light." He conjured a second glowing sphere and set it above Liam's head. "It will stay with you. If you need me, yell."

"Aye."

"I'll be quick," Mal promised. He touched the boy's arm, and started into the ruined tavern.

Graystone cracked beneath his weight. Timbers groaned. The tavern had fallen in upon itself. The rush of soot and ash and snow had left tiny hillocks about the floor. Mal kicked through the refuse.

Standing in the center of the building, he could see the twilight sky above his head. The tavern's second floor was gone.

"What do you see?" Liam called.

"Nothing," he called back. "Yet."

He sent his light higher into the air, until the glow illuminated the entire remains of the building. Standing in one place, he turned this way and that, searching.

No bones, no evidence of the Widow's charred body.

No sign of Siobahn.

Mal sucked in a breath and began a new search, eyes shut. He let the fingers of his power crawl over every piece of ash, along every cracked stone. Still, he felt nothing, not even an echo of the murders he'd witnessed a season earlier.

Teeth gritted tight, he tried again, opening his center wide, dropping walls, desperation overruling caution.

Siobahn!

Nothing. And then, something. A faint tug, a wavering image on the backs of his eyelids. The Widow's shade, shifting before her hearth, and ghostly flames still burning, smoke rising through a chimney that had crumbled and fallen to pieces in the fire.

He opened his eyes and regarded the hearth. Alone in the ash and splinters it looked like a monument, a large stone box blackened by heat.

He didn't see the Widow's ghost, but if he narrowed his eyes, he could still glimpse the ghostly flames, and when he picked his way carefully across fallen timbers, he could feel heat on his face.

"What is it?" Liam called again. Mal didn't answer.

He crouched on his toes, peering into the hearth. The andirons were still there, apparently bolted to the floor. The Widow's prized wood had burned away to nothing. Ash filled the back of the box, covered the stone floor, coated the walls.

But the andirons were free of soot, the metal smooth and polished.

Ignoring the now blistering heat of ghostly flame, Mal stuck one gloved hand into the hearth and grabbed the closest andiron.

Searing heat made him yelp. He yanked his hand back just as Liam rushed into the building.

"My lord?"

"Have a care," Mal cautioned. "The ground is pitted in places. Move slowly."

"I heard you shout," the boy said, edging gingerly along the foundation.

"The hearth is spelled," Mal explained. "It burns to the touch."

Liam stopped at Mal's side. He squinted into the hearth.

"I used to climb in there, when I was tiny. To help the Widow clean. She could almost stand up in it."

"I thought she never put the fires out."

"She did, twice a year. On the Aug's birthdate, and on Washing Day."

"Summer and spring," Mal murmured. Sweat trickled down his nose. "Do you feel the heat?" he asked.

"Nay." Liam looked from Mal's dampened face to the black hearth.

"Can you put your hand in there? Touch the irons?"

"Aye," the boy said, and demonstrated.

"Doesn't hurt?" In spite of himself, Mal smiled.

"Nay."

"Well." Mal set his hands on his knees and thought. "Pull on the irons. See if you can get them free."

Liam shot Mal an incredulous stare, but tugged gamely on the andirons with both hands.

"They're tight," he reported after a breathless moment. "Tight to the floor."

"Turn them," Mal suggested on a whim. "Like the knobs on the doors at court."

Liam grunted, and shook his head. Then he stuck his head into the hearth, and scrambled all the way in.

Mal's heart skipped. But the lad seemed perfectly

comfortable. He sat on his knees between the andirons, and sneezed.

"You're a mess," Mal said. "See anything?"

The boy sneezed again. He shook his head. "Smells like grease."

"Come out," Mal ordered. He didn't like seeing the boy among phantom flames.

Liam started to slip out, then paused. "Wait."

"What is it?"

"There's a keyhole!" Liam said, excited.

"What?" Mal leaned toward the hearth, then flinched away from the roaring flames. "Where?"

"In the floor."

As Mal watched, Liam brushed away soot, exposing stone. The keyhole was there, set into the floor.

"Why would anyone put a lock in the bottom of the Widow's hearth?" Liam wondered.

"A safe hole?" Mal suggested. "To hide coins or jewels or other treasure. Can you open it?"

"Nay," he hedged.

"Avani told me you had a way with the picks."

"I do," the lad said. "But this lock is fancy."

"Very well, then." Mal refused to feel defeat. "Come out."

Liam slithered across stone. "Can't you unlock it with a spell?"

"No. The hearth has been trapped against cants. The flames are there as warning." He ran gloved fingers through his hair, glancing around. "There must be a key somewhere."

"The Widow kept a ring of keys on her belt," said Liam. Then he choked, eyes wide. "And another closed in her shed!"

"Her shed?"

"Her vegetable shed! I remember. She kept a ring on a peg on the wall. Behind her turnips. She didn't know I saw. She'd whup me when I tried to steal potatoes."

"Where?" demanded Mal.

"Down the hill, behind the tavern," Liam said eagerly. "Do you think it's still standing?"

Mal didn't dare hope. He straightened, brushing dirt from his trousers. "Let's take a look."

Liam nodded. He clamored over timbers, leading the way.

The night smelled of stale smoke. The grass behind the tavern was scorched black. Liam slid down a small slope, Mal's light dancing above his head. Mal walked after, hand on his sword. The ground was slick, but when he heard Liam shout, he broke into a run, slipping until he reached the lad's side.

"What is it?"

Liam had his knife in his hand. His teeth were bared in a quivering snarl. "I saw something move."

"Where?"

"There!" The boy pointed with his blade. "Behind the shed."

Mal turned. The Widow's vegetable shed had survived the fire, if barely. The stone walls were blackened, and the door burnt away to hinges, but the structure remained upright.

He made his way slowly around the small building.

"A corpse," he called to the boy. He looked down at the contorted face.

Liam stayed rooted to the slope.

"It moved," he insisted.

Mal nudged the body with his foot. It was fresher than most they had found; blood had dried and flies set in, but the flesh had not yet begun to rot.

A gust of spring wind sent the man's torn tunic flapping.

"Just the wind blowing." He walked back around the shed.

"How did he die?" Liam demanded, still quivering.

"Like all the others," Mal replied. He took the lad's arm, steering him around to the front of the shed. "Show me where the Widow kept her keys."

The keys were still there, on a peg in the stone wall. They hung on a bronze ring. Mal counted eleven, of differing sizes and shapes.

He took the ring from the wall and started back up the hill.

"Is the key there?" Liam asked, hurrying after.

"I don't know. You'll have to try each one."

Liam did, with a boy's enthusiasm—fright forgotten.

The ninth key fit, and turned. Liam whistled in appreciation.

"Tumbler's well oiled, my lord. Someone's cared for it recently."

"Leave the key in the lock and crawl out," Mal ordered.

Liam didn't argue. He hopped from the hearth, then looked expectantly at Mal.

"Reach in and see if you can lift the floor out."

Liam frowned. "Lift the *floor* out?"

"Use the irons as handles," Mal explained. "Straight up. The stone should come free."

Obediently, Liam grabbed the irons. He tugged, groaning. The stone shifted slightly, grating, but wouldn't come free. Liam groaned again, thin arms straining. When he released the irons, the square of stone dropped back into place.

"Too heavy," the lad gasped.

"I'll do it."

Liam looked decidedly alarmed. "But, my lord, you said—"

"I know."

Mal took the boy's place at the hearth. Staring into the faint flames, he fixed the position of the andirons in his head, then shut his eyes and reached.

Pain burst in his hands. He could feel his gloves cooking, his flesh blistering. He bit his tongue until he tasted blood. He fumbled along the floor of the hearth, trying to find the andirons.

He couldn't feel anything past the flame in his fingertips.

"You've got them!" Liam cried, muffled by the roar of angry flames. "Pull, my lord!"

Mal locked his knees and heaved, eyes still squeezed shut. He didn't want to look into the hearth, to see the flames lick at his hands. He pulled, and heard stone scrape.

"Almost, my lord!"

Mal set his teeth, and pulled again. Then he staggered and fell onto his knees in the ash. He was free of the flames, the andirons still gripped in his hands.

Liam dropped at his side. He studied the square of stone Mal had pulled up with the irons.

"It's a door," he said. "How did you know?"

"A guess." Mal blinked sweat from his eyes.

He dropped the stone. Lifting his throbbing hands, he found them intact, the gloves still cool, flesh untouched.

"Are you burnt?" Liam worried.

"Nay," Mal said. He climbed to his feet. "What have we uncovered?"

The phantom flames had gone out. The ash on the walls and the earth was cool. At the very center of the hearth a square hole gaped, a shaft only a little wider than Mal's shoulders.

"It's dark." Liam peered into the shaft. "I don't see anything."

Mal sent his light into the hole. Liam crawled forward and leaned over the edge, looking after the glowing ball. He gasped.

"I see handholds, my lord! Way down in the dark. It's a ladder!"

Mal peered over his shoulder. "So it is."

"Will we climb in?"

"Let me go first." Mal gripped the sharp lip of the shaft. His voice echoed away into the depths.

"I think it's very deep," Liam said. "It looks very deep, doesn't it, my lord?"

"Aye," Mal muttered.

He slung his booted feet into the shaft.

EVERIN SAT ON the hard floor beside Avani.

He gripped her shoulder tightly, trying to steady the tremor in her limbs. She felt him there, and wanted to shake him off. She couldn't find the strength.

He'd tricked her, she thought. Walked her right into a trap, like a ewe to slaughter.

The pain in her skull was easing, shards of yellow light blinking out. She could hear the throb of her heart in her temples, steady. Yet she couldn't open her eyes, couldn't yet draw her sword and slit Everin's bearded throat.

"Take deep breaths," he ordered. "Faolan says the pain will ease. He's gone to get you some ale."

Avani coughed. She swallowed bile. She tried to move her head. She couldn't. But her eyelids were slowly becoming less heavy.

Through slitted lids she could just make out her sword where it lay on the floor, inches from her knees. She'd dropped it when the yellow stone had lashed out and bruised her skull.

Her fingers twitched, and fell far short of the blade. Everin didn't seem to notice. There was a clatter as the bald youth came striding back into the room. Jacob rode his shoulder.

"The bird was clawing at my door," he said, in the thick brogue of a flatland peasant. "So I let him in. He's yours, is he?"

"Aye." Everin set his palm against Avani's spine and forced her into a sitting position, propping her shoulders up with his hands.

Faolan nodded. He set a battered clay bowl at Avani's side.

"Drink," Everin said. He clasped her hands around the bowl, and urged the cup to her mouth. In spite of herself, she drank thirstily.

The ale was bitter, but it warmed her stomach and chased most of the pain from her head.

"Better," Everin said as if he knew. "You can open your eyes, Avani. Faolan's covered his torque."

"My lord said the yellow gems weren't spelled," Avani croaked. She forced her lids open, and blinked at the youth's hairless jaw.

Jacob sat on Faolan's shoulder as if he belonged.

"Malachi is wise in his way," Everin replied. "But he is a young man, in a very young kingdom."

Avani took another swallow of ale. She eyed her sword.

Casually, Everin reached out and drew the weapon to his side.

"We are guests here, black eyes," he warned.

"You tricked me!" Avani accused.

"I didn't," returned Everin, gruff. "If only you'd shut your lovely mouth and listen, I'll explain."

Avani gritted her teeth. She set the bowl back on the floor and glared. Everin smiled through his beard.

"I told you I knew a shortcut," he said. "It wasn't trickery. Faolan guards the entrance to the passages. They begin in his cellar."

"Passages?" Avani ventured.

"Aye. A grand network of underground tunnels. They spread beneath the mountains, beneath the scarlet wood, and in a handful of places, beneath Wilhaiim. Most of the entrances on this side of the mountains have been sealed up, for safety's sake. Faolan keeps one of the few remaining open."

"Passages beneath the skin of the world?" Avani scoffed to hide the pounding of her heart. "Impossible."

"The hells," Faolan said, smiling sweetly. "Every story has its root in truth. These tunnels have existed long before the theists consigned the damned to the bowels of the earth."

"Oh, *ai*?" Avani met the man's flat stare. "And who dug them, then?"

"You won't believe me until you see for yourself," Everin said. "Faolan will open the tunnel at dawn. Until then, you should sleep."

"Dawn is only a few hours away," Faolan promised.

Avani didn't waste time on fear. She sprang from the floor, drawing her knife in one smooth motion. She lunged at Everin. The bearded man grunted in surprise.

Jacob screamed and flew in her face, wings beating. Faolan grabbed her by the belt, yanking her back and away from Everin.

Hissing, she whirled, dodging Jacob's claws, and turned her blade on Faolan. The acolyte backed away, arms lifted, lips moving, forming soft syllables.

Avani threw herself forward, slashing at air.

And Everin set himself between her blade and Faolan. Avani's knife bit his arm, slicing leather and flesh. The bearded man tripped her with the ease of a trained soldier. He sent her sprawling back across the floor, her knife skittering away out of reach.

For the first time, Avani saw true fear in his yellow eyes.

"Don't ever," Everin said very precisely, "attack one of the *aes si* with your open blade."

Avani snarled. Her back hurt, and she was having trouble catching her breath. Jacob hunched on the floor a hand's breadth away, glaring.

Everin helped Faolan to his feet, murmuring softly. The acolyte sent a neutral glance in Avani's direction, then quietly left the room.

Everin shut the door, then turned.

"He'll return at dawn. Will you sleep?"

"You'll kill me as soon as I shut my eyes."

The anger drained from Everin's face. He slumped against the wall.

"Why would you think so? Have I not already saved your life several times over?"

Avani rolled carefully onto her knees. She refused to answer, refused to look at him.

"Faolan didn't know you had the one of the yellow stones with you, Avani," Everin said gently. "Neither did I. Where is it?"

Avani hesitated. Croaking, Jacob stabbed at her pack with his beak.

"Ah," Everin smiled at the raven. "You're lucky, Avani. Had it been on your person, you might have suffered more than a headache. The stone in Faolan's torque is raw, untempered, and apt to make use of any open conduit nearby. Keep the ring tucked there, away from your flesh. Who gave it to you?"

"I found it," Avani admitted, shocked by Jacob's betrayal. "In Andrew's coldroom."

That seemed to surprise Everin. He glanced away, and pressed three fingers against the oozing scratch on his arm.

"You've been lying all along," Avani accused. "You were never his son at all."

The man's head whipped back around. He studied Avani narrowly. "Aye?"

"Andrew's heir. You were never his son. You've had everyone well and truly fooled, even the king."

Everin didn't reply, but Avani read the truth in his stance.

"You're the son of the Aug."

His beard bristled, and his yellow eyes gleamed. Jacob left the ground and settled on the big man's shoulder, beak clacking.

"You are," Avani breathed. She scooted backward, pressing her spine against the wall. "You are. I saw it, I dreamed it, the Goddess spoke clearly, and I was too addlepated to see."

"Avani." Sighing, he reached out, but she flinched away, scraping the back of her skull on the rough wall.

"Don't touch me. You're dead, long dead."

"Nay." The man almost shuffled his feet in dismay.

"Why are you here?" Avani demanded. She couldn't help herself, she laughed her nerves aloud. "You said you wanted to enlist, as a Kingsman! A Kingsman!"

"As a wee lad I begged my sire to let me join the guard," he admitted. "He would not allow it. Later, much later, I chose a desert lord's army instead." He rolled his shoulders. "I'm here to stop the murders."

"And you'd know how to do that, would you?" she spat.

"I know now. I suspected, before. But when you told me of the bones, and showed me the bit of fabric, and the pearl baubles, then I knew."

"The bones? The bones in Andrew's coldroom?"

"Aye." For once, he didn't smile. "Siobahn's bones."

"The *bhut's* bones. Cursed bones." She stared into Everin's yellow eyes, and then she knew.

"*Ai*, Goddess," she groaned, and fisted her hands against her brow. "I was right, was I? I was right all along."

"Aye," Everin replied. "You were right all along."

AVANI CURLED AGAINST the wall and dreamed.

In her sleep she walked upon packed clay, down a curving tunnel carved from the bones of the earth. Green moss coated the walls, soft as silk. Ferns dripped from the ceiling, brushing the top of her head.

The air was chill and musty. The Hennish gloves she wore did little to keep her hands warm.

She kept her left hand firmly on the pommel of her sword. Magus-light bobbed against the ceiling.

The tunnel dipped sharply into the earth. A bronze gate, crafted in whorls and curls, stood open, against dry stone walls. The clay beneath her feet turned to slate, smooth tiles cut and laid with a craftsman's precision.

The air warmed.

"My lord. Is that light ahead?" Liam whispered, so quietly she had to strain to hear him. His hand gripped her sleeve like a lifeline.

"I don't know." She squinted along the passage. "It appears so."

She paused, thinking, and then nodded at the boy.

"Stay still," she ordered, then snuffed both of the glowing spheres.

Darkness dropped heavy about her shoulders. Liam made a small sound of distress.

"Just wait," she said.

Then her eyes adjusted, and the gloom seemed to lighten. There was a glow, ahead, far down the tunnel.

She concentrated, questing carefully ahead. Still she sensed nothing.

She looked down at the ring on her finger, watched the facets reflect faint light, and frustration made her want to punch stone walls.

"My lord," Liam whispered. He jostled her arm.

"Aye," she replied, irritated back into the rough accent of her childhood. "Ready?"

The lad nodded.

"Ahead, then."

She walked along the tunnel, the heels of her boots clicking on slate.

The light grew slowly as they approached a bend in the tunnel. Liam's steps began to drag, and her own slowed in response. She was not afraid, but long ago she'd learned the wisdom of caution.

They stopped together on the edge of darkness and light, where the glow shifted from soft to bright, and gloom receded. Here, the air was heated almost uncomfortably. She felt sweat trickle down the back of her neck.

The boy trembled against her thigh. She touched the top of his head in reassurance.

"Wait here."

"Nay," Liam protested. "Please, my lord. Don't leave me behind."

She swallowed a sigh.

"Together then," she relented. Taking the boy's fingers in her free hand, she stepped forward.

The passage curved into a great cavern, a swell at the end of the tunnel, shaped like a teardrop and larger even than Renault's throne room. The air thrummed, and sourceless white light made her eyes sting.

She wiped them with the back of her wrist, and tried to see.

Stone teeth pierced the air, grown from the floor, many taller than a man, some entirely decorated with intricately carved patterns. The columns sparkled in the light, sharp and lovely, and behind every one faces, inhuman faces. Watching, waiting, eyes wide and empty.

Liam screamed, and his hand was ripped from her own. She whirled, but he was gone.

"Liam!"

Enraged, gripping her sword, she strode through the light, a challenge.

"Malachi."

The voice stopped her; beloved, despised.

Siobahn.

Shock glued her to the floor. She looked up, through the stinging light, and into the face of her Goddess.

Chapter Twenty-One

FAOLAN LED THE WAY down a seemingly endless stretch of stone steps, almost straight into the depths of the earth. Avani descended carefully in his wake. Everin followed at her back, and the raven rode still on his shoulder.

A familiar bronze key hung from a cord on Remy's belt, twirling gently as he walked.

She'd seen the acolyte use the bit of bronze to open a hidden door in the wall of his basement, heard the click as the key had thrown an unseen latch.

Everin flicked a glance at Faolan. The big man had given her back her sword and her knife. Avani knew better than to try the blades. Even an islander had sense enough not to attack the legendary Virgin King.

"*Eochair.* The guardian keys. There are very few left," he said. "You found the one given into my care."

"Thom had it."

The stairway was narrow, the steps smooth. As they

descended, the walls lit, and then fell dark again after their passing. It was a cant, Avani guessed, not unlike the glow of coldroom ceilings.

"Whoever killed your Thom had it," Everin corrected. "It was stolen from me, a season ago. I was careless. It's not like to happen again."

"You lost it," Avani said. "And I found it."

The stairway ended so abruptly she almost stepped on Faolan's bare heels. The tunnel ahead was wide, the floor stone.

"And I found you," Everin retorted. "And *you* lost it."

Avani growled. Faolan glanced over his shoulder, smile bland. The tunnel forked. They took the left branch.

"Do you live here?" Avani asked the acolyte. "Underground, in these tunnels?"

"Faolan lives in Whitcomb," Everin answered.

Faolan looked back at Everin, and then at Avani.

"An acolyte guards the outside door," he said, simply. "But I grew up to manhood in the mounds. My family still runs beneath the earth."

Avani's shoulder blades twitched uneasily. She walked several heartbeats in silence. Faolan's feet made no sound on the stones. He smelled ripe to her senses, harmless, like apples in the fall.

But when he moved it was with the fluid ease of a predator. And she was sure she'd seen a glint of fang behind his lip when he'd smiled.

"Did you kill them?" she demanded. "All of them?"

Everin's hand gripped the back of her neck in warning. Faolan didn't look around, or slow his sinuous gait.

"Not," he said, "because we wished it, though mortal blood is very sweet."

Avani stumbled. Everin kept her from falling.

"You're too blunt, black eyes," he said, low. "Have care, or it will get you murdered with the rest."

"Yet you," Avani pointed out, "against all possibilities, are still alive."

Faolan laughed, clear as a bell. Everin's fingers twitched against the nape of Avani's neck. She shivered.

"Andrew was the start of it," the acolyte said. The path forked again. Faolan led them down the right-hand path. "He grew up a peasant, in the King's Forest. When he was a child, he found a way into one of our mounds. He spent some time in our halls, too much time. He became greedy. He was banished."

"Andrew never forgot," said Everin. "The barrows take hold of a man, sometimes unto madness. A child, once exposed to the *aes si*, is never the same. He never stopped searching for a way back."

"Your mortal king gave him the ring with the yellow stone," Faolan said without inflection. "Andrew used it to find the door at Whitcomb. I denied him entrance."

"And left him alive."

Faolan stopped. He stared at Everin. "It was a mistake. My first mistake."

"You of all people should have known he'd find another way in."

"Trickery," Faolan's smile showed needle sharp teeth. "He cheated. No mortal may pass without a key."

"You hadn't the foresight to restrict the dead, none of

you," Everin's own teeth flashed. "*That* was your first mistake." He looked at Avani. "Andrew sent Siobahn into the mounds to steal one of *eochair*. Happens she stole mine."

"Goddess," Avani breathed. "Andrew sent Siobahn into the ground?"

Faolan's head swiveled. He pinned her with empty eyes.

"There are no gods," he replied, "but us."

AVANI FOLLOWED BECAUSE she had to. The endless, snaking tunnels would have her lost easily, and she refused to wander like a mad thing in the dark, trapped in the bowels of the earth.

They walked until her feet began to hurt, and her stomach to growl, and then Everin stopped.

"We will rest for a while, here," he decided. "The tunnels have a magic of their own, but still we have a way yet to go."

As easily as that, he sat cross-legged on the ground.

Avani didn't argue. She sat on her sack as far from the man as she could, and rested her head on her knees. Faolan walked on a few paces more, and then stopped and waited, motionless.

"We haven't much time to spend," Everin murmured. "There is a war raging already, under the Downs. If Siobahn wins, Stonehill will be but a verse in a far larger slaughter."

"Liam—"

"If he's alive, we'll find him in the middle of it."

Avani turned her head until her cheek rested on one knee.

"Why?" she asked. "She killed them all? And Kate?"

"And Andrew." Everin nodded. "She was far stronger than he realized, far more than a handy tool. He'd bound her too completely to Mal, in bringing her back. She had a magus to draw upon." He spread his large hands, studied his fingers. "Mayhap Andrew tried to stop her, in the end."

"And she poisoned him." Avani stiffened. "The *agraine* on the sword that cut my lord?"

"Was an accident, I imagine. She still needs him, aye, needs his strength. And she loves him. Aye, and that is the root of all our trouble."

"What does she want?"

Everin's beard split in a wry smile. "Can you not guess, black eyes?"

"My lord," Avani said, remembering the inescapable garden Siobahn had set in Mal's head. "She wants my lord. Love."

"Life," Faolan corrected. "She wants to live again, to retrieve that which she threw away so carelessly."

AVANI COULDN'T REST. Soon Everin stood. As they walked on, the big man began to hum, a soft roll of sound that echoed its way along stone floors.

Jacob left Everin's shoulder for her own. She refused to acknowledge him.

"I dreamed of you," she said at last, to stop the humming. "Of your grave. Is there no one buried beneath the slab?"

"Nay. Naught but a sack full of rocks."

"Why?"

"It was time for me to die. Every king must die."

"But you didn't."

"No," he agreed.

"Why?" she persisted.

Everin sighed. Faolan watched from under lashless lids.

"There was a pretender in the court," the bearded man explained. "A sly little man with no real relation to royalty. He wanted the crown. In the dead of night he slaughtered the royal guard and slit my father's throat as he lay sleeping. My mother wouldn't lose her true love, so she struck a bargain with the folk in the mounds."

"Sometimes," said Faolan, "the gods listen."

"Life. Love." Everin shook his head. "My father's life for mine own. I was but a babe in her belly; I imagine it was an easy choice. Mayhap she thought she'd only miscarry. The Aug lived on to rule. Ra'vadin was ostensibly locked away in Wilhaiim's deepest dungeon. In truth my father exiled him beneath the earth, to serve as my tutor.."

"Ra'vadin? Ra'vadin was your pretender?"

"Read him, have you?"

"I thought he was beloved of the Virgin King." Avani said, baffled.

"So he was. He taught me my letters, and my history, and how to woo a lover with poetry. A handy thing, when a man is lonely. Several lifetimes lonely, and bored. The *aes si* are lively hosts, but have little interest in mortal philosophies, and until I struck my own bargain with the folk,

Ra'Vadin was the only exposure to human doctrine I was allowed."

"Time passes," Faolan replied. "Kingdoms rise and fall. Islands sink. What is man to us, that his philosophy should matter?"

"Still, it is my world, and I have missed it," Everin said, brittle. "I will not see it rent apart because you misjudged Andrew."

"She has the magus, his yellow stone, and your key. Without the key she might be manageable."

"She has all of *you*," returned Everin, "and your monstrous hunger."

Faolan only bared sharp teeth. "She used your key to free us upon the world, little king. Or did you think the acolytes are set to protect gods from man?" He laughed again. "You are children, striving for courage in the dark. The lies you tell yourselves keep nightmares at bay."

"Nothing keeps the nightmares at bay," corrected Everin. "But with Avani's help, I intend to wake from this one."

"Why me?" Avani clenched her fingers around the pommel of her knife.

"Because you, island witch, have found a way into Mal's very center," Everin said simply. "Even I have not managed that, and not for lack of trying. You'll find a way to cut the binding Andrew worked."

"*Ai*, and if I haven't the strength?" She reached up, touching Jacob's feathers for courage. His claws bit into her shoulder.

Everin shrugged slightly. "Then I must kill the man,

and hope for the best. He makes the ghostie what she is, and we cannot allow this mucking about to continue."

"Mucking about." Avani swallowed hard. "I won't let you hurt my lord."

"Then we are in agreement," he replied.

SIOBAHN'S BONES LAY spread on the floor, the skeleton still wrapped in bits of faded satin. A small troop of white-skinned monsters guarded the bones. They held notched swords or sharpened sticks in long-fingered hands, and showed fangs as Mal approached.

Siobahn stood among them, smiling.

Two of the creatures separated from their brothers. They wore animal pelt and silk, and their long hair was knotted and greasy, their round eyes shadowed.

Liam hung between them. The lad had stopped screaming. When the monsters dropped him at Siobahn's feet, he lay unmoving.

Mal beat back rage and disbelief.

"Siobahn," he said. "What have you done?"

Siobahn stepped over Liam, drifting closer. Her escort skittered in her wake. Mud streaked the spirit's brow and stained the hem of her wedding gown. She studied Mal. When she smiled, his heart lurched.

"Malachi. I meant to surprise you." She clasped her hands. "How did you find me?"

"The spell you set upon Kate's body."

Her mouth twisted. "I left no spell."

"A vision took me. I saw Stonehill, and heard you call."

"I left no cant." She tapped one slippered foot. Then she stilled, fingers clenching. "Andrew told you."

"No. Andrew won't speak."

The clench of her lips eased.

"I banished him," she allowed. "And set a *sidhe* in his place. They are very clever mimics, when need arises."

Mal flicked a glance at her fanged guard. The creatures stared back, impassive.

"You banished him?" he repeated carefully.

"I've grown strong." Her smile was full of affection. "Your love has made me strong. Andrew told me. Andrew taught me how to use it."

Use me, Mal thought. Rage froze to ice in his veins. His heart shattered, but the pain was distant.

"Why?" He took a casual step forward. He couldn't see Liam. The *sidhe* gathered too closely about Siobahn.

"He wanted me whole again," she said. "He knew you needed me whole. He'd discovered a new people, a new magic, beneath the Downs. He promised me; it would make me whole again, give me life."

"No," Mal said numbly. "Siobahn, you know better. It's impossible."

"He saw it," Siobahn retorted. She stamped a foot. "When he was a child, one of the people took him into the mounds. He saw it, there, a dead babe come back to life. *They* did it, with nothing more than a handful of clay and a simple cant."

Out of the corner of his eye Mal saw one of the monsters smile. The creature appeared no different than its flat-eyed brothers, no more or less than a piece of the crowd. But when it smiled, the hair on Mal's scalp rose.

"Andrew said he'd make them help me, if I helped him first. He needed one of those little keys. To get back into the tunnels. He was desperate for it, gone quite mad."

"But Andrew's dead."

Siobahn nodded, petulant. "I killed him. He was reluctant to give up his all secrets, when he was alive. But that was easily remedied, and now he's dead – and a weak shade at that – and I've all the knowledge I need."

"No."

Siobahn turned. The *sidhe* parted before her, revealing Liam and the pitiful skeleton.

"That babe died in war," Siobahn said. "The folk are always warring amongst themselves, Andrew said. They had the infant's body, perfect but for a gash at the top of his skull."

She stood over her bones, pensive. Mal took another step in her direction. Two *sidhe* blocked his path. Their long fingers ended in sharp, curving claws.

"They brought the child back. He lived again. But he was less than he had been, and the parents wouldn't take him. So they exiled him, alive and hale and squalling, beyond the doors. Andrew saw it. And he kept track of the child, after."

She wasn't looking at the skeleton, Mal realized. Her smile was for Liam, lying limp on stone, and her smile was a rictus of greed.

"Siobahn." He hoped to distract. "Did you kill the Kingsmen on the Downs?"

She tossed her head. "Not me. The *sidhe* are very territorial."

"Kate?"

Her sigh was full of regret. "She'd grown suspicious. She guessed too much, and she meant to go to you with her concerns. You, or the island witch." The last she spat.

Mal wouldn't let himself think of Avani.

"The walking corpses on the Downs? What of them, Siobahn?"

"A dead man is little more than clay in the hands of the folk, easy to enchant. The poisoned blade was meant for the boy, Mal. Part of a bargain made. I didn't know you would be so foolish as to take the wound instead."

"The trap in the keep pantry? The one hidden in Andrew's boot?"

Siobahn showed her teeth in a rictus of irritation. "The *sidhe* will play their games. Like unruly children, they'll tear wings off a butterfly just to see how it bleeds."

The *sidhe* shifted minutely, little more than the sighing of breeze through grass. Siobahn didn't notice. Mal did. He felt cold perspiration break on his brow.

"Siobahn," he said, low. "You've been misled. Andrew lied to you. These creatures haven't your interests in mind. Come away." He held out a hand.

She twitched her gown. The muddy hem skimmed over Liam.

"He's muddling the power in this place, I can feel it. They sent him away for good reason. He should have died upon the Downs, with your witch."

Her burning blue eyes were cold when she smiled. "Andrew didn't lie. You did. You promised to love me forever, and forever is cold and dark and frightening, and if not for Andrew's spell of binding, you'd have let me go long ago."

Mal drew his sword. Siobahn didn't flinch. The *sidhe* shifted again.

"You won't hurt me, Mal," said his wife. "You love me. You can't help it. And you're strong, Andrew was right. Your strength is like nectar, like sweet wine, and it pumps within my dead heart. The *sidhe* will do what I ask, have done as I ask, because of you. And because I unlocked their gate."

She nudged Liam with a toe.

"The child is trouble," she mused absently. "Kill him."

"No!" Mal lunged.

Siobahn lifted her hand and felled him with a word.

The breath squeezed from his lungs. He tripped and went down. The slate floor rose up to meet him, bruising. His sword rang, spinning across tile.

The *sidhe* moved, flowing over Liam, gathering like flies on spoiled meat.

Mal tried to shout, but his throat was closed. Siobahn used his power against him, relentless. He was lessened almost to nothing. She held his center. She was clever, she'd had him for seasons, if not years, and he'd been all but unaware.

Her strength astounded him. Her greed was terrifying. And the emptiness in her heart made him want to weep.

Siobahn knelt on the floor at his side. He felt the soft touch of her hand as she stroked his cheek.

She said, "You'll wait here, until it's over. And then, when I'm whole again, then you'll understand."

She touched his face one more time. Her skirt rustled as she rose. Mal tried to speak her name, but still he couldn't move. She rose, and moved away. He heard the dry whisper of the *sidhe* as they followed after.

He felt despair settle and crush him against the ground. Siobahn began to murmur. The stone grew warm against his flesh.

Eyes closed, he drifted. Siobahn's voice rose and fell. Mal felt stretched and thin, unraveled. The air grew thick and hot. Mal's clothes stuck in places to his damp skin.

Then something sharp pierced the flesh of his thumb, as cold as a shard of ice. The pain ran down his bones in his arm. His heart jolted, and his lids flew open.

The raven bit him again, this time on the cheek, dangerously near his right eye. More pain surged like lightning through his skull.

Jacob tilted his head, regarding Mal with interest. Blood dripped from his beak.

Avani! Mal remembered.

The raven only gnashed its beak.

Avani! He tried to reach for her, but Siobahn had locked him way inside his own skull, walled him away from the world. He couldn't get out.

Until the raven bit him again, on the bridge of his nose between his eyes, and the sheer unearthly agony sent Mal surging to his knees.

Avani! He thought the raven had shattered his mind.

As soon as the walls broke, Avani found him, slicked over his center, a salve to his broken core. She filled the gaps, repaired the wounds, made him whole. He clutched at her with invisible fingers, gathered her close.

He couldn't let her go. He needed her there, in his heart, setting him free, making him stronger than he'd ever thought he could be.

Mal stood up, Jacob clutching his shoulder. Slowly, carefully, Mal summoned his sword from the floor. It flew from the shadows to his hand.

He glanced once over his shoulder, and saw Avani in truth, standing frozen at the mouth of the tunnel, made brilliant by the glare, Everin propping her upright.

He saw himself through her eyes, a lithe man all in black, face bloodied, the promise of vengeance set on his mouth. And Liam, sprawled lifeless on the floor; and beyond, the *sidhe* gathered about Siobahn.

Avani cried out and staggered toward Liam. Mal's vision doubled, and the surge of grief was Avani's. Then he was himself again, the bridge between them muted, focused to a steady pull of power.

He turned. Siobahn looked up. He felt her reach out to bind him again. He slapped her down with a twitch of his mind. She gasped, rocking a step back.

Then her face changed. With a hard word she sent the *sidhe* over the stone to meet him.

Mal met them eagerly. The ring of blade against blade sent madness singing through his blood. The first, he cut down quickly, easily. The next two fell before his sword. He spoke a quick cant, and two more of the creatures dropped, dissolving into a noxious puddle on the floor.

They howled, feral, and jumped upon him. They used their teeth and their nails, and knives made of bone and bronze.

He was meant to die there, beneath the world, betrayed and broken.

Instead, he drew more strength from Avani.

"Enough," he said, and lifted his ringed hand. The stone flashed.

The *sidhe* fell back, silent, his blood on their nails and in their mouths. They slid away from his hand, watching, waiting. The heat of their magic made their pale skin gleam wetly.

"Enough, Siobahn," Mal said.

She looked up at him across her own skeleton. Her blue eyes burned with sorrow or hatred.

He walked forward, the *sidhe* drifting in his wake, and scattered her bones with a scrape of his boot. He held out a gloved hand.

Siobahn closed her delicate fingers hard about his own.

AVANI'S LEGS WERE shaking. Her mouth bled where she'd bitten through her lower lip.

She cradled Liam in her lap and wept. Her heart still beat behind her ribs, and her breath fluttered the lad's hair, but her mind drifted there across the room, in Mal's skull. She felt disjointed, split in half.

"He's yet alive," Everin murmured.

"So much blood," Avani wiped at Liam's face, even as she felt Siobahn struggle with Mal.

"They marked him," Faolan replied. "With nail and tooth, they tasted him."

"He needs a healing."

"I've a salve in my sack." Avani fumbled for her bag. Everin stopped her hand.

"The lad needs more than salve."

Avani flinched as Siobahn scorched Mal with his own fire. Everin looked quickly at her face. He shook his head.

"You're too tangled with that man, black eyes. If he goes down, he'll take you with him."

"He needs my help." Avani blinked hard as the world doubled and then wavered.

"He needs you, aye, but you cannot sever Andrew's binding. He has to do it himself, child."

Avani was lost now behind Mal's eyes. Siobahn struggled still, refusing to give up.

Across the room, the vocent and his wife stood frozen, linked only by fingers, but the force of their battle shook the floor.

Everin pulled hard on a lock of Avani's hair. The small, startling pain drew her attention, and she gazed into yellow eyes.

"Come all the way back," he ordered. "Take care of yon lad, and let the vocent finish his own war."

Faolan, too, peered into her face.

"Take the child up," he said. "He doesn't belong here."

Avani looked down at Liam. She saw his eyes roll beneath bloodstained lids. The *sidhe* had scarred him, scribed lines into his skin, whirls and patterns, peeled away narrow pieces of flesh.

He moaned, stirring..

"*Ai,*" she said.

She released Mal, dividing, settling wholly back into her own body.

The shock of separation made tears well in her eyes. She dashed them away.

"Come," Faolan ordered. "Quickly. Before they remember."

He lifted the boy and strode away.

"Go," Everin said. "I'll stay with your lord."

Avani looked at Mal, rooted in silent battle, at the *sidhe*, watching avidly.

Everin drew his own sword, and set it point down on stone.

"I'll stay," he said again. "Go. Hurry."

She turned and ran after Liam.

MAL FELT AVANI's retreat. His bones ached with the emptiness she left behind.

Still, he didn't call her back.

Siobahn stood unmoving in his grip, while she fluttered and fought in the cage of his magic.

Let me go! She beat at him with images of fury, loss, and longing, love.

I can't, he said, soft.

His sorrow frightened her more than his returning strength.

I'll kill you! I'll make them kill you!

The *sidhe* lurked, a hum in the air. He could almost hear their hunger.

He wasn't afraid. He felt nothing but resignation.

No, he said. *It's over.*

And he severed Andrew's binding, quickly, cleanly, a slice of an invisible knife behind his eyes and through his core. The link frayed, and snapped.

Siobahn screamed.

"You are only myself," he told the spirit, watching steadily as she flickered. "You have always, only, been myself."

She stared at him, uncomprehendingly. Then she twisted in his grip, and flew to strike at his face with her small fists.

Mal snuffed Siobahn out, as he might any other hapless shade.

She frayed away into nothing. Her scream echoed for one last heartbeat between his ears, and then she was gone.

He staggered. Everin held him up.

"Steady," the bearded man warned. "Here they come."

FAOLAN BATHED LIAM with water from the Widow's well.

The scratches on the boy's flesh were deep, but not to the bone. The knots and whorls were almost beautiful. He twitched beneath their ministrations, but didn't wake.

"They scarred him," she realized. "They never meant to kill him."

"He's lucky," Faolan said, binding the deepest of the wounds with strips torn from his own tunic. "My people are fickle."

The ground shook beneath their feet. A rock fell from

the side of the well into the depths. Avani heard its distant splash.

"What of my lord?" she asked, afraid. "Will they kill *him*?"

"They might," the *aes si* replied, "easily."

Avani rose to her feet, reaching for her knife.

"Stay." Faolan tossed her a flat stare. It was midday above ground, and sunlight made his bald head stark and ugly. "You, they will devour, a tender piece of meat. Stay, and let Everin prevail upon them."

"Can he?"

The acolyte shrugged fluidly. "He has a talent for it."

The ground shook again. Avani sank to her knees at Liam's side and waited.

THEY CLIMBED FROM the earth not through the Widow's hearth, but through a smaller gate not far from the Widow's vegetable shed. The passage was narrow. Mal had to crawl on hands and knees, his sword sheathed in his hand.

There was another gate, this one little taller than a child.

"Use the key," Everin said. "Lock it. They haven't the strength now, but be sure they'll try it later."

Mal couldn't help himself; he laughed.

Siobahn's key was slick with *sidhe* ichor. He'd found it by her bones, beneath a scrap of rotting fabric. Mal pulled a glove from his hand with his teeth and used bare fingers to turn the key in the latch. The ground shook again as he did so, and soil fell in his eyes.

"They're very angry," Mal said unnecessarily.

"They're alive," Everin returned, sharp. "And should be grateful for the privilege."

They crawled a few lengths more and then burst into fresh air. Someone, possibly the Widow, had covered the mouth of the tunnel with branches of flowering holly. The branches were long dead, leaves curling, and the thorns scraped Mal's bare hand.

He rose to his feet, sheathed his sword, and looked up the hill at the remains of the tavern.

"Keep the lad safe," Everin suggested, brushing dirt from his jerkin. There were scratches on his face, but not from the holly. The *sidhe* had been free with claw and tooth. "He's your bargaining chip."

"I won't trade the boy's life for mine own."

"For your king's?" Everin asked. He started up the hill, and spoke over his shoulder. "For Wilhaiim's? Avani's? Don't make promises you can't keep, Lord Vocent."

Mal hung the key on its cord around his neck. Then he spoke a cant to hide the tunnel mouth, shifting the old holly branches into the semblance of solid graystone.

When he turned back, Avani was halfway down the hill, and still running.

She barreled into his chest, nearly knocking him onto the Downs. His arms came around her automatically. She fit against him as if she belonged. He shifted his hands to her shoulders and gripped her tight.

"You're alive," she spoke into his breastbone.

"Of course," he decided to be amused. For now, he

could spare her worry. "Is not a vocent the most powerful man alive?"

"Arrogant." She looked up, mouth trembling.

"And stubborn," Mal agreed.

He rested his chin atop her head and listened to her breathe.

THEY TOOK SHELTER in Avani's home, warmed by spiced cider, away from the stink of the corpses that lay still strewn across the Downs.

Liam slept cradled in Everin's lap in the cellar, warmed by one of Avani's blankets. When the lad stirred and opened his eyes, he smiled to see the big man there, and then dropped back into a healing sleep.

Avani wondered what the boy would remember when he woke fully.

"Tell him the truth," Mal counseled. "All of it. He's young enough to make of it what he will. Children are resilient."

"What will they say at court?" Avani worried.

She sat cross-legged on a pile of torn pillows, basking in the heat of her wood stove. A mug of cider soothed her hands.

"Whatever Renault puts out." Mal stood in her doorway, watching spring rain fall across her stoop. The key to the mounds hung on its cord around his neck. "Likely the other lads will look at him in awe."

Avani couldn't read his expression. She touched his mind, and found him closed against her.

Temper, she thought, *or sorrow*.

"Did you know?" He turned from the door. The holes Jacob had put in his face were crusted with dried blood.

"No. The Widow always said he was a crofter's orphan she'd taken up as a babe."

"I guessed," Mal said. "But far too late, only as Siobahn told his tale. I should have known. I couldn't find him in the forest when he tracked me. And they let him live, didn't they, when they devoured Stonehill."

"The acolyte said he was lucky." Avani buried her nose in her mug. "I'll allow myself the luxury of believing some of that luck may rub off on you, my lord."

Mal left the door. He strode across the room, looming over her.

"You should come back with us," he said. Emotion turned his accent thick.

Avani's own throat closed.

"No." She shook her head, swallowed. "I belong here, for now."

He scoffed. "Alone on unforgiving mountains, with corpses moldering all around, and the *sidhe* beneath the rock."

"You did close the passage?" She smiled a little at his temper. "I won't be alone. Everin will help me clear the Downs of the dead. He believes in fixing mistakes."

"Mighty Everin," he mocked. "You don't truly believe he's the son of the Aug?"

She shrugged. "Whatever he is, there's a thing or two he can teach me. And Faolan. *He* won't leave the Downs until he's atoned."

"I can teach you!" He paced back and forth over her rugs. "We need you, in Wilhaiim, Avani. Renault needs you. And he won't wait forever."

She set her mug on her thigh, waiting for more, but he wouldn't speak what she knew was in his heart. Perhaps he couldn't. Perhaps the loss, the betrayal, smothered all else.

"I'll come back," she promised. "What choice do I have, ai? When I'm ready. Give me time. The *sidhe* have a strong magic. Will you keep their knowledge from your king?"

"The *sidhe* are dangerous," he snarled. "You'll stay away from them."

"You closed the passage," she reminded him again. "You have the key."

He waved an impatient hand.

"Give me time," she insisted, though she knew it was he who needed space. "Will you send my idol back to me, as soon as you return?"

"Aye. And all of your *salwar*. I'll remember. And rosemary from Kate's garden." His voice broke.

She went to him, then, setting her mug on the floor. He pulled her in, buried his face in her hair, then against her throat. His mouth touched the curve of her jaw.

At last he set her aside.

"All the innocents, their deaths weigh on my shoulders." He scrubbed at the wound between his eyes, bringing fresh blood to the surface.

Avani stepped back across her rugs, leaving him alone in front of the stove. She bent to pick up her cider, brushing tears from her cheeks with the back of her hand, and hoped he didn't see her sorrow.

"You'll come home," he pressed. "When you're ready?"

"*Ai*, home." The word eased her. "When I'm ready, I'll come home, and mayhap carry the secrets of the folk in my sack."

He almost smiled, then. She felt it.

"*Ai*," he said, and then, very briefly, his power brushed her center, a lover's caress.

SHE SAW THEM off at dawn, the vocent and his squire. She stood on the stoop, watching the two straight figures as they climbed slowly away across the Downs. The sky was blue and clear, and new grass poked green stems about her home.

She refused to shed more tears.

"They'll heal each other," Everin said over her shoulder. "Malachi and his king. And the boy will grow into his heritage."

"If they make it to Wilhaiim without incident." Avani hugged herself.

"They will," said Faolan. He sat in the new grass, and eyed Jacob as the raven pranced on her roof.

"You know this?"

"I do." He smiled, showing pointed teeth. "Because I am *aes si*, and we are the gods of the earth."

She met his flat stare without fear.

"We shall see," she said. "*Ai*, we shall see."

Dawn

HE DREAMED OF great caverns, and barrows, and the ripe stench of deep earth.

He walked endless tunnels, bootheels striking over slate, or sticking in old mud.

He wore a string of rubies on his breast, and a second chain of true gold, and suspended from the gold links, a vocent's yellow ring.

He spoke a new language, an older language. When he dreamed, the strange words burbled meaninglessly from his lips.

When he grew tired of the heart of the earth, he climbed up through the tunnels to fresh air, and ran on summer grass. The village pen kept new lambs.

When time allowed, he spent time in his little house on the slope, among brilliant rugs, with only his Goddess as company.

And when he woke from dreams of earth and sky, he woke to the stale darkness of his suite, heart pounding.

But his anguish was silent, and the raven sleeping on the windowsill didn't stir, nor the boy, curled on his hearth.

MAL MISSED HER. He knew he saw through her eyes as often as his own. He didn't allow it during the day, but at night his resolve weakened.

He wondered if she dreamed of his life. He never felt her in his skull. Her *jhi* guarded his rooms, and the lad she'd rescued from Stonehill grew before his eyes toward manhood.

As summer waned, he found his way for the first time back through the Royal Gardens, chasing a hunch. It took him very little time to find the small wooden chest buried in Kate's plot of herbs.

He split the chest open and found rolls of parchment: Andrew's notes on the *sidhe*. He took the parchment back with him to his rooms, and spent days bent over at his desk, studying.

The nights grew short.

Mal took a sheaf of parchment with him to the grave-yard and sat on Siobahn's slab. He'd seen to it her bones had been safely returned. If her spirit lingered, he never saw it.

Her grave had become a place to think.

The king joined him much later. He carried a clutch of fall crocuses in his hand.

"You spend too much time here," he chided.

"As do you," Mal returned, without looking up from his reading.

"What is it this time?" Renault asked.

"Barrow maps. They've spread themselves beneath our kingdom. Beneath our kingdom, and beyond."

Renault laid the crocuses carefully on Siobahn's slab.

"If Andrew's to be believed, they've lived under the skin of the earth far longer than you or I have walked above it," the king said. "Why fear them now?"

Mal pulled his attention from the parchment, glancing at his king. "They believe themselves gods. They've tasted our flesh, they're remembering blue sky and fresh air. It stirs them. If they can find another way out, they will."

"You're dreaming again."

"Not mine. Avani's."

Renault grunted. "Are you certain you're not dreaming the results of too rich a supper?"

Mal smiled slightly. "We've a connection, Avani and I."

The king glanced down at the flowers on Siobahn's grave.

"Aye," he said. And then, "Mayhap it's time to bring the island witch back to court."

"If she will come," Mal agreed.

"Aye," Renault repeated. "See that she does."

Acknowledgments

Thanks to Paul, Katherine, and Aidan for clearing out when I needed to work. To Mary and Eric for the tranquility of the house at Loon Lake. To the Wilson Lunch Ladies for Tequila Thursdays, and the Barn Crew for Chaps brunch dates. Also, thanks to Kelly O'Connor for the words of encouragement, and for the loan of her excellent editorial skills, and to the rest of the Harper Voyager team, for making everything come together so wonderfully.

About the Author

SARAH REMY writes fiction to keep real life from getting out of hand. She lives in Spokane, Washington, where she shows horses, works at a local elementary school, and rehabs her old house. Follow her on Twitter at @sarahremywrites.